NEW YORK TIMES BESTSELLING AUTHOR

JOANN ROSS

It Happened One Week

D0207541

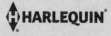

ISBN-13: 978-1-335-66251-4

Recycling programs for this product may not exist in your area.

It Happened One Week
First published in 1996.
This edition published in 2023.
Copyright © 1996 by JoAnn Ross

She Dreamed of a Cowboy
First published in 2021.
This edition published in 2023.
Copyright © 2021 by Joanna Sims

For questions and comments about the quality of this book, please contact us at CustomerService@Harlequin.com.

Harlequin Enterprises ULC
22 Adelaide St. West, 41st Floor
Toronto, Ontario M5H 4E3, Canada
www.Harlequin.com

Printed in U.S.A.

CONTENTS

New York Times and *USA TODAY* bestselling author **JoAnn Ross** has been published in twenty-seven countries. A member of Romance Writers of America's Honor Roll of bestselling authors, JoAnn lives with her husband and three rescued dogs—who pretty much rule the house—in the Pacific Northwest. Visit her at joannross.com.

Books by JoAnn Ross

The Inheritance

Honeymoon Harbor

Summer on Mirror Lake
Snowfall on Lighthouse Lane
Herons Landing

Honeymoon Harbor Novellas

Home to Honeymoon Harbor
Once Upon a Wedding
Just One Look

Visit the Author Profile page
at Harlequin.com for more titles.

IT HAPPENED ONE WEEK

JoAnn Ross

To Dianne Moggy—who provided the inspiration.

Prologue

Satan's Cove

The letters had been painstakingly carved into the shifting silver sands. Although she could see them from the top of the jagged cliff overlooking the Pacific Ocean, fifteen-year-old Amanda Stockenberg could not make out the message.

As she descended the stone steps to the beach, slowly at first, then faster, until she was nearly running, the words became clearer.

Dane loves Amanda.

Despite the fact that she'd spent most of last night crying, Amanda began to weep.

He was waiting for her in their secret, private place. Just as he'd promised. Just as she'd hoped.

Smugglers' Cave, carved by aeons of wind and ocean

out of the rocky seaside cliffs, had long been rumored to be one of the local sites where pirates had once hidden stolen booty before moving it inland.

Amanda wasn't interested in the legends about the pirates' nefarious behavior. And despite the violence that supposedly occurred here, to her, Smugglers' Cave was the most romantic place on earth.

It was here, on a star-spangled July Fourth night, while the glare of fireworks lit up the night sky, that Dane first kissed her. Then kissed her again. And again. Until she thought she'd literally melt from ecstasy.

"I thought you wouldn't come," she cried, flinging herself dramatically into his strong dark arms. Her avid mouth captured his. The kiss was hot and long and bittersweet.

"I told you I would," he reminded her, after they finally came up for air.

"I know." Her hands were linked together around his neck. Her young, lithe body was pressed against his so tightly that it would have been impossible for the morning ocean breeze to come between them. "But I was so afraid you'd be mad at me."

"Mad?" Dane looked honestly surprised by the idea. "Why would I be mad at you?"

"For leaving." Just thinking about her imminent departure caused the moisture in Amanda's sea blue eyes to overflow.

"You don't have any choice, sweetheart." With more tenderness than she would have imagined possible, he brushed her tears away with his fingertips. "We've both known that from the beginning."

"That doesn't make it any less awful!" she wailed.

"No." Despite his brave words, Dane's dark eyes

were every bit as bleak as hers as he traced her trembling, downturned pink lips with a tear-dampened finger. "It doesn't."

The tender touch left behind a taste of salt born of her overwhelming sorrow. "We could run away," she said desperately, grabbing his hand and holding it tightly between both of hers. "Just you and I. Somewhere no one could ever find us. To Wyoming. Or Florida."

"Don't think I haven't been tempted." His lips curved at the idea, but even as distressed as she was, Amanda noticed that the smile didn't reach his eyes. "But running away is never the answer, princess."

She was too desperate, too unhappy, to listen to reason. "But—"

"We can't." His tone, while gentle, was firm. "As attractive as the idea admittedly is, it's wrong."

"How can love be wrong?"

Dane sighed, looking far older, far more world-weary than his nineteen years. "You're only fifteen years old—"

"I'll be sixteen next week."

"I know." This time the reluctant smile turned his eyes to the hue of rich, warm chocolate. "But you still have your entire life ahead of you, honey. I'm not going to be responsible for ruining it."

"But you wouldn't!" she cried on a wail that scattered a trio of sea gulls. "You'd make it better. Perfect, even."

As much as she'd first resisted joining her family for this annual summer vacation on the Oregon coast, the moment she'd first seen Smugglers' Inn's sexy young bellhop, lifeguard, and all-around handyman, Amanda had changed her mind.

Over the past four glorious weeks, her life had been

focused on Dane Cutter. He was all she wanted. All she would ever want. She'd love him, Amanda vowed, forever.

But now, she didn't want to waste time talking. Not when their time together was coming to an end, like sands falling through some hateful hourglass. Rising on her toes, she pressed her lips against his once more.

The morning mist swirled around them; overhead, sea gulls squawked stridently as they circled, searching for mussels in the foaming surge. Caught up in emotions every bit as strong—and as old—as the forces that had formed the craggy coastline, neither Dane nor Amanda heard them.

The ocean's roar became a distant buzz in Amanda's ears. For this glorious suspended moment, time ceased to have meaning. The hungry kiss could have lasted a minute, an hour, an eternity.

Finally, the blare of a car horn managed to infiltrate its way into Amanda's consciousness. She tried to ignore it, but it was soon followed by the sound of an irritated male voice cutting through the fog.

Dane dragged his mouth from hers. "Your father's calling." He skimmed his lips up her cheeks, which were damp again from the cold ocean mist and her tears.

"I know." She swiped at the tears with the backs of her trembling hands, looking, Dane thought, more like an injured child than the almost-grown-up woman she insisted that she was. Unwilling, unable to leave, she twined her arms around his neck again and clung.

For not the first time since her arrival in Satan's Cove, Dane found himself sorely tested. For not the first time, he reminded himself that she was far too young for the thoughts he kept having, the feelings he kept experiencing. But even as his mind struggled to hold on to that crucial fact—like a drowning man clinging to a piece of driftwood in a storm-tossed sea—his body was literally aching for fulfillment.

Dane was not inexperienced. He'd discovered, since losing his virginity to a sexy blond Miss Depoe Bay the summer of his sixteenth year, that sex was easy to come by. Especially during vacation season, when the beaches were filled with beautiful girls looking for a summer fling.

But he'd never wanted a girl as he wanted Amanda. What was worse, he'd never *needed* a girl as he needed Amanda. Accustomed to keeping a tight rein on his emotions, Dane wasn't at all comfortable with the effect Amanda Stockenberg had had on him from the beginning.

Finally, although it was nearly the hardest thing he'd ever had to do—second only to refusing her ongoing, seductive pleas to make love these past weeks—Dane gently, patiently, unfastened Amanda's hold on him.

"You have to go," he said again, prying her hands from around his neck. He kissed her fingers one at a time. "But it's not over, princess. Not unless you want it to be."

Distraught as she was, Amanda failed to hear the question—and the uncharacteristic lack of assurance—in his guarded tone.

"Never!" she swore with all the fervor of a young woman in the throes of her first grand love. "I promise."

Her father called out again. The van's horn blared. Once. Twice. A third time.

Giving Dane one last desperate kiss, Amanda spun

around, sobbing loudly as she ran up the rock stairs. She did not—could not—look back.

He stood there all alone, hands shoved deep into the pockets of his jeans, and watched her leave, resisting the urge to call out to her. He heard the van drive off, taking her far away from Satan's Cove. Away from him.

Dane stayed on the windswept beach for a long, silent time, watching as the relentless ebb and flow of the tide slowly, inexorably, washed away the love letter he'd written in the drifting silver sand.

Chapter 1

Portland, Oregon
Ten years later

"This can't be happening. Not to me. Not now!" Amanda Stockenberg stared in disbelief at the television screen where towering red-and-orange flames were engulfing the Mariner Seaside Golf Resort and Conference Center located on the Oregon coast.

"It *is* lousy timing," her administrative assistant, Susan Chin, agreed glumly. It had been Susan who'd alerted Amanda to the disaster, after hearing a news bulletin on the radio.

"That has to be the understatement of the millennium," Amanda muttered as she opened a new roll of antacids.

Hoping for the best, but fearing the worst, she'd left a meeting and run down the hall to the conference room.

Now, as the two women stood transfixed in front of the television, watching the thick streams of water prove ineffectual at combating the massive blaze, Amanda could see her entire career going up in smoke right along with the five-star resort.

She groaned as the hungry flames devoured the lovely cedar-shake shingled roof. The scene shifted as the cameras cut away to show the crews of helmeted firemen valiantly fighting the fire. From the grim expressions on their soot-stained faces, she sensed that they knew their efforts to be a lost cause.

And speaking of lost causes...

"It's obvious we're going to have to find a new site for the corporate challenge," she said, cringing when what was left of the wooden roof caved in with a deafening roar. Water from the fire hoses hit the flames, turned to steam and mixed with the clouds of thick gray smoke.

"I'd say that's a given," Susan agreed glumly. "Unless you want to have the group camping out on the beach. Which, now that I think about it, isn't such a bad idea. After all, the entire idea of this coming week is to present the creative teams with challenges to overcome."

"Getting any of the managers of *this* company to work together as a team is going to be challenge enough." Amanda sank into a chair, put her elbows on the long rectangular mahogany conference table and began rubbing at her temples, where a headache had begun to pound. "Without tossing in sleeping in tents on wet sand and bathing out of buckets."

Advertising had been a cutthroat, shark-eat-shark business since the first Babylonian entrepreneur had gotten the bright idea to chisel the name of his company onto a stone tablet. Competition was always fierce, and everyone knew that the battle went not only to the most creative, but to the most ruthless.

Even so, Amanda felt the employees of Janzen, Lawton and Young took the idea of healthy competition to unattractive and often unprofitable extremes. Apparently, Ernst Janzen, senior partner of the company that had recently purchased Amanda's advertising agency, seemed to share her feelings. Which was why the idea of corporate-management teams was born in the first place.

In theory, the concept of art, copy and marketing working together on each step of a project seemed ideal. With everyone marching in unison toward the same finish line, the firm would undoubtedly regain superiority over its competitors.

That was the plan. It was, Amanda had agreed, when she'd first heard of it, extremely logical. Unfortunately, there was little about advertising that was the least bit logical.

The agency that had hired her directly after her graduation from UCLA, Connally Creative Concepts, or C.C.C., had made a name for itself by creating witty, appealing and totally original advertising that persuaded and made the sale through its ability to charm the prospect.

Although its location in Portland, Oregon, was admittedly a long way from Madison Avenue, some of the best copywriters and art directors in the country had been more than willing to leave Manhattan and take pay cuts in order to work long hours under the tutelage of Patrick Connally. C.C.C. had been like a family, Patrick Connally playing the role of father to everyone who came for inspiration and guidance.

Unfortunately, two years ago Patrick Connally had died of a heart attack at the age of seventy-five, after a heated game of tennis. His widow, eager to retire to Sun City, Arizona, had sold the agency to another company. Eight months after that, the new owner merged the united agencies with yet a third creative shop.

Unsurprisingly, such multiple mergers in such a short span of time resulted in the dismissal of several long-time employees as executives trimmed excess staff. A mood of anxiety settled over the offices and morale plummeted as everyone held their collective breath, waiting to see who was going to be "downsized" next.

After the initial purge, things had seemed to be settling down until the advertising wars kicked up again. A six-month battle that played out daily in the newspapers and on the internet had resulted in an unfriendly takeover by the international mega-agency of Janzen, Lawton and Young, and those employees who'd been breathing at last, found their livelihoods once again in jeopardy.

Janzen, Lawton and Young had long had a reputation for the most artless and offensive commercials to run in America. But it also boasted the highest profits in the business. In order to keep profits up to the promised levels, a new wave of massive staff cuts had hit the agency.

Morale plummeted to new lows.

Unsurprisingly, the same creative people who had once been responsible for some of the most innovative—and effective—advertising in the business, turned on one another.

A recent case in point was today's client meeting. The creative group had been assigned to propose a new concept for a popular line of gourmet ice cream. From day one, the members of the recently established team had been at each other's throats like a pack of out-of-control pit bulls.

"I can't believe you seriously expect me to be a part of this presentation," Marvin Kenyon, the head copywriter, had complained after viewing the animated sequence proposed by award-winning art director Julian Palmer.

"It's a team effort," Amanda reminded him mildly. "And you *are* a valuable member of the team."

The copywriter, who'd won his share of awards himself, folded his arms over the front of his blue oxford-cloth shirt and said, "I categorically refuse to share blame for something as sophomoric and static as that animation sequence."

"Sophomoric?" Julian Palmer rose to his full height of five feet five inches tall. What he lacked in stature, he more than made up for in ego. "Static? Since when are you an expert on visuals?"

"I know enough to see that if we present your idea, we'll blow the account for sure," Marvin retorted. "Hell, a baboon with a fistful of crayons could undoubtedly create a more visually appealing storyboard."

Julian arched an eyebrow as he adjusted the already perfect Windsor knot in his Italian-silk tie. "This from a man who creates—" he waved the printed sheets Marvin had handed out when he'd first arrived in the presentation room like a battle flag "—mindless drivel?"

"Drivel?" Marvin was on his feet in a shot, hands

folded into fists as he came around the long, polished mahogany table.

"Marvin," Amanda protested, "please sit down. Julian didn't mean it, did you, Julian?"

"I never say anything I don't mean," the artistic director replied. "But in this case, I may have been mistaken."

"There, see?" Amanda soothed, feeling as if she were refereeing a fight between two toddlers in a kindergarten sandbox. "Julian admits he was mistaken, Marvin. Perhaps you can amend your comment about his work."

"I *was* wrong to call it drivel," Julian agreed. "That's too kind a description for such cliché-ridden rubbish."

"That does it!" Marvin, infamous for his quicksilver temper, was around the table like a shot. He'd grabbed hold of his team member's chalk-gray vest and for a moment Amanda feared that the two men were actually going to come to blows, when the conference-room door opened and the client arrived with Don Patterson, the marketing manager, on his heels.

"Am I interrupting something?" the longtime client, a man in his mid-fifties whose addiction to ice cream had made him a very wealthy man, asked.

"Only a momentary creative difference of opinion," Amanda said quickly. "Good afternoon, Mr. Carpenter. It's nice to see you again."

"It's always a pleasure to see you again, Ms. Stockenberg." The portly entrepreneur took her outstretched hand in his. His blue eyes warmed momentarily as they swept over her appreciatively. "I'm looking forward to today's presentation," he said as his gaze moved to the uncovered storyboard.

Wide brow furrowed, he crossed the room and began

studying it for a long silent time. Since it was too late to begin the presentation as planned, the team members refrained from speaking as he took in the proposed campaign. Amanda didn't know about the others, but she would have found it impossible to say a word, holding her breath as she was.

When Fred Carpenter finally did speak, his words were not encouraging. "You people have serviced my account for five years. I've dropped a bundle into your coffers. And this is as good as you can come up with? A cow wearing a beret?"

"Let me explain the animation," Julian said quickly. Too quickly, Amanda thought with an inner sigh. He was making the fatal mistake of any presenter: appearing desperate.

"Don't worry, the art can be rethought," Marvin interjected as Julian picked up the laser pen to better illustrate the sequence. "Besides, it's the words that'll sell your new, improved, French vanilla flavor, anyway." He paused, as if half expecting a drumroll to announce his message. "A taste of Paris in every spoonful."

"That's it?" the snack-food executive asked.

"Well, it's just the beginning," Marvin assured him. Moisture was beading up on his upper lip, his forehead. Another rule broken, Amanda thought, remembering what Patrick Connally had taught her about never letting the client—or the competition—see you sweat. "See, the way I envision the concept—"

"It's drivel," Julian said again. "But the team can fix that, Fred. Now, if we could just get back to the art."

"It's not drivel," Marvin exploded.

"Marvin," Amanda warned softly.

"I've seen cleverer copy written on rolls of novelty toilet paper," the art director sniffed.

"And I've seen better art scrawled on the sides of buildings down at the docks!"

Amanda turned toward the client who appeared less than amused by the escalating argument. "As you can see, Mr. Carpenter, your campaign has created a lot of in-house excitement," she said, trying desperately to salvage the multimillion-dollar account.

"Obviously the wrong kind," Carpenter said. "Look, I haven't liked how all these mergers resulted in my account being put into the hands of the same agency that handles my competitors. It looks to me as if you guys have been instructed by your new bosses to soften your approach—"

"The hell we have," both Julian and Marvin protested in unison, agreeing for once. Amanda tried telling herself she should be grateful for small favors.

"Then you've lost your edge," the self-proclaimed king of ice cream decided.

"That's really not the case, Fred," Don Patterson, the marketing member of the team, finally interjected. A man prone to wearing loud ties and plaid sport jackets, he was nevertheless very good at his job. "Perhaps if Julian and Marvin went back to the drawing board—"

"There's no point. We've had five great years working together, you fellows have helped make Sweet Indulgence the second-bestselling ice cream in the country. But, the team over at Chiat/Day assures me that they can get me to number one. So, I think I'm going to give them a try."

He turned toward Amanda, who could literally feel the color draining from her face. "I'm sorry, Ms. Stockenberg. You're a nice, pretty lady and I'd like to keep my account here if for no other reason than to have an excuse to keep seeing you. But business is business."

"I understand." With effort, Amanda managed a smile and refrained from strangling the two ego-driven creative members of the ill-suited team. "But Don does have a point. Perhaps if you'd allow us a few days to come up with another concept—"

"Sorry." He shook his head. "But things haven't been the same around here since all the mergers." His round face looked as unhappy as hers. "But if you'd like," he said, brightening somewhat, "I'll mention you to the fellows at Chiat/Day. Perhaps there's a spot opening up over there."

"That's very kind of you. But I'm quite happy where I am."

It was what she'd been telling herself over and over again lately, Amanda thought now, as she dragged her mind from the disastrous meeting to the disaster currently being played out on the television screen.

"You know," Susan said, "this entire challenge week isn't really your problem. Officially, it's Greg's."

"I know." Amanda sighed and began chewing on another Tums.

Greg Parsons was her immediate supervisor and, as creative director, he was the man Ernst Janzen had hand-selected for the job of instituting the team concept. The man who had moved into the executive suite was as different from Patrick Connally as night from day. Rather than encouraging the cooperative atmosphere that had once thrived under the founder of C.C.C., Greg ruled the agency by intimidation and fear.

From his first day on the job, he'd set unrealistic profit

targets. This focus on profits diverted attention from what had always been the agency's forte—making clients feel they were getting superior service.

Apparently believing that internal competition was the lifeblood of success, he instigated political maneuvering among his top people, pitting one against the other as they jockeyed for key appointments.

Although such intrigue usually occurred behind the scenes, one of the more visible changes in policy was the conference table at which Amanda was sitting. When she'd first come to work here, the room had boasted a giant round table, the better, her former boss had declared, to create the feeling of democracy. Now, five days a week, the staff sat around this oblong table while Parsons claimed the power position at the head.

Although it might not seem like such a big thing, along with all the other changes that had taken place, it was additional proof that C.C.C. had lost the family feeling that had been so comfortable and inspirational to both employees and clients.

Desperate to salvage his foundering career, Parsons had come up with the idea of taking the teams to a resort, where, utilizing a number of outward-bound-type game-playing procedures he'd gleaned from his latest management-training course, the various independent-minded individuals would meld into one forceful creative entity.

"The problem is," Amanda said, "like it or not, my fortunes are tied to Greg."

"Lucky him. Since without you to run interference and do all his detail work, he'd undoubtedly have been out on his Armani rear a very long time ago," Susan said.

"That's not very nice."

"Granted. But it's true."

Amanda couldn't argue with her assistant's pithy analysis. From the time of Greg's arrival from the Dallas office three months ago, she'd wondered, on more than one occasion, exactly how the man had managed to win the corporate plum of creative director. It certainly hadn't been on merit.

Then, six weeks after he'd moved into the expensively redecorated executive office, the question was answered when Susan returned from a long lunch with the other administrative assistants where she'd learned that Greg just happened to be married to Ernst Janzen's granddaughter. Which, Amanda had agreed, explained everything.

It was bad enough that Greg was frightfully incompetent. Even worse was the way he saw himself as a modern-day Napoleon—part dictator, part Don Juan. And although she'd deftly dealt with his less-than-subtle passes, her refusal had earned Amanda her superior's antipathy. He rode her constantly, belittling her work even as he routinely took credit for her ideas in upper-level corporate meetings.

It was no secret that the man was unhappy in Portland. He constantly berated the entire West Coast as hopelessly provincial. It was also common knowledge that he had his eye on a superior prize—that of national creative director and vice president. Along with the requisite increase in salary and numerous perks, the coveted slot also came with a corner-window penthouse office on Manhattan's famed Madison Avenue.

"I still don't see why you put up with the man," Susan said, her acid tone breaking into Amanda's thoughts.

"It's simple. I want his job."

"It should have been yours in the first place."

Once again, Amanda couldn't argue with the truth. While she hadn't specifically been promised the creative director's spot when she was first hired, there'd been every indication that Patrick Connally considered her on the fast track to success.

She'd worked hard for the past four years, forgoing any social life, giving most of her time and energy to the company.

The sacrifices had paid off; there had been a time, not so long ago, when the job of creative director had looked like a lock. Until Greg Parsons arrived on the scene.

"Blood's thicker than water. And unfortunately, Greg happens to be married to Mr. Janzen's granddaughter."

"Talk about sleeping your way to the top," Susan muttered.

"Unfortunately, family ties seem to have gotten Greg this far." Amanda frowned up at the oil portrait of the new creative director hanging on the wall. The ornate, gilt-framed painting featured Parsons in one of his dress-for-success chalk-striped suits, holding a cigar.

"But," she continued, "after the problems he's had instituting the team concept, he's stalled in the water."

Susan arched a jet eyebrow. "Are you saying you think he's on the way out?"

"Unfortunately, I don't think—unless Jessica Janzen Parsons wises up and divorces him—there's any chance of that. So, I've come up with a plan to get the guy out of my life—and out of town—once and for all."

"Please tell me it involves tar and feathers."

"Not quite." Actually, although she'd never admit it, Amanda found the idea of running Parsons out of town on a rail—like in the good old days of the Wild West—eminently appealing.

"Actually, it's simple. Or at least it was," she amended with another bleak glance toward the television screen. "Until the resort went up in smoke."

"Let me guess. You were going to lure the bastard out onto the cliff behind the resort late one night, hit him in the head with his precious new PING nine iron, then shove him into the ocean. Where, with any luck, he'd be eaten by killer sharks."

Despite all her problems, Amanda smiled. "As attractive as that scenario may be, the sharks would probably spare him because of professional courtesy. Besides, I've come to the conclusion that the easiest way to get Greg out of my hair is to give him what he most wants."

"Don't tell me that you're going to go to bed with him?"

"Of course not." Amanda literally shuddered at the unpalatable idea. "Actually, I've decided to get him promoted."

A slow, understanding grin had Susan's crimson lips curving. "To Manhattan."

Amanda returned the smile with a cocky, confident grin of her own. "To Manhattan."

Amanda couldn't deny that losing the conference-center resort to fire was a setback. After all, without someplace to hold the corporate challenge, Greg couldn't prove that his idea had merit. Which in turn would keep him here in Portland indefinitely.

But it wasn't the first challenge she'd overcome in her rise up the advertising corporate ladder. Amanda doubted it would be her last.

A part of her hated the idea of Greg Parsons getting

any more credit, when in reality, if the upcoming week proved a success, it would be her doing. A stronger part of her just wanted him gone. She would swallow her pride, along with her ego, if it meant getting the obnoxious man out of her life.

Now all she had to do was find some other location for the challenge. Which wasn't going to be easy, considering this was the high tourist season on the Oregon coast.

Could she do it? Amanda asked herself as she pointed the remote toward the television and darkened the screen.

You bet.

Satan's Cove

"We've got a problem."

Dane Cutter stopped in the act of nailing down cedar shingles and glanced over the steep edge of the roof. "So why don't you tell me something I don't know?"

He'd been the proud owner of Smugglers' Inn for two months. Well, if you wanted to get technical, he and the bank actually owned the century-old landmark building. Since he'd signed the final papers, Dane doubted a single day had gone by that he hadn't had to overcome some new catastrophe.

Having paid for an extensive professional inspection of the building that, because of competition from larger, fancier resorts catering to the corporate trade, had fallen into disrepair during his time away from Satan's Cove, Dane knew the problems he was taking on. And although they were considerable, he'd foolishly expected to have some time to do all the necessary renovations.

Thus far, he'd tackled the inn's ancient plumbing and electrical systems, evicted countless field mice and killed more spiders than he cared to think about.

He'd also replaced the ancient gas oven, replastered the algae-filled swimming pool, and was in the process of replacing the shingles that had blown away during last night's storm.

The next thing on his lengthy list—barring any further emergencies—was replacing the ancient gas heater, after which he planned to resand and seal the oak floors in the public rooms, then resurface the tennis court.

Since reopening last week, he'd reassured himself at least daily that it was just as well potential guests weren't exactly beating down his door. Although he admittedly needed all the bookings he could get to make the hefty mortgage payments, he also needed time to restore the inn to its former glory.

Reva Carlson grinned up at him. "Technically it's a bit of good news and some bad news. I suppose it's all in how you look at it."

"Why don't you give me the good news first?"

The way things had been going, after the storm and the burst pipe that had left the inn without water for twenty-four hours, Dane figured he could use a little boost. Hell, what he needed was a miracle. But he was willing to settle for whatever he could get.

"Okay." Reva's grin widened. "It looks as if we're going to meet this month's mortgage payment, after all."

"We got a booking?" If he'd had his choice, he would have kept the inn closed until all the needed repairs could be done. Unfortunately, his cash flow being what it was, he'd been forced to open for limited occupancy.

"We've sold out the entire place," Reva revealed proudly.

She was right. This was definitely a case of good and bad news. "Not including the tower room?" The last he'd looked into the hexagonal-shaped room that boasted a bird's-eye view of the Pacific Ocean, the wallpaper had been peeling off the walls.

"Of course not. You're good, boss, but you're not exactly a miracle worker. However, every other room, every bed, every last nook and cranny of Smugglers' Inn is going to be taken over by some Portland ad agency for an entire week."

Dane rapidly went over a mental list of repairs he'd have to accomplish in order to accommodate such a crowd.

"So, when are these ad people scheduled to arrive, anyway?"

"You could at least pretend to be pleased," she complained. "Besides, it's not that bad. We've plenty of time to get ready."

"What, exactly, do you consider plenty of time?"

"Three days."

"Three days?" He dragged his hand through his hair.

"Well, technically four. Including this one."

It was already four in the afternoon. "Damn it, Reva—"

"You're the one who's been bitching about needing bookings," she reminded Dane. "Well, now you've got some. Or would you rather me call the woman back and tell her that we're full?"

Reminding himself that the difficult could be accomplished immediately, while the impossible might take a bit longer, he said, "You did good, lady."

Another thought, beyond the necessary repairs, occurred to him. "You'd better warn Mom." He'd taken his mother out of a forced retirement and put her back in the remodeled kitchen, where she had happily begun stocking the pantry and whipping up recipes that rivaled those of any five-star resort in the country.

"I already did," she assured him, reminding him why he'd hired the former night manager away from the world-famous Whitfield Palace hotel chain. "Which reminds me, she told me to tell you that you'll have to drive into town for supplies."

"Tell her to make out a list and I'll do it as soon as I finish with the roof."

Dane returned to his hammering. And even as he wondered exactly how he was going to get everything done in time for the arrival of all those guests, he allowed himself to believe that things around Smugglers' Inn were definitely beginning to look up.

Chapter 2

Portland

"You were right about every motel, hotel, resort and cottage up and down the coast being booked to the rafters," Susan reported to Amanda. "Every place with the exception of Smugglers' Inn, which, I'll have to admit, made me a little nervous. But the woman from the Satan's Cove visitors' bureau assured me that it's listed on the historical register."

"It is," Amanda murmured, thinking back to that wonderful summer she'd spent at Satan's Cove.

The memory was, as always, bittersweet—part pleasure and part pain. She'd never been happier than she'd been that summer of her first love. Nor more heartbroken than on the day she'd driven away from Smugglers' Inn—and Dane Cutter—back to Los Angeles with her family.

He'd promised to write; and trusting him implicitly, Amanda had believed him. For the first two weeks after arriving home, she'd waited for a letter assuring her that she was not alone in her feelings—that the kisses they'd shared, along with the desperate promises, had been more than just a summer romance.

When three weeks passed without so much as a single postcard, Amanda had screwed up enough nerve to telephone Dane at the inn. But the woman working the desk informed her that he'd left Satan's Cove to return to college. No, the woman had insisted, in a bored tone, he hadn't left any forwarding address.

She'd thought about asking to talk to his mother, who'd been the inn's cook. But youthful pride kept her from inquiring further. So, believing she'd simply been one more conquest for a drop-dead-gorgeous college boy who already had more than his share of girls throwing themselves at him, Amanda tried to write the intense, short-lived romance off to experience.

And mostly, she'd been successful. But there were still times, when she would least expect it, that she'd think back on that summer with a mixture of wistfulness and embarrassment.

"I'm surprised they could take us," she said now, recalling the inn's popularity. Her father had had to book their rooms six months in advance. "They must have had a huge cancellation."

"According to the reservations clerk, the place has been closed for several years," Susan revealed. "Apparently it's recently changed hands. This is the new owner's first season."

"I'm not sure I like the sound of that," Amanda muttered. Even in an industry built on ego and turf, the agency had become a nest of political intrigue and backbiting. The corporate team challenge week was going to be tough enough without them having to serve as some novice innkeeper's shakedown summer season.

"You can always call Popular Surplus and order up the tents."

Despite her concerns, Amanda laughed. The truth was, she really didn't have any other choice. She could put twenty people—none of whom got along very well in the best of circumstances—into tents on the beach, eating hot dogs cooked over an open fire, or she could trust the new owner of Smugglers' Inn to know what he or she was doing.

After all, how bad could it be? The landmark inn, located on one of the most scenic stretches of Pacific Coast, was pretty and cozy and wonderfully comfortable. She thought back on the lovely flower-sprigged wallpaper in the tower room she'd slept in that long-ago summer, remembered the dazzling sunsets from the high arched windows, recalled in vivid detail the romance of the crackling fires the staff built each evening in the stone fireplace large enough for a grown man to stand in.

"Smugglers' Inn will be perfect," she said firmly, as if saying the words out loud could make them true. "I don't know why I didn't think of it in the first place."

"Probably because you've had a few other things on your mind," Susan said, proving herself to be a master of understatement. "And although I have no doubt you can pull this thing off, I'm glad I'll be holding down the fort here while you lead the troops in their wilderness experience."

That said, she left Amanda to worry that this time she'd actually bitten off more than she could chew.

Never having been one to limit herself to a normal, eight-hour work schedule, Amanda remained at her desk long into the night, fine-tuning all the minuscule details that would ensure the challenge week would be a success.

But as hard as she tried to keep her mind on business, she could not keep her unruly thoughts from drifting back to the summer of her fifteenth year.

She'd fallen in love with Dane the first time she'd seen him. And although her parents had tried to convince her otherwise, she knew now, as she'd known then, that her feelings had been more than mere puppy love.

It had, admittedly, taken Dane time to realize they were a perfect match. But Amanda had steadfastly refused to give up her quest. She pursued him incessantly, with all the fervor of a teenager in the throes of a first grand love.

Everywhere Dane went, Amanda went there, as well, smiling up at him with a coy Lolita smile overbrimming with sensual invitation. After discovering that one of his duties was teaching a class in kayaking, despite her distaste for early morning awakenings, she showed up on the beach at six-thirty for lessons. Although the rest of the class was sensibly attired for the foggy sea air in jeans and sweatshirts, she'd chosen to wear a hot-pink bikini that barely covered the essentials.

And that was just the beginning. During Dane's lifeguarding stint each afternoon, she lounged poolside, wearing another impossibly scant bikini, her golden skin glowing with fragrant coconut oil. Grateful for childhood diving lessons, she would occasionally lithely rise from the lounge to treat him to swan dives designed to show off her budding female figure.

She tormented him endlessly, pretending to need his assistance on everything from a flat bicycle tire to fastening her life jacket before going out on a sight-seeing boat excursion.

Adding local color to the inn's reputation had been the legend—invented by a former owner—that it was haunted by a woman who'd thrown herself off the widow's walk after her fiancé's ship was sunk by pirates off the rocky shoals. One night, Amanda showed up at Dane's room, insisting that she'd seen the ghost.

It would have taken a male with inhuman strength to resist her continual seduction attempts. And, as Dane later confessed, he was, after all, only human.

Which was why, seven days after Amanda Stockenberg's arrival at Smugglers' Inn, Dane Cutter succumbed to the inevitable. However, even as they spent the star-spangled nights driving each other insane, Dane had steadfastly refused to make love to her.

"I may be too damn weak where you're concerned, princess," he'd groaned during one excruciatingly long petting session, "but I'm not reckless enough to have sex with a minor girl."

She'd sworn that no one would ever know, promised that she'd never—ever—do anything to get him in trouble. But on this point, Dane had proved frustratingly intractable.

And although, as the years passed, Amanda begrudgingly admitted that he'd done the right and noble thing, there were still times, such as tonight, when she was sitting all alone in the dark, that she'd think back over the bliss she'd experienced in Dane Cutter's strong young arms and wish, with all her heart, that he hadn't proved so strong.

Satan's Cove

The day before the group was due to arrive at Smugglers' Inn, Dane was beginning to think they just might make it.

The roof was now rainproof, the windows sparkled like diamonds, and every room in the place—with the exception of the tower room, which he'd written off as impossible to prepare in such short time—was white-glove clean. And although the aroma of fresh paint lingered, leaving the windows open another twenty-four hours should take care of that little problem.

His mother had definitely gone all out in the kitchen. The huge commercial refrigerator was stuffed with food and every shelf in the pantry was full. Kettles had been bubbling away on the new eight-burner stove nearly around the clock for the past two and a half days, creating mouth-watering scents.

Using the hefty deposit Reva had insisted upon, he'd hired additional staff and although the kids were as green as spring grass, they were bright, seemingly hard-working and unrelentingly cheerful.

He was passing the antique registration desk on his way to the parlor, planning to clean the oversize chandelier, when the sound of a stressed-out voice garnered his instant attention.

"I'm sorry, ma'am," Mindy Taylor, the nineteen-year-old cheerleader, premed student and local beauty queen he'd hired, said in an obviously frustrated voice. "But—"

She sighed and held the receiver a little away from her ear, indicating that it was not the first time she'd heard the argument being offered on the other end of the line.

"Yes, I can appreciate that," Mindy agreed, rolling her expressive eyes toward the knotty-pine ceiling. "But I'm afraid it's impossible. No, it's not booked, but—"

Dane heard the renewed argument, although he couldn't make out the words.

"It's a woman from that Portland advertising agency." Mindy covered the mouthpiece with her hand to talk to Dane. "She's insisting on the tower room, even though I told her that it wasn't available."

Dane held out his hand. "Let me talk to her."

"That's okay." Perfect white teeth that Dane knew had cost her parents a fortune in orthodontia flashed in the dazzling smile that had earned Mindy the Miss Satan's Cove title two years running. As this year's Miss Oregon, she'd be competing in the national pageant, which made her a local celebrity.

"It'll be good practice for Atlantic City. I need to work on my patience," she admitted. "Sometimes I think if I'm asked one more stupid question by one more judge I'm going to scream.

"I understand your feelings," Mindy soothed into the receiver as she tried yet again. "But you see, Ms. Stockenberg, Smugglers' Inn has been closed for the past few years, and—"

"Wait a minute," Dane interrupted. "Did you say Stockenberg?"

The name hit him directly in the gut, reminding him of the time he'd been standing behind the plate and his cousin Danny had accidentally slammed a baseball bat into his solar plexus.

"Excuse me, but could you hold a moment, please?"

Mindy put her hand over the mouthpiece again and nod-ded. "That's right."

"Not Amanda Stockenberg?" It couldn't be, Dane told himself, even as a nagging intuition told him it was true.

"That's her." Mindy appeared surprised Dane knew the name. "The guest list the agency sent along with their deposit lists her as an assistant creative director.

"I put her in the cliff room, but she's insisting on being moved to the tower. Something about it having sentimental meaning. I explained that it was impos-sible, but—"

"Let her have it."

"What?" Eyes the color of a sun-brightened sea wid-ened to the size of sand dollars.

"I said, book Ms. Stockenberg into the tower room." His tone was uncharacteristically sharp and impatient.

Mindy was not easily cowed. Especially by a man she'd been able to talk into playing Barbie dolls back in his teenage baby-sitting days, when their mothers had worked together at this very same inn. "But, Dane, it's a terrible mess."

She wasn't telling him anything he didn't already know. "Don't worry," he said, softening his voice and his expression. "I'll take care of it."

Mindy eyed him with overt curiosity. Then, as the voice on the other end of the phone began talking again, she returned her attention to the conversation.

"It seems I was mistaken, Ms. Stockenberg," she said cheerfully, switching gears with a dexterity that had Dane thinking she'd ace her Miss America inter-view. "As it happens, the tower room is available after all. Yes, that is fortunate, isn't it?"

She turned to the new computer Dane was still paying for. Her rosy fingernails tapped on the keys, changing Amanda Stockenberg from the cliff room to the tower suite.

"It's all taken care of," she assured Dane after she'd hung up. Her expressive eyes held little seeds of worry. "It's none of my business, but I sure hope you know what you're doing."

"If I knew what I was doing, I wouldn't have bought the inn in the first place." His crooked grin belied his complaint. After years of traveling the world for the Whitfield Palace hotel chain, there was no place he'd rather be. And nothing he'd rather be doing. "If you see Reva, tell her I had to run into town for some wallpaper."

"Ms. Stockenberg mentioned little blue flowers," Mindy said helpfully.

"I remember."

And damn it, that was precisely the problem, Dane told himself two hours later as he drove back to Smugglers' Inn from the hardware store in Satan's Cove with the newly purchased wallpaper. He remembered too much about Amanda Stockenberg's long-ago visit to Satan's Cove.

The only daughter of a wealthy Los Angeles attorney and his socialite wife, Amanda had come to the Oregon coast with her family for a month-long vacation.

Pampered and amazingly sheltered for a modern teenager, she'd obviously never met anyone like him. Unfortunately, during his years working at Smugglers' Inn—part-time while in high school, then summers and vacations to put himself through college—Dane had run across too many rich girls who considered him along the same lines as a summer trophy.

Dane's own father, scion of a famous Southern department-store family, had been a masculine version of those girls. Rich and spoiled, he'd had no qualms about taking what he wanted, then moving on after the annual Labor Day clambake, leaving behind a young, pregnant waitress.

Although Mary Cutter—a quiet, gentle woman who'd gone on to be a cook at the inn—had brought Dane up not to be bitter about his father's abandonment, he'd decided early on that it was better to stick with your own kind.

Which was why he'd always avoided the temptation of shiny blond hair and long, tanned legs. Until Amanda Stockenberg arrived on the scene.

She pursued him endlessly, with the single-mindedness of a rich, pretty girl accustomed to getting her own way. She was part siren, part innocent; he found both fascinating.

When she showed up at his door in the middle of the night during a thunderstorm, swearing she'd seen the ghost reputed to haunt the inn, Dane took one look at her—backlit by flashes of lightning, clad in a shorty nightgown—and all his intentions to resist temptation flew right out the window.

Being male and all too human, he allowed her into his room.

"That was your first mistake," he muttered now, at the memory of the sweet lips that had kissed him senseless. His second mistake, and the one that had cost him dearly, had been letting Amanda Stockenberg into his heart.

They did not make love—she was, after all, too young. And even if he'd wanted to—which, Lord help him, he did—he knew that by legal standards Amanda was jailbait. And from the no-holds-barred conversation Stockenberg had with Dane when even he could no longer ignore his daughter's outrageously flirtatious behavior, Dane knew the attorney would not be averse to filing statutory rape charges on any boy who dared take Amanda to bed.

Dane's mother, remembering her own youthful summer romance, had worried about his succumbing to his raging hormones and blowing his chances at finishing college.

"Don't worry, Mom," he'd assured her with the cocky grin that had coaxed more than one local beauty into intimacy. "I won't risk prison for a roll in the hay with a summer girl."

With that intent firmly stated, he'd managed to resist Amanda's pleas to consummate their young love. But drawn to her in ways he could not understand, Dane had spent the next three weeks sneaking off to clandestine trysts.

Dane and Amanda exchanged long slow kisses in the cave on the beach, forbidden caresses in the boathouse, passionate promises in the woods at the top of the cliff overlooking the sea, and on one memorable, thrilling, and terrifying occasion, while her parents slept in the room below them, they'd made out in Amanda's beloved tower room with its canopied bed and flower-sprigged walls.

Although he'd tried like hell to forget her, on more than one occasion over the past years, Dane had been annoyed to discover that her image had remained emblazoned on his mind, as bright and vivid—and, damn it, as seductive—as it had been a decade ago.

"It's been ten years," he reminded himself gruffly as he carried the rolls of paper and buckets of paste up the narrow, curving staircase to the tower room.

And, damn it, he'd dreamed about her over each of those ten years. More times than he could count, more than he'd admit. Even to himself.

"Hell, she's probably married."

It took no imagination at all to envision some man—a rich, suave guy with manicured fingernails and smooth palms that had never known the handle of a hammer, a man from her own social set—snapping Amanda up right after her debut.

Did girls still have formal debuts? Dane wondered, remembering a few he'd worked as a waiter during college—formal affairs in gilded hotel ballrooms where lovely rich girls donned long elbow-length gloves, their grandmothers' pearls and fancy white dresses that cost nearly as much as a semester's tuition, and waltzed with their fathers. He'd have to ask Mindy. The daughter of a local fisherman, she'd certainly met her share of society girls at various beauty pageants. On more than one occasion she'd complained to Dane that those rich girls only entered as a lark. Their futures, unlike hers, didn't depend on their winning the scholarship money. The fact that Amanda still had the same name as she had that long-ago summer meant nothing, Dane considered, returning his thoughts to Amanda Stockenberg's marital status. Married women often kept their maiden names for professional reasons.

His jaw clenched at the idea of Amanda married to some Yuppie who drove a BMW, preferred estate-bottled wine to beer, bought his clothes from Brooks Brothers, golfed eighteen holes on Saturday and sailed in yachting regattas on Sundays.

As he'd shopped for the damn wallpaper, Dane had hoped that he'd exaggerated the condition of the tower room when he'd measured the walls after Amanda's telephone call. Unfortunately, as he entered it now, he realized that it was even worse.

He wasn't fixing it up for sentimental reasons, Dane assured himself firmly. He was only going to the extra trouble because he didn't want Amanda to think him unsuccessful.

He pulled the peeling paper from the walls, revealing wallboard stained from the formerly leaky roof. Water stains also blotched the ceiling, like brown inkblots in a Rorschach test. The pine-plank floor was badly in need of refinishing, but a coat of paste wax and some judiciously placed rugs would cover the worst of the damage.

A sensible man would simply turn around and walk out, close the door behind him and tell the lady, when she arrived, that the clerk had made a mistake; the tower room wasn't available.

For not the first time since he'd gotten the idea to buy Smugglers' Inn, Dane reminded himself that a sensible man would have stayed in his executive suite at the New Orleans home office of the Whitfield Palace hotel chain and continued to collect his six-figure salary and requisite perks.

I'll bet the husband plays polo. The thought had him snapping the plumb line with more force than necessary, sending blue chalk flying. Dane had not forgotten Amanda's father's boastful remarks about the polo ponies he kept stabled at his weekend house in Santa Barbara.

What the hell was he doing? Dane asked himself as he rolled the paper out onto a board placed atop a pair of sawhorses and cut the first piece. Why torture himself with old memories?

He slapped the paste onto the back of the flowered paper and tried not to remember a time when this room had smelled like the gardenia cologne Amanda had worn that summer.

When something was over and done with, you forgot it and moved on.

Wasn't that exactly what she had done?

After promising him "forever," Amanda Stockenberg had walked out of his life without so much as a backward glance.

And ten years later, as he climbed the ladder and positioned the strip of paper against the too-heavy blue chalk line, Dane was still trying to convince himself that it was only his pride—not his heart—that had been wounded.

Although many things in Amanda's life had changed over the past ten years, Smugglers' Inn was not one of them. Perched on the edge of the cliff overlooking the Pacific Ocean, the building's lit windows glowed a warm welcome.

"Well, we're here, folks," the driver of the charter bus announced with a vast amount of cheer, considering the less-than-ideal circumstances of the trip. A halfhearted round of applause rippled down the rows.

"It's about time," Greg Parsons complained. He

speared Amanda a sharp look. "You realize that we've already lost the entire first day of the challenge."

Having been forced to put up with her supervisor's sarcasm for the past hour, Amanda was in no mood to turn the other cheek.

"That landslide wasn't my fault, Greg." They'd been stuck on the bus in the pouring rain for five long, frustrating hours while highway crews cleared away the rock and mud from the road.

"If we'd only left thirty minutes earlier—"

"We could have ended up beneath all that mud."

Deciding that discretion was the better part of valor, Amanda did not point out that the original delay had been caused by Kelli Kyle. The auburn-haired public-relations manager had arrived at the company parking lot twenty-five minutes after the time the bus had been scheduled to depart.

Watercooler rumors had Kelli doing a lot more for Greg than plotting PR strategy; but Amanda's working relationship with Greg was bad enough without her attacking his girlfriend.

She reached into her purse, took out a half-empty roll of antacids and popped two of the tablets into her mouth. Her stomach had been churning for the past twenty miles and a headache was threatening.

Which wasn't unusual when she was forced to spend the entire day with Greg Parsons. Amanda couldn't think of a single person—with the possible exception of Kelli Kyle—who liked the man.

The first thing he'd done upon his arrival in Portland was to prohibit staffers from decorating their office walls and cubicles with the crazy posters and wacky decorations that were a commonplace part of the creative environment at other agencies. When a memo had been sent out two months ago, forbidding employees even to drink coffee at their desks, Amanda had feared an out-and-out rebellion.

The hand grenade he kept on his desk and daily memos from *The Art of War* also had not endeared him to his fellow workers.

"Let's just hope we have better luck with this inn you've booked us into," he muttered, scooping up his crocodile attaché case and marching down the aisle. "Because so far, the corporate challenge is turning out to be an unmitigated disaster."

Unwilling to agree, Amanda didn't answer. The welcoming warmth of the fire crackling in the large stone fireplace soothed the jangled nerves of the challenge-week participants, as did the glasses of hot coffee, cider and wine served on a myrtle-wood tray by a handsome young man who vaguely reminded Amanda of Dane Cutter.

The young girl working behind the front desk was as pretty as the waiter was handsome. She was also, Amanda noticed, amazingly efficient. Within minutes, and without the Miss America smile fading for a moment, Mindy Taylor had registered the cranky, chilled guests into their rooms, handed out the keys and assigned bellmen to carry the luggage upstairs.

Finally it was Amanda's turn. "Good evening, Ms. Stockenberg," Mindy greeted Amanda with the same unfailing cheer she had the others. "Welcome to Smugglers' Inn."

"It's a relief to be here."

The smile warmed. "I heard about your troubles getting here from Portland." She tapped briskly on the computer as she talked. "I'm sure the rest of your week will go more smoothly."

"I hope so." It sure couldn't get any worse.

"You're in the tower room, as requested." Mindy handed her the antique brass key. "If you don't mind waiting just a moment, Kevin will be back and will take your suitcases up for you."

"That's not necessary," a male voice coming from behind Amanda said. "I'll take care of Ms. Stockenberg's luggage."

No, Amanda thought. *It couldn't be!*

She slowly turned around, taking time to school her expression to one of polite surprise. "Hello, Dane."

Although a decade had passed, he looked just the same. But better, she decided on second thought. Dark and rugged, and so very dangerous. The kind of boy—no, he was a man now, she reminded herself—that fathers of daughters stayed awake nights worrying about.

His shaggy dark hair was still in need of a haircut, and his eyes, nearly as dark as his hair, were far from calm, but the emotions swirling in their midnight depths were too complex for Amanda to decipher. A five-o'clock shadow did nothing to detract from his good looks; the dark stubble only added to his appeal.

His jeans, white T-shirt and black leather jacket were distractingly sexy. They also made her worry that standards might have slipped at the inn since the last time she'd visited.

"Hello, princess." His full, sensual mouth curved in a smile that let her know the intimacy implied by the long-ago nickname was intentional. "Welcome to Smugglers' Inn." His gaze swept over her. "You're looking more lovely than ever."

Actually, she looked like hell. To begin with, she was too damn thin. Her oval face was pale and drawn. Her beige linen slacks and ivory top, which he suspected probably cost as much as the inn's new water heater, looked as if she'd slept in them; her hair was wet from her dash from the bus, there were blue shadows beneath her eyes, and sometime during the long trip from Portland, she'd chewed off her lipstick.

Dane knew he was in deep, deep trouble when he still found her the most desirable woman he'd ever seen.

Amanda struggled to keep Dane from realizing that he'd shaken her. All it had taken was his calling her that ridiculous name to cause a painful fluttering in her heart.

How could she have thought that she'd gotten over him? Dane Cutter was not a man women got over. Not in this lifetime. Her hand closed tightly around the key.

"Thank you. It's a relief to finally be here. Is the dining room closed yet? I know we're late, but—"

"We kept it open when it was obvious you'd gotten held up. Or, if you'd prefer, there's room service."

The idea of a long bath and a sandwich and cup of tea sent up to her room sounded delightful. "That's good news." The first in a very long and very trying day.

"We try to make our guests as comfortable as possible."

He scooped up both her cases, deftly tucked them under his arm and took her briefcase from her hand. It was biscuit-hued cowhide, as smooth as a baby's bottom, with her initials in gold near the handle. "Nice luggage."

She'd received the Louis Vuitton luggage from her parents as a graduation present. Her mother had been given a similar set from her parents when she'd married. And her mother before her. It was, in a way, a family tradition. So why did she suddenly feel a need to apologize?

"It's very functional."

His only response to her defensive tone was a shrug. "So I've heard." He did not mention that he'd bought a similar set for his mother, as a bon voyage gift for the Alaskan cruise he'd booked her on last summer. "If you're all checked in, I'll show you to your room."

"I remember the way." It had been enough of a shock to discover Dane still working at the inn. Amanda didn't believe she could handle being alone in the cozy confines of the tower room with him. Not with the memory of their last night together still painfully vivid in her mind.

"I've no doubt you do." Ignoring the clenching of his stomach, Dane flashed her a maddening grin, letting her know that they were both on the same wavelength. The devil could probably take smiling lessons from Dane Cutter. "But someone needs to carry your luggage up and Jimmy and Kevin are tied up with other guests."

"There's no hurry." Her answering smile was as polite as it was feigned. Although she'd never considered herself a violent person, after the way Dane had treated her, dumping her without a single word of explanation, like he undoubtedly did the rest of his summer girls, her hands practically itched with the need to slap his face. "I'll just go on up and they can bring my bags to the tower whenever they're free."

"I have a feeling that might be a while." He nodded his head toward the doorway, declaring the subject closed.

Not wanting to create a scene in front of the avidly interested young clerk, Amanda tossed her damp head and marched out of the room.

This was a mistake, she told herself as she stood beside Dane in the antique elevator slowly creaking its way up to the third floor. The next few days were the most important in her life. Her entire career, everything she'd worked so hard to achieve, depended on the corporate challenge week being a success. She couldn't allow herself to be distracted.

Unfortunately, Smugglers' Inn, she was discovering too late, held far too many distracting memories.

"I'm surprised to find you working here," she murmured, trying to ignore the familiar scent of soap emanating from his dark skin.

He chuckled—a low, rich tone that crept under her skin and caused her blood to thrum. "So am I." He put the bags on the floor, leaned against the back wall and stuck his hands in his pockets. "Continually."

Amanda thought about all the plans Dane had shared with her that summer. About how he was going to get out of this isolated small coastal town, how he planned to make his mark on the world, how he was going to be rich by his thirtieth birthday.

She did some rapid calculations and determined him to be twenty-nine. Obviously, if his unpretentious clothing and the fact that he was still carrying bags for guests at the inn were any indication, if Dane hoped to achieve even one of those goals, he'd have to win the lottery.

"Looks as if you've done all right for yourself." His measuring glance swept over her. "Assistant creative director for one of the top advertising firms in the country. I'm impressed."

"Thank you."

"Tell me, do you have a window office?"

"Actually, I do." Realizing that he was daring to mock her success, she tossed up her chin. "Overlooking the river."

"Must be nice. And a corporate credit card, too, I'll bet."

"Of course." She'd been thrilled the first time she'd flashed the green American Express card granted only to upper-level management personnel in an expensive Manhattan restaurant. It had seemed, at the time, an important rite of passage. Having been born into wealth, Amanda wanted—needed—to achieve success on her own.

"High-backed swivel desk chair?"

Two could play this game. "Italian cream leather."

She refused to admit she'd bought the extravagant piece of office furniture for herself with last year's Christmas bonus.

Of course, the minute Greg Parsons had caught sight of it, after returning from a holiday vacation to Barbados, he'd rushed out and bought himself a larger, higher model. In jet leather. With mahogany trim.

Dane whistled appreciatively. "Yes, sir, you've definitely come a long way. Especially for a lady who once professed a desire to raise five kids in a house surrounded by a white picket fence, and spend summers putting up berries and long dark winters making more babies in front of a crackling fire."

How dare he throw those youthful fantasies back into her face! Didn't he realize that it had been *him* she'd fantasized about making love to, *his* babies she'd wanted?

After she'd been forced to accept the fact that her

dreams of marrying Dane Cutter were only that—stupid, romantic teenage daydreams—she'd gone on to find a new direction for her life. A direction that was, admittedly, heavily influenced by her father's lofty expectations for his only child.

"People grow up," she said. "Goals change."

"True enough," he agreed easily, thinking how his own life had taken a 180-degree turn lately. "Speaking of changes, you've changed your scent." It surrounded them in the enclosed space, more complex than the cologne that had haunted his dreams last night. More sensual.

"Have I?" she asked with feigned uninterest. "I don't remember."

"Your old cologne was sweet. And innocent." He leaned forward, drinking it in. "This makes a man think of deep, slow kisses." His breath was warm on her neck. "And hot sex on a steamy summer night."

His words, his deep voice, the closeness of his body to hers, all conspired to make her knees weak. Amanda considered backing away, then realized there was nowhere to go.

"I didn't come here to rehash the past, Dane." Her headache was building to monumental proportions. "This trip to Satan's Cove is strictly business."

"Yeah, I seem to recall Reva saying something about corporate game-playing stunts."

Her remarkable eyes were as blue as a sunlit sea. A careless man could drown in those wide eyes. Having succumbed to Amanda Stockenberg's siren call once before, Dane had no intention of making that mistake again. Although he knew that to touch her would be dangerous, he couldn't resist reaching out to rub the pads of his thumbs against her temples.

Amanda froze at his touch. "What do you think you're doing?"

Her voice might have turned as chilly as the rain falling outside, but her flesh was warming in a way he remembered all too well. "Helping you get rid of that headache before you rub a hole in your head."

He stroked small, concentric circles that did absolutely nothing to soothe. One hand roamed down the side of her face, her neck, before massaging her knotted shoulder muscle.

His hand was rough with calluses upon calluses, hinting at a life of hard, physical work rather than the one spent behind a wide executive desk he'd once yearned for. It crossed Amanda's mind that in a way, she was living the successful, high-powered life Dane had planned for himself. Which made her wonder if he was living out her old, discarded dreams.

Was he married? Did he have children? The idea of any other woman carrying Dane Cutter's baby caused a flicker of something deep inside Amanda that felt uncomfortably like envy.

"You sure are tense, princess." His clever fingers loosened the knot even as they tangled her nerves.

She knew she should insist he stop, but his touch *was* working wonders on her shoulder. "Knotted muscles and the occasional headache come with the territory. And don't call me *princess.*"

Dane knew the truth of her first statement all too well. It was one of several reasons he'd bailed out of corporate life.

"How about the occasional ulcer?" He plucked the

roll of antacids from her hand, forestalling her from popping another tablet into her mouth.

"I don't have an ulcer."

"I suppose you have a doctor's confirmation of that?"

She tossed her head, then wished she hadn't when the headache stabbed like a stiletto behind her eyes. "Of course."

She was a liar. But a lovely one. Dane suspected that it had been a very long time since Amanda had taken time to visit a doctor. Her clothes, her title, her luggage, the window office with the high-backed Italian-leather chair, all pointed to the fact that the lady was definitely on the fast track up the advertising corporate ladder.

Her too-thin face and the circles beneath her eyes were additional proof of too many hours spent hunkered over advertising copy and campaign jingles. He wondered if she realized she was approaching a very slippery slope.

He was looking at her that way again. Hard and deep. Just when Amanda thought Dane was going to say something profound, the elevator lurched to a sudden stop.

"Third floor, ladies' lingerie," he said cheerfully. "Do you still wear that sexy underwear?"

She wondered if he flirted like this with all the female guests, then wondered how, if he did, he managed to keep his job. Surely some women might complain to the management that the inn's sexy bellhop brought new meaning to the slogan Service With a Smile.

"My underwear is none of your business." Head high, she stepped out of the elevator and headed toward the stairway at the end of the hall, leaving him to follow with the bags.

"I seem to remember a time when you felt differently."

"I felt differently about a lot of things back then. After all, I was only fifteen." The censorious look she flashed back over her shoulder refused to acknowledge his steadfast refusal to carry their teenage affair to its natural conclusion.

"I recall mentioning your tender age on more than one occasion," he said mildly. "But you kept insisting that you were all grown-up."

Not grown-up enough to hold his attention, Amanda thought grimly. As she climbed the stairs to the tower room, she decided she'd made a major mistake in coming to Smugglers' Inn.

Her focus had been clear from the beginning. Pull off the corporate challenge week, get the obnoxious Greg Parsons promoted out of her life, then move upward into his position, which should have been hers in the first place.

Awakening old hurts and reliving old memories definitely hadn't been part of the plan.

And neither had Dane Cutter.

Chapter 3

The first time Amanda had seen the tower room, she'd been entranced. Ten years hadn't lessened its appeal.

Delicate forget-me-nots bloomed on the walls, the high ceiling was a pale powder blue that had always reminded her of a clear summer sky. More blue flowers decorated the ribbon-edged curtains that were pulled back from the sparkling window and matched the thick comforter.

"The bed's different," she murmured.

"Unfortunately, during the time the inn was closed, it became a termite condo and had to go."

"That's too bad." She'd loved the romantic canopy. "But this is nice, too." She ran her hand over one of the pine-log posts that had been sanded to a satin finish.

"I'm glad you approve."

He'd taken the bed from his own room this morning. Now, watching her stroke the wooden post with her slender fingers, Dane felt a slow, deep ache stir inside him.

"I'd suggest not getting too near the woodwork," he warned. "The paint's still a bit sticky."

That explained the white specks on his jeans. A pang of sadness for lost opportunities and abandoned dreams sliced through Amanda.

"Well, thank you for carrying up my bags." Her smile was bright and impersonal as she reached into her purse.

An icy anger rose inside him at the sight of those folded green bills. "Keep your money."

All right, so this meeting was uncomfortable. But he didn't have to get so nasty about it. "Fine." Amanda met his strangely blistering look with a level one of her own. "You realize, I suppose, that I'm going to be here at the inn for a week."

"So?" His tone was as falsely indifferent as hers.

"So, it would seem inevitable that we'd run into each other from time to time."

"Makes sense to me."

It was obvious Dane had no intention of helping her out with this necessary conversation. "This is an important time for me," she said, trying again. "I can't afford any distractions."

"Are you saying I'm a distraction?" As if to underscore her words, he reached out and touched the ends of her hair. "You've dyed your hair," he murmured distractedly.

"Any man who touches me when I don't want him to is a distraction," she retorted, unnerved at how strongly the seemingly harmless touch affected her. "And I didn't dye it. It got darker all on its own."

"It was the color of corn silk that summer." He laced his fingers through the dark gold hair that curved beneath her chin. "Now it's the color of caramel." He held a few strands up to the light. "Laced with melted butter."

The way he was looking at her, the way he kept touching her, caused old seductive memories to come barreling back to batter at Amanda's emotions.

"Food analogies are always so romantic."

"You want romance, princess?" His eyes darkened to obsidian as he moved even closer to her.

As she tried to retreat, Amanda was blocked by the edge of the mattress pressing against the backs of her knees. Unwilling desire mingled with a long-smoldering resentment she'd thought she'd been able to put behind her.

"Damn it, Dane." She put both hands on his shoulders and shoved, but she might as well have been trying to move a mountain. He didn't budge. "I told you not to call me *princess*."

"Fine. Since it's obvious that you've grown up, how about *contessa?*"

It suited her, Dane decided. *Princess* had been her father's name for a spoiled young girl. *Contessa* brought to mind a regal woman very much in charge of her life, as Amanda appeared to be.

The temper she'd kept on a taut leash during a very vexing day broke free. "You know, you really have a lot of nerve." Her voice trembled, which made her all the more angry. She did not want to reveal vulnerability where this man was concerned. "Behaving this way after what you did!"

"What I did?" His own temper, worn to a frazzle from overwork, lack of sleep, and the knowledge that

Amanda was returning to Satan's Cove after all these years, rose to engulf hers. "What the hell did I do? Except spend an entire month taking cold showers after some teenage tease kept heating me up?"

"Tease?"

That did it! She struck out at him, aiming for his shoulder, but hitting his upper arm instead. When her fist impacted with a muscle that felt like a boulder, the shock ran all the way up her arm.

"I loved you, damn it! Which just goes to show how stupid a naive, fifteen-year-old girl can be."

What was even more stupid was having wasted so much time thinking about this man. And wondering what she might have done to make things turn out differently.

His answering curse was short and rude. "You were too self-centered that summer to even know the meaning of the word *love*." Impatience shimmered through him. "Face it, contessa, you thought you'd get your kicks practicing your feminine wiles on some small-town hick before taking your newly honed skills back to the big city."

He would have her, Dane decided recklessly. Before she left Smugglers' Inn. And this time, when she drove away from Satan's Cove, he'd keep something of Amanda for himself. And in turn, leave her with something to remember on lonely rainy nights.

"I loved you," she repeated through clenched teeth. She'd never spoken truer words. "But unfortunately, I was stupid enough to give my heart away to someone who only considered me a summer fling."

Thank heavens she'd only given her heart. Because

if she'd given her body to this man, she feared she never would have gotten over him.

Which she had.

Absolutely. Completely.

The hell she had.

The way he was looking at her, as if he couldn't decide whether to strangle her or ravish her, made Amanda's heart pound.

"You were a lot more than a summer fling." His fingers tightened painfully on her shoulders. His rough voice vibrated through her, causing an ache only he had ever been able to instill. "When I went back to college, I couldn't stop thinking about you. I thought about you during the day, when I was supposed to be studying. I thought about you at night, after work, when I was supposed to be sleeping. And all the time in between."

It was the lie, more than anything, that hurt. All right, so she'd misinterpreted their romance that long-ago summer. Amanda was willing to be honest with herself. Why couldn't he be equally truthful?

"It would have been nice," she suggested in a tone as icy as winter sleet, "if during all that time you were allegedly thinking of me, you thought to pick up a pen and write me a letter. An email. Hell, one of those postcards with the lighthouse on it they sell on the revolving rack downstairs next to the registration desk would have been better than nothing."

"I did write to you." He was leaning over her, his eyes so dark she could only see her reflection. "I wrote you a letter the day you left. And the next day. And for days after that. Until it finally got through my thick head that you weren't going to answer."

The accusation literally rocked her. The anger in his

gritty voice and on his face told Amanda that Dane was telling the truth. "What letters? I didn't get any letters."

"That's impossible." His gaze raked over her snow-white face, seeking the truth. Comprehension, when it dawned, was staggering. "Hell. Your parents got to them first."

"Apparently so." She thought about what such well-meaning parental subterfuge had cost her. What it had, perhaps, cost Dane. Cost them both.

"You know, *you* could always have written to *me,*" Dane said.

"I wanted to. But I couldn't get up the nerve."

He arched a challenging eyebrow. But as she watched reluctant amusement replace the fury in his eyes, Amanda was able to breathe again.

"This from a girl nervy enough to wear a polka-dot bikini horseback riding just to get my attention?" The ploy had worked. The memory of that cute little skimpily clad butt bouncing up and down in that leather saddle had tortured Dane's sleep.

The shared memory brought a reluctant smile from Amanda. She'd paid for that little stunt. If Dane's mother hadn't given her that soothing salve for the chafed skin on the insides of her legs, she wouldn't have been able to walk for a week.

"It was different once I got back home," she admitted now. "I kept thinking about all the older girls who worked at the inn, and went to college with you, and I couldn't imagine why you'd bother carrying a torch for a girl who'd only just gotten her braces off two weeks before coming to Satan's Cove."

Damn. He should have realized she might think that. But at the time, he'd been dazzled by the breezy self-confidence he'd assumed had been bred into Amanda from generations of family wealth.

Oh, he'd known she was too immature—her passionate suggestion that they run away together had been proof of that. But it had never occurred to him that she wasn't as self-assured as she'd seemed. She had, after all, captured the attention of every male in Satan's Cove between the ages of thirteen and ninety. She'd also succeeded in wrapping him—a guy with no intention of letting any woman sidetrack his plan for wealth and success—around her little finger.

Looking down at her now, Dane wondered how much of the girl remained beneath the slick professional veneer Amanda had acquired during the intervening years.

"I did work up my nerve to call you once," she said quietly. "But you'd already gone back to school and the woman who answered the phone here said she didn't have your forwarding address."

"You could have asked my mother."

Her weary shrug told him that she'd considered that idea and rejected it.

Dane wondered what would have happened if his letters had been delivered. Would his life have turned out differently if he'd gotten her call?

Never one to look back, Dane turned his thoughts to the future. The immediate future. Like the next week.

"It appears we have some unfinished business." His hand slipped beneath her hair to cup the back of her neck.

"Dane—" She pressed her palm against his shirt and encountered a wall of muscle every bit as hard as it had been when he was nineteen. There was, she decided recklessly, definitely something to be said for a life of physical work.

"All this heat can't be coming from me." His fingers massaged her neck in a way that was anything but soothing as his lips scorched a trail up her cheek. "The sparks are still there, contessa." His breath was warm against her skin. "You can't deny it."

No, she couldn't. Her entire body was becoming hot and quivery. "Please." Her voice was a throaty shimmer of sound. "I can't concentrate when you're doing that."

"Then don't concentrate." His mouth skimmed along her jaw; Amanda instinctively tilted her head back. "Just feel." When his tongue touched the hollow of her throat, her pulse jumped. "Go with the flow."

"I can't," she complained weakly, even as her rebellious fingers gathered up a handful of white cotton T-shirt. "This week is important to me."

"I remember a time when you said *I* was important to you." The light abrasion of his evening beard scraped seductively against her cheek as his hands skimmed down her sides.

"That was then." She drew in a sharp breath as his palms brushed against her breasts and set them to tingling. In all her twenty-five years Dane was the only man who could touch off the fires of passion smoldering deep inside her. He was the only man who could make her want. And, she reminded herself, he'd been the only man who'd ever made her cry. "This is now."

"It doesn't feel so different." He drew her to him. "*You* don't feel so different."

He wanted her. Too much for comfort. Too much for safety. The way she was literally melting against him made Dane ache in ways he'd forgotten he could ache.

"This has been a long time coming, Amanda." His hands settled low on her hips. "We need to get it out of our systems. Once and for all."

She could feel every hard male part of him through her clothes. He was fully, thrillingly aroused. Even as she tried to warn herself against succumbing to such blatant masculinity, Amanda linked her fingers around his neck and leaned into him.

"I don't know about *your* system," she said breathlessly, as his tongue skimmed up her neck, "but mine's doing just fine."

"Liar." His lips brushed against hers. Teasing, testing, tormenting.

Desire throbbed and pooled between her thighs. Flames were flicking hotly through her veins. She'd never wanted a man the way she wanted Dane Cutter right now. Worse yet, she'd never *needed* a man the way she needed him at this moment.

Which was why she had to back away from temptation. When, and if, she did make love to Dane, she wanted to make certain she knew exactly what she was doing. And why.

She needed to be certain that the desire coursing through her veins was not simply a knee-jerk response to the only man who'd ever made her burn. She had to convince herself that she wasn't succumbing to the seduction of the romantic setting, old memories, and sensual fantasies.

After suffering the resultant pain from her impulsive, teenage behavior, Amanda had acquired a need for an orderly, controlled life. Unfortunately, there was nothing orderly or controlled about the way Dane Cutter made her feel.

"I need to think," she protested weakly. "It's been a long and frustrating day and I'm exhausted, Dane."

"Fine." He'd give her that. There would, Dane told himself, be other times. "But before I go, let me give you something to think about."

Amanda knew what was coming. Knew she should resist. Even as she warned herself to back away now, before she got in over her head, another voice in the back of her mind pointed out that this was her chance to prove she was no longer a foolish young girl who could lose her heart over a simple kiss.

Since the second option seemed the more logical, Amanda went with it. She stood there, her palms pressed against his chest, as he slowly, deliberately, lowered his mouth to hers.

It was definitely not what she'd been expecting.

The first time he'd kissed her, that long-ago night when she'd come to his room, clad in her sexiest nightie, Dane had been frustrated and angry—angry at her for having teased him unmercifully, angry at himself for not being able to resist.

His mouth had swooped down, causing their teeth to clang painfully together as he ground his lips against hers. He'd used his mouth and his tongue as a weapon and she'd found it shocking and thrilling at the same time.

Later, as the days went by, Dane had grown more and more sexually frustrated, and it had showed. Although his kisses were no longer tinged with anger, they were riddled with a hot, desperate hunger that equaled her own.

Although the attraction was still there a decade later,

it was more than apparent to Amanda that the years had mellowed Dane, taught him patience. And finesse.

He cupped her face in his hands and she trembled.

He touched his mouth to hers and she sighed.

With a rigid control that cost him dearly, Dane forced himself to take his time, coaxing her into the mists by skimming kisses from one side of her full, generous mouth to the other.

"Dane—"

Ignoring her faint protest, he caught her bottom lip in his teeth and tugged, causing a slow, almost-languid ache.

Prepared for passion, she had no defenses against this exquisite, dreamy pleasure. Amanda twined her arms tighter around his neck and allowed herself to sink into his kiss.

"Oh, Dane..."

"Lord, I like the way you say my name." His breath was like a summer breeze against her parted lips. "Say it again."

At this suspended moment in time, unable to deny Dane anything, Amanda softly obliged.

"Your voice reminds me of warm honey." He soothed the flesh his teeth had bruised with his tongue. "Sweet and thick and warm."

He angled his head and continued making love to her with his mouth. The tip of his tongue slipped silkily between her lips, then withdrew. Then dipped in again, deeper this time, only to withdraw once more.

Every sense was heightened. Every nerve ending in her body hummed.

His clever, wicked tongue repeated that glorious movement again and again, each time delving deeper, seducing hers into a slow, sensual dance. The rest of the world drifted away. Until there was only Dane. And the pure pleasure of his mouth.

Damn. This wasn't going the way he'd planned. The rich, warm taste of her was causing an ache in his loins far worse than the teenage horniness he'd suffered the last time he'd been with Amanda like this. Sweat broke out on his forehead as he felt the soft swell of her belly pressing against his erection.

Her throaty moans were driving him crazy and if she didn't stop grinding against him that way, stoking fires that were already close to burning out of control, he was going to throw her down on that bed and rip away those travel-rumpled clothes.

He imagined sliding his tongue down her throat, over her breasts, swirling around the hard little nipples that were pressing against his chest, before cutting a wet swath down her slick, quivering stomach, making her writhe with need; then lower still, until he was sliding it between her legs, gathering up the sweet taste—

"Hell."

Jerking his mind back from that perilous precipice, Dane literally pushed himself away from her. For his sake, not hers.

It had happened again! Ten minutes alone with Amanda and he'd nearly lost it. What was it about this woman? Even at nineteen he'd been far from inexperienced. Yet all it had taken then—and, apparently, all it took even now—was a taste of her succulent lips, the feel of her hot, feminine body pressed against his, to bring him to the brink of exploding.

Her head still spinning, her body pulsing, Amanda stared at Dane and watched as his rugged face closed up.

He jammed his hands into the pockets of his jeans with such force that her eyes were drawn to the brusque movement. Heaven help her, the sight of that bulge pressing against the faded denim caused something like an ocean swell to rise up from her most feminine core.

Realizing what she was staring at, Dane again cursed his lack of control. "I'm not going to apologize." His voice was distant, and amazingly cold for a man who, only moments earlier, had nearly caused them both to go up in flames.

"I wouldn't ask you to." She dragged her hair back from her temples, appalled by the discovery that her hands were shaking. "I'm no longer a teenager, Dane. You don't have to worry about my father showing up at the door with a shotgun."

Dane almost laughed. He wondered what she'd say if he told her that he found the idea of an irate father far less threatening than what he was currently feeling.

"You're tired." And she had been for some time, if the circles beneath her eyes were any indication. "We'll talk tomorrow. After you've had some rest."

"There's no need to—"

"I said, we'll talk tomorrow."

Amanda stiffened, unaccustomed to taking such sharp, direct orders from any man. Before she could argue, he said, "Just dial three for room service. The cook will fix anything you'd like. Within reason."

With that, he was gone. Leaving Amanda confused. And wanting.

As he descended the narrow, curving stairway, Dane assured himself that his only problem was he'd been taken by surprise. Initially, he hadn't expected Amanda to show up from the shadows of the past. Then, when she had arrived, he certainly hadn't expected such a knee-jerk, gut-wrenching physical reaction.

By tomorrow morning, Dane vowed, he'd have control of his body.

What was worrying the hell out of him was the problem he feared he was going to have gaining control over his heart.

Chapter 4

Amanda was not in a good mood the following morning, as she went downstairs to prepare for the kickoff meeting. Her headache had returned with a vengeance and her stomach was tied up in knots. She'd spent the night tossing and turning, reliving old memories of her days—and nights—at Smugglers' Inn.

And then, when she had finally fallen asleep shortly before dawn, her dreams had been filled with the man who had, impossibly, become an even better kisser. The sensual dreams had resulted in her waking up with an unhealthy curiosity about all the women with whom Dane had spent the past ten years practicing his kissing technique.

After a false turn, she found the conference room Susan had reserved. Ten years ago, the room had been a sleeping porch. The oversize green screens had been replaced with glass, protecting occupants from the unpredictable coastal weather without taking away from the dazzling view, which, at the moment, was draped in a soft silver mist.

It was absolutely lovely. Greg would find nothing to complain about here. The only problem would be keeping people's minds off the scenery and focused on the challenge.

Drawn by the pull of the past, she walked over to the wall of windows and gazed out, trying to catch a glimpse of the cave where she and Dane had shared such bliss.

Both relieved and disappointed to see the fog blocked the view of that stretch of beach, she turned her back on the sea and crossed the room to a pine sideboard where urns of coffee and hot water for tea had been placed. Beside the urn were baskets of breakfast breads, and white platters of fresh fruit.

Amanda poured herself a cup of coffee and placed some strawberries onto a small plate. When the fragrant lure proved impossible to resist, she plucked a blueberry muffin from one of the baskets, then set to work unpacking the boxes of supplies.

As she separated T-shirts bearing the team challenge logo into red and blue stacks, Amanda wondered what Dane was doing.

Although she remembered him to have been an early riser, she doubted he'd have arrived at the inn. Not after the late hours he'd worked yesterday. Which was just as well, since she still hadn't sorted out her feelings. All the agonizing she'd done during the long and sleepless night had only confused her more.

Last night, alone with him in the tower room that had

been filled with bittersweet memories, it had felt as if no time at all had passed since that night they'd lain in each other's arms, driving each other to painful distraction, whispering tender words of love, vowing desperate promises.

This morning, Amanda was trying to convince herself that stress, exhaustion and the surprise of seeing Dane again had been responsible for her having responded so quickly and so strongly to him. To his touch. His kiss.

Memories of that enticing kiss flooded back, warming her to the core. "You have to stop this," she scolded herself aloud.

It was imperative that she concentrate on the difficult week ahead. If she allowed her thoughts to drift constantly to Dane Cutter, she'd never pull off a successful challenge. And without a successful challenge, not only would she lose her chance for promotion, she could end up being stuck with Greg Parsons for a very long time.

"And that," she muttered, "is not an option."

"Excuse me?"

Having believed herself to be alone, Amanda spun around and saw a woman standing in the doorway. She was casually dressed in navy shorts, a white polo shirt and white sneakers. If it hadn't been for her name, written in red script above her breast, Amanda would have taken her for a guest.

"I was just talking to myself," she said with embarrassment.

"I do that all the time." The woman's smile was as warm and friendly as Mindy Taylor's had been last night. "Sometimes I even answer myself back, which was beginning to worry me, until Dane said that the time to worry was if I began ignoring myself."

She crossed the room and held out her hand. "I'm Reva Carlson. And you must be Amanda Stockenberg."

Having observed the frenzied activity that had gone into preparing the tower room, then hearing how Dane had insisted on carrying Amanda's bags last night, Reva was more than a little interested in this particular guest. As was every other employee of Smugglers' Inn.

"You're the conference manager Susan spoke with," Amanda remembered.

"Among other things. The management structure around this place tends to be a bit loose."

"Oh?" Amanda wasn't certain she liked the sound of that. One of the advantages of the Mariner Seaside Golf Resort and Conference Center had been an assistant manager whose sole function had been to tend to the group's every need.

"Everyone's trained to fill in wherever they're needed, to allow for optimum service," Reva revealed the management style Dane had introduced. "Although I'm embarrassed to admit that I've been barred from the kitchen after last week's fire."

"Fire?" After having watched her first choice of resort go up in flames, Amanda definitely didn't like hearing that.

"Oh, it wasn't really that big a deal." The shoulders of the white knit shirt rose and fell in a careless shrug. "I was merely trying my hand at pears flambé. When I poured just a smidgen too much brandy into the pans, things got a little hot for a time." Her smile widened. "By the time the fire department showed up, Dane had things under control."

When even the sound of his name caused a hitch in her breathing, Amanda knew she was in deep, deep trouble. "Dane was working in the kitchen?"

"Sure." Another shrug. "I told you, we're pretty loose around here. And Dane's amazingly handy at everything. He shot the pan with the fire extinguisher, and that was that. But in the meantime, I've been banned from any further cooking experiments, though Mary did promise to let me frost a birthday cake for one of our guests tomorrow."

"Mary?" At the familiar name, Amanda stopped trying to picture Dane in an apron, comfortable in a kitchen. "Mary Cutter?"

"That's right." Reva tilted her head. "Sounds as if you know her."

"I used to." Amanda couldn't quite stop the soft sigh. "I came here with my parents on a vacation ten years ago."

"Mindy mentioned something about that." Reva's friendly gaze turned speculative. "I guess Dane must have been working here at the time, too." Her voice went up on the end of the sentence, turning it into a question.

It was Amanda's turn to shrug. "I suppose. It was a long time ago, and there was quite a large staff, so it's hard to remember everyone."

From the knowing expression in the convention manager's eyes, Amanda had the feeling she wasn't fooling her for a moment. "I do remember his mother made the best peach pie I've ever tasted." She also, Amanda had discovered this morning, baked dynamite blueberry muffins.

"Mary's peach pie wins the blue ribbon at the county fair every year." Returning to her work mode, Reva glanced around the room. "Do you have everything you need?"

"I think so." Amanda's gaze took another slow sweep around the room, trying to seek out any lapses Greg might catch.

"If you think of anything—anything at all—don't hesitate to call on any of us. I have to run into town on some errands, but Dane's around here somewhere."

"I'm sure we'll be fine," Amanda said quickly. Too quickly, she realized, as Reva's gaze narrowed ever so slightly.

"Well, good luck." Reva turned to leave. "With everything."

Matters taken care of to her satisfaction, Reva Carlson returned to her own work, leaving Amanda with the feeling that the woman's parting comment had little to do with the upcoming challenge exercises.

After she finished unpacking the boxes, Amanda headed down the hall to the kitchen, to thank Mary Cutter for the superb Continental breakfast, when she heard her name being called.

Believing it to be someone from the agency, she turned, surprised to see two familiar faces.

"Miss Minnie? Miss Pearl?" The elderly sisters had been guests the last time Amanda had stayed at the inn.

"Hello, dear," one of them—Minnie or Pearl, Amanda couldn't remember which was which—said. Her rosy face was as round as a harvest moon and wreathed in a smile. "We heard you'd come back. It's lovely to see you again."

"It's nice to see you, too. It's also a surprise."

"I don't know why it should be," the other sister

said. "With the exception of the three years the inn was closed—"

"A terrible shame," the other interrupted. "As I was telling Dane just yesterday—"

"Sister!" A scowl darkened a sharp, hatchet face. "I was speaking."

"I'm sorry, sister." There was a brief nod of a lavender head that had been permed into corkscrews; the pastel hue complemented the woman's pink complexion. "I was just pointing out to Amanda how sad it was that such a lovely inn had been allowed to fall into disrepair."

"You'd never know that to look at it now," Amanda said.

"That's because Dane has been working around the clock," the thinner of the two sisters huffed. It was more than a little obvious she resented having her story sidetracked. "As I was saying, with the exception of those three unfortunate years, we have been visiting Smugglers' Inn for the last sixty-four years."

"I believe it's only been sixty-three, sister."

A forceful chin thrust out. "It's sixty-four."

"Are you sure?"

"Of course. I remember everything that happened that year," the other snapped with the certainty of a woman who'd spent forty-five years as the research librarian for the Klamath County Library in southern Oregon.

The term *sibling rivalry* could have been invented to define Minnie and Pearl Davenport. Recalling all too well how these arguments could go on all day, Amanda repeated how nice it was to see the women again and escaped into the kitchen.

This room, too, was as she remembered it—warm

and cheerful and immensely inviting. Fragrant, mouth-watering steam rose from the pots bubbling away on the gleaming stove; more copper pots hung from a ceiling rack and the windowsill was home to a row of clay pots filled with fresh green herbs.

An enormous refrigerator that hadn't been there the last time Amanda had sneaked into the kitchen for a heart-to-heart talk with Mary Cutter was open.

"Hello?"

A dark head popped out from behind the stainless-steel door. "Amanda, hello!" Dane's mother's expression was warm and welcoming. She closed the refrigerator and opened her arms. "I was hoping you'd get a chance to escape those boring old business meetings and visit with an old friend."

As she hugged the woman, Amanda realized that Mary Cutter had, indeed, become a friend that summer. Even though, looking back on it, she realized how concerned Mary had been for Dane. As she would have been, Amanda admitted now, if some sex-crazed, underage teenage girl had been chasing after her son.

"They're not that bad." Amanda felt duty-bound to defend the group.

"Oh?" Releasing her, Mary went over to the stove and poured two cups of coffee. She put them on the table, and gestured for Amanda to sit down. "Then why do you have those dark circles beneath your eyes?"

Amanda unconsciously lifted her fingers to the blue shadows she thought she'd managed to conceal successfully this morning. It was bad enough having to deal with Dane and their past, which now seemed to be unsettled. By the time the corporate challenge week was over, she'd undoubtedly be buying concealer by the carton.

"I've been working long hours lately."

"You're not sleeping very well, either, I'd suspect. And you have a headache."

"It's not that bad," Amanda lied as Mary reached out and rubbed at the lines carving furrows between her eyes.

The older woman's touch was gentle and more maternal than any Amanda had ever received from her own mother. Then again, the Stockenbergs never had been touchers. The Cutters—mother and son—definitely were.

Mary's smile didn't fade, but the way she was looking at her, hard and deep, made Amanda want to change the subject. "I just ran into Miss Minnie and Miss Pearl," she said. "But I couldn't remember which was which."

"Minnie is the one with white hair and an attitude. Pearl has lavender hair and hides Hershey's Kisses all over the inn."

"Why would she do that?"

"Because the poor dear has an enormous sweet tooth. And Minnie has her on a diet that would starve a gerbil." Mary flashed a quick grin that was remarkably like her son's, although it didn't have the capability to affect Amanda in such a devastating manner. "I feel so sorry for Pearl. She's been sneaking in here for snacks ever since they arrived last week."

"Well, I can certainly understand that. I had a muffin that was just short of heaven."

"I'm so pleased you enjoyed it." Mary's eyes skimmed over Amanda judiciously. "You're a bit thin, dear. We'll have to see what we can do about fattening you up a little."

"A woman can never be too thin," Amanda said, quoting one of her sleek mother's favorite axioms.

"Want to bet?" a deep voice asked from the doorway.

Amanda tamped down the little burst of pleasure brought about by the sight of Dane, clad again in jeans. Today's shirt was faded chambray; his shoes were high-topped sneakers.

Mary greeted him with a smile. "Good morning, darling."

"Morning." He crossed the room on a long, easy stride and kissed his mother's cheek. "Do I smell sugar cookies?"

"It's my new cologne," Mary said with a laugh. "The saleswoman said it has vanilla in it." She shook her head in mock regret. "She also said men would find it impossible to resist. I'm afraid I was oversold."

"Never met a man yet who didn't like sugar cookies," Dane said agreeably. His grin slipped a notch as his attention turned to Amanda. "Good morning."

Amanda had watched the way he brushed his finger down his mother's cheek in a casual, intimate gesture that was as natural to him as breathing. Once again she was reminded how different the Cutters were from the Stockenbergs. It would be wise to keep those differences in mind over the next several days.

"Good morning." Her tone was friendly, but cool. She could have been speaking to a stranger at a bus stop.

"Sleep well?" His tone was as studiously casual as hers.

"Like a baby," she lied. She pushed herself up from the table. "Well, I really do have to get back to work. I just wanted to stop in and say hi," she told Mary. "And to thank you for the lovely breakfast."

"It's been lovely seeing you again, dear." Dane's mother took Amanda's hand in both of hers. "I realize you're going to be extremely busy, but I hope you can find time to visit again."

"I'd like that." It was the truth.

Without another word to Dane, Amanda placed her cup on the counter, then left the kitchen.

"Well, she certainly has grown up to be a lovely young lady," Mary said.

"Really?" Dane's answering shrug was forced. "I didn't notice."

Mary poured another cup of coffee and placed it in front of him. "Reva says she has a very responsible position at that advertising agency."

This earned little more than a grunt.

"I couldn't help noticing she's not wearing any ring on her left hand."

Dane's face shuttered. "No offense, Mom, but I really don't want to talk about Amanda."

"Of course, dear," Mary replied smoothly. But as she turned to the stove and poured pancake batter into an iron skillet, Mary Cutter was smiling.

Despite instructions that they were to meet at eight o'clock sharp, the team members straggled into the conference room. By the time everyone had gotten coffee, fruit and pastries and taken their seats, it was twenty-eight minutes past the time the kickoff had been scheduled to begin.

"Well, this is certainly getting off to a dandy start," muttered Greg, who was sitting beside Amanda at the pine trestle table at the front of the room. "Didn't you send out my memo letting the troops know I expected them to be prompt?"

"Of course." Amanda refrained from pointing out that if one wanted troops to follow orders, it was helpful if they respected their commanding officer. "We arrived awfully late last night," she said, seeking some excuse for the tardy team members. "Everyone was probably a little tired this morning."

His only response to her efforts was a muttered curse that did not give Amanda a great deal of encouragement.

Greg stood and began to outline the week's activities, striding back and forth at the front of the room like General Patton addressing the soldiers of the Third Army. He was waving his laser pointer at the detailed flowchart as if it were Patton's famed riding crop. The troops seemed uniformly unimpressed by all the red, blue and yellow rectangles.

As he set about explaining the need for consistent process and implementation, even Amanda's mind began to wander, which was why she didn't hear the door open at the back of the room.

"I'm sorry to interrupt," one of last night's bellmen, who bore an amazing resemblance to Brad Pitt, said. "But Ms. Stockenberg has a phone call."

"Take a message," Greg snapped before Amanda could answer.

"He says it's urgent."

"I'd better take it," Amanda said.

"Just make it quick. I intend to get on schedule."

"I'll be right back." Amanda resisted the urge to salute.

The news was not good. "But you have to come,"

she insisted when the caller, the man she'd hired to conduct the physical adventure portion of the weekend, explained his predicament. "I understand you've broken your leg. But surely you can at least sit on the beach and instruct—"

She was cut off by a flurry of denial on the other end of the line. "Oh. In traction? I'm so sorry to hear that." She reached into her pocket, pulled out the antacids she was never without and popped one into her mouth.

"Well, of course you need to rest. And get well soon." She dragged her hand through her hair. "There's no need to apologize. You didn't fall off that motorcycle on purpose."

She hung up the phone with a bit more force than necessary. "Damn."

"Got a problem?"

Amanda spun around and glared up at Dane. "I'm getting a little tired of the way you have of sneaking up on people."

"Sorry." The dancing light in his eyes said otherwise.

"No." She sighed and shook her head. "I'm the one who should apologize for snapping at you. It's just that I really need this week to go well, and before we can even get started on the kayak race, my adventure expert ends up in the hospital."

"That *is* a tough break."

She could hear the amusement in his voice. "Don't you dare laugh at me."

"I wouldn't think of it." He reached out and rubbed at the parallel lines his mother had smoothed earlier. "I don't suppose a hotshot businesswoman—with her own window office and fancy Italian-leather chair—would need any advice?"

The soothing touch felt too good. Too right. Amanda backed away. "At this point, I'd take advice from the devil himself." Realizing how snippy she sounded, she felt obliged to apologize yet again.

"Don't worry about it. People say things they don't mean under stress." Which he knew only too well. Dane had found it enlightening that the temper he'd developed while working for the Whitfield Palace hotel chain seemed to have vanished when he'd bought the inn, despite all the problems refurbishing it had entailed. "How about me?"

"How about you, what?"

"How about me subbing for your kayak guy?"

Remembering how he'd taught her to paddle that double kayak so many years ago, Amanda knew it was the perfect solution. Except for one thing.

"Don't you have work to do?"

Dane shrugged. "It'll keep."

"I wouldn't want you to get in trouble."

"Why don't you let me worry about that, contessa? Besides, we all kind of pitch in where needed around here."

That was exactly what Reva had told her. And Amanda was grateful enough not to contest that ridiculous name. "Thank you. I really appreciate your help."

"Hey, that's what we're here for." He grinned and skimmed a dark finger down the slope of her nose. "Service With a Smile, that's the motto at Smugglers' Inn."

The knot of tension in her stomach unwound. It was impossible to worry when he was smiling at her that way. It was nearly impossible to remember that the man represented a dangerous distraction.

Relieved that she'd overcome the first hurdle of the

week, and putting aside the nagging little problem of what she was going to do about the rest of the scheduled adventure exercises, Amanda returned to the conference room and began handing out the challenge-team shirts.

"What the hell are these?" Don Patterson, the marketing manager, asked.

"They're to denote the different teams," Amanda explained. "Reds versus blues."

"Like shirts versus skins," Marvin Kenyon, who'd played some high school basketball, said.

"Exactly."

"I wouldn't mind playing shirts and skins with Kelli," Peter Wanger from the computer-support division said with a leer directed toward the public-relations manager, who was provocatively dressed in a pair of tight white jeans and a thin red top. The scoop neck barely concealed voluptuous breasts that, if they hadn't been surgically enhanced, could undoubtedly qualify as natural wonders of the world.

"Watch it, Peter," Amanda warned. "Or you'll have to watch that video on sexual harassment in the workplace again."

"Oh, Peter was just joking," Kelli said quickly, sending a perky cheerleader smile his way. "It doesn't bother me, Amanda."

That might be. But it did bother Greg. Amanda watched her superior's jaw clench. "Amanda's right," he growled. If looks could kill, Peter would be drawn and quartered, then buried six feet under the sand. "Just because we're not in the office doesn't mean that I'll stand for inappropriate behavior."

It sounded good. But everyone in the room knew that what was really happening was that Greg had just stamped his own personal No Trespassing sign on Kelli Kyle's wondrous chest.

"Talk about inappropriate," Laura Quinlan muttered as Amanda handed her a red T-shirt. "My kid's Barbie doll has tops larger than that bimbo's."

At thirty-six, Laura was a displaced homemaker who'd recently been hired as a junior copywriter. Amanda knew she was struggling to raise two children on her own after her physician husband had left her for his office assistant—a young woman who, if Laura could be believed, could be Kelli Kyle's evil twin.

Secretly agreeing about the inappropriateness of Kelli's attire, but not wanting to take sides, Amanda didn't answer.

"I can't wear this color," Nadine Roberts complained when Amanda handed her one of the red shirts. "I had my colors done and I'm a summer."

"This week you're an autumn." Amanda tossed a blue shirt to Julian Palmer.

"You certainly chose a graphically unsatisfying design," he complained.

"We should have come to you for help," she said, soothing the art director's easily ruffled feathers. Personally, she thought the white Team Challenge script just dandy. "But I knew how overworked you've been with the Uncle Paul's potato chip account, and didn't want to add any more pressure."

"The man's an idiot," Julian grumbled. "Insisting on those claymation dancing barbecue chips."

"It worked for the raisin growers," Kelli reminded everyone cheerfully. Despite all the rumors that had circulated since the woman's arrival two weeks ago, no one could accuse her of not being unrelentingly upbeat.

Amanda had been surprised to discover that beneath that bubbly-cheerleader personality and bimbo clothing, Kelli possessed a steel-trap mind when it came to her work. Which made it even more surprising that she'd stoop to having an affair with a man like Greg.

Not that there was actually any proof, other than gossip, that they were sleeping together, she reminded herself. However, given Greg's Lothario tendencies, along with all the time the pair spent together in his office with the door closed, Amanda certainly wouldn't have bet against the possibility.

Julian stiffened and shot Kelli a look that suggested her IQ was on a level with Uncle Paul's. "Potato chips," he said, "are not raisins."

No one in the room dared challenge that proclamation.

"Wait a damn minute," Marvin Kenyon complained when Amanda handed him a blue shirt. "I categorically refuse to be on *his* team." He jerked a thumb in Julian's direction.

Amanda opened her mouth to answer, but Greg beat her to the punch. "You'll be on whatever team I tell you you're on," he barked from the front of the room. "In case I haven't made myself clear, people, challenge week isn't about choice. It's about competition. Teamwork.

"And effective immediately, you are all going to work together as teams. Or at the end of the week, I'll start handing out pink slips. Do I make myself clear?"

He was answered by a low, obviously unhappy mumble.

Smooth move, Greg, Amanda thought.

The worst problem with mergers was their effect

on the employees. Even more so in advertising, where people were the agency's only real assets.

The rash of changeovers had caused dislocation, disaffection, underperformance and just plain fear. Which explained why more and more accounts were leaving the agency with each passing day. It was, after all, difficult to be creative when you thought you were going to be fired.

There were times, and this was definitely one of them, when Amanda wished she'd stuck to her youthful dreams of creating a family rather than an ad for a new, improved detergent or a toothpaste that supposedly would make the high school football quarterback ask the class wallflower to the prom.

When the idea of home and children once again brought Dane to the forefront of her mind, she shook off the thought and led the group out of the room, down to the beach where the first challenge activity was scheduled to take place.

Chapter 5

"Oh, my God," Laura said as the group reached the beach and found Dane waiting. "I think I'm in love."

While Greg had been harassing the troops and Amanda had been handing out T-shirts, Dane had changed into a black neoprene body glove. The suit somehow seemed to reveal more of him than if he were stark-naked.

His arms, his powerful legs, his chest, looked as if they had been chiseled from marble. No, Amanda decided, marble was too cold. Dane could have been hewn from one of the centuries-old redwoods found in an old-growth forest.

"That man is, without a doubt, the most drop-dead-gorgeous male I've ever seen in my life." Kelli was staring at Dane the way a religious zealot might stare at her god. "Oh, I do believe I'm going to enjoy this week."

"We're not here to enjoy ourselves," Greg ground

out. "It's not a damn holiday." He turned his sharp gaze on Amanda. "That's the guy you hired to lead the adventure exercises?"

Call her petty, but Amanda found watching Greg literally seething with masculine jealousy more than a little enjoyable. Less enjoyable was the realization that Kelli's and Laura's lustful looks and comments had triggered a bit of her own jealousy.

"Not exactly."

Blond brows came crashing down. "What does that mean?"

"I'll explain later." She cast a significant glance down at her watch. "You're the one who wanted to stay on schedule, Greg. Come with me and I'll introduce you."

The introductions were over quickly, neither man seeming to find much to like about the other.

"The plan," Amanda explained to Dane, "as it was originally laid out to me, works like a relay race. Team members pair up, two to a kayak, paddle out to the lighthouse, circle it, then return back to the beach where the next group takes their places in the kayak and follows the same course. The best combined times for the two out of three heats is declared the winner."

Dane nodded. "Sounds easy enough."

"Easy for you to say. You haven't seen this group in action."

Seeing her worried expression and remembering what she'd told him about this week being vastly important to her, Dane understood her concern.

"Don't worry, Ms. Stockenberg," he said in his best businesslike tone, the one that had served him well for all those years in the big city, "before the week's over, you'll have turned your group into a lean, mean, advertising machine."

"That's the point," Greg Parsons snapped.

Amanda, who'd detected the sarcasm in Dane's tone, didn't respond. Instead, she introduced Dane to the others, then stood back and ceded control to the man she hoped could pull it off.

He didn't raise his voice above his usual conversational tone, but as he began to explain the basics of kayaking, Amanda noticed that a hush settled over the suddenly attentive group. Even the men were hanging on every word.

It was more than the fact that he was a stunningly good-looking male specimen. As amazing as it seemed for a man who'd been content to stay in the same job he'd had in high school, Dane Cutter definitely displayed leadership potential, making Amanda wonder yet again what had happened to sidetrack all his lofty career goals.

Perhaps, she considered, once this week was over and she'd earned the position of Northwest creative director, she'd offer Dane a job in management. After all, if he actually managed to pull this disparate, backbiting group into cohesive teams, helping him escape a dead-end life in Satan's Cove would be the least she could do.

Then again, she reminded herself firmly when she realized she was thinking too much like her autocratic father, there was no reason for Dane to be ashamed of having chosen a life of manual labor. It was, she admitted reluctantly, more honest than advertising.

Dane gave the teams a brief spiel about the versatility of kayaks, demonstrated forward and bracing strokes, explaining how the foot-operated rudder would help steer in crosswinds or rough seas, and skimmed over the wood-paddles-versus-fiberglass argument.

Amanda was not surprised to discover that despite the introduction of high-tech models, Dane remained an advocate of wood. The fact that he obviously felt strongly about a century-old inn proved he was a traditionalist at heart.

When he asked for questions, Kelli's hand shot up. "Shouldn't we be wearing wet suits like yours?" she asked.

"It's not really necessary," Dane assured her, making Amanda extremely relieved. She figured the sight of Kelli Kyle in a neoprene body glove could easily cause at least two heart attacks.

"But what if we get wet?"

"One can only hope," Peter murmured, earning laughter from several of the men and another sharp glare from Greg. At the same time, Amanda worried that Kelli in a wet T-shirt could be even more distracting than Kelli in a snug neoprene suit.

"Hopefully that won't prove a problem," Dane said with an answering smile.

"I've seen kayaking on the Discovery channel." This from Nadine Roberts. "And they always tip over."

"That technique is called an Eskimo roll. And you don't have to worry about learning it for this exercise," Dane told her.

"What if we don't intend to learn it? What if we roll anyway?" An auditor in the accounting department, Nadine was not accustomed to letting things slide.

"Never happen." Dane's grin was quick and reassuring. "You're thinking of the Inuit cruiser style, which is designed for speed and minimum wind interference.

You'll be in double touring kayaks, which are extremely stable. Think of them as floating minivans."

"My minivan is a lot bigger," Laura argued.

"People," Greg interjected sharply, "we're wasting valuable time here." He turned toward Dane. "As fascinating as all this might be," he said, his sarcastic tone indicating otherwise, "we don't have all day. So, if you're through with the instructions, Cutter, it's time to get this show on the road."

"It's your show," Dane said agreeably. But Amanda could see a simmering irritation in his dark eyes. "I'll need a volunteer for a demonstration." His seemingly casual gaze moved over the group before landing on Amanda. "Ms. Stockenberg," he said, "how about helping me with a little show-and-tell?"

Every head on the beach had turned toward her. Knowing that refusal would garner unwanted interest, Amanda shrugged. "Fine."

She took the orange life jacket Dane held out to her and put it on over her challenge T-shirt.

"Need any help with that?" he asked, reminding her of the time she'd pretended to need him to fasten the ties for her.

"I'm fine, thank you."

"Actually," he murmured, for her ears only, "you're a helluva lot better than fine, contessa."

Her temper flared, predictably. Remembering where she was, Amanda tamped it down.

"You'll need this." He handed her a helmet not unlike the one she wore when rollerblading or biking. "There are a lot of rocks around the lighthouse."

"I thought you said there's no risk of capsizing," she argued as she nevertheless put the white helmet on.

"Good point. But it never hurts to be prepared."

Good point, she echoed mentally as she watched him drag the kayak toward the water. If she'd been prepared to discover Dane still working here, she wouldn't be suffering from these unsettling feelings.

Within minutes of being afloat, she began to remember the rhythm he'd so patiently taught her that long-ago summer. Holding the blade of the wooden paddle close to her chest, her hands a bit more than shoulders' width apart, she plunged the blade in cleanly, close to the hull, pulling back with her lower hand, using torso rotation rather than arm strength, punching forward with her upper hand at the same time. When the blade of the paddle reached her hip, she snapped it out of the water and stroked on the other side.

Stab, pull, snap. Stab, pull, snap. Behind her, she could feel Dane moving in concert. *Stab, pull, snap.* "Not bad," Dane said. "For someone who probably considers the rowing machine at the gym roughing it."

Since his remark hit close to the truth, Amanda opted not to take offense. "I can't believe it's coming back so fast." *Stab, pull, snap. Left, right, left, right.* Although the touring kayak was built for stability, not speed, they were skimming through the surf toward the lighthouse. "I suppose it's like riding a bicycle."

"Or kissing," Dane suggested. *Stab, pull, snap.* The paddles continued to swish through the water. "We always did that well together, too. Ten years ago. And again, last night."

His words stopped her cold. "I don't want to talk about last night." Unnerved, she forgot to pull the paddle out until it had drifted beyond her hip. When she did, she caused the boat to veer off course.

The brisk professional ad executive was back. Dane was tempted to flip the kayak just to teach her a lesson. And to cool himself off. Didn't she know what she'd done to him last night? Didn't she realize how all it had taken was the taste of those succulent lips and the feel of that soft body against his to cause time to go spinning backward and make him feel like a horny, sex-starved teenager again?

"Tough," he deftly corrected, setting them straight again. Didn't she know that showing up this morning in that soft cotton T-shirt and those shorts that made her legs look as if they went all the way up to her neck was like waving a red flag in front of a very frustrated bull?

When he felt his hand tighten in a death grip on the smooth wooden shaft, he flexed his fingers, restraining the urge to put them around her shoulders to shake her.

"Because I have no intention of spending the next five nights lying awake, thinking about might-have-beens."

His tone was gruff, but Amanda was no longer an easily cowed fifteen-year-old girl. She began to shoot him a glare over her shoulder, but the lethal look in his eyes had her missing yet another stroke.

"You agreed to teach the kayaking just to get me alone with you, didn't you?"

"I could see from that schedule you and Mr. Slick have devised for the week that having you to myself for any decent length of time was going to be difficult, if not impossible," he agreed without displaying an iota of guilt about utilizing such subterfuge. "Fortunately, I've always prided myself on managing the impossible. Like resisting making love to a painfully desirable teenager."

"Dane..." Words deserted her as something far more dangerous than anger rose in those dark eyes.

They were behind the lighthouse now, out of view of the challenge-team members waiting for them back on the beach.

Dane stopped stroking and laid his paddle across the kayak. "I've thought about you, Amanda. I've remembered how you felt in my arms, how you tasted, how my body would ache all night after I'd have to send you back to your room."

"Don't blame me. *You're* the one who didn't want to make love."

"Wrong. What I wanted to do and what I knew I had to do were two entirely different things, contessa. But just because I was trying to do the honorable thing— not to mention staying out of jail—doesn't mean that I haven't imagined how things might have been different. If we'd met at another time."

"It wouldn't be the same." It was what she'd been telling herself for years. "That summer was something apart, Dane. Something that belongs in its own time and its own place. It doesn't even seem real anymore. And it certainly doesn't fit in our real lives."

She wasn't saying anything Dane hadn't told himself innumerable times. The problem was, he hadn't bought the argument then. And he wasn't buying it now.

"Are you saying you haven't thought about me?"

"That's exactly what I'm saying." It was the first and only lie she'd ever told him.

"Never?"

"Never."

He considered that for a moment. "All right. Let's

fast-forward to the present. Tell me you didn't feel anything last night, and I'll never mention it again."

"I didn't mean for that to…" She shook her head. "It just happened," she said weakly.

"Tell me."

She swallowed and looked away, pretending sudden interest in a trio of dolphins riding the surf on the horizon. There was a tug-of-war going on inside her. Pulling her emotionally toward Dane, pushing her away. Pulling and pushing. As it had done all during the long and lonely night.

"Tell me you haven't thought about how it could be," he continued in a low, deep voice that crept beneath her skin and warmed her blood. "Tell me you haven't imagined me touching you. You touching me. All over. Tell me that you don't want me."

Amanda knew that the easy thing, the safe thing, would be to assure him that the kiss they'd shared had been merely pleasant. But certainly nothing to lose sleep over. Unable to lie, she did the only thing she could think of. She hedged.

"You're certainly not lacking in ego." She tried a laugh that failed. Miserably.

"Tell me." His soft, gently insistent tone, touched with a subtle trace of male arrogance, was, in its own way, more forceful than the loudest shout. Once again Amanda wondered why Dane was wasting such talents here, at a small inn in a small coastal town, miles from civilization.

"I can't." She closed her eyes and shook her head.

Dane let out a long relieved breath that Amanda, caught up in the grips of her own turmoiled emotions, did not hear. So he'd been right. She wanted him, even as she didn't want to want him. He knew the feeling all too well.

"Have dinner with me tonight."

Was there anyone in the world who could resist that deep velvet voice? She certainly couldn't.

"I can't." Her voice shimmered with very real regret. "Greg and I have to go over today's results at dinner. And try to come up with substitutes for the bike race, backpacking trip and rock climb, now that we've lost our adventure leader."

"That's no problem. I'll do it."

The part of her who was desperate for the challenge week to be a success wanted to jump at his offer. Another, even stronger part of her, the part she feared was still a little bit in love with Dane, could not put his job in jeopardy on her account.

"I can't let you do that."

"I told you, it's no big deal."

"You won't think so if you lose your job."

Dane shrugged. "Jobs are easy to come by." His smile, while warm, was unthreatening. "Now, dinner with a beautiful woman, that's well worth throwing caution to the wind for.

"I'm volunteering for purely selfish reasons, Amanda. If I help out with the rest of the challenge week, you won't have to spend so much of your evenings with that cretin you're working so hard to get promoted back East, so I can be with you."

Her eyes widened. "How did you know I was trying to get Greg promoted to Manhattan?"

Amanda desperately hoped that he hadn't overheard any of the team members discussing such a possibility. She hadn't wanted anyone but Susan to know about her plan to win Greg Parsons's job. The job, she reminded herself, that should have been hers.

He watched the fear leap into her eyes and wondered if she realized that the goal she was chasing was not only illusive, but not worth the struggle.

"Don't worry. It was just a wild shot in the dark." He wanted to touch her—not sexually, just a hand to her cheek, or her hair, to soothe her obviously jangled nerves. "It's you city folks who are big on corporate intrigue. Out here in the boonies, we tend to spend more time trying to decide whether to take our naps before dinner or afterward."

Amanda still hadn't gotten a handle on Dane. But she knew he wasn't the country bumpkin he was pretending to be.

"I'd love to have you take over leading the corporate challenge. Of course, the agency will insist on paying you."

The figure she offered would pay for the new furnace the inn needed if he wanted to stay open year-round. Pride had Dane momentarily tempted to turn it down. He remembered just in time that the money would not come out of Amanda's pocket, but from the corporate checkbook of a very profitable advertising agency.

"That sounds more than reasonable. It's a deal."

"Believe me, Dane, you're saving my life."

He watched the worry lines ease from her forehead and wished that all her problems could be so simple to solve. He also wondered how bad those headaches would become, and how many cases of antacids she'd have to chew her way through before she realized that advertising wasn't real life.

"So, now that we've solved that problem, what about dinner?"

"I honestly can't."

She paused, running through a mental schedule. Now that they didn't have to come up with new activities, she and Greg didn't have all that much to cover. Besides, he'd undoubtedly want to get away early in order to sneak off to Kelli's room. Which, she'd noticed, conveniently adjoined his.

"How about dessert? We have to get together," he reminded, "so you can fill me in on the rest of the activities the leader you originally hired had planned for the week."

Telling herself that she'd just have to keep things on a strictly business level, Amanda said, "With your mother in the kitchen, how can I turn down dessert?"

"Terrific." His smile was quick and warmed her to the core. "I'll meet you down by the boathouse."

The boathouse had been one of their secret meeting places. Amanda knew that to be alone with Dane in a place that harbored so many romantic memories was both foolhardy and dangerous.

"Something wrong with the dining room?"

"It's too public."

"That's the idea."

"Ah, but I was under the impression that part of the corporate challenge agenda was to keep the teams off guard. So you can observe how they respond to unexpected trials."

Amanda vaguely wondered how Dane knew so much about corporate game-playing strategy. "So?"

"So, if we go over the events you have planned in any of the public rooms, some of the team members might overhear us."

He had, she admitted reluctantly, a good point.

"There's always my room," he suggested when she didn't immediately answer.

"No," she answered quickly. Too quickly, Dane thought with an inward smile. It was obvious that they were both thinking about the first time she'd shown up at his door.

"Okay, how about the tower room?"

Not on a bet. "The boathouse will be fine."

"It's a date."

"It's not a date." Amanda felt it important to clarify that point up front. "It's a business meeting."

Dane shrugged. "Whatever." Matters settled to his satisfaction, he resumed paddling.

As Amanda had suspected, other than complain about the outcome of the first challenge event, Greg was not inclined to linger over dinner. Forgoing appetizers, he got right to the point of their meeting as he bolted through the main course.

"Today was an unmitigated disaster." His tone was thick with accusation.

"It wasn't all that bad," she murmured, not quite truthfully. The race hadn't been as successful as she'd hoped.

Unsurprisingly, Julian and Marvin had not meshed. They never managed to get their stroking rhythm in sync, and although each continued to blame the other loudly, their kayak had gotten so out of control that it had rammed into the one piloted by Laura and Don at the far turn around the lighthouse. Fortunately, Dane was proved right about the stability of the craft. But although neither kayak overturned, once the four were back on the beach, the three men almost came to blows.

Needless to say, Greg's subsequent cursing and shouting only caused the friction level to rise even higher. The only thing that had stopped the altercation from turning into a full-fledged brawl was Dane's quiet intervention. Amanda had not been able to hear what he was saying, but his words, whatever they were, obviously did the trick. Although their boatmanship didn't improve much during the second heat, the combatants behaved like kittens for the remainder of the afternoon.

"It was a disaster," Greg repeated. He pushed his plate away and took a swig from the drink he was never without. "I don't have to tell you that your career is on the line here, Amanda."

She refused to let him see how desperately she wanted the week to be successful. If he knew how important it was to her, he might try to sabotage her participation.

"If I remember correctly, this entire scheme was *your* idea."

"True." He turned down a second cup of coffee from a hovering waitress, and declined dessert. "But my job's not in jeopardy so long as *I'm* the one who eats a family holiday dinner with Ernst Janzen every Christmas." He placed his napkin on the table and rose.

"Make it work, Amanda," he warned, jabbing a finger toward her. "Or you'll be out on the street. And your assistant will be pounding the pavement, looking for a new job right along with you."

She felt the blood literally drain from her face. It was just an idle threat. He couldn't mean it, she assured herself. But she *knew* he did.

It was one thing to blow her plans for advancement. She was also willing to risk her own career. But to be suddenly responsible for Susan's job, six months before her assistant's planned wedding, was more pressure than Amanda needed.

"I expect tomorrow's exercise to be a model of efficiency and collaboration," he said. "Or you can call Susan and instruct her to start packing both your things into boxes."

With that threat ringing in her ears, he turned on his heel and left the dining room.

The long day, preceded by a sleepless night, had left Amanda exhausted. Her dinner with Greg had left her depressed. And although she'd been secretly looking forward to being alone with Dane, now that the time had arrived, Amanda realized she was more than a little nervous.

Butterflies—no, make that giant condors—were flapping their wings in her stomach and she'd second-guessed her agreement to meet with him at least a dozen times during dinner.

Admittedly stalling, she was lingering over dinner when Mary appeared beside the table, a small pink bakery box in her hand.

"How was your meal?"

Amanda smiled, grateful for the interruption that would keep her from having to decide whether or not to stand Dane up again. Which would be difficult, since they were scheduled to spend the remainder of the week working on the challenge together.

"Absolutely delicious." The salmon pasta in white-wine sauce had practically melted in her mouth. "I'll probably gain ten pounds before the week is over."

"From what Dane tells me, with the week you have planned, you'll undoubtedly work off any extra calories."

Mary held out the box. "I thought you and Dane might enjoy some carrot cake."

For ten years Amanda had been searching for a carrot cake as rich and sweet as Mary Cutter's. For ten years she'd been constantly disappointed.

"Make that twelve pounds," she complained weakly, eyeing the box with culinary lust.

Mary's look of satisfaction was a carbon copy of her son's. Although not as direct as Dane, in her own way, Mary Cutter could be a velvet bulldozer. "As I said before, a few extra pounds couldn't hurt, dear."

Running her hand down Amanda's hair in another of those maternal gestures Amanda had never received from her own mother, Mary returned to the kitchen, leaving Amanda with two pieces of carrot cake and a date for which she was already late.

She was on her way across the front parlor when someone called her name. Turning, she viewed the gorgeous young woman who'd been on duty last night, standing behind the desk.

"Yes?"

"I hate to ask, especially since you're a paying guest and all, but would you mind doing me a favor?" Mindy Taylor asked.

"If I can."

"Could you tell Dane that the furnace guy promised to begin work on Friday?"

Two things crossed Amanda's mind at nearly the same time. The first being that her meeting with Dane seemed to be common knowledge. The second being the fact that along with his other duties, Dane appeared to be in charge of maintenance.

"If I see him," she hedged.

"Great." Mindy flashed her dazzling Miss Satan's Cove smile. "Isn't it great how things work out?"

"What things?"

"Well, if the Mariner resort hadn't burned down, your advertising agency wouldn't have come here in the first place. Then, if your adventure leader hadn't spun out on his Harley on that rain-slick curve, you wouldn't have needed to hire Dane to fill in, and the inn would have to close after Labor Day."

Last night, Amanda had been impressed with Mindy's seeming combination of intelligence and beauty. Tonight she wondered if she'd made a mistake in judgment.

"I don't understand what hiring Dane to lead the challenge week has to do with Smugglers' Inn being able to remain open after Labor Day."

"Without a new furnace, we would have had to shut down for the winter."

"But what does that have to do with Dane?"

It was Mindy's turn to look at Amanda as if she was lacking in some necessary intelligence. "Because he's using the check from your agency to buy the new furnace."

"But why would Dane…" Comprehension suddenly hit like a bolt of lightning from a clear blue summer sky. "Dane's the new owner of Smugglers' Inn."

"Lock, stock and brand-new gas furnace," Mindy cheerfully confirmed.

Chapter 6

A full moon was floating in an unusually clear night sky, lighting Amanda's way to the boathouse. At any other time she might have paused to enjoy the silvery white path on the moon-gilded waters of the Pacific Ocean, or stopped to gaze up at the millions of stars sparkling overhead like loose diamonds scattered across a black velvet jeweler's cloth.

But her mind was not on the dazzling bright moon, nor the silvery water, nor the stars. Amanda was on her way to the boathouse to kill Dane Cutter.

He was waiting for her, just as he'd promised. Just as he had so many years ago. Unaware of the pique simmering through her, Dane greeted her with a smile that under any other conditions she would have found devastatingly attractive.

"I was getting worried about you."

She glared up at him, a slender, furious warrior with right on her side. "I got held up."

"So I see." Lines crinkled at the corners of his smiling eyes. "I hope that's Mom's carrot cake."

She'd forgotten she was still carrying the pink box. "It is." She handed it to him. Then reached back and slammed her fist into his stomach.

He doubled over with a grunt of surprise, dropping the cake box. "Damn it, Amanda!"

He gingerly straightened. She was standing, legs braced, as if intending to pound him again. He waited until he was sure his voice would be steady.

"You get one free shot, contessa. That's it. Try another cheap stunt like that and I'll have no choice but to slug you back."

"You wouldn't dare!" He might be a liar, but the man she'd fallen in love with ten years ago would never strike a woman. Then again, she reminded herself, apparently there was a lot she didn't know about the man Dane Cutter had become.

"I wouldn't risk putting it to the test." His dark eyes were hard. Implacable.

Dane saw her hand move to her stomach and damned himself for having caused another flare-up of her obviously touchy nerves.

But damn it, he hadn't started this. His plans for the evening had been to start out with some slow, deep kisses. After that, he'd intended to play things by ear, although if they ended up in bed, he certainly wasn't going to complain.

The worst-possible-case scenario was that they might waste valuable time together actually talking about her damn challenge-week events. One thing he hadn't planned on was having a fist slammed into his gut.

"You know, you really ought to see a doctor about that."

She frowned, momentarily thrown off track. "About what?"

"You could have an ulcer."

Following his gaze, she realized that the way her hand was pressed against the front of her blouse was a sure giveaway that she wasn't as much in control as she was trying to appear. "I don't have an ulcer."

"You sure? They can treat them with antibiotics, so—"

"I said, I don't have any damn ulcer."

Dane shrugged. "Fine. Then I'd suggest you work on your attitude."

"My attitude?" Her hands settled on her hips. "How dare you question *my* attitude. After what you've done!"

"What, exactly, have I done? Other than to offer to pull your fat out of the fire? Corporately speaking, that is."

Physically, she didn't appear to have an ounce of fat on her—one of the things he was hoping his mother's cooking could change. Amanda's society mother had been wrong; there was such a thing as a woman being too thin.

"That wasn't exactly the act of pure selflessness you made it out to be at the time," she countered with a toss of her head. "Not when you consider the new furnace for the inn. Which is scheduled to be installed Friday, by the way."

"Ah." It finally made sense. "Who told you?"

Amanda didn't know which made her more angry.

That Dane had lied to her in the first place, or that he appeared so cavalier at having gotten caught.

"That doesn't matter," she said between clenched teeth. "What matters is that you lied to me."

Now that he knew what all the storm and fury was about, Dane found himself enjoying the murder in her eyes. It spoke of a passion he had every intention of experiencing before this week was over.

"I'd never lie to you, Amanda."

She folded her arms and shot him a disbelieving look. "I don't recall you telling me that you were the new owner of Smugglers' Inn."

"I don't recall you asking."

Frustrated and furious, Amanda let out a huff of breath. "It's not the sort of question one asks a person one believes to be a bellman."

Her words were dripping icicles. Although hauteur was not her usual style, having been on the receiving end of her mother's cool conceit for all of her twenty-five years, Amanda had learned, on rare occasions, to wield the icy weapon herself. Tonight was one of those occasions.

Dane revealed no sign of having been fatally wounded. "You know, that snotty attitude doesn't suit you, contessa." Ignoring her warning glare, he reached out and stroked her hair. "It's too remote." Stroked her cheek. "Too passionless." Stroked the side of her neck. "Too untouchable."

That was precisely the point, damn it! Unfortunately, it wasn't working. Seemingly undeterred by her fury, he was jangling her nerves, weakening her defenses. Reminding herself that she was no longer a naive, hopelessly romantic young fifteen-year-old, Amanda moved away from his beguiling touch.

"You let me think you were still just an employee." Although his touch had regrettably cooled her ire, the thought that he might have been laughing at her still stung.

Just an employee. He wondered if she knew how much like her rich, snobbish mother those words sounded. "I suppose I did." Until now, Dane hadn't realized that he'd been testing her. But, he admitted, that was exactly what he'd been doing.

"Does it really make that much of a difference? Whether I work at the inn? Or own it?" Her answer was suddenly uncomfortably important.

Amanda had worked long enough in the advertising jungle to recognize a verbal trap when she spotted one. "That's not the point," she insisted, sidestepping the issue for the moment.

He lifted an eyebrow. "May I ask what the point is, then? As you see it?"

"You were pretending to be something you weren't."

"We all pretend to be something—or someone—we aren't from time to time."

Like that long-ago summer when she'd pretended to be the Lolita of Satan's Cove. She hadn't fooled Dane then. And she didn't now. Although he had no doubt that she was more than capable of doing her job, he also knew that she wasn't the brisk, efficient advertising automaton she tried so hard to appear.

"I don't." She jutted her chin forward in a way that inexplicably made Dane want to kiss her. Then again, he'd been wanting to kiss her all day long.

Thinking how ridiculous their entire situation

was turning out to be, Dane threw back his head and laughed.

"I hadn't realized I'd said anything humorous," she said stiffly.

Her vulnerability, which she was trying so hard to conceal, made him want to take her into his arms. "I'm sorry." He wiped the grin from his face. "I guess you've spent so many years perfecting your career-woman act that you've forgotten that it really isn't you."

His accusation hit like the sucker punch she'd slammed into his stomach. The familiar headache came crashing back. "It isn't an act."

"Of course, it is." As he watched the sheen of hurt, followed by a shadow of pain, move across her eyes, Dane damned himself for putting them there. Laying aside his romantic plans, he began massaging her throbbing temples, as he had last night.

"I don't want you to touch me," she complained.

"Sure you do. The problem is you don't want to *want* me to touch you." His fingertips were making circles against her skin. Igniting licks of fire, burning away the pain. "Would it make you feel any better if I promised not to seduce you tonight?"

"As if you could," she muttered, trying to ignore the delicious heat that his caresses were creating.

Dane didn't answer. They both knew there was no need.

He abandoned his sensual attack on her headache, sliding his hands down her neck, over her shoulders, and down her arms. Amanda did not resist as he linked their fingers together.

"For the record, I think you're intelligent, creative,

and ambitious. You believe you think you know what you want—"

"I do know," she insisted.

"And you're not going to stop until you get it," he said, ignoring her firmly stated correction. "Whatever the cost."

"I have every intention of becoming Northwest regional creative director of Janzen, Lawton and Young." Determination burned in her eyes and had her unconsciously lifting her chin. "Once I get rid of Greg Parsons, just watch me go."

He smiled at that, because tonight, despite the change in plans, was not a night for arguing. "Believe me, I have no intention of taking my eyes off you."

Alerted by the huskiness in his tone, Amanda blew out a breath. "Am I going to have trouble with you?"

His answer was a slow masculine grin. "I certainly hope so." He moved closer. "Lots and lots of it."

She pulled a hand free and pressed it against his shoulder. "Damn it, Dane—"

He touched a finger against her mouth, cutting off her weak protest. "If you can forget what we had together, Amanda, you're a helluva lot stronger person than I am."

With effort, she resisted the urge to draw that long finger into her mouth. "It's over. And has been for years."

"That's what you think." He lifted the hand he was still holding and pressed his lips against her knuckles. Their eyes met over their linked hands—his, hot and determined; hers, soft and wary. "It's just beginning, Amanda. And we both know it."

Those words, so quietly spoken, could have been a

promise or a threat. Needing time to think, not to mention space in which to breathe, Amanda tugged her hand free and backed away. Both physically and emotionally.

"I only came down here to discuss the challenge."

Frustration rose; Dane controlled it. For now. "You're the boss," he said agreeably.

"Not yet," Amanda corrected. "But I will be." Because her unpleasant conversation with Greg was still in her mind, her shoulders slumped. "If I'm not fired first."

He wondered if she had any idea how vulnerable she could appear and decided that bringing it up now, after what even he would have to admit had not been the most successful of days, would serve no purpose.

Dane wanted to put his arm around her, to soothe more than seduce, but knew that if he allowed himself to touch her again, all his good intentions would fly right out the window. That being the case, he slipped his hands into the pockets of his jeans to keep them out of trouble.

"I can't see that happening."

"Believe me, it's a distinct possibility." She hadn't thought so, before today. Oh, she'd considered herself so clever with her little plan to get Greg promoted. Caught up in the logistics of getting the horrid man out of Portland, she hadn't given enough thought to the inescapable fact that half the challenge team actively disliked the other half. "After what happened today."

She dragged her hand through her hair. "Speaking of which, I suppose I ought to thank you."

"And here I thought you wanted to knock my block off."

"I did. Still do," she admitted. "But, as angry as I am at you for not being entirely honest with me, I can't overlook the fact that you were probably the only thing standing between me and the unemployment line today."

She sighed and shook her head as she stared out over the gilded sea. "From the way Julian, Marvin, Don, and Greg were behaving, you'd think we'd all come here to play war games."

"Business is probably as close to war as most people get," Dane said. "Other than marriage."

His grim tone suggested he was speaking from experience. A thought suddenly occurred to her. "You're not married, are you?"

Dane swore. Annoyance flickered in his dark eyes, and drew his lips into a hard line. "Do you honestly believe that if I had a wife, I'd be planning to take you to bed?"

"Planning is a long way from doing." As she'd learned, only too well. She'd had such plans for this week!

"That may be true for some people. But I've developed a reputation for being tenacious." He cupped her chin between his fingers, holding her gaze to his. "I'm going to have you, contessa. And you're going to love it."

The last time she'd allowed him to bait her, she'd ended up kissing him as if there were no tomorrow. Afraid that the next time she wouldn't be able to stop with a mere kiss, Amanda jerked her head back, folded her arms across her chest and reminded herself that it was important at least to pretend to remain cool.

"You may be accustomed to women succumbing to your seduction techniques, Dane. But I have no intention of joining the hordes. I'm also a tougher case than you're obviously accustomed to."

"Victories are always more satisfying when they don't come easily. And you haven't answered my question."

Discounting his arrogant male statement about taking her to bed, despite the fact that he was also confusing, beguiling, and distracting her, Amanda sensed that Dane was a caring, compassionate individual. And although he had misled her, she knew, from past experiences, that he was also an honorable man. Most men would have taken what she was literally throwing at him ten years ago without a backward glance when the summer was over. But Dane was not most men.

"I suppose I can't imagine you committing adultery."

"Well, I suppose that's a start. Perhaps I ought to have someone write a reference letter. How about my mother? She'd love an opportunity to sing my praises."

"That's not the way I remember it."

"Ten years ago she was a single mother concerned her son was about to repeat her own romantic mistake." Because he could not continue to stand this close to Amanda without touching, he reached out and twined a strand of her hair around his finger.

"These days, she's a mother who's begun to worry that her son isn't ever going to provide her with the grandchildren she's so eager to spoil."

That was yet another difference between the Stockenbergs and the Cutters. Amanda's mother refused even to discuss the possibility of becoming a grandmother anytime in this century. While her father had warned her on more than one occasion of the dangers of falling prey to the infamous "baby track" that would hinder her success.

"How do you feel about that?" she asked.

"Actually, I think it's a pretty good idea. With the right woman, of course."

She couldn't help thinking of a time when she'd dreamed of having children with this man. She also had no intention of asking Dane what type of woman fit his criteria. Deciding that the conversation was drifting into dangerous territory, she opted to change the subject.

"May I ask a question?"

"Shoot."

"What did you say to Greg and the others today? To stop them from brawling on the beach?"

Dane shrugged. "Not that much. I merely pointed out to Parsons that he had too much riding on this week to risk getting into a fistfight with his employees."

That was why Greg had marched away, steam practically coming from his ears, Amanda decided. "But what about Julian and Marvin? They were at each other's throats after that disastrous first heat, but by the end of the day they were behaving as if they were candidates for the Kayaking Olympic Team."

Dane knew he was treading in dangerous waters again. He didn't want to lie to Amanda. But if he told her the truth about his conversation with the art director and head copywriter, she'd undoubtedly want to slug him again.

She'd also be furious that he'd interfered, little mind the fact that she'd needed some help at the time. Especially since her egocentric supervisor was obviously not only a bully, but an incompetent idiot to boot.

"I said pretty much the same thing to them I did to Parsons." He forced himself to meet her lovely, serious eyes. "I suggested this week was going to be long and tough enough to get through without complicating things with useless feuds.

"I also mentioned that since management, in its own ignorance, tended to take things like this ridiculous corporate challenge week seriously, it made sense to save their differences for the creative arena where it mattered, bury their individual hatchets and cooperate by trying to win the thing together."

"I'm impressed."

"It's not that big a deal."

It was the truth, so far as it went. What he'd failed to mention was that he'd also told the two combatants that if they didn't shape up and do their best to make this week a success, he'd throw them both off the cliff. Then drown them.

Although they'd resorted to bluster, from the uneasiness in their eyes, he realized that they'd half believed he might actually do it. And, although he wasn't violent, such behavior was undeniably tempting. If it helped Amanda.

Watching her today, seeing how seriously she took her work, understanding how important it was to her that she pull off this week, Dane knew that in order to get what *he* wanted, he would have to see that Amanda got what *she* wanted. And what she wanted, it seemed, was Greg Parsons's job. That being the case, he intended to move heaven and earth—and a portion of the Oregon coast, if necessary—to ensure her success.

"Believe me, Dane, it was a very big deal." Thinking back on what he'd done for her—for no other reason than that he'd wanted to help—Amanda felt guilty. "I'm sorry I hit you."

Her hand was on his arm. Dane covered it with his.

"You were right. I haven't exactly been the most forthright guy in the world the past couple of days. But I never meant to hurt you. Or to make you feel I was having fun at your expense."

His hand was darker than hers. Larger. And warmer. When she began imagining it moving over her body, touching her in places that were aching for just such a sensual touch, Amanda knew that no matter how hard she tried to deny it, Dane was right. Before this week was over, they would become lovers.

That idea was thrilling and terrifying at the same time.

"There's something I don't understand," she murmured.

"What's that?"

"What made you decide to buy the inn? After swearing that you couldn't wait to get away from Satan's Cove, I'm surprised to find you still here."

"Not still."

"Pardon me?"

"I said, I'm not still here. I'm back."

"Oh." That made a bit more sense, she supposed. "What did you do in between?"

Dane took encouragement from the fact that she cared about how he'd spent his life during those intervening years. "A little of this. A little of that."

"That's not very enlightening."

"I suppose not." He gave her a long look. "I guess I just can't figure out why you'd care. Since you've already said you haven't thought about me since that summer."

"I may have thought of you," she admitted, realizing that there was no way she'd be able to keep up the subterfuge. "From time to time."

Dane didn't answer. He just stood there, looking down at her, a frustratingly inscrutable look on his face, as the tension grew thicker and thicker between them.

"All right!" She threw up her hands in surrender. "I lied. I thought about you a lot, Dane. More than I should have. More than I wanted.

"Every man I've ever gone out with, I've ended up comparing to you. Once I dated a man for six months because, believe it or not, if I closed my eyes, his voice reminded me of yours.

"I go to work, and if I'm not careful, my mind will drift and I'll think of you and wonder where you are, and what you're doing. And at night—" On a roll now, she began to pace. "At night I'll lie in bed, and you'll be lying there beside me, kissing me, touching me, loving me.

"And then I'll wake up, and realize it was only a dream. But it doesn't seem like a dream, damn it. It seems real! And then, last night, I was tired and cranky, and worried, and all of a sudden I heard this voice I've dreamed about time and time again, and I turned around and there you were, and this time you weren't a dream.

"You were real. Wonderfully, marvelously real! And it was all I could do not to throw myself in your arms and beg you to make love to me—with me—for the rest of my life!

"So, there." She stopped in front of him, close enough that he could see the sheen of tears in her expressive blue eyes. "Now you know. Is that what you wanted to hear me say? Is your almighty male ego satisfied now?"

She was trembling. Once again the need to comfort warred with the desire to seduce. Once again comfort won out. "Yes. It's what I wanted to hear."

He put his hands on her shoulders and drew her to him. And although she remained stiff, she wasn't exactly resisting, either.

He cupped her chin again. "But only because it's a relief to know that I wasn't the only one feeling that way."

Amanda read the truth in his warm, loving gaze and felt even more like weeping. Her emotions were in a turmoil. She couldn't think straight. She could only feel. She wrapped her arms around his waist and clung. "Really?"

"Really." His smile was that crooked, boyish one that had once possessed the power to make her young heart turn somersaults. It still did.

"And if you think it's dumb dating a guy for six months because he sounds like someone else, how about marrying someone because she has the same laugh as a girl you once loved?"

"You didn't!"

"Guilty." His grin turned sheepish. "I was young and determined to get you out of my system when I met Denise."

Denise. Dane had been married to a woman named Denise. A woman with her laugh. Amanda hated her. "What happened?"

"It's a long story."

"I'm not in any hurry to be anywhere." On the contrary, a very strong part of Amanda wished she could stop time and make this night last forever.

There'd been a moment, during her passionate speech about how many times she'd thought of him over the intervening years, that Dane had thought perhaps tonight would turn out to be the night he finally made love to Amanda. Now that he'd made the mistake of bringing up his ex-wife, he knew he'd have to remain patient a bit longer.

Reminding himself that Amanda was worth waiting for, Dane took her hand and led her over to a rowboat tied to the pier.

"We may as well get reasonably comfortable," he said. "Because this is going to take a while."

Chapter 7

Dane's fingers curved around her waist as he lifted her easily into the boat. Amanda sat down on the bench seat, leaned back against the bow and waited.

Dane sat down beside her. When he began talking, his words were slow and measured.

"I liked Denise from the moment I met her. Along with the all-important fact that she had your laugh, she was also beautiful and smart and sexy. And the only woman I'd ever met who was every bit as driven to succeed as I was."

"She sounds like an absolute paragon."

Dane would have had to be deaf not to hear the female jealousy in Amanda's dry tone. He chuckled as he put his arm around her shoulder, encouraged when she did not pull away.

"Unfortunately, except for our work, we didn't have

a single solitary thing in common. Six months later, when neither of us had much to laugh about, we decided to call it quits before our disastrous marriage ruined a very good working relationship."

"I can't imagine working with an ex-husband."

Dane shrugged. "It hadn't been a typical marriage from the beginning. I'd married her to get over you and she married me on the rebound after her divorce from a miserable first marriage. Right before the split, I was promoted into a position that involved a lot of traveling. After a time, it was as if our marriage had never happened and we found we could be friends again. Two years ago, I introduced her to an old college friend of mine who's a stockbroker in San Francisco. They clicked right off the bat, got married, and I got a note from her last week announcing her pregnancy. So things worked out for the best."

"You said you were young?"

Dane sighed. Although he'd overcome any regrets he'd once harbored over his marriage, revealing such irresponsible behavior to the one woman he wanted to impress was proving more than a little embarrassing.

"I graduated from University of Oregon the summer after I met you," he said. "Mom was there, of course, along with Denise—who was my supervisor during my apprentice program at Whitfield. We went out to dinner, then after I took Mom back to her hotel, Denise invited me out for a drink to celebrate.

"One toast led to another, and another, and a few more, then we bought a bottle of champagne—a magnum—and the next thing I remember we were waking up in a motel room in Reno, Nevada.

"Denise couldn't remember much of anything, either,

but the signed certificate from a justice of the peace on the dresser spoke for itself, so after several cups of strong coffee and a great many aspirin, we figured, since we'd always gotten along so well at the office, we might as well try to make a go of it."

Amanda didn't know which part of the story—so unlike the Dane she'd known who'd driven her crazy with his self-control—she found most amazing. "You actually married your boss?"

This time his grin was more than a little sheepish. "Women aren't the only ones who can sleep their way to the top of the company."

Since she knew he was joking, Amanda overlooked his blatantly chauvinistic remark. "She must have been older."

"About twelve years. But that didn't have anything to do with the breakup. We were just mismatched from the get-go."

In all his travels around the world, Dane had met a great many chic women, but none of them had oozed sophistication like his former wife. Denise preferred Placido Domingo to Garth Brooks, champagne cocktails at the symphony to hot dogs at the ballpark, and given the choice between spending an afternoon at a stuffy art museum with her uptown friends or fly-fishing on a crystal-clear Oregon river, she'd choose Jackson Pollack over rainbow trout any day.

Dane had often thought, over these past months since his return to Satan's Cove, that if he and Denise hadn't broken up that first year, they definitely would have divorced over his need to leave the city for this wildly beautiful, remote stretch of Oregon coast. Since there could have been children involved by this point, he was grateful they'd cut their losses early.

So stunned was Amanda by the story of Dane's marriage, it took a while for something else he'd said to sink in.

"You said she was your supervisor at Whitfield. Whitfield as in the Whitfield Palace hotel chain? 'When Deluxe Will No Longer Do'?" she asked, quoting the world-famous slogan. "*That's* where you were working?"

"I was in the intern program at Whitfield while I was in college and they hired me full-time after graduation."

This was more like it. This fit the burning need Dane had professed to escape Satan's Cove. This was the man, when she'd daydreamed about Dane, she'd imagined him to be. "What did you do there?"

"A bit of everything. Whitfield makes its managerial prospects start at the bottom and work in all the different departments. I was assigned to the custodial department my sophomore year at U of O, worked my way up to housekeeping my junior year, reservations my senior year, then spent the summer after graduation in the kitchen."

"That's the summer you were married." Even knowing that it hadn't worked out, Amanda realized that she hated the idea of any other woman sharing Dane's life. Let alone his bed.

It should have been her, Amanda thought with a surprisingly furious burst of passion. It could have been her, if her parents hadn't manipulated things to keep them apart. Or if her feelings hadn't been so wounded and his pride so stiff.

Unaware of her thoughts, Dane nodded. "That's it. By Christmas I was on my way to being single again."

Denise's petition for divorce—they'd agreed she'd be the one to file—had arrived at his office on December 23. He'd spent the next two days in Satan's Cove with his mother.

The morning after Christmas, he was on a plane to Paris. And after that Milan. Then Zurich. And on and on until he was spending so much of his life at 30,000 feet, he'd often joked—not quite humorously—that he should just give the postal service his airline schedule.

"And then you began traveling." Amanda recalled the earlier condensed version. "Still for Whitfield?"

"When Denise and I split, I'd just gotten promoted to assistant director of guest relations, working out of the New Orleans headquarters. Essentially, it was my job to visit each hotel at least twice a year and pull a surprise inspection."

"You must have been popular," Amanda said dryly.

"I like to think I bent over backward to be fair. But I will admit to being tough. After all, guests pay big bucks to stay at a Whitfield Palace. It's important they feel they're getting their money's worth."

"I stayed at the Park Avenue Whitfield last month," Amanda revealed, "on a trip back to Manhattan. The New York agency handles their advertising account." With luck and Dane's help, Greg Parsons would soon be transferring to those renowned Madison Avenue offices. "It really was like being in a palace."

Although she'd grown up with wealth, Amanda hadn't been able to keep from staring at the sea of marble underfoot or the gleaming crystal chandeliers overhead. She'd had the impression that at any minute, a princess would suddenly appear from behind one of the gilded pillars.

"That's the point," Dane said.

"True." Whoever had named the worldwide hotel chain had definitely hit the nail right on the head.

Amanda also remembered something else about her stay at the flagship hotel. Her room, furnished with genuine antiques and boasting a view of the leafy environs of Central Park, had been comfortably spacious. And the marble bathrooms had an amazing selection of French milled perfumed soaps, shampoos and lotions. In addition, the staff had been more than accommodating. Still, even with all that, Amanda had felt vaguely uncomfortable during her three-day stay.

"You know," she said thoughtfully, "as luxurious as the Park Avenue Whitfield is, I like what you've done with Smugglers' Inn better. It's more comfortable. Cozier."

His slow, devastating grin reached his eyes. "That's the point." Dane was undeniably pleased that she understood instinctively the mood he'd wanted to create. "I'm also glad you approve."

"I really do." He was looking at her as if he wanted to kiss her again. Her heart leaped into her throat. Then slowly settled again. "It's lovely, Dane. You should be very proud."

The sea breeze fanned her hair, causing it to waft across her cheek. Dane reached out to brush it away and ended up grabbing a handful. "Speaking of lovely..."

He pulled her closer with a gentle tug on her hair.

"It's too soon," she protested softly.

Personally, Dane thought it was about ten years too

late. "Just a kiss." His mouth was a whisper from hers. "One simple kiss, Amanda. What could it hurt?"

She could feel herself succumbing to the temptation in his dark eyes, to the promise of his silky breath against her lips, to the magic in the fingers that had slipped beneath her hair to gently massage the nape of her neck.

A simple kiss. What could it hurt?

"Just a kiss," she whispered in a soft, unsteady breath. Her lips parted of their own volition, her eyes fluttered shut in anticipation of the feel of his mouth on hers. "You have to promise."

He slid the fingers of his free hand down the side of her face. "I promise." He bent his head and very slowly, very carefully, closed the distance.

The stirring started, slow and deep. And sweet. So achingly, wonderfully sweet.

There was moonlight, slanting over the sea, turning it to silver. And a breeze, feathering her hair, whispering over her skin, carrying with it the salt-tinged scent of the sea. Somewhere in the distance a foghorn sounded; the incoming tide flowed over the rocks and lapped against the sides of the boat that was rocking ever so gently on the soft swells.

His lips remained night-cool and firm while hers heated, then softened. Amanda's hand floated upward, to rest against the side of his face as Dane drew her deeper and deeper into a delicious languor that clouded her mind even as it warmed her body to a radiant glow.

Although sorely tempted, Dane proved himself a man of his word, touching only her hair and the back of her neck. With scintillating slowness, and using only his mouth, he drew out every ounce of pleasure.

A soft moan slipped from between Amanda's heated lips. No man—no man except Dane—had ever been able to make her burn with only a kiss. He whispered words against her mouth and made her tremble. He murmured promises and made her ache.

Dane had spent most of the day hoping that he'd overreacted to last night's encounter. A man accustomed to thinking with his head, rather than his heart—or that other vital part of his anatomy that was now throbbing painfully—he'd attempted to make sense out of a situation he was discovering defied logic.

Despite all the intervening years, despite all the women he'd bedded since that bittersweet summer, Dane found himself as inexplicably drawn to Amanda as ever.

The first time they'd been together like this, his desire had been that of a boy. Last night, and even more so now, as he shaped her lips to his, forcing himself to sample their sweet taste slowly, tenderly, Dane knew that this desire was born from the age-old need of a man for his mate.

Because he could feel himself rapidly approaching that dangerous, razor-thin line between giving and taking, Dane lifted his head. Then waited for Amanda to open her eyes.

Those wide eyes he'd never been able to put out of his mind were clouded with unmistakable desire as she stared up at him in the moonlight.

He could have her, Dane knew. Right here, he could draw her into his arms and crush her mouth to his until she was senseless, until she couldn't speak, couldn't think, couldn't breathe. And couldn't run away.

Although he'd never considered himself a masochist, Dane fantasized about the way her body would feel next to his, beneath his, on top of his. He wanted her in every way possible.

The problem was, Dane realized with a stunned sense of awareness, he also wanted her forever.

She murmured a faint, inarticulate protest as he brushed one last quick kiss against her parted lips, then stood.

"Just a kiss," he reminded her, holding out his hand to help her to her feet.

Amanda needed all the assistance she could get. Her mind was still spinning from that devastating, heart-swelling kiss and she wasn't certain if her legs would hold her. She wanted Dane. Desperately. Worse yet, she needed him. Absolutely. For not the first time in her life, Amanda found herself damning his iron control.

"This is getting impossible," Amanda said.

Watching the myriad emotions storm in her eyes—desire, confusion, frustration—Dane vowed that there would be a time when he would take more. But for tonight, that kiss would have to be enough.

"What's that?" he asked mildly.

"You. Me. And what's happening between us. I had my life planned. I knew what I wanted. But ever since I arrived back in Satan's Cove, I can't understand what I'm feeling."

Sympathy stirred as the hair she'd ruffled with unsteady fingers fell back into place. "I think the problem is that you understand exactly what you're feeling."

"All right," she said on a frustrated sigh. "You're right. I do know. But you have to understand that I'm not that silly teenager who threw herself at you ten years ago, Dane. I've worked hard to get where I am. My entire life, from the day I chose a major in college, has revolved around advertising."

Personally, Dane thought that was about the saddest thing he'd ever heard, but not wanting to get into an argument over the art and artifice of the advertising marketplace, he kept silent.

"I've given up so many things, made so many sacrifices, not to mention plans—"

"They say life is what happens when you're making plans," he interjected quietly.

Amanda stared up at him and shook her head. "Yes. Well."

She, who'd always been so smug about her ease with words, could not think of a single thing to say. Still unnerved by the kiss they'd shared, and uneasy at the way he was looking down at her, so calm, so comfortable with who he was and where he was, Amanda dragged her gaze back out to sea. A boat drifted by on the horizon, the running lights looking like fallen stars on the gleaming black water.

They stood there, side by side, looking at the ocean, all too aware of the closeness of the other.

"Damn it," she said with a sudden burst of frustration. "You, of all people, should understand. You obviously didn't succeed at Whitfield because you married your supervisor. You had to have worked hard."

"Sixteen to eighteen hours a day," he agreed. "Which is one of the reasons I quit."

"Yet I'll bet there are still days when you put in that many hours."

"Sure." Dane thought about the hours he'd spent fixing up the tower room. Just for her. He'd told himself at the time that the work had been done out of ego, because he wanted her to see what a success he'd made of the place. But now Dane suspected that his motives had been far more personal.

"But I said long hours were *one* of the reasons I quit Whitfield," he reminded her. "There were others."

"Such as?" Amanda was genuinely interested in whatever roads Dane had taken that had led him all over the world before returning to Satan's Cove.

"I wasn't overly fond of corporate structure." That was the truth. "And corporate structure wasn't overly fond of me."

That was a major understatement. Fortunately, he'd been successful enough that the guys in the pin-striped suits in the executive towers had overlooked his independent streak. Most of the time.

Granted, he'd thoroughly enjoyed the work in the beginning. Especially the travel. For a young man who'd grown up in an isolated coastal town of less than two hundred people, his early years at the hotel chain had been an exhilarating, eye-opening experience.

But newness faded over time and the day he'd realized he was close to suffocating in the luxurious eighteenth-floor corner window suite of the glass tower that dominated New Orleans's central business district, he'd turned in his resignation.

Eve Whitfield Deveraux—who'd inherited control of the hotel chain from her father—had asked him to reconsider. Having married a maverick herself, the hotel CEO appreciated having someone she could always count on to tell her the truth. There were already too many sycophants around her, she'd told him on more than one occasion. What she needed was a few more rebels like Dane Cutter.

As much as he'd genuinely liked her, Dane couldn't stay. So he'd cashed in his stock options and his IRA, closed his money-market and checking accounts, and returned home.

Dane realized that while his mind had been drifting, Amanda had been quietly waiting for him to continue.

"Besides," he said, "working long hours these days is a helluva lot different. Because Smugglers' Inn is mine. It's not some trendy real-estate investment I plan to sell to some foreign development company in a few years for a quick profit.

"I've put more than money into the place, though to be truthful, it's just about cleaned out my bank account, which is the only reason I decided to take that money from your agency.

"But I don't really mind the broken heaters and clogged pipes and leaky roofs, because I'm building something here, Amanda. I'm building a home. For myself and my family.

"Because as much of a rush as it admittedly was at first, flying all over the world, staying in presidential suites, having everyone snap to attention the moment my car pulled up in front of a Whitfield Palace hotel, the novelty eventually wore off.

"That was when I realized that what I truly wanted, more than money, or power, or prestige, was someone to come home to at the end of the day.

"Someone to walk along the beach with in the twilight of our years. Someone who'll love me as much as I'll love her—and our children, if we're lucky enough to have them."

He'd definitely been on a roll. It was, Dane considered as he felt himself finally running down, probably the longest speech he'd ever given. And, he thought, perhaps his most important.

Amanda didn't speak for a long time. Dane's fervent declaration, while sounding well-thought-out, had definitely taken her by surprise. Since arriving at Smugglers' Inn, she'd been trying to make the various aspects of Dane mesh in her mind.

The young man she'd first fallen in love with had been the most driven individual she'd ever met. And that included her father, who was certainly no slouch when it came to workaholic, success-at-all-cost strategies.

Remembering all Dane's lofty dreams and plans and ambitions, when she'd mistakenly believed he'd never left Satan's Cove, she hadn't been able to understand how he could have failed so miserably in achieving his goals.

Then she'd discovered he actually owned the landmark inn. And, as lovely as it admittedly was, she couldn't help wondering how many people could so easily turn their back on power and prestige.

"That picture you're painting sounds lovely."

"You almost sound as if you mean that."

He wondered if she realized it was almost the exact same picture she'd painted for him so many years ago. It was, Dane considered, ironic that after all these years apart they were back here in Satan's Cove, still attracted to one another, but still at cross purposes. It was almost as if they'd entered a parallel universe, where everything—including their individual dreams and aspirations—was reversed.

"Of course I mean it. I also admire you for knowing yourself well enough to know what's right for you."

"I think I hear a *but* in there."

"No." She shook her head. "Perhaps a little envy."

"I don't know why. Seems to me you're in the catbird seat, contessa. All you have to do is get Parsons out of your way and you're definitely back on the fast track."

"So why does it feel as if the lights at the end of the tunnel belong to an oncoming train?" She was not accustomed to revealing weakness. Not to anyone. But tonight, alone at the edge of the world with Dane, it somehow seemed right.

"Because you're tired." Dane couldn't resist touching her. "Because change is always disruptive," he murmured as he began kneading her tense, rocklike shoulders. "And with the takeovers and mergers, you've been going through a lot of changes lately.

"Not to mention the fact that Parsons is the kind of jerk who'd stress out Deepak Chopra. And along with trying to juggle this stupid corporate challenge week, you're being forced to confront feelings you thought you'd put behind you long ago."

His talented fingers massaged deeply, smoothing out the knots. "If I were a better man, I'd leave you alone and take a bit of the pressure off. But I don't think I'm going to be able to do that, Amanda."

She knew that. Just as she knew that deep down inside, she didn't really want Dane to give up on her.

"I just need a little more time." She was looking up at him, her eyes eloquently pleading her case. When she allowed her gaze to drift down to his mouth—which she could still taste—Amanda was hit with an arousal more primal and powerful than anything she'd ever known.

She imagined those firmly cut lips everywhere on her body, taking her to some dark and dangerous place she'd only ever dreamed about. "To think things through."

It wasn't the answer he wanted. Unfortunately, it *was* the answer he'd been expecting.

Dane's response was to cup the back of her head in his hand and hold her to a long, deep kiss that revealed both his hunger and his frustration. And, although she was too caught up in the fire of the moment to recognize it, his love.

"Think fast," he said after the heated kiss finally ended.

Still too aroused to speak, Amanda could only nod.

Chapter 8

Amanda was more than a little relieved when the next day began a great deal more smoothly than the previous day's kayak races. When team members woke to a cool, drizzling rain streaming down the windows that necessitated putting off the bike race until afternoon, she was prepared to switch gears.

Taking the indoor equipment from her store of supplies, she divided the teams into subgroups and put everyone to work building a helicopter from pieces of scrap paper, cardboard, rubber bands and Popsicle sticks. Although speed was of the essence, it was also important that the constructed vehicle manage some form of brief flight.

"I still don't get the point of this," Laura complained as yet another attempt fatally spiraled nosefirst into the rug.

"You're blending science and art," Amanda explained

patiently yet again. "Advertising is a subtle, ever-changing art that defies formularization."

"That's what it used to be," Luke Cahill muttered as he cut a tail rotor from a piece of scarlet construction paper. "Until the invasion of the MBA's." A rumpled, casual man in his mid-thirties, he possessed the unique ability to pen a catchy tune and link it with an appealing advertising idea.

Amanda had always considered Luke to be the most easygoing person working at the agency. She realized the recent stress had gotten to him, as well, when he glared over at Don Patterson, the financially oriented marketing manager, who stopped remeasuring the length of the cardboard helicopter body to glare back.

"However much you artsy types would like to spend the day playing in your creative sandboxes, advertising is a business," Don countered. "I, for one, am glad to see this agency finally being run as a profit-making enterprise."

"You won't *have* any profits if the product suffers," Luke snapped back. "Advertising is more than numbers. It's our native form of American anthology."

"He's right," Marvin Kenyon said. "Advertising—and life—would be a helluva lot easier if it could be treated like science—A plus B equals C—but it can't.

"Life is about change, damn it. And advertising reflects that. The best advertising, the kind we *used* to do for C.C.C., can even act as an agent for change."

Greg, who was sitting off to the side, watching the group, applauded, somehow managing to make the sound of two hands coming together seem mocking.

"Nice little speech, Kenyon." He poured himself a drink—his second of the morning—and took a sip. "But if you're not part of the solution you're part of the problem. If you can't get with the program, perhaps you don't belong in advertising."

"Not belong?" This from Julian. "You *do* realize that you're talking to a man who has twenty-nine years' experience creating witty, appealing, and totally original advertising that makes the sale through its ability to charm prospective buyers?"

As she heard the art director stand up for the head copywriter, Amanda felt a surge of excitement. As foolish as these games had seemed at first, something was happening.

Until the pressures brought about by first the mergers, then the takeover, C.C.C. had been viewed throughout the advertising world as a flourishing shop.

Unfortunately, because of the political machinations that were part and parcel of becoming a bigger agency, Marvin and Julian had started sniping at each other, causing morale to tailspin as sharply and destructively as Laura's failed helicopter model.

But now, thanks to Greg's threat, Julian had just felt the need to stand up for his former creative partner. And although she wondered if they'd ever regain the sense of "family" that had been the hallmark of Connally Creative Concepts, Amanda hoped such behavior was a sign that the creative members of the agency would resume encouraging each other, spurring their colleagues to even greater achievements, as they'd done in the past.

"We can't ignore the fact that we're in a service business," she said. "Unfortunately, no matter how creative our advertising is, if we don't possess the organization to effectively service our clients, we'll fail."

"That's what I've been trying to say," Don insisted.

"On the other hand," Amanda said, seeking a middle ground, "we could have the best media buying and billing system in the world but if creativity suffers because everyone's getting mired down in details, we won't have any clients to bill. And no profits. Which, of course, eventually would mean no salaries."

She reached out and picked up the helicopter the blue team had just finished and held it above her head. When she had their undivided attention, she let it go. The copter took off on a sure, albeit short flight, ending atop a bookcase.

"That was teamwork, ladies and gentlemen," she said with a quick, pleased grin. "Science and creativity, meshing into one efficient, artistic entity."

Dane had slipped into the back of the room during the beginning of the argument. He'd convinced himself that Amanda wasn't really happy in her work; that deep down inside, where it really counted, she was still the young girl who wanted to have babies and make a comfortable home for her family.

Now, having observed the way she'd deftly turned the discussion around, he was forced to admit that perhaps Amanda really did belong exactly where she was.

It was not a very satisfying thought.

Her spirits buoyed by the successful helicopter project, Amanda found herself thoroughly enjoying the excellent lunch of grilled sockeye salmon on fettucini, black bean salad, and fresh-baked sourdough bread, the kind that always reminded her of San Francisco's famed Fisherman's Wharf. Dessert was a blackberry cobbler topped with ice cream. The berries, Mary told the appreciative guests, had been picked from the bushes growing behind the inn; the ice cream, which was almost unbearably rich with the unmistakable taste of real vanilla beans, was homemade.

"It's a good thing I'm only spending a week here," Amanda said when she stopped by the kitchen to thank Dane's mother again for helping make the week a success.

"Oh?" With lunch successfully behind her, Mary had moved on to preparing dinner and was slicing mushrooms with a blindingly fast, deft stroke that Amanda envied, even as she knew she'd undoubtedly cut her fingers off if she ever dared attempt to duplicate it. "And why is that, dear?"

"Because I'd probably gain a hundred pounds in the first month." She still couldn't believe she'd eaten that cobbler.

"Oh, you'd work it all off," Mary assured her easily. "There's enough to do around here that burning calories definitely isn't a problem."

"I suppose you're right." Amanda had awakened this morning to the sound of hammering. Although the sun was just barely up, when she'd looked out her window she'd seen Dane repairing the split-rail fence that framed the front lawn and gardens. "Dane certainly seems to be enjoying it, though."

"He's happy as a clam."

"It's nice he's found his niche."

"It's always nice to know what you want out of life," Mary agreed easily. "Even nicer if you can figure out a way to get it."

"You must have been proud of him, though. When he was working for the Whitfield Palace hotel chain."

Amanda had the feeling that if she'd made the life-style reversal Dane had chosen, her father would have accused her of dropping out. Amanda's father remained vigilant for any sign that his daughter might be inclined to waver from the straight-and-narrow path he'd chosen for her—the one that led directly to an executive suite in some Fortune 500 company.

Never having been granted a son, Gordon Stockenberg had put all his paternal dreams and ambitions onto Amanda's shoulders. And except for that one summer, when she'd fallen in love with a boy her father had found totally unsuitable, she'd never let him down.

"I'd be proud of Dane whatever he chose to do." Mary piled the mushrooms onto a platter and moved on to dicing shallots. "But I have to admit that I'm pleased he's come home. Not only do I enjoy working with my son, it was obvious that once he became a vice president at Whitfield, he began feeling horribly constrained, and—"

"Vice president?"

"Why, yes." Mary looked up, seeming surprised that Amanda hadn't known.

"Dane was actually a vice president at Whitfield Palace hotels?" After last night's conversation, she'd realized he'd been important. But a vice president?

"He was in charge of international operations," Mary divulged. "The youngest vice president in the history of the hotel chain. He was only in the job for a year, and Mrs. Deveraux—she's the CEO of Whitfield—wanted him to stay on, especially now that she and her husband have begun a family and she's cut back on her own travel, but Dane has always known his own mind."

Once again Amanda thought of her boastful words about her window office and her lovely, expensive Italian-leather chair. Unfortunately, as much as she wanted to be irritated at Dane for having let her make a fool of herself, she reluctantly admitted that it hadn't really been his doing. She'd been so eager to prove how important she was....

A vice president. Of International Operations, no less. She groaned.

"Are you all right, dear?"

Amanda blinked. "Fine," she said, not quite truthfully. She took out her roll of antacids. Then, on second thought, she shook two aspirin from the bottle she kept in her purse.

Mary was looking at Amanda with concern as she handed Amanda a glass of water for the aspirin. "You look pale."

"I'm just a little tired." And confused. Not only did she not really know Dane, Amanda was beginning to wonder if she even knew herself.

"You're working very hard." The stainless-steel blade resumed flashing in the stuttering coastal sunlight coming in through the kitchen windows. "Dane told me how important this week is to you."

"It is." Amanda reminded herself exactly how important. Her entire career—her life—depended on the challenge week's being a success.

"He also told me you're very good at motivating people."

"Dane said that?" Praise from Dane Cutter shouldn't mean so much to her. It shouldn't. But, it did.

"I believe his exact words were, barring plague or pestilence, you'll have your promotion by the end of the week."

"I hope he's right."

Mary's smile was warm and generous. "Oh, Dane is always right about these things, Amanda. He's got a sixth sense for business and if he says you're going to win your creative director's slot, you can count on it happening."

It was what she wanted, damn it. What she'd worked for. So why, Amanda wondered as she left the kitchen to meet the members of the team, who were gathering in the parking lot for their afternoon bicycle race, did the idea leave her feeling strangely depressed?

The mountain bikes, like the team-challenge T-shirts and accompanying slickers, were red and blue.

"At least they look sturdy," Julian decided, studying the knobby fat tires.

"And heavy," Kelli said skeptically. "What's wrong with a nice, lightweight ten-speed?"

"Kelli has a point, Amanda," Peter interjected with what Amanda supposed was another attempt to make points with the sexy public-relations manager. "Why can't we just use racing bikes?"

"In the first place, you're not going to be sticking to the asphalt." Amanda handed everyone a laminated map of the course. "You'll need a sturdy bike for all the detours over gravel and dirt roads and creekbeds."

When that description earned a collective groan, Amanda took some encouragement from the fact that everyone seemed to share the same reservations. That, in its own way, was progress.

"Think of it as touring new ground," she suggested optimistically.

"That's definitely pushing a metaphor," Marvin complained over the laughter of the others.

Amanda's grin was quick and confident. "That's why I leave the copywriting to you."

She went on to explain the rules, which involved the riders leaving the parking lot at timed intervals, following the trail marked on the maps, then returning to the inn, hopefully in time for dinner. She would ride along as an observer and, if necessary, a referee. Once everyone was back, the collective times would determine which team had won.

"Any questions?" she asked when she was finished.

"I have one." Laura was adjusting the chin strap on her helmet with the air of someone who'd done this before. "Since it's obvious you can't be at every checkpoint, how are you going to ensure some people don't skip a segment?"

"Are you accusing people of not being honest?" Don complained.

"You're in advertising marketing, Don," Luke reminded. "I'd say a lack of forthrightness goes with the territory."

When everyone laughed, Amanda experienced another surge of optimism. Only two days ago, such a comment would have started a fight. Things were definitely looking up!

"Not that I don't trust everyone implicitly," Amanda said, "but now that you bring it up, there will be referees at all the checkpoints to stamp the appropriate section of your map." She had arranged with Dane to hire some of his off-duty employees.

"Is Mindy going to be one of those referees?" Peter asked hopefully.

"Mindy Taylor will be working the second segment," Amanda revealed.

"There go our chances," Don grumbled as he pulled on a pair of leather bicycle gloves. "Because with Miss America working the second checkpoint, Peter will never get to number three."

There was more laughter, and some good-natured teasing, along with the expected complaints from Peter, which only earned him hoots from his fellow teammates and the opposing team.

"Well," Amanda said, glancing down at her stopwatch, "if everyone's ready, we'll send off the first team."

"Oh, look!" Kelli exclaimed, pointing toward the inn. "Here comes Dane." Amanda found the public-relations manager's smile far too welcoming. "Hey, coach," Kelli called out, "any last advice?"

Since the course was easily followed and everyone knew how to ride a bike, Amanda had decided it wouldn't be necessary for Dane to come along. He was, however, scheduled to lead the upcoming backpacking trip and rock-climbing expedition.

"Just one." He rocked back on his heels and observed the assembled teams with mild amusement. "Watch out for logging trucks."

Marvin frowned. "I didn't realize they were logging this part of the coast."

"Well, they are. And those drivers aren't accustomed to sharing the back roads. Stay out of their way. Or die."

With that ominous warning ringing in everyone's ears, the teams pedaled out of the parking lot.

She was going to die. As she braked to a wobbly stop outside the inn, Amanda wondered if she'd ever recover the feeling in her bottom again.

"You made good time," Dane greeted her. He was up on a ladder, painting the rain gutter. He was wearing cutoff jeans and a white T-shirt. "Considering all the extra miles Kelli said you put in riding back and forth between teams."

"You'd think adults could conduct a simple bike race without trying to sabotage one another, wouldn't you?"

Amanda frowned as she remembered the fishing line members of the blue team had strung across a particularly rocky stretch of path.

"You wanted them working together," he reminded her. "Sounds as if that's exactly what they were doing."

"I wanted them to cooperate," she muttered. "Not reenact Desert Storm." The red team had, naturally, sought to retaliate. "Thanks for the suggestion to take along the extra tire tubes. I still haven't figured out where they got those carpet tacks."

"I've got a pretty good guess." Dane had found evidence of someone having been in the workshop.

"Well, other than a few bumps and bruises, at least no one got hurt," Amanda said with a long-suffering sigh. "You were also right about those trucks, by the way. They're scary."

"Like bull elk on amphetamines." As he watched her gingerly climb off the bike, Dane wiped his hand over his mouth to hide his smile. "You look a little stiff."

How was it that she had no feeling at all in her rear, yet her legs were aching all the way to the bone? "That's an understatement." She glared at the now muddy mountain bike that had seemed such a nifty idea when the original challenge coach, who'd conveniently managed to avoid taking part in the week's activities, had first suggested it. "I swear that seat was invented by the Marquis de Sade."

"If you're sore, I can give you a massage. To get the kinks out," he said innocently when she shot him a stern look. "I've got pretty good hands. If I do say so myself." He flexed his fingers as he grinned down at her from his perch on the ladder.

Amanda had firsthand knowledge of exactly how

good those hands were. Which was why there was absolutely no way she was going to take Dane up on his offer.

"Thanks, anyway. But I think I'll just take a long soak in a hot bath." Suddenly uncomfortably aware of how dirty and sweaty she must look, she was anxious to escape.

"Suit yourself." He flashed her another of those devastating smiles, then returned to his painting.

She was halfway up the steps when he called out to her.

"Yes?" She half turned and looked up at him. He was so damn sexy, with that tight, sweat-stained T-shirt and those snug jeans that cupped his sex so enticingly. He reminded her of the young Brando, in *A Streetcar Named Desire*. Rough and dangerous and ready as hell.

It crossed Amanda's mind that if Eve Deveraux had ever seen her vice president of international operations looking like this, she probably would have offered to triple his salary, just to keep him around to improve the scenery.

"If you change your mind, just let me know."

"Thank you." Her answering smile was falsely sweet. "But I believe that just might be pushing your hospitality to the limit."

"We aim to please." The devilish grin brightened his dark eyes. "Service With a Smile. That's our motto here at Smugglers' Inn."

She might be confused. But she wasn't foolish enough to even attempt to touch that line. Without another word, she escaped into the inn.

Enjoying the mental image of Amanda up to her neck in frothy white bubbles, Dane was whistling as he returned to work.

Chapter 9

After a long soak and a brief nap, Amanda felt like a new woman. During her time in the claw-footed bathtub, she'd made an important decision. The next time Dane tried to seduce her, she was going to let him.

Having already spent too much time thinking of him, she'd come to the logical conclusion that part of her problem regarding Dane was the fact that they'd never made love.

Tonight, Amanda vowed as she rose from the perfumed water, toweled off and began dusting fragrant talcum powder over every inch of her body, she was going to remedy that nagging problem.

She dressed carefully for dinner, in an outfit she'd providentially thrown into her suitcase at the last minute—a broomstick gauze skirt that flowed in swirls the color of a summer sunrise, and a matching scoop-necked top with crisscross lacing up the front. The bright hues brought out the heightened color in her cheeks.

She paused in front of the mirror, studying her reflection judiciously. Her freshly washed hair curved beneath her chin, framing her face in gleaming dark gold. Anticipation brightened her eyes, while the fullness of the skirt and blouse suggested more curves than she currently possessed.

"You'll do," she decided with a slow smile ripe with feminine intent. Spritzing herself one last time with scent, she left the tower room, heading downstairs to dinner. And to Dane.

He wasn't there! Amanda forced a smile and attempted to make small talk with the other people at her table as the evening droned on and on. On some level she noted that her meal of shrimp Provençal and tomato, mushroom and basil salad was excellent, but the food Mary Cutter had obviously labored over tasted like ashes in Amanda's mouth.

She wasn't the only person inwardly seething. Greg, who was seated at the neighboring table, did not even bother to conceal his irritation at the fact that Kelli was also absent from the dining room. He snapped at his table companions, glared at the room in general and ordered one Scotch after another.

Finally, obviously fed up, Miss Minnie marched up to the table and insisted that he display more consideration.

"This is, after all," she declared with all the haughty bearing of a forceful woman accustomed to controlling those around her, "supposed to be a civilized dining room."

Greg looked up at her through increasingly bleary eyes. "In case it's escaped your notice," he said, the alcohol causing him to slur his words, "the firm of Janzen, Lawton and Young happens to have booked every room in this inn, with the exception of the suite occupied by you and your sister."

His jaw was jutted out; his red-veined eyes were narrowed and unpleasant. "That being the case, if you have a problem with my drinking, I would suggest that you just hustle your skinny rear end upstairs and order room service."

A hush fell over the dining room. Shocked to silence for what Amanda suspected was the first time in her life, Miss Minnie clasped a blue-veined hand to the front of her dove-brown silk dress.

Out of the corner of her eye, Amanda saw Mary emerging from the kitchen at the same time Mindy was entering from the lobby. Feeling somehow to blame— she was responsible for the horrid man having come to Smugglers' Inn, after all—Amanda jumped to her feet and went over to Greg's table.

"You owe Miss Minnie an apology, Greg," she said sternly. She bestowed her most conciliatory smile upon the elderly woman. "It's been a long day. Everyone's tired. And out of sorts."

"Don't apologize for me, Amanda," Greg growled, continuing to eye the elderly woman with overt contempt.

"But—"

"He's right," Miss Minnie agreed in a voice that could have slashed through steel. "There's no point in trying to defend such uncouth behavior. It would be like putting a top hat and tails on an orangutan and attempting to teach him how to waltz." She lifted her white head and marched from the room.

A moment later, Miss Pearl, who'd been observing the altercation from across the room, hurried after her sister, pausing briefly to place a plump hand on Amanda's arm.

"Don't worry, dear," she said. "My sister actually enjoys these little tiffs." Dimples deepened in her pink cheeks. "She insists it keeps her blood flowing." With that encouragement ringing in Amanda's ears, she left the room.

Perhaps Miss Minnie found such altercations beneficial, but this one had sent Amanda's blood pressure soaring. "That was," she said, biting her words off one at a time, "unconscionable behavior."

"Don't take that holier-than-thou tone with me, Amanda," Greg warned. "Because, in case it's escaped that empty blond head of yours, I can fire you. Like that." He attempted to snap his fingers, but managed only a dull rubbing sound that still managed to get his point across. Loud and clear.

"You're representing the agency, Greg. It seems you could try not to be such a bastard. At least in public."

"It's not *me* you need to worry about, sweetheart," he drawled as he twisted his glass on the tablecloth. "We both know that what's got you so uptight tonight is that our host is off providing personal service to the missing member of our challenge team."

No. As furious as she'd been at Dane, Amanda couldn't believe that the reason he hadn't come to dinner was because he preferred being with Kelli Kyle. Her eyes unwillingly whipped over to Laura—who was Kelli's roommate. When Laura blushed and pretended a sudden interest in the tablecloth, Amanda realized that about this, at least, Greg wasn't lying.

"You're wrong," she managed to say with a composure she was a very long way from feeling. "But there's nothing so unusual about that, is there? Since I can't think of a single thing you've been right about since you arrived in Portland.

"You're stupid, Greg. And mean-spirited. Not to mention lazy. And one of these days, Ernst Janzen is going to realize that nepotism isn't worth letting some incompetent bully destroy his empire."

Amazingly, the knot in her stomach loosened. She might have lost her job, but she'd finally gotten out feelings she'd been keeping bottled up inside her for too long.

When the other diners in the room broke out in a thundering ovation, she realized she'd been speaking for everyone. Everyone except, perhaps, the missing Kelli.

"And now, if you'll excuse me," she said, lifting her head, "I've another matter to take care of."

As fate would have it, Amanda passed Kelli coming into the inn as she was coming out.

"Hi, Amanda," Kelli said with her trademark perky smile. "Isn't it a lovely evening?"

Amanda was not inclined to bother with pleasantries. "Where's Dane?"

The smile faded and for a suspended moment, Kelli appeared tempted to lie. Then, with a shrug of her shoulders, she said, "On the beach."

Amanda nodded. "Thank you."

"Anytime."

Intent on getting some answers from Dane, as she marched away, Amanda didn't notice Kelli's intense, thoughtful look.

She found Dane at the cave. The place where those long-ago pirates had allegedly stashed their treasure. The place she'd always thought of as *their secret sanctuary.* He'd lit a fire and was sitting on a piece of driftwood beside it, drinking a beer. The lipstick on the mouth of the empty bottle beside the log told its own story.

"Hello, contessa." His smile was as warm as any he'd ever shared with her. "I've been waiting for you."

As confused as Amanda had been about everything else, the one thing she'd thought she could believe for certain was that Dane was an honorable man. To discover otherwise was proving terribly painful.

"Why don't you tell that to someone stupid enough to believe you." She'd tried for frost and ended up with heat. Instead of ice coating her words, a hot temper made them tremble.

Amanda's bright gauze skirt was almost transparent in the firelight. Dane found it difficult to concentrate on her anger when his attention was drawn to her long, firm legs.

He slowly stood. "I think I'm missing something here."

"I can't imagine what." Amanda sent him a searing look. "Unless it's your scorecard." When he gave her another blank look, she twined her fingers together to keep from hitting him as she'd done the other night. "To keep track of all your women."

"What women? I don't—"

"Don't lie to me!" When he reached out for her, she gave him a shove. "I passed Kelli on the way down here." Her voice rose, shaky but determined. "She told me where to find you."

"I see." He nodded.

She'd hoped he would explain. On her way down the steps to the beach, she'd prayed that he would have some logical reason for being alone on a moonlit beach, or worse yet, in this cozy cave, with a woman like Kelli Kyle.

Her imagination had tossed up scenario after scenario—perhaps the faucet was dripping in Kelli's bathroom, or perhaps her shutters had banged during last night's brief storm. Perhaps...

Perhaps she'd decided that Dane would make a better lover than Greg Parsons.

Ignoring the anger that was surrounding Amanda like a force field, Dane put his hands on her shoulders. "I can explain."

"That's not necessary." She shrugged off his touch and turned away. "Since it's all perfectly clear. 'Service With a Smile.' Isn't that what you said?"

He spun her around. "Don't push it, Amanda."

Threats glittered in his dark gaze, frightening her. Thrilling her. "And don't *you* touch *me*."

She was still gorgeous. Still stubborn. And so damn wrong. "I'll touch you whenever I want."

"Not after you've been with her. But don't worry, Dane, I understand thoroughly. Kelli was just a fling for you. Like you would have been for me."

Temper, need, desire, surged through him. "You still know what buttons to push, don't you, sweetheart?"

Before she could answer, his head swooped down. Unlike the other times he'd kissed her over the past few days, this time Dane wasn't patient.

His mouth crushed hers with none of his usual tenderness. The hard, savage pressure of his lips and teeth grinding against hers was not a kiss at all, but a branding.

Fear battered, pleasure surged. She tried to shake her

head, to deny both emotions, but his hand cupped the back of her head, holding her to the irresistible assault.

All the passions Amanda had suppressed, all the longings she'd locked away, burst free in a blazing explosion that turned her avid lips as hungry as his, had her tongue tangling with his, and had her grabbing handfuls of his silky hair as she gave herself up to the dark. To the heat. To Dane.

He pulled back, viewed himself in her passion-clouded eyes, then took her mouth again.

This time Amanda dived into the kiss, matching his speed, his power. She'd never known it was possible to feel so much from only a kiss. She'd never known it was possible to need so much from a man.

Having surrendered to the primitive urges coursing through her blood, she clung to Dane as she went under for the third time, dragging him down with her.

Somehow—later she would realize that she had no memory of it happening—they were on their knees on the blanket he'd laid on the sand when he'd first arrived at the cave, and his hand was beneath her skirt while she was fumbling desperately with the zipper at the front of his jeans.

Despite the danger of discovery—or perhaps, she would consider later, because of it—as those clever, wicked fingers slipped beneath the high-cut elastic leg of her panties, seeking out the moist warmth pooling between her legs, Amanda wanted Dane. Desperately.

There were no soft words. No tender touches. His hands were rough and greedy. And wonderful. As they moved over her body, creating enervating heat, Amanda gasped in painful pleasure, reveling in their strength, even as she demanded more.

A fever rose, rushing through her blood with a heat that had nothing to do with flames from the nearby fire. Her need was rich and ripe and deep, causing her to tear at his clothing as he was tearing at hers. She wanted—needed—the feel of flesh against flesh. Her skin was already hot and damp. And aching.

There was a wildness in Dane that thrilled her. A violence that staggered Amanda even as she strained for more. This was what she'd wanted. This mindless passion that she'd known, instinctively, only he could create.

She hadn't wanted gentle. Or tender. What she'd sought, what she'd been waiting for all of her life, was this heat. This madness. This glory.

Dane Cutter knew secrets—dark and dangerous secrets. Tonight, Amanda swore, he would teach them to her.

She was naked beneath him, her body bombarded by sensations her dazed mind could not fully comprehend. When his harshly curved lips closed over her breast, she locked her fists in his jet hair and pressed him even closer.

She said his name, over and over. Demands ripped from her throat. "Take me," she gasped, arching her hips upward as something dark and damning curled painfully inside her. "Now. Before I go mad."

She was wet and hot. Her flesh glowed in the flickering orange light from the flames. She looked utterly arousing.

She was not the only one about to go mad. His long fingers urgently stroked that aching, swollen bud between her quivering thighs with wicked expertise. Within seconds she was racked by a series of violent shudders that left her breathless.

Trembling, she stared up at Dane, momentarily stunned into silence, but before she could recover, his hands had grasped her hips, lifting her against his mouth. He feasted greedily on the still-tingling flesh. She was pulsing all over, inside and out. Amanda clung to Dane, unable to do anything else as he brought her to another hammering climax.

Her body was slick and pliant. His was furnace-hot. Dane wanted Amanda with a desperation like nothing he'd ever known. There was no thought of control now. For either of them.

Hunger had them rolling off the blanket and onto the sand, hands grasping, legs entwined, control abandoned. As the blood fired in his veins and hammered in his head, Dane covered her mouth with his and plunged into her, swallowing her ragged cry.

For a suspended moment as he encountered the unexpected barrier, Dane turned rigid, his burning mind struggling to make sense of the stunning message riveting upward from his pounding loins. But before he could fully decode it, a red haze moved over his eyes and he was moving against her, burying himself deep within her heat.

Sensations crashed into passion, passion into love, with each driving stroke. It was more than Amanda could have imagined, more than she'd ever dreamed. The pain she'd expected never came. Instead, there was only glorious heat and dazzling pleasure.

She wrapped her legs around Dane's lean hips, pressed her mouth against his and hung on for dear life.

Just when she thought she couldn't take any more, he was flooding into her. Then entire worlds exploded.

Her mind was numb, her body spent. She lay in his

arms, her hair splayed over his chest, her lips pressed over his heart, which seemed to be beating in rhythm with her own.

Although the stinging pulsating had begun to diminish, Amanda's entire body remained devastatingly sensitized. His hand, resting lightly at the base of her spine, seemed to be causing her body to glow from inside with a steady, radiant heat.

"Why the hell didn't you tell me?" Emotions churned uncomfortably inside Dane. Of all the stupid mistakes he'd made concerning this woman, this one definitely took the cake.

Amanda knew there was no point in pretending ignorance. She knew exactly what he was talking about. Besides, she'd made her decision and had no intention of apologizing for it.

"I didn't think it mattered." She closed her eyes and wished that this conversation could have waited until she was ready to return to the real world. And her real life.

"She didn't think it mattered." He grabbed hold of her hair—not gently—and lifted her composed gaze to his. "My God, Amanda, I practically raped you."

The fire was burning down, but there was still enough light for her to see the guilt in his dark eyes.

"It wasn't anything near rape." Amanda refused to let Dane take away what he'd given her. Refused to let him reject what she'd given him.

"I sure as hell didn't use any finesse."

"I know." She stretched, enjoying the feel of his muscular legs against her thighs. "And it was wonderful." Actually, it was better than wonderful. But there were not enough words in all the world to describe what she was feeling.

"I was too damn rough." His dark eyes, already laced with chagrin, turned bleak with self-disgust. He frowned as he viewed the bruises already beginning to form on her arms, her hips, her thighs.

He brushed his knuckles over the tops of her breasts, which were also marred with angry smudges. "A woman's first time should be special." He touched the tip of his tongue to a nipple and heard her sigh.

"It *was* special." She lifted her hands to comb them through his hair, but a lovely lethargy had settled over her, infusing her limbs, and she dropped them back to her sides. "The most special thing that ever happened to me."

Her softly spoken words could not quite expunge his feelings of guilt. "It was too fast."

She laughed at that. The rich, satisfied sound of a woman in love. "Don't worry," she murmured against his neck as she pressed her body against his, rekindling cooling sparks. "We can do it again." She ran her tongue in a provocative swath down his neck. "And this time, you can take all night."

It was an offer he was not about to refuse. But having already screwed up what should have been one of the most memorable occasions of her life, Dane intended to do things right.

Wanting to set a more romantic stage—and on a practical level, wanting to wash off the sand he feared was embedded in every pore—he suggested moving to the house. To his room.

Amanda immediately agreed. "But I'd rather we make love in the tower room." Her smile, as she refastened the lacy bra he'd ripped off her, was as warm as any a woman had ever shared with any man. "It already has warm memories for me. I love the idea of making more."

He suddenly realized that he definitely wasn't pleased by the thought that she'd soon be leaving Satan's Cove. Whatever they did together tonight in the refurbished tower room would simply become another memory that she'd look back on with fondness over the coming years.

"Dane?" She witnessed the shadow moving across his eyes, watched his lips pull into a taut line. "Did I say something wrong? If I'm pushing you—"

"No." Her hands had begun to flutter like frightened birds. He caught them by the wrists, lifted them to his mouth and kissed them. "I want you, Amanda. I have from the moment you walked in the door. The problem is, I don't know what you want."

"I want you." The answer was echoed in the sweet warmth of her smile.

Dane couldn't help himself. He had to ask. "For how long?"

He could not have said anything worse. Amanda flinched inwardly even as she vowed not to let him see he'd scored such a direct hit. Obviously, she considered, now that he'd discovered she'd been a virgin, he was concerned she'd take what had happened between them, what was about to happen again, too seriously.

He'd already professed the belief that he should have done more—as if such a thing was humanly possible— to make her first lovemaking experience special. Now, it appeared he was afraid of becoming trapped in a permanent relationship he hadn't initially bargained for.

"If you're asking if I'm going to call my father and have him show up in Satan's Cove with a shotgun, you don't have to worry, Dane." She withdrew her hands from his and backed away, just a little.

As he watched her trying to relace the blouse he'd torn open, Dane experienced another pang of regret for having treated her so roughly.

"Just because I chose to make love with you, doesn't mean that I'm foolish enough to get all misty-eyed and start smelling orange blossoms and hearing Lohengrin." Her voice was remarkably calm, given the fact that she was trembling inside.

Once again he found himself missing the young girl who wanted nothing more from life than to spend her days and nights making babies with him. On the heels of that thought came another.

"Hell." This time he dragged both hands through his hair. "I didn't use anything."

He'd put the condoms in his pocket before coming down here, but then he'd gotten sidetracked by Kelli Kyle. Then, when Amanda had arrived, she'd been so busy spitting fire at him and had made him so angry, he'd completely forgotten about protection.

Smooth move, Cutter, he blasted himself. Even in his horny, hormone-driven teenage days, he'd never behaved so irresponsibly.

He looked so furious at himself, so frustrated by the situation, that Amanda wrapped her arms around his waist and pressed a brief kiss against his scowling mouth. "It's okay. It's a safe time of the month for me."

He'd heard that one before. "You know what they call people who use the rhythm method of family planning, don't you?"

She tilted her head back and looked up at him. "What?"

"Parents." He shook his head again, thinking that tonight was turning out to be just one disaster after another. "I'm sorry."

"I do wish you'd stop saying that," she said on a soft sigh. "Truly, Dane, it would take a miracle to get me pregnant tonight. And besides, it was only one time."

Dane wondered how many pregnant women had ended up reciting that old lament. "Things aren't the same as they were that summer, Amanda. There's a lot more to be worried about than pregnancy, as serious as that is."

His expression was so somber, Amanda almost laughed. "I don't need a lecture, Dane. I know the risks. But I also know you. And trust you."

"Sure. That's why you went ballistic when you realized I'd been drinking beer out here with Parsons's PR manager."

She'd been hoping that wouldn't come up. She still couldn't believe that she'd behaved like a teenager who'd just caught her date necking with another girl in the parking lot outside the senior prom.

"I *was* jealous," she admitted reluctantly.

"Join the club." He smiled and ran the back of his hand down the side of her face in a slow, tender sweep. "When Jimmy was adjusting your bike pedals today, I just about saw red."

The Brad Pitt look-alike had been unusually attentive. At the time, Amanda had been flattered by his obvious admiration. Especially when the inn was overrun with young girls who could compete with Mindy for her Miss Satan's Cove crown.

"You're kidding."

"I'd already decided that if he touched your leg one more time, I'd fire him."

Amanda laughed at that, finding Dane's confession surprising and wonderful. "I suppose having a crush on an older woman is natural at nineteen."

"I wouldn't know." He gathered her close and kissed her smiling mouth. Lightly. Tenderly. Sweetly. As he'd planned to do all along. "When *I* was nineteen I was so bewitched by a sexy young siren, I wouldn't have thought of looking at anyone else."

It was exactly what she'd been hoping he'd say. Rising up on her toes, she twined her arms around his neck and clung.

"By the way," Dane said when the long, heartfelt kiss finally ended, "I had a life-insurance physical when I bought this place. You don't have to worry about any diseases."

"I wasn't worried." She watched him carefully put out the fire. When he crouched down, his jeans pulled tight against his thighs, making her all too aware of how wonderful those strong, firm legs had felt entwined with hers. "May I ask one question without sounding like a jealous bitch?"

"You could never sound like a bitch." Satisfied with his efforts, he stood again. "But shoot."

"What *was* Kelli doing down here?"

Dane shrugged. "Damned if I know." Seeing the disbelief on her face, he mistook it for another stab of feminine pique. "But if she was trying to lure me into her bed, she sure had a funny way of going about it."

"Oh?" Amanda believed that was exactly what Kelli had had in mind. Obviously she'd tired of Greg and was looking for some way to pass the time until returning to

Portland. What better diversion than a man for whom the word *hunk* had been invented?

"She spent the entire time it took her to drink that beer talking about you," he revealed.

"Me?" That was a surprise. "Why on earth would she be interested in me? And what did she say?"

"It was more what she wanted me to say." He rubbed his chin thoughtfully. The conversation had seemed strange at the time. Looking back, it didn't make any more sense.

Unless, of course, Greg was using her to pump him to discover any flaws he might use against Amanda in their corporate warfare. "She asked a lot of questions about how I thought you were conducting the challenge week. If you'd mentioned your feelings about the value of the games. And whether or not you had discussed individual team members with me."

"That doesn't make any sense," Amanda mused. "Perhaps Greg's using her as a spy. To discover my weak points. And to find out if I'm trying to unseat him."

"That'd be my guess." Even as Dane agreed, he thought that although the explanation made sense, it hadn't seemed to fit Kelli Kyle's probing questions. Putting the nagging little problem away for now, he ran his hands through Amanda's tousled hair, dislodging silvery grains of sand.

"Are we through talking about business?"

"Absolutely." She beamed up at him. "Are you going to make love to me again?"

"Absolutely." And, after a long interlude spent beneath the shower in the bath adjoining the tower room, that's exactly what Dane did.

With a restraint that she never would have guessed

possible, he kept the pace slow and this time when he took her, the ride was slow and long and heartbreakingly gentle. But no less dizzying.

Amanda had mistakenly believed that in that whirlwind mating in the cave, Dane had taught her everything he knew about love. Before the sun rose the following morning, she realized that she'd been wrong.

Her first heady experience, as dizzying as it had proved to be, had only been a prelude to the most glorious night any woman could have known.

A night she knew she would remember for the rest of her life.

Chapter 10

It was the coo of a pigeon sitting on her windowsill that woke her. Amanda stretched luxuriously and felt her lips curve into a slow, satisfied smile. For the first time in her life she knew exactly how Scarlett had felt the morning after Rhett had carried her up all those stairs.

Although she felt a pang of regret to find herself alone in bed, she decided that Dane must have slipped away to prevent gossip. Not that anyone would actually come all the way up here to the tower room. But it was thoughtful of him all the same.

It certainly wouldn't help matters to have the team members gossiping about her and Dane sleeping together. Not that either of them had gotten much sleep.

Besides, they both had a busy day today. Amanda was taking the team out on a deep-sea fishing trip, while Dane caught up on some much-needed grounds work.

She climbed out of the high log bed, aware of an unfamiliar stiffness. *To think you've wasted all that time on the stair stepper,* she scolded herself lightly. *When there are far better ways to work out.*

Perhaps, she considered with an inward grin, she should take Dane back to Portland with her at the end of the challenge. *Maybe, with the raise that comes with the creative director's slot, I could hire him to be my personal trainer.* And dear Lord, how *personal* he'd been!

Even as she found the idea more than a little appealing, it brought home, all too clearly, that their time together was coming to an end. If everything went according to plan, in two short days she'd be getting back on that bus and returning to Portland, where hopefully she'd move into Greg's office. While Dane would stay here, in Satan's Cove, living the bucolic life of a coastal innkeeper.

The thought of losing him, just when she'd found him again, was not a pleasant one. But unwilling to spoil what brief time they had left together, Amanda decided to take yet another page out of Scarlett O'Hara's story and think about that tomorrow.

She went into the adjoining bathroom, which was now overbrimming with memories of the long hot shower they'd taken together last night.

This morning, as she stood beneath the streaming water, she wondered if she'd ever be able to take a shower again without remembering the feel of Dane's strong, sure hands on her body, or the taste of his lips on hers, or the dazzling, dizzying way his mouth had felt when he'd knelt before her and treated her to lovemaking so sublime she'd actually wept.

When memories began flooding her mind and stimulating her body yet again, Amanda decided it was time to get to work. She turned off the water and slipped into the plush white robe—reminiscent of those favored by the Whitfield Palace hotels—hanging on the back of the door.

She found Dane pouring coffee. The scent of the rich dark brew, along with the aroma of Mary Cutter's freshly baked croissants, drew her like a magnet.

"You weren't kidding about special service."

"With a smile." He handed her a cup of steaming coffee, but before she could drink it, he bent his head and kissed her. "I knew it."

"What?" How was it that he could set her head spinning with a single kiss? Although she doubted they'd had more than three hours' sleep, Amanda had never felt more alive.

"That you'd be drop-dead gorgeous in the morning." His eyes took a slow tour of her, from her wet caramel-colored hair down to her toes, painted the soft pink of the inside of a seashell. Beads of water glistened on the flesh framed by the lapels of the bulky white robe. Dane was struck with an urge to lick them away.

"Flatterer." She laughed and dragged a hand through her damp hair. "And if you don't stop looking at me that way, I'll miss the fishing boat."

"If you've ever smelled a fishing boat, you'd know that would be no great loss." His own smile faded. "I've been thinking about the final challenge event."

Amanda nodded. It had been on her mind, as well. "The cliff climb."

"You realize there isn't much room for error in rock climbing."

"I know." She sat down at the skirted table and tore

off a piece of croissant. It was as flaky as expected, layered with the sweet taste of butter. "I trust you to keep things safe."

"I'm not in the survival business." He sat down as well, close enough that their knees were touching.

"I know that, too." After last night, Amanda couldn't find it in her to worry about anything. "But so far, you've done a wonderful job."

"You haven't been so bad, yourself, sweetheart. The way you've kept those team members from going for one another's throats would probably earn you a top-level job in the diplomatic corps, if you ever decide to give up advertising."

She wondered what he'd say if he knew she thought about exactly that on an almost daily basis lately. One of the things that had drawn her to advertising in the first place was that it was a service business, a business that prospered or failed on how it served its clients.

With all the recent megamergers, there seemed to be very little benefit to clients. In fact, more than one old-time C.C.C. client had proclaimed to be upset by a supposed conflict of interest now that the same huge agency was also handling their competitors' advertising.

"You know," she murmured, "a lot of people—mostly those in New York—used to consider C.C.C. old-fashioned. And perhaps it was." Which was, she'd often thought lately, one of the things she'd loved about Connally Creative Concepts. "But it was still an agency where clients' desires were catered to.

"These days, it seems that if you can't win new accounts by being creative, you buy them by gobbling up other, more innovative shops. But the forced combination inevitably fails to create a stronger agency."

"Instead of getting the best of both worlds, you get the worst of each," Dane guessed.

"Exactly." Amanda nodded. "Creativity becomes the last item on the agenda. And, although I hate to admit it, the advertising coming out of Janzen, Lawton and Young these days shows it. In the pursuit of profits, our clients have become an afterthought. They're getting lost in the shuffle."

"It's not just happening in advertising," Dane observed. "The workplace, in general, has become increasingly impersonal."

Which was another of the reasons he'd left the world of big business. Although, under Eve Whitfield Deveraux's guidance, the Whitfield Palace hotel chain routinely topped all the Best 100 Corporations to Work For lists, it was, and always would be, a profit-driven business.

"Every day I arrive at my office, hoping to rediscover the business I used to work in." Amanda had been so busy trying to keep things on an even keel at work, she hadn't realized exactly how much she'd missed the often-frantic, always-stimulating atmosphere of C.C.C. "But I can't. Because it's disappeared beneath a flood of memos and dress codes and constantly changing managerial guidelines."

She sighed again. "Would you mind if we tabled this discussion for some other time?" The depressing topic was threatening to cast a pall over her previously blissful mood.

"Sure." It was none of his business anyway, Dane told himself again. What Amanda chose to do with her life was no one's concern but her own. Knowing that he was utterly hooked on this woman who'd stolen his heart so long ago, Dane only wished that were true.

"May I ask you something?"

There was something in his low tone that set off warnings inside Amanda. She slowly lowered her cup to the flowered tablecloth. "Of course."

"Why me? And why now?"

Good question. She wondered what he'd say if she just said it right out: *Because I think—no, I know—that I love you.*

She put her cup down and stared out at the tall windows at the sea, which was draped in its usual silvery cloak of early morning mist.

"When I was a girl, I was a romantic."

"I remember." All too well.

"I believed that someday a handsome prince would come riding up on his white steed and carry me off to his palace, where we'd live happily ever after." Dane had had a Harley in those days instead of a white horse, but he'd fit the romantic fantasy as if it had been created with him in mind. He still did.

"Sounds nice," Dane agreed. "For a fairy tale." Speaking of fairy tales, he wondered what would happen if, now that he finally had her back again, he just kept Amanda locked away up here in the tower room, like Rapunzel.

"For a fairy tale," she agreed. "I also was brought up to believe that lovemaking was something to be saved for the man I married."

"A not-unreasonable expectation." Dane considered it ironic that he might have Gordon Stockenberg to thank for last night.

"No. But not entirely practical, either." She ran her fingernail around the rim of the coffee cup, uncomfortable with this discussion. Although they'd been as intimate as two people could be, she was discovering that revealing the secrets of her heart was a great deal more difficult than revealing her body.

"If we'd made love that summer, I probably would have found it easier to have casual sex with guys I dated in college. Like so many of my friends.

"But you'd made such a big deal of it, I guess I wanted to wait until I met someone I could at least believe myself to be in love with as much as I'd been in love with you."

Which had never happened.

"Then, after I graduated, I was so busy concentrating on my work, that whenever I did meet a man who seemed like he might be a candidate, he'd usually get tired of waiting around and find some more willing woman."

"Or a less choosy one."

She smiled at that suggestion. "Anyway, after a time, sex just didn't seem that important anymore."

"You *have* been working too hard."

Amanda laughed even as she considered that now that she'd experienced Dane's magnificent lovemaking, sex had taken on an entirely new perspective.

"Anyway," she said with a shrug designed to conceal her tumultuous feelings, "perhaps it was old unresolved feelings reasserting themselves, but being back here again with you, making love to you, just felt so natural. So right."

"I know the feeling." He covered her free hand with his, lacing their fingers together. "You realize, of course, that you could have saved me a great many cold showers if you'd just admitted to wanting me that first night?"

The way his thumb was brushing tantalizingly against the palm of her hand was creating another slow burn deep inside Amanda. "Better late than never."

"Speaking of being late…" He lifted her hand to his lips and pressed a kiss against the skin his thumb had left tingling. "How much time do we have before you're due at the dock?"

She glanced over at the clock on the pine bedside table and sighed. "Not enough."

"I was afraid of that." He ran the back of his hand down her cheek. "How would you like to go into town with me tonight?"

The opportunity to be alone with Dane, away from the prying eyes of the others, sounded sublime. "I'd love to."

"Great. Davey Jones's Locker probably isn't what you're used to—I mean, the tablecloths are white butcher paper instead of damask and the wine list isn't anything to boast about. But the food's pretty good. And the lighting's dark enough that we can neck in the back booth between courses."

Her smile lit her face. "It sounds absolutely perfect."

Other than the fact that the sea had turned rough and choppy by midafternoon, and Dane had been right about the smell of fish permeating every inch of the chartered fishing boat, the derby turned out better than Amanda had honestly expected.

The teams seemed to be meshing more with each passing day, and at the same time the competitive viciousness displayed on the bike race had abated somewhat. At least, she considered, as the boat chugged its way into the Satan's Cove harbor, no one had thrown anyone overboard.

As team members stood in line to have their catch weighed and measured, Amanda noticed that Kelli was missing. She found her in the restroom of the charter office, splashing water on her face. Her complexion was as green as the linoleum floor.

"Whoever thought up this stupid challenge week should be keelhauled," the public-relations manager moaned.

Since the week had been Greg's idea, Amanda didn't answer. "I guess the Dramamine didn't work." Prepared for seasickness among the group, Amanda had given Kelli the tablets shortly after the boat left the dock, when it became obvious that the woman was not a natural-born sailor.

"Actually, it helped a lot with the seasickness. I think it was the smell of the fish that finally got to me." She pressed a hand against her stomach. "I'm never going to be able to eat salmon or calamari again."

"I'm sorry," Amanda said, realizing she actually meant it. "Is there anything I can do?"

"No." Kelli shook her head, then cringed, as if wishing she hadn't done so. "I just want to get back to the inn, go to bed, pull the covers over my head and if not die, at least sleep until morning."

"That sounds like a good idea. I'll ask Mary Cutter to fix a tray for you to eat in your room."

If possible, Kelli's complexion turned an even sicklier hue of green. "I don't think I could keep down a thing."

"You need something in your stomach. Just something light. Some crackers. And a little broth, perhaps."

Although obviously quite ill, Kelli managed a smile. "You know, everything I've been told about you suggests you're a dynamite advertising executive. Yet, sometimes, like during that stupid helicopter session, you seem to be a born diplomat."

"Thank you." Amanda was surprised to receive praise from someone so close to her nemesis.

"You don't have to thank me for telling the truth," Kelli said. "But there's another side to you, as well. A softer, nurturing side. So, what about children?"

The question had come from left field. "What about them?"

"Do you intend to have any?"

"I suppose. Someday."

"But not anytime soon?"

"Getting pregnant certainly isn't on this week's agenda," Amanda said honestly.

For some reason she could not discern, Kelli seemed to be mulling that over. Amanda waited patiently to see what the woman was up to.

"You don't like me much, do you?" Kelli asked finally.

"I don't really know you."

"True. And spoken like a true diplomat. By the way, Dane was a perfect gentleman last night."

"I can't imagine Dane being anything but a gentleman."

"What I mean is—"

"I know what you mean." Amanda didn't want to talk about Dane. Not with this woman.

Kelli reached into her canvas tote, pulled out a compact and began applying rose blush to her too-pale cheeks. "You love Dane, don't you?"

"I really don't believe my feelings are anyone's business but my own."

"Of course not," Kelli said quickly. A bit too quickly, Amanda thought. "I was just thinking that advertising is a very unstable business, and if you were to get involved with our sexy innkeeper, then have to move back East—"

"I doubt there's much possibility of that. Besides, as exciting as New York admittedly is, I'm comfortable where I am."

Kelli dropped the blush back into the bag and pulled out a black-and-gold lipstick case. "Even with Greg as creative director?"

She'd definitely hit the bull's-eye with that question.

"Greg Parsons isn't Patrick Connally," Amanda said truthfully. "And his management style is a great deal different." Sort of like the difference between Genghis Khan and Ghandi. "But, as we've pointed out over these past days, advertising is all about change."

"Yes, it is, isn't it?" Kelli looked at Amanda in the mirror. Her gaze was long and deep. Finally, she returned to her primping. After applying a fuchsia lipstick that added much-needed color to her lips, she said, "I suppose we may as well join the others."

As they left the restroom together, Amanda couldn't help thinking that their brief conversation wasn't exactly like two women sharing confidences. It had strangely seemed more like an interview. Deciding that she was reading too much into the incident, she began anticipating the evening ahead.

Amanda hadn't been so nervous since the summer of her fifteenth year. She bathed in scented water that left her skin as smooth as silk, brushed her newly washed hair until it shone like gold and applied her makeup with unusual care. Then she stood in front of the closet, wondering what she could wear for what was, essentially, her first real date with Dane.

She'd only brought one dress, and she'd already worn it last night. Besides, somehow, the front ties had gotten torn in their frantic struggle to undress. And although she had no doubt that the patrons of Davey Jones's Locker wouldn't complain about her showing up with the front of her blouse slit down to her navel, she figured such sexy attire would be overkill for Satan's Cove.

Although she'd been underage, hence too young to go into the bar/restaurant the last time she'd visited the coastal town, from the outside, the building definitely did not seem to be the kind of place where one dressed for dinner.

With that in mind, she finally decided on a pair of black jeans and a long-sleeved white blouse cut in the classic style of a man's shirt. Some gold studs at her ears, a gold watch, and a pair of black cowboy boots completed her ensemble.

"Well, you're not exactly Cinderella," she murmured, observing her reflection in the antique full-length mirror. "But you'll do."

So as not to encourage unwanted gossip, she'd agreed to meet Dane in the former carriage house that had been turned into a garage. As she entered the wooden building, his eyes darkened with masculine approval.

"You look absolutely gorgeous, contessa."

She was vastly relieved he hadn't seen her when she'd arrived from the boat, smelling of fish, her face pink from the sun, her nose peeling like an eleven-year-old tomboy's and her hair a wild tangle.

"I hope this is appropriate." She ran her hands down

the front of her jeans. "I thought I'd leave my tiara at home tonight."

"All the better to mingle with your subjects," he agreed, thinking that although she'd cleaned up beautifully, he still kind of liked the way she'd looked when she'd returned from the fishing derby today.

He'd been in the garden, tying up his mother's prized tomato plants, when he'd seen her trying to sneak into the lodge, her complexion kissed by the sun and her tangled hair reminding him of the way it looked when she first woke up this morning after a night of passionate lovemaking.

"I got to thinking," he said, "that perhaps, after a day on a fishing boat, taking you out for seafood wasn't the best idea I've ever had."

"Don't worry about me." Her smile was quick and warm and reminded him of the one he'd fallen for when he was nineteen. "I've got a stomach like a rock. And I adore seafood."

"Terrific. Iris has a way with fried oysters you won't believe."

"I love fried oysters." She batted her lashes in the way Scarlett O'Hara had made famous and a fifteen-year-old girl had once perfected. "They're rumored to be an aphrodisiac, you know."

"So I've heard. But with you providing the inspiration, contessa, the last thing I need is an aphrodisiac."

He drew her into his arms and gave her a long deep kiss that left her breathless. And even as he claimed her mouth with his, Dane knew that it was Amanda who was claiming him. Mind, heart and soul.

Satan's Cove was laid out in a crescent, following the curving shoreline. As Dane drove down the narrow main street, Amanda was surprised and pleased that the town hadn't changed during the decade she'd been away.

"It's as if it's frozen in time," she murmured as they drove past the cluster of buildings that billed themselves as the Sportsman's Lodge, and the white Cape Cod–style Gray Whale Mercantile. "Well, almost," she amended as she viewed a window sign on another building that advertised crystals and palm readings. A For Rent sign hung in a second-story window above the New Age shop.

"Nothing stays the same." Dane said what Amanda had already discovered the hard way at C.C.C. "But change has been slow to come to this part of the coast."

"I'm glad," she decided.

"Of course, there was a time when Satan's Cove was a boomtown. But that was before the fire."

"Fire?"

"Didn't you learn the town's history when you were here before?"

"I was a little preoccupied that summer," she reminded. "Trying to seduce the sexiest boy on the Pacific seaboard. Visiting dull old museums was not exactly high on my list of fun things to do."

Since he'd had far better places to escape with her than the town museum, Dane decided he was in no position to criticize.

"With the exception of Smugglers' Inn, which was located too far away, most of the town burned down in the early nineteen-thirties. Including the old Victorian whorehouse down by the docks. Well, needless to say, without that brothel, the fishermen all moved to Tillamook, Seaside and Astoria."

"Amazing what the loss of entrepreneurs can do to

a local economy," she drawled sapiently. "So what happened? Didn't the women come back after the town was rebuilt?"

"By the time the city fathers got around to rebuilding in the mid-thirties, the prohibitionists had joined forces with some radical religious reformers who passed an ordinance forbidding the rebuilding of any houses of ill repute.

"After World War II, alcohol returned without a battle. And so did sex. But these days it's free." He flashed her a grin. "Or so I'm told."

Even though she knew their time was coming to an end, his flippant statement caused a stab of purely feminine jealousy. Amanda hated the idea of Dane making love to any other woman. But short of tying him up and taking him back to Portland with her, she couldn't think of a way to keep the man all to herself.

She was wondering about the logistics of maintaining a commuter relationship—after all, Portland was only a few hours' drive from Satan's Cove—when he pulled up in front of Davey Jones's Locker.

From the outside, the weathered, silvery gray building did not look at all promising. Once inside, however, after her eyes adjusted to the dim light, Amanda found it rustically appealing.

Fish, caught in local waters, had been mounted on the knotty-pine-paneled walls, yellow sawdust had been sprinkled over the plank floor and behind an L-shaped bar was a smoky mirror and rows of bottles.

"Dane!" A woman who seemed vaguely familiar, wearing a striped cotton-knit top and a pair of cuffed white shorts, stopped on her way by with a tray of pilsner glasses filled with draft beer. Her voluptuous breasts turned the red and white stripes into wavy lines. "I was wondering what it would take to get you away from that work in progress."

She flashed Dane a smile that belonged in a toothpaste commercial and her emerald eyes gleamed with a feminine welcome Amanda found far too sexy for comfort. Then her eyes skimmed over Amanda with unconcealed interest.

"Just grab any old table, you two," she said with an airy wave of her hand. "As soon as I deliver these, I'll come take your drink order."

With that, she was dashing across the room to where a group of men were playing a game of pool on a green-felt-topped table. The seductive movement of her hips in those tight white shorts was nothing short of riveting.

"Old friend?" Amanda asked as she slipped into a booth at the back of the room.

"Iris and I dated a bit in high school," Dane revealed easily. "And when I first returned to town. But nothing ever came of it. We decided not to risk a great friendship by introducing romance into the relationship."

Relief was instantaneous. "She really is stunning." Now that she knew the woman wasn't a threat, Amanda could afford to be generous.

"She is that," Dane agreed easily. "I've seen grown men walk into walls when Iris walks by. But, of course, that could be because they've had too much to drink."

Or it could be because the woman had a body any *Playboy* centerfold would envy. That idea brought up Dane's contention that she was too thin, which in turn had Amanda comparing herself with the voluptuous Iris, who was headed back their way, order pad in hand. The outcome wasn't even close.

"Hi," she greeted Amanda with a smile every bit as warm as the one she'd bestowed upon Dane. "It's good to see you again."

Amanda looked at the stunning redhead in confusion. "I'm sorry, but—"

"That's okay," Iris interrupted good-naturedly. "It's been a long time. I was waiting tables at Smugglers' Inn the summer you came for a vacation with your parents."

Memories flooded back. "Of course, I remember you." She also recalled, all too clearly, how jealous she'd been of the sexy redheaded waitress who spent far too much time in the kitchen with Dane. "How are you?"

"I'm doing okay. Actually, since I bought this place with the settlement money from my divorce, I'm doing great." She laughed, pushing back a froth of copper hair. "I think I've found my place, which is kind of amazing when you think how badly I wanted to escape this town back in my wild teenage days."

She grinned over at Dane. "Can you believe it, sugar? Here we are, two hotshot kids who couldn't wait to get out of Satan's Cove, back home again, happy as a pair of clams."

"Iris was making a pretty good living acting in Hollywood," Dane revealed.

"Really?" Although she'd grown up in Los Angeles, the only actors she'd ever met were all the wannabes waiting tables at her favorite restaurants. "That must have been exciting."

"In the beginning, I felt just like Buddy Ebsen. You know—" she elaborated at Amanda's confused look "—'The Beverly Hillbillies.' Movie stars, swimming pools… Lord, I was in hog heaven. I married the first guy I met when I got off the bus—an out-of-work actor. That lasted until I caught him rehearsing bedroom scenes with a waitress from Hamburger Hamlet. In our bed.

"My second marriage was to a director, who promised to make me a star. And I'll have to admit, he was doing his best to keep his promise, but I was getting tired of being the girl who was always murdered by some crazed psycho. There's only so much you can do creatively with a bloodcurdling scream.

"Besides, after a time, a girl gets a little tired of her husband wearing her underwear, if you know what I mean."

"I can see where that might be a bit disconcerting," Amanda agreed. She'd never met anyone as open and outgoing as Iris. She decided it was no wonder the woman had chosen to leave the art and artifice of Hollywood.

"After my second divorce, I got fed up with the entire Hollywood scene and realized, just like Dorothy, that there's no place like home."

"I just realized," Amanda said, "I've seen one of your films."

"You're kidding!"

"No. I went to a Halloween party a few years ago and the host screened *Nightstalker.*"

"You've got a good eye," Iris said. "I think I lasted about three scenes in that one."

"But they were pivotal," Amanda said earnestly, remembering how Iris's character—a hooker with a heart of gold—had grabbed her killer's mask off, enabling a street person rifling through a nearby Dumpster to get a glimpse of his scarred face. Which in turn, eventually resulted in the man's capture.

"I knew I liked you." Iris flashed a grin Dane's way. "If I were you, I'd try to hold on to this one."

"Thanks for the advice." Dane didn't add that that was exactly what he intended to do.

Chapter 11

Although the ambience was definitely not that of a five-star restaurant, and the food was not covered in velvety sauce or garnished with the trendy miniature vegetable-of-the-week, Amanda couldn't remember when she'd enjoyed a meal more.

There was one small glitch—when Julian, Marvin, and Luke Cahill had unexpectedly shown up. Fortunately, they appeared no more pleased to see her than she was to see them, and after a few stiltedly exchanged words, settled into a booth across the room.

Amanda wondered what the three were doing together. They could be plotting strategy, were it not for the fact that Marvin and Julian were on the blue team and Luke was on the red.

As much as she had riding on the corporate challenge, for this one night Amanda refused to think about her plan for success. After all, here she was, on her first real date with the man she'd always loved, and she wasn't going to spoil things trying to figure out this latest bit of corporate intrigue.

Instead, she took a sip of the house white wine, smiled enticingly over the heavy rim of the glass, and allowed herself to relax fully for the first time since arriving in Satan's Cove.

It was late when they returned to the inn. The moon and stars that had been so vivid the other night were hidden by a thick cloud of fog.

Someone—undoubtedly Mindy—had left a lamp in the downstairs reception parlor on; it glowed a warm welcome. The lights in the upstairs windows were off, revealing that the other guests had gone to bed.

Amanda didn't invite Dane up to her room. There was no need. Both of them knew how the night would end.

The elevator was cranking its way up to the third floor when Dane turned and took her in his arms. "I'd say tonight went pretty well," he murmured against her cheek. "For a first date."

"Better than well." She sighed her pleasure as she wrapped her arms around his waist. "I can't remember when I've enjoyed myself more."

"I'm glad." His lips skimmed up to create sparks at her temple. Dane didn't add that he'd worried she'd find Davey Jones's Locker too plebeian for her city tastes.

"And just think—" she leaned back a bit, sensual amusement gleaming in her eyes "—the night's still young."

Actually, that wasn't really the case. But Dane wasn't about to argue. After all the sleep he'd lost fixing up the inn, he wasn't about to complain about losing a bit more if it meant making love again to Amanda.

Lowering his head, he touched his lips to hers. At first briefly. Then, as he drew her closer, the kiss, while remaining tender, grew deeper. More intimate. More weakening.

Her limbs grew heavy, her head light. Amanda clung to him, wanting more. She'd never known an elevator ride to take so long.

The cage door finally opened. Hand in hand, they walked to the stairwell at the end of the hallway. It was like moving in a dream. A dream Amanda wished would never end.

They'd no sooner entered the tower room than Dane pulled her close and kissed her again. Not with the slow self-control of a man who knew how to draw out every last ounce of pleasure, but with the impatient demand of a lover who realized that this stolen time together was rapidly coming to an end.

With a strength and ease that once again bespoke the life of hard, physical work he'd chosen over shuffling papers, Dane scooped her up in his arms and carried her across the plank floor to the bed, which had been turned down during their absence. A mint, formed in the unmistakable shape of the inn, had been left on the pillow. Dane brushed it onto the floor with an impatient hand and began unbuttoning Amanda's blouse.

"No." It took an effort—her bones had turned to syrup—but she managed to lift her hands to his.

"No?" Disbelief sharpened his tone, darkened his eyes.

She laid a calming hand against his cheek and felt the tensed muscle beneath her fingertips. "It's my turn."

Unconsciously, she skimmed her tongue over her lips, enjoying the clinging taste of him. "To make love to you."

It was at that moment, when every atom in his body was aching to take Amanda—and take her now—that Dane realized he could deny this woman nothing.

His answering smile was slow and warm and devilishly sexy. "I'm all yours, contessa." He'd never, in all his twenty-nine years, spoken truer words.

He rolled over onto his back, spread out his arms and waited.

Never having undressed a man—last night's frantic coupling in the cave didn't really count, since Amanda still couldn't remember how they'd ended up naked—she was more than a little nervous. But, remembering how his bare torso had gleamed like bronze in the firelight, she decided to begin with his shirt.

With hands that were not as steady as she would have liked, she tackled the buttons one by one. She'd known he was strong—his chest was rock hard and wonderfully muscled. But it was his inner strength that continued to arouse her. Just as it was his loyalty, integrity and steely self-confidence that Amanda had fallen in love with.

When she reached his belt, she had two choices—to unfasten his jeans or tug the shirt free. Unreasonably drawn to the enticing swell beneath the crisp indigo denim of the jeans that had become his dress slacks when he'd changed lifestyles, Amanda stuck to her vow to keep things slow.

Dane was moderately disappointed when she took the easy way out and pulled his shirt free of his waistband—until she folded back the plaid cotton and pressed her silky lips against his bare chest. Her mouth felt like a hot brand against his flesh, burning her claim on him, just as she'd done so many years ago.

"I'm not very experienced." Her lips skimmed down the narrow arrowing of ebony chest hair, leaving sparks. "You'll have to tell me what you like." Retracing the trail her mouth had blazed, she flicked her tongue over a dark nipple. The wet heat caused a smoldering deep in his loins, which threatened to burst into a wildfire.

"That's a dandy start," he managed in a husky voice roughened with hunger.

"How about this?" She bestowed light, lazy kisses back down his chest, over his stomach.

"Even better," he groaned, when she dipped her tongue into his navel. His erection stirred, pushing painfully against the hard denim barrier. Realizing that it was important to cede control to Amanda, Dane ignored the ache and concentrated on the pleasure.

He could have cursed when she suddenly abandoned her seduction efforts. Relief flooded through him as he realized she was only stopping long enough to take off his shoes and socks.

For a woman who a little more than twenty-four hours ago had been a virgin, Amanda was definitely making up for lost time.

"I've never noticed a man's feet before," she murmured, running her hands over his. "Who could have guessed that a foot could be so sexy?"

He began to laugh at that outrageous idea, but when she touched her lips to his arch, lightning forked through him, turning the laugh into a choked sound of need.

"Lord, Amanda—" He reached for her, but she deftly avoided his hands.

She touched her mouth to his ankle, felt the thundering of his pulse and imagined she could taste the heat of his blood beneath her lips.

Realizing that she was on the verge of losing control of her emotions, Amanda shifted positions, to lie beside him. She returned her mouth to his face, kissing her way along his rigid jaw as her hands explored his torso, exploiting weaknesses he'd never known he possessed.

She left him long enough to light the fire he'd laid while she'd been out on the fishing boat. Then she proceeded to undress. She took as much time with her buttons as she had with his. By the time the white shirt finally fluttered to the floor, Dane had to press his lips together to keep his tongue from hanging out. As he observed her creamy breasts, unbearably enticing beneath the ivory lace bra, Dane discovered that ten years hadn't lessened his reaction to the sexy lingerie that had driven a sex-crazed nineteen-year-old to distraction.

She sat down in the wing chair beside the bed, stuck out a leg and invited him to pull off the glove-soft cowboy boot. Dane obliged her willingly. The left boot, then the right, dropped to the floor.

The jeans were even tougher to get off than the boots. "I should have thought this through better," she muttered as she tugged the black denim over her hips, irritated she'd lost the sensual rhythm she'd tried so hard to maintain.

"You certainly don't have to apologize, contessa." The sexy way she was wiggling her hips as she struggled to pull the tight jeans down her legs had Dane feeling as if he was about to explode. "Because it definitely works for me."

Their gazes touched. His eyes were dark with desire,

but tinged with a tender amusement that eased her embarrassment.

She had to sit down in the chair again to drag the jeans over her feet, but then she was standing beside the bed, clad only in the lacy bra and panties. The soft shadow beneath the skimpy lace triangle between her thighs had Dane literally biting the inside of his cheek.

"Don't stop now."

Thrilled by the heat flashing in his midnight-dark eyes, along with the hunger in his ragged tone, Amanda leaned forward, unfastened the back hooks of the bra, then held it against her chest for a suspended moment. With her eyes still on his, she smiled seductively.

As she raised her hands to comb them through her hair in a languid gesture, the lace bra fell away.

Unbearably aroused, Dane drank in the sight of her creamy breasts. While not voluptuous, they were smooth and firm. He remembered, all too well, how perfectly they had fit in his hands. In his mouth.

Watching him watch her, Amanda experienced a rush of power—followed by a wave of weakness. Although far more nervous now than when she'd begun the impromptu striptease, Amanda was determined to see it through. She hooked her fingers in the low-cut waistband, drawing the lace over her hips and down her legs.

"You are absolutely gorgeous." The truth of his words was echoed in his rough voice.

"And you're overdressed." Returning to the bed, she knelt over him, struggling with his belt buckle for a few frustrating seconds that seemed like an eternity.

Success! She dragged his jeans and white cotton briefs down his legs, then kissed her way up again.

"You're killing me," he moaned as her hand encircled his erection.

"Now you know how I felt." His sex was smooth and hot. "Last night." She lowered her head, and her hair fell over his hips like a gleaming antique-gold curtain as she swirled her seductive tongue over him.

Curses, pleas, or promises, Dane wasn't sure which, were torn from his throat. For the first time in his life, he understood what it was to be completely vulnerable.

She touched. He burned.

She tasted. He ached.

Amanda straddled Dane, taking him deep inside her, imprisoning him willingly, wonderfully, in her warmth.

Their eyes locked, exchanging erotic messages, intimate promises that neither had dared put into words.

Then, because they could wait no longer, she began to move, quickly and agilely, rocking against him, driving him—driving herself—toward that final glorious crest.

Although their time together was drawing to an end, neither Amanda nor Dane brought up the subject of what would happen once the challenge week ended. By unspoken mutual agreement, they ignored the inevitable, intent on capturing whatever pleasure they could. Whenever they could.

On the overnight backpacking trip, while the others tossed and turned, unaccustomed to sleeping on the ground, Dane slipped into Amanda's tent. Their lovemaking, while necessarily silent, was even more thrilling because of the risk of discovery. And when she couldn't remain quiet at the shattering moment of climax, Dane covered her mouth with his, smothering her ecstatic cry.

Time passed as if on wings. On the day before she was scheduled to leave, while Dane was on the beach, preparing for the final event of the challenge week—the cliff climb—Amanda was alone in her room, her eyes swollen from the tears she'd shed after he'd left her bed.

The knock on her door had her wiping her damp cheeks. "Yes?"

"Amanda?" It was Kelli. "May I speak with you?"

Although they hadn't exchanged more than a few words since the fishing-boat incident, Amanda had gotten the impression that Kelli had been watching her every move, which had only increased her suspicions that the public-relations manager was spying for Greg.

"Just a minute." She ran into the adjoining bathroom, splashed some cold water on her face and pulled a brush through her hair. Then she opened the door.

"I'm sorry to bother you, but…" Kelli's voice drifted off as she observed Amanda's red-rimmed eyes. "Is something wrong?"

"No." When Kelli arched an eyebrow at the obvious lie, Amanda said, "It's personal."

Kelli's expression revealed understanding. "Love can be a real bitch, can't it?"

"Is it that obvious?" Amanda thought she and Dane had been so careful.

"Not to everyone," Kelli assured her.

Amanda decided it was time to get their cards on the table. "That's probably because not everyone has been watching me as closely as you."

If she'd expected Kelli to be embarrassed, Amanda would have been disappointed.

"That's true. But none of the others were sent here from Manhattan to evaluate the office."

"So you *are* a company spy?"

"*Spy* is such a negative word, don't you think?" Kelli suggested mildly. "I prefer to think of myself as a troubleshooter."

"Then you ought to shoot Greg Parsons," Amanda couldn't resist muttering.

"I've considered that. But my recommendation is going to be to fire him, instead."

"You're kidding!" Amanda could have been no more surprised than if Kelli had told her that Martians had just purchased the agency. "But he's family."

"Not for long," Kelli revealed. "It seems his wife has gotten tired of his philandering and is about to file for divorce. Obviously, Mr. Janzen isn't eager to employ the man who's broken his granddaughter's heart."

"It probably helps that he's incompetent to boot."

"That is a plus," Kelli agreed. "Which is, of course, where you come in." She paused a beat. For effect, Amanda thought. "You're the obvious choice to replace Greg as regional creative director."

"I'd hoped that was the case."

"I've already informed the partners that you'd be terrific at the job. But after receiving my daily emails, they've instructed me to offer you another position.

"You also know that all the recent mergers and downsizing has created a great deal of anxiety."

"Of course."

"Your Portland office is not unique. Janzen, Lawton and Young has been experiencing the same problems with all its new worldwide acquisitions. Which is why the partners have come up with the idea of creating the post of ombudsman. Which is where you come in.

"If you decide to accept the position, you'll achieve

upper-management status and be required to travel between offices, creating the same good feeling and teamsmanship you've managed with this group."

"I'd rather have a root canal than repeat this challenge week."

Kelli grinned. "After that fishing trip, I'm in your corner on that one. Actually, the partners think the challenge week was overrated and undereffective. They believe that you could achieve the same results simply by visiting each office and employing your diplomatic skills to assure the employees that the mergers are in everyone's best interests."

"Even if I don't believe they are?" Amanda dared to ask.

"You're in advertising," Kelli reminded her with one of her perky trademark smiles. "Surely you're not averse to putting a positive spin on things. As you've done to get Marvin and Julian working together this week. You weren't lying when you stressed how important it was for the creative people and the accounting people to work together, were you?"

"Of course not, but—"

"Take some time to think it over," Kelli suggested. She went on to offer a salary that was more than double what Amanda was currently making. "Of course, you'll have a very generous expense account. Since image is important in advertising, all upper-level employees travel first class."

"It sounds tempting," Amanda admitted. She thought about what her father would say when she called him with the news.

"Believe me, you'll earn every penny."

"If I decide not to accept—"

"The job of creative director for the Northwest region is still yours."

"How much time do I have?"

"The partners would like your answer by the end of next week. Sooner if possible."

With that, Kelli flashed another self-assured grin and turned to leave. She was in the doorway when she looked back. "I'd appreciate you not saying anything about this to Greg."

"Of course not," Amanda murmured, still a bit stunned by the out-of-the-blue offer. It was more than she'd dared hope for. More than she'd dreamed of. So why wasn't she ecstatic?

Chapter 12

The rock cliffs towered above the beach, looking cold and gray and forbidding.

"Who'll take care of my kids when I die?" Laura asked, her lack of enthusiasm obvious.

"No one's going to die," Dane assured her.

"This isn't fair to the women," Nadine complained. "I've seen rock climbers on the Discovery channel, and they're mostly all men."

"It's true that some climbing—like overhangs—requires strength in the shoulders and arms. But the fact that women aren't usually as strong in those areas isn't as important as you'd think," Dane said. "Since women tend to be smaller than men, they don't need as much strength. In fact, on the average, smaller people have a better strength-to-weight ratio, which is what's important in climbing."

"That's easy for you to say," Nadine muttered, casting a disparaging glance at Dane's muscular arms.

"It's true. Climbing is done primarily with the legs and feet because they're stronger. You can stand for hours at a time on your feet, but even the strongest man can only hang from his arms for a few minutes. The most essential element of climbing is balance."

While the group eyed the cliff with overt suspicion, Dane explained the basics of rock climbing. "One of the most important things to remember," he told the team members, "is that although the tendency is to look up for handholds, you should keep your hands below your shoulders and look down for footholds.

"Balance climbing, which is what you'll be doing, is like climbing stairs, although today you'll be climbing more sideways than vertically. You find a place for your foot, settle into a rest step, then make a shift of your hips and move on to the next step, always striving to keep your body poised over one foot.

"You can pause, or rest supported by both feet. You can also lift your body up with both legs, but never advance a foot to the next hold until you're in balance over the resting foot."

"What about ropes?" Laura, still unconvinced, asked.

"There's an old adage—'It's not the fall that hurts, it's the sudden stop.' If a rope stops a fall too fast, you can end up with a broken body. Or, a rope can pull loose and let you continue to fall. So, although you'll be equipped with a rope harness, since there are plenty of ledges and handholds, you shouldn't need to use the rope on this climb."

"We're not going to rappel?" Luke asked.

"Not today." Dane's assurance drew murmurs of relief.

After more explanation of terms and techniques,

Dane climbed up the side of the cliff to set the woven climbing rope while the others watched.

"He makes it look so easy," Laura said.

"Kobe Bryant makes hoops look easy, too," Luke added. "But I wouldn't be stupid enough to play one-on-one with the guy."

"It's tricky," Kelli allowed. "But this cliff is only a grade one."

"What does that mean?" Julian asked. "And how do you know so much about it?"

"I've been climbing since my teens," she answered the second question first. "As for the rating, climbs are divided into grades from one to six. A grade one, like this one, will only have one to two pitches. A grade six, like some of the routes on El Capitan, can have more than thirty pitches."

"Terrific," Julian muttered. "The red team's brought in a ringer."

"I've already decided to take myself off the team," Kelli revealed, as Dane came back down the rocks with a deft skill that Amanda admired, even as her heart leaped to her throat.

"That's not necessary," Marvin said. "I've been climbing since college. And while I haven't done El Capitan, I think I can do my bit for the blue team."

With the competitive balance restored, the final challenge event began. To everyone's surprise, the climb went amazingly well. Even Laura, who'd sworn that she wouldn't be able to get past the first rest stop, managed to make her way to the top, then back down again.

The final participant was Julian, who was making record time when, eager to reach the top of the cliff, he leaned too far into the slope, pushing his feet outward, causing him to slip. Sensing he was about to slide, he grabbed for a handhold, causing a small avalanche of pebbles.

Everyone watching from below breathed a united sigh of relief as the rope looped around his waist held.

"There's a ledge six inches to the left of you," Dane called out. "Just stay calm. You can reach it with no trouble."

Dangling against the cliff, Julian managed to edge his left foot sideways until it was safely on the ledge.

"That's it," Dane said encouragingly. "Now, put the heel of your right foot on that outcropping just below where it is now."

Although he was trembling visibly, Julian did as instructed.

"It's going to be okay," Dane assured Amanda and the others. "He's not in any danger." He lifted his cupped hands again. "Now, all you have to do is come back down the way you went up and you're home free."

Later, Amanda would decide that the next moment was when Julian made his mistake. He looked down, viewed the gathered team members far below, realized exactly how close he'd come to falling—and literally froze.

Dane was the first to realize what had happened. He cursed.

"I'd better go bring him down."

"No," Marvin said. "He's my teammate. I can talk him the rest of the way up."

"It's just a game," Amanda protested. "Winning isn't worth risking anyone's life."

"I know that." Marvin gently pried her fingers off his arm. "But there's more at risk than winning, Amanda. Julian will never forgive himself if he gives up now."

That said, he repeated the ascent path he'd worked out the first time he'd scaled the cliff. Within minutes he was perched on a rock horn beside the art director and although it wasn't possible to hear what they were saying, it was obvious the two men were engaged in serious conversation.

When Julian looked down again, Amanda drew in a sharp breath, afraid that he'd panic and lose his balance again. But instead, he turned his attention back to the rock wall and began slowly but surely moving upward, with Marvin right behind him, offering words of encouragement and pointing out possible paths.

When Julian reached the top of the cliff, cheers rang out from the team members below.

"Talk about teamwork," Kelli murmured to Amanda. "You've definitely pulled it off, Amanda. I hope you're seriously considering the partners' offer."

"How could I not?" Amanda answered.

As Julian and Marvin made their way back down the cliff, Dane came over to stand beside Amanda. "I couldn't help overhearing Kelli. Congratulations. You'll be great."

She looked up at him with confusion. "You know?"

It was Dane's turn to be confused. "Know what? I assumed you'd been offered Parsons's job."

"I was." She glanced around, not wanting the others to hear. "But it's turned out to be a bit more complicated."

She didn't want to discuss the amazing offer with Dane until they were alone and she could attempt to discern how he felt about her possibly moving to New York.

If he asked her to stay, she would. Already having missed one opportunity with this man, she was not about to blow another.

Something was wrong. Dane felt it deep in his gut. He was going to lose her again.

The ride back to the inn was a boisterous one. Although the blue team had won the week's event on points, even their opponents were fired up by Julian and Marvin's cooperative team effort. By the time the van pulled into the parking lot of the inn, everyone had decided to go into Satan's Cove to celebrate having ended the week on such a high note.

"Are you sure you don't want to come with us?" Kelli asked an hour later, after the trophies had been handed out.

"It's been a long day," Amanda demurred. "I have a lot to think about. I think I'll just stay here."

"If you're sure."

"I'm sure."

Kelli glanced at Dane, who'd come into the room during the awards ceremony, then back at Amanda. "It's a fabulous offer, Amanda."

"I know."

"But then again, men like Dane Cutter don't come into a girl's life every day."

"I know that, too." She'd had two chances with Dane. How many more would she be lucky enough to be given?

"Well, I don't envy you your choice, but good luck." Kelli left the room to join the others, who were gathering in the reception foyer for their trip to town.

Unbearably nervous, Amanda stood rooted to the spot as Dane walked toward her.

"Your hands are cold," he said as he took both of them in his.

"It's the weather." Rain streaked down the windows, echoing her mood. "It'll be good when you get the new furnace installed."

"Yes." It wasn't the chill outside that had turned her fingers to ice, but a nervousness inside, Dane decided.

"Would you like to talk about it?" he asked quietly.

Amanda swallowed past the lump in her throat. "Actually," she said, her voice little more than a whisper, "I would. But first I'd like to make love with you."

Dane needed no second invitation.

Alone in the tower room, Dane and Amanda undressed each other slowly, drawing out this suspended time together with slow hands and tender touches.

The candles she'd lit when they'd first entered the room burned low as they moved together, flowing so effortlessly across the bed, they could have been making love in an enchanted world beneath the sea.

Whispered words of love mingled with the sound of rain falling on the slate roof; soft caresses grew more urgent, then turned gentle again as they moved from patience to urgency, returning to tenderness, before continuing on to madness. All night long.

The candles stuttered out. The rain stopped, the moon began to set. And despite their unspoken efforts to stop time, morning dawned. Gray and gloomy.

Amanda lay in Dane's arms, feeling more loved than she'd ever felt in her life. And more miserable.

"Are you ready to talk about it?" he asked quietly.

As his thumb brushed away the errant tear trailing down her cheek, she squeezed her eyes tight and helplessly shook her head.

"We have to, Amanda." His voice was as calm and self-controlled as it had been ten years ago, making her feel like a foolish, lovestruck fifteen-year-old all over again. "We can't put it off any longer."

"I know."

With a long sigh, she hitched herself up in bed. Dane

wondered if she realized how beautiful she was, with her face, flushed from making love, framed by that tousled dark gold cloud of hair. Her eyes were wide and laced with more pain than a woman who'd spent the night making mad, passionate love should be feeling. She dragged her hand through her hair. "I don't know where to start."

He sat up as well and put his arm around her shoulder. "How about at the beginning?"

This wasn't going to be good. Dane's mind whirled with possibilities, trying to get ahead of the conversation so he could supply an argument to any reason she might try to give for leaving.

"Kelli *is* a company spy. But not for Greg."

"She works for the home office." All the pieces of the puzzle that had been nagging at him finally fell into place.

"Yes."

"When did you find out?"

"Right before the rock climb. She told me Greg was going to be fired. And that his job was mine, if I wanted it."

"Which you do." Dane decided there were worse things than commuter marriages. Portland wasn't that far away, and if her job made her happy...

"I thought I did." Her fingers, plucking at the sheets, revealed her nervousness. Dane waited.

"She offered me another position."

"Oh?" His heart pounded hard and painfully in his chest. "In Portland?"

Her words clogged her throat. Amanda could only shake her head.

"The job's in Manhattan," Dane guessed flatly.

"Yes." She shook her head again. "No."

"Which is it? Yes? Or no?" An impatience he'd tried to control made his tone gruff.

"My office would be in Manhattan. But I'd be traveling most of the time. In an ombudsman position."

It made sense. Having watched her in action, Dane knew she'd be a natural. And Lord knows, if the lack of morale the employees of the former C.C.C. agency had displayed when they'd first arrived at Smugglers' Inn was indicative of that of the international firm's other acquisitions, they were in desperate need of an effective ombudsman.

"That's quite an offer."

"Yes." Her voice lacked the enthusiasm he would have expected. "I think I could be good at it."

"I know you'd be great." It was, unfortunately, the absolute truth.

"And the salary and benefits are generous."

When she related them to Dane, he whistled. "That would definitely put you in the big leagues." Which was where her father had always intended her to be.

"I've dreamed of ending up on Madison Avenue, of course," Amanda admitted. "But I never thought my chance would come this soon. My parents would probably be proud of me," she murmured, echoing his thoughts.

"They'd undoubtedly be proud of you whatever you did." It wasn't exactly the truth. But it should be.

Her crooked, wobbly smile revealed they were thinking the same thing.

"When do you have to give the partners your answer?"

"By the end of next week." *Tell me not to go,* she begged him silently.

Dane wanted to tell her to turn the offer down. He

wanted to insist she stay here, with him, to make a home during the day and babies at night, as they'd planned so many years ago.

But, just as he'd had to do what was right for him, Dane knew that Amanda could do no less for herself.

"It's a terrific opportunity," he forced himself to say now. "I'm sure you'll make the right choice."

Because he feared he was going to cry, Dane drew her back into his arms, covered her mouth with his, and took her one last time with a power and a glory that left them both breathless.

Not wanting to watch Amanda walk out of his life for a second time, later that morning Dane went down to the beach, seeking peace.

In the distance, he heard the bus taking the corporate team—and Amanda—away.

He knew that Eve Deveraux would be happy to give him a job at the Park Avenue Whitfield Palace. But, although it would allow him to be with Amanda, Dane was honest enough with himself to admit that there was no way he could return to the rat race of the city.

During his last years at Whitfield, he'd become driven and impatient. He hadn't liked that hard-edged individual, his mother definitely hadn't, and he knew damn well that Amanda wouldn't, either. Which made his choice to go to Manhattan no choice at all.

He saw the words written in the sand from the top of the cliff, but the mist kept him from being able to read them.

As he climbed down the stone steps, the words became clearer.

Amanda loves Dane.

"I love you." The soft, familiar voice echoed her

written words. Dane turned and saw Amanda standing there, looking like his every dream come true.

"We found something together the other night in the cave, Dane. Something that's far more valuable to me than any alleged pirate's treasure. I want to stay. Here, in Satan's Cove with you." Her heart was shining in her eyes. "If you'll have me."

As much as he wanted to shout out *Yes!,* Dane knew they'd never be happy if she felt her decision was a sacrifice.

"What about New York?"

"It's a great place to visit."

"But you wouldn't want to live there."

"Not on a bet."

He felt a rush of relieved breath leave his lungs. "What about the job of creative director?"

"You're not going to make this easy for me, are you?" she asked with a soft smile.

"I don't think a decision this important *should* be easy."

"True." She sighed, not having wanted to get into the logistics of her decision right now. "The problem is, if I move into Greg's job, I'd still be working for a huge agency. Which wasn't why I got into advertising in the first place.

"After you left the room this morning, I had some visitors. Marvin, Julian, and Luke. They've been as unhappy as I have with the profit craze that's taken over the industry lately. They also decided Satan's Cove was a perfect place to open a shop.

"They've arranged to lease the offices above the crystal store and asked me to join them." Her smile was beatific, reminding Dane of how she looked after they'd made love.

"As much as I love the idea of you staying here, with me," Dane said, "I have to point out there aren't many prospective accounts in Satan's Cove, sweetheart."

"They've already contacted former clients who are unhappy with the way things have been going, and want to sign on. A lot of our business can be done by phone and email, with the occasional trip into the city.... And speaking of local clients, I thought you might consider redoing your brochure."

"What's wrong with my brochure?"

"It's lovely. But it could use some fine-tuning. Why don't I give you a private presentation later?" She'd also come up with a nifty idea for Davey Jones's Locker she intended to run by Iris.

Putting advertising aside for now, Amanda twined her arms around Dane's neck and pressed her smiling lips to his.

As they sealed the deal with a kiss, the last of the fog burned off.

Amanda loves Dane.

The brilliant sun turned the love letter she'd written in the sand to a gleaming gold nearly as bright as Dane and Amanda's future.

* * * * *

Joanna Sims is proud to pen contemporary romance for Harlequin Special Edition. Joanna's series, The Brands of Montana, features hardworking characters with hometown values. You are cordially invited to join the Brands of Montana as they wrangle their own happily-ever-afters. And, as always, Joanna welcomes you to visit her at her website, joannasimsromance.com.

Books by Joanna Sims

Harlequin Special Edition

The Brands of Montana

A Match Made in Montana
High Country Christmas
High Country Baby
Meet Me at the Chapel
Thankful for You
A Wedding to Remember
A Bride for Liam Brand
High Country Cowgirl
The Sergeant's Christmas Mission
Her Second Forever
She Dreamed of a Cowboy

The Montana Mavericks: Six Brides for Six Brothers

The Maverick's Wedding Wager

Visit the Author Profile page
at Harlequin.com for more titles.

SHE DREAMED OF A COWBOY

Joanna Sims

Dedicated to my beloved father:

Even though you don't read my books
because of the naughty scenes, every hero has
a little bit of you in him. I love you to pieces
and I am so proud to be your daughter.

Prologue

"Do you realize that I am on the verge of answering a very important question that has plagued womankind for centuries?" Customer-service representative Skyler Sinclair tugged on the golden blond wig she had donned. The hair was thick and straight and cascaded down to the middle of her back.

Skyler spun around to face her father, her heavy mane of blond hair swinging around her shoulders in the most satisfying way. "Do blondes *really* have more fun?"

Chester Sinclair was standing just inside the front door of her garage apartment, his arms crossed in front of his chest and his brooding dark eyes a match for the frown on his face.

"Why the wig?" her father asked. "You've never been ashamed of your hair or your scars."

"I'm not ashamed." Skyler turned back to her reflection to adjust the wig a bit more. "I'm just not about to show up in Bozeman, Montana, looking like Skyler the Cancer Patient."

"You *are* a cancer patient," her father reminded her.

"Correction. I *was* a cancer patient. Now I'm a cancer victor!" She punched the air like she was a boxer training for a fight. "I'm a cancer-crushing badass, that's what I am!"

In the middle of her tiny living room, Skyler planted her feet on the ground, hands on her hips, and lifted her chin like she was a superhero. After a second of holding the pose, she suddenly felt weak and dizzy, like her legs were going to buckle right out from underneath her. With a self-effacing laugh, Skyler folded herself into a nearby chair with a deep sigh. "Well, maybe not back to superhero status just yet."

As he had been from the second she was first diagnosed with a rare form of lung cancer, Chester was at her side.

"You *are* a cancer-crushing badass." Chester kneeled on one knee by the chair. "But you've got to be careful, Skyler. Don't overdo it. You're still so weak. Wait awhile, let all this virus stuff blow over and then go. It's not the right time."

"Time," Skyler said in a wistful voice as she tugged off the blond wig to expose her own patchy strawberry blond locks. "Time is a funny thing, Dad. I used to think I had all the time in the world. Now I know that I don't." She met her father's eyes. "None of us do. I always had an excuse why I didn't have time to do this or to do that. I was forever putting things off because—" she shrugged "—let's face it, I was too afraid to try."

She patted his hand to reassure him. "I'm not afraid anymore, Dad. Cancer taught me the most valuable life lesson. All we have is right now. The time is *now*. Not tomorrow, not next week or next year. *Now*. I can't wait. I *won't* wait. I can't waste this second chance I've been given by beating this thing."

"Montana is too damn far away." Chester sat back on his heels with a grumble.

When the light-headedness subsided, Skyler pushed herself upright. "That was always one of my excuses for not going. Too far away, not enough money, not enough time. But you know that I've always dreamed of Montana." Skyler heard an emotional catch in her own voice. "Always. I've dreamed of the horses and the mountains and the wide-open spaces. Fresh air. I've dreamed of what it must be like to camp out under the stars with a herd of cattle grazing nearby…" Her voice trailed off a bit. "The smell of a campfire. I've dreamed of that life ever since I was a little girl. Don't you see? Montana isn't going to be just being some unfulfilled wish on my bucket list. It's going to be my dream come true."

Chapter One

"I'm here now, so let me go," Hunter Brand said to his father as he strode into the lobby of the Bozeman Yellowstone International Airport.

"Represent the family well, son," Jock Brand reiterated for what seemed like the one hundredth time. "Remember that, like it or not, you represent Sugar Creek Ranch."

Hunter hung up the phone, slipped it into his back pocket and then pulled the black bandanna he had tied around his neck up over his nose and mouth. How in the world had he managed to pull this summer detail? Babysitting a spoiled city girl who'd convinced her father to let her play cowgirl for a summer? Sugar Creek wasn't a vacation spot for bored socialites; it was a multimillion-dollar cattle operation. They did real work on the ranch and Hunter couldn't fathom why Jock had decided, seemingly out of the blue, to open the ranch to a tourist for the summer.

"Excuse me." Hunter smiled with his eyes at the pretty young woman at the information booth. "Did a private charter arrive from New York City?"

Hunter thought that he detected a hint of sympathy in the young woman's eyes when she pointed toward a baggage carousel where a slight woman with long blond hair was standing. The woman had a collection of suitcases, which looked like they were covered in vintage floral wallpaper, balanced precariously on a luggage cart. Her back to him, his tourist was staring up at a T. rex skull mounted at the center of the carousel.

"Thank you." Hunter tipped his hat to the young woman.

While he walked toward his summer ward, Hunter took in the expensive cowgirl hat, boots and dark denim designer jeans that hadn't seen a speck of dirt or work since their purchase. As he drew closer, the more irritated he became. The tourist looked like she could be snapped in half by a strong gust of wind. And then a thought popped into his brain. Maybe his summer wasn't ruined after all; this woman wouldn't be able to handle ranch work. Especially if he threw some of the tougher, dirtier, smellier jobs her way right off the bat— she wouldn't last one week, much less an entire summer. He'd have her racing back to her posh life in the city before the end of the week. Who could blame him if he gave her the experience she said that she wanted?

It was with that thought in his mind that Hunter greeted the tourist.

"Are you Skyler Sinclair?"

The woman gave a little start and then spun around

with a laugh. It was a sweet, tinkling, joyous laugh that he immediately liked in spite of his intention to dislike everything about her.

"Yes." Skyler looked up at him, the corners of her eyes crinkling with a smile. "I am."

For a split second that seemed like slow motion, their eyes met and held. Skyler was wearing a mask, which drew his attention wholly to her large violet-blue eyes. Lovely, wide, expectant eyes that appeared to be completely without artifice. Then those eyes widened with a flash of recognition.

"Hunter Brand." Skyler said his name with a breathiness that stroked his ego in just the right way.

Hunter cringed inwardly. He had never met Skyler, but she seemed to know him. When he was a teenager, he had participated in a reality TV show, *Cowboy Up!*, and he'd never managed to live that down. After all these years, there were still fan clubs dedicated to him. God help him, he hoped Skyler wasn't a stalker.

Skyler must have read the question in his eyes because, filling in the silence between them, she explained, "I saw your picture on the Sugar Creek Ranch website."

Hunter wasn't sure if he believed that was the whole story, but it was good enough for now.

"This is amazing." Skyler pointed to the T. rex skull. "The nice woman at the information booth over there said that the Museum of the Rockies is open. Do you think I'll have time to go there?"

"I don't know," he hedged. "There's an awful lot of work that needs to get done at the ranch. You ready to head out?"

"Absolutely," Skyler said enthusiastically, and he

was kind of surprised that her apparent disappointment about the museum had dissipated so quickly. "I can't wait to see the ranch."

Skyler had to work to keep up with Hunter; some called her stature petite, but she was just short and her legs always had to work double time to match the stride of a taller person like Hunter. As she walked beside the cowboy, Skyler's mind was whirling with giddy teen-age-girl, fantasy-come-to-life thinking.

Hunter Brand!

Even with the bandanna covering the lower part of his face, she had recognized him instantly. Those eyes were unmistakable. She couldn't believe that *the* Hunter Brand, her absolute favorite cowboy on *Cowboy Up!*, was the one to come get her from the airport. She had an entire wall of her bedroom dedicated to Hunter Brand and now he was pushing her luggage cart through the airport? How could her Montana adventure have started any more perfectly? It couldn't have.

She couldn't *wait* to video-chat with her best friend, Molly; Molly had also had a teenage fantasy about marrying Hunter. She was going to lose her mind.

Once outside, Hunter lowered the bandanna and Skyler was able to see his entire handsome face. Yes, he had aged from his time on the show and that age had done him good. The man had a beautifully chiseled jawline, a slight dimple in his chin, prominent cheekbones and a perfectly straight, strong nose. Golden skin, jet-black hair peeking out from beneath his well-worn cowboy hat and just the deepest sapphire-blue eyes. There wasn't any other word that she could think of to describe the grown-up Hunter Brand other than *hunk*.

Hunter dropped the tailgate of his blue Chevy truck and began to toss her baggage into the bed.

"You brought a lot of stuff," her companion said as he hoisted the largest bag into the back of his truck.

"I wasn't sure what to bring," she said, feeling a bit self-conscious over the sheer number of bags she had brought. It did seem excessive now that she was actually here.

Hunter paused and looked at her dead in the face. "For ranch work? Jeans, boots, hat, T-shirts, underwear and plenty of socks."

"Check and check." She made little check marks in the air with a self-effacing laugh.

"I'm not sure you quite understand what you've signed up for here," Hunter said.

It didn't take a genius to read the subtext: Hunter thought she was soft—a real pushover. She could almost hear an unsaid "little lady" hanging in the air between them.

"Don't you worry your pretty little head about me for one second," Skyler said as she picked up one of her medium-size bags. "I can pull my own weight."

Skyler grunted as she attempted to pick up the heavy bag high enough to get it into the truck bed. Unable to get the bag into the truck, and well aware of Hunter's eyes on her, she pushed the bag against the tailgate and squatted down so she could get some leverage. But, even with the extra leverage, she just couldn't get the darn bag into the stupid truck.

"Need a hand?"

Smug.

"Sure. If you want.," she said quickly, trying to cover up how breathless she felt from this simple, mundane task.

With one hand, Hunter easily pushed the bag into the back of the truck. Hunter closed the tailgate with a smirk on his lips.

"Pull your own weight," he said with a deadpan expression. "I can see that."

"I didn't say I could *lift* my own weight, now did I?" Skyler quickly clarified. "No. I don't think I *did* say that."

Once inside the truck, Hunter rolled all of the windows down to let the fresh air into the cab on the way to Sugar Creek.

"I get tired of wearing this mask," she said. "I tested negative. How about you?"

It felt odd to say it, but she felt like it had to be said nonetheless.

"I tested negative a couple of weeks back and other than picking you up today, I haven't seen a soul."

"That must be why you drew the short straw and had to come to the airport to pick me up, huh?"

"I have marching orders to keep you safe while you're at Sugar Creek Ranch. It's a job like any other."

"Do you mind if I take off my mask?" she asked.

"No."

Gratefully, Skyler took off her mask and breathed in the fresh Montana air, unimpeded, for the first time in her life. She glanced over at Hunter; he had slipped the bandanna down from his face. And then she sighed. It was a long, happy sigh. She didn't know if she was sighing because of the beauty of Montana, the freshness of the air or the handsomeness of Hunter's profile.

Skyler held on to her hat so it wouldn't get blown off and leaned her head out of the window with her eyes closed. She breathed in deeply as the wind rushed over her face, loving the smell of the Montana air.

With another sigh, she sat upright in the seat. "I don't think I've seen a more beautiful view."

Hunter nodded silently.

"And to think you wake up to all of this every day of your life." After several attempts to have a conversation with Hunter, Skyler took the hint and focused on communicating with people who actually *wanted* to talk to her. She called her dad and then Molly. She texted tons of pictures of the Montana landscape and posted them to her social-media pages.

"That's my brother Gabe's spread right there." Hunter startled her by speaking for the first time in thirty minutes. "Little Sugar Creek."

"It's lovely."

Hunter slowed the truck down and turned onto a gravel drive. "And this here is Sugar Creek Ranch."

Skyler could only internally describe the feeling she was having driving onto Sugar Creek property for the first time as similar to waking up on Christmas morning. There was all of the same eagerness and anticipation, and the excitement of knowing that something wonderful was about to be unwrapped.

The rolling pastures were filled with tall grass bending slightly from a balmy late afternoon breeze, and the breathtaking mountains looked like a living postcard. It was heavenly. It was...

"Holy cow!" Skyler was jerked to the side a bit, her hat falling askew on her head when Hunter hit a huge pothole.

"The rain has just torn this road all to pieces," Hunter explained, swerving to avoid another pothole. "We've got an order of crush and run coming in the next couple of weeks."

"Crush and run?"

"Crushed-up rock to fill in the potholes."

"Oh."

Hunter glanced over at her. "That might just be one of your first jobs. Dragging the crush and run."

Skyler reached for the dashboard to stabilize her body with one hand and hold on to her hat with the other; the truck was bobbing and weaving around so much that she actually began to feel a bit seasick.

"Whatever you need me to do, I will do it." Skyler closed her eyes and fought the feeling of seasickness.

"You okay over there?" She heard Hunter ask the question as he thankfully pulled off the main, pothole-riddled road onto a less bumpy drive.

"Yes. Just a touch of benign positional vertigo, is all. Nothing to worry about." She kept her eyes tightly closed.

Hunter slammed on the brakes in a way that made Skyler wonder if he was deliberately making her problem worse. The truck jerked to a halt, which made her head snap back against the headrest, and her hat fell forward over her face.

"We're here," he said.

Skyler pushed up the brim of her hat so she could see her summer home-away-from-home. Off the main road, they had driven through a canopy of trees to an opening. Tucked away in the woods there was a private oasis with rustic storage buildings, a horse stable, pastureland and a quaint cabin complete with a front porch and rocking chairs.

"This is mine?"

"Yep." Hunter hopped out of the truck.

"All mine?"

"All yours."

"For the whole summer?" She opened the passenger door, her eyes darting from one spot to another. She had grown up in the city; she loved it and was accustomed to sharing a small amount of square footage with a large amount of people. She had never imagined having this much square footage all to herself.

"This—" she pushed the door slowly shut behind her "—is amazing. Truly amazing."

Hunter was already hauling her bags out of the back of his truck; he seemed like he was in a hurry to be rid of her. It stung a little that *the* Hunter Brand hadn't immediately fallen head over heels for her, as per her thousands of teenage fantasy reels she had played in her head. But that disappointment was overtaken by the sheer beauty all around her. If she had any doubt about her decision to come to Montana so soon after she'd been given the "all clear for now" by her team of doctors, those doubts were gone. This part of the world, so quiet and peaceful, filled with the scent of pine in the air, was exactly the place she needed to be to fully recover. This was somewhere she could build her strength, emotionally and physically.

Skyler wanted to explore the grounds and take some pictures for her friends, but followed Hunter's lead instead and tugged one of her suitcases out of the bed of the truck. She let it land on the ground with a thud and then dragged it behind her. The suitcase wheels hit some rocks and twigs along the way, tipping the bag sideways. By the time she reached the porch steps, she was winded, perspiring and a little bit dizzy. She forced herself not to show on the outside how weak she was feeling on the inside. Her pride wanted to hide her vulnerability from Hunter; not that she should care what her teenage crush thought about her…and yet, she kind of did. Kind of.

Grunting and pulling and bracing her legs so she could tug the suitcase to the top of the steps before Hunter returned to find her, once again, struggling, Skyler finally managed to drag the bag onto the porch. For a moment, she closed her eyes and caught her breath. Lord have mercy, the surgery and chemo had sapped her completely of her stamina and strength.

Without a word, Hunter came over, scooped up the bag at her feet, lifted it onto his shoulder like a sack of potatoes and went back into the cabin. Skyler followed him inside and watched as he dropped her last bag unceremoniously on top of her other bags he had stacked in the living room near an antique wood-burning stove.

"Your family keeps this cabin for guests like me?" It was cozy and woodsy with shiplap walls, a vaulted ceiling in the living room and overstuffed furniture perfect for curling up for a nap. There was a small kitchen off the living room—a little outdated but clean and functional.

"There's never been a guest like you before."

"You've never had a guest like me before?" Skyler ran her hands across the hand-carved, butcher-block countertop.

"No." Hunter adjusted his hat on his head. "You're the first."

As if to indicate he was finished with that topic, he turned his body slightly away from her and pointed down the hallway. "Bedroom. Bathroom. If you like TV you're out of luck. Jock installed a hot spot." Hunter pointed to a device on the counter. "Password is on the back."

"Okay," Skyler said quietly, her mind still stuck on the idea that the Brand family had never had a guest like her before.

"I stocked the fridge with some staples—the vegetables we grow on site, so there's always more where that came from. We can go into town tomorrow and pick up anything else you think you might need."

Hunter stood with his hands on his hips for a minute, looked around for a second and then nodded toward the front door. "Let me take you on a quick tour outside before I go."

Skyler trailed behind him, through the front door, down the porch steps, still mulling over the fact that she was the *first*.

"So, is this *your* cabin?" She had a horrible feeling in her gut that she had displaced him from his own home.

"No," Hunter replied. "This was my brother Liam's cabin. All of us have a stake on the ranch. This is his. He's out at the Triple K Ranch with his wife, Kate. He still keeps his old trucks in this shed right here." He indicated one of the buildings. "So you might see him out here working on them."

"What's in there?" Skyler pointed to a large building next to the garage.

"My brother Shane built an obstacle course in there."

"Wow," Skyler said. "That's impressive."

"Yeah," Hunter agreed. "Shane was a sergeant in the army. He recreated a lot of the obstacles they had in boot camp."

"My father was a gunnery sergeant in the marines."

For the first time, Hunter looked at her with a modicum of interest. "Is that right?"

She nodded. "He worked on tanks and amphibious vehicles."

"Jock had me move some of the horses down from the main barn for your use."

"I have *horses*?"

"Yes." Hunter walked quickly toward the barn. "Jock was under the impression that you can ride."

Two summers at Circle F Dude Ranch were about to come in handy.

"I know my way around a barn," she said confidently.

"Good," he said tersely. "Because starting tomorrow, these two horses are your responsibility for the rest of the summer."

"Why start tomorrow when we have today right now?"

Her comment stopped him in his tracks for a moment. "If you're ready to get to work, there's always work to do."

"I'm ready to work."

She was exhausted and already sweaty under her clothes; the wig was hot and she hated it. But tomorrow waited for no woman.

Something akin to respect flashed in Hunter's striking blue eyes. They were even deeper and bluer in person than they ever had been on TV or in pictures.

"You might want to change into some work clothes then," he advised over his shoulder as he headed toward the barn.

She gave up trying to match his pace, wanting to save some sliver of energy for the barn work. She could collapse totally and completely after Hunter left. "These *are* my work clothes."

They entered the barn, which was old and felt "left behind." There were layers of dust on overturned buckets, and dried-out currycombs left on a tack trunk between the stalls. The wash rack had a layer of hay and dirt plugging the drain; there were cobwebs in almost every corner. The barn could be cleaned up with a little effort and elbow grease. Most important were the beautiful creatures that had been brought to the barn just for her.

"This here is Zodiac." Hunter's tone was much gentler when he was with the horses. The tall chestnut-brown horse with a black mane and tail whickered at them and then nibbled at Hunter's shirt.

"Hi, Zodiac." Skyler let the horse smell her hand. "You are so handsome."

"He's a great cow pony." Hunter gave the horse a pat on the neck. "He'll take care of you out there."

Skyler nodded as if she understood his meaning, but she wasn't sure what Hunter meant by "out there." No doubt she would find out soon enough.

"And this sweet girl is Dream Chaser." Hunter smiled affectionately at the mare across the aisle from Zodiac. "She's as pretty as they come and as sure-footed on the trail as any I've known."

"Hi, Dream Chaser." Skyler pet the mare's neck. She was smaller and stockier than Zodiac, with bright blue eyes and a white blaze on her face, with a brown body and white on her legs.

"I brought a couple of bales of hay down from the main barn just to hold them over. We'll go get more tomorrow and load up the feed room."

"Okay." It seemed like Hunter intended to just fold

her right into the work at the ranch, and that suited her just fine.

Hunter disappeared out the back of the barn and returned with a wheelbarrow, a pitchfork and a shovel.

"If you grab the manure, I'll get the urine." He handed her the pitchfork.

The old pitchfork was constructed of wood and steel, and it was a whole lot heavier than it looked. When she took it in her hands, the unanticipated weight of it made her lower her hands a bit before she lifted it.

If he noticed her struggling with the pitchfork, he didn't show it. They mucked the stalls and gave the two horses some hay and feed. Then Hunter showed her how to get water from the garage over to the barn.

"I hooked up this hose for the time being." Hunter tugged on the heavy hose to pull it into the barn. "I'm not sure what's wrong with the water pipes in here— I'll have to look in to it later—but for now, this will work." He stopped just inside the barn, turned on the water and let it stream out onto the gravel in front of the barn. "Make sure you let the water run for a while—the sun heats up the hose and you don't want to be giving the horses hot water in their buckets."

By the time they dumped the stall pickings in a compost pile, Skyler didn't have a dry spot on her body. Every crevice was soaked with sweat. Her new boots had been christened with horse manure and mud, her clothes were stuck to her skin, and yet, she felt elated. Exhausted and elated. It had taken all of her mental and physical strength to finish the chores, but she had persevered. She hadn't given up, and she was proud of herself.

"I've got jobs waiting on me," Hunter said at the

bottom of the porch steps. "I'll see you tomorrow first thing."

Skyler leaned against the porch railing as much for stability as comfort.

"Hunter?" She said his name to get his attention.

He turned back to her, his eyebrows raised slightly with a question.

"Why do you think Jock agreed to let me come?" She was still stuck on the idea that it wasn't typical for the Brand family to have guests like her at the ranch. With everything going on in the world, why would Hunter's father agree to it?

Hunter repositioned his hat on his head. "You'll have to ask him that yourself, Skyler. Jock didn't ask for my permission and he didn't factor in my opinion to his final decision."

"So you don't think I should be here." She posed it more as a statement of obvious fact rather than a question. She could read his behavior toward her easy enough.

"We aren't a dude ranch," Hunter said matter-of-factly. "My number is on the refrigerator. If you need me, text me."

Skyler crossed her arms in front of her body. "I will. Thank you."

Right before he climbed behind the wheel of his truck, he said, "Get some rest, Skyler. The day starts before dawn and doesn't end until after dark."

Chapter Two

Skyler's first night in the cabin was not ideal. The early evening had been filled with exploration, some unpacking, foraging in the refrigerator and finally talking on the phone while rocking on the front porch. As dusk gave way to night, the realization that she was out in the middle of nowhere began to set in. Other than the small light over the barn, there wasn't any light illuminating the buildings surrounding the cabin. There were a couple of lights on the cabin facing out toward the yard, but the range was very small. Beyond that light, complete and total darkness. And, in the darkness, odd noises that made her feel like a sitting duck. There were predators out there, she was sure of it. Even her total exhaustion from the day of travel and barn work couldn't overtake her nervousness. She dozed off for an hour or two, but would awaken the moment there was a howl or scratching noise or thump on the roof.

She had barely dozed off for the fourth time when loud banging on her front door sent her shooting upright in bed. Her heart was racing and she felt the awful feeling of adrenaline pumping all over her body.

"Skyler!" Hunter yelled. "Time to go to work!"

She cursed, threw off the covers, jumped out of bed and stubbed her toe on the nightstand while she fumbled to turn on the light. She found her phone turned it on and read with fuzzy eyes that is was just after four in the morning.

More banging on her door only served to make her more anxious as she hopped on one leg to pull on her jeans. She snatched the wig off the bedpost and managed to get it onto her head.

"Skyler!"

"Lord, you are an annoying man." Skyler had one sock on and one sock off as she raced to the bathroom to find her wayward bra.

"I'm coming!" she shouted at the top of her lungs. "Stop banging on the door!"

More knocking.

Somehow Skyler managed to get into her bra and pull on a T-shirt; she checked her reflection in the mirror only to realize that the wig was askew.

"Lovely."

She fixed the wig, then picked up her boots on the way to the door. "I swear, if you do not stop banging on my door, I will…"

Skyler tried to open the door, but had too many things in her hands, so she dropped the sock and boots, unlocked the door and the yanked it open.

"Good morning," Hunter said nonchalantly.

"Good morning?"

"That's what I said."

Skyler scooped up her boots and sock and walked over to the couch, leaving the door open and Hunter standing in the doorway.

"It's not even five o'clock in the morning," Skyler complained while she pulled on her other sock. "It's not even light outside yet."

"I told you we start before dawn around here."

"I heard you." She pushed her foot into a boot. "I thought it was a metaphor."

For the first time, Hunter actually smiled at her, and that smile almost made it worth it to be up at this ungodly hour. The straight white teeth and the dimples sucked her right back in to her teenage fantasy crush.

What a hunk. An annoying hunk. But a total hunk nonetheless.

"A metaphor for what?" he asked.

"I don't know." She stood up and stomped her foot into her boot; her hair fell into her face and she threw it over her shoulder, irritated. "Life."

"No. I was giving you the facts of life here on the ranch."

There was a moment of silence in the room that broken by the sound of her stomach loudly growling.

"I need to grab something to eat," she said, stating the obvious.

"Critters first."

"Critters first?" she repeated. "Meaning?"

"The animals can't feed themselves. You eat after they eat."

"Oh." She frowned. "How many are in the buffet line ahead of me?"

Another dimpled smile. "Hundreds."

Not wanting to give him the opportunity to milk one more ounce of enjoyment out of her apparent misery, Skyler grabbed an apple out of the refrigerator, then got her phone and her hat, and joined him on the porch.

"Ready."

Hunter checked his watch. "You're late."

"How can I be late when *you* didn't tell me what time to be ready?" She trotted after him.

He flipped on the light in the barn aisle. "I said before dawn. It's before dawn."

"Well." She smiled at the image of Zodiac and Dream Catcher blinking their eyes sleepily in the light, their heads hanging low over the stall gate. "Maybe we could drill down on a specific time for tomorrow. Maybe *that* would be helpful."

"Sure," Hunter said in an uncharacteristically agreeable tone of voice. "Let's drill down on, let's say, four a.m. every day."

Skyler's shoulders slumped. "Every morning?"

He handed her a large plastic scoop. "Fill this with feed to the top and then split it between the two of them. After they're done eating, they can go out to the pasture."

She looked at the scoop in her hand.

"And, yes," he added, "every morning. Unless, of course, you think that the horses could do without eating one day so you can have a spa day."

Skyler talked back to him in her head, thinking of all sorts of snarky things she could say in response. But in reality, she zipped her lip, fed the horses and sprayed them both with fly spray, glad that she had muscle memory from summer camp, and then haltered each horse and took them out to the adjacent pasture. The moon was still in the sky; it was still completely dark outside.

"That wasn't too bad. What's next?" she asked with her most cheerful, perky, you-can't-get-me-down voice.

"Follow me."

"You know how to drive a tractor?" Hunter asked his shadow.

"Sure," Skyler said evenly. "That's how I get to work every morning. Tractor."

He found himself smiling again, but had his back to her so she couldn't see it. Skyler, he had quickly discovered, shared his caustic wit and tendency to be a smart-ass. Yet another thing he liked about the tourist.

"Hop up there," Hunter said.

Skyler climbed into the tractor seat and looked around to familiarize herself with the different components; she would have to scoot forward in order to reach the pedals, but other than that, it was a pretty comfortable seat.

"First, you'll want to…" Hunter began.

Skyler moved the gear to Neutral, stepped on the clutch, turned the key to first notch, waited for a red light to come on and then after the red light went off, she cranked the engine.

"…move the gear into Neutral, step on the clutch, wait for the glow light to…" Hunter stopped talking and started watching.

She sent him a pleased grin. "After the Marines, Dad opened a garage and worked on plenty of diesel engines. I haven't driven a tractor, but I have driven a semi."

"Well…" Hunter said slowly, "I'll be damned."

A sliver of light from the sun rising up behind the

far-off mountains was glowing pink as Hunter hopped into the trailer hitched to the tractor.

"Put her in gear and drive up this path." Hunter sat down on top of the bales of hay stacked in the tractor. "We'll feed this herd first and then move on to the next."

For the next several hours, they worked together. Rain had been scarce so they were throwing hay in the fields to keep the cows well-fed. It was tedious work, but Skyler enjoyed it. Her misery from lack of sleep and being up early was overshadowed by the sound of cows mooing for their breakfast and the feeling of purpose that driving the tractor had given her. They finished with the cows and then Hunter directed her to drive the tractor to a field of horses.

"Watch this," Hunter said after she drove the tractor through the open gate. He closed the gate behind them, hopped back on the trailer and then whistled loudly.

Now the sun was sending off a soft yellow glow over the rolling hills before her. And then, off in the distance, faint at first, was the sound of pounding. Then she saw them—a herd of horses galloping in the horizon. They were whinnying and kicking up their heels, their ears forward, their necks arched, legs pumping as they raced across the field.

Skyler was mesmerized by the sight; it was if she was seeing horses in the wild, because they were so free. It moved her to tears.

"I have never seen anything that beautiful before."

"It never gets old," Hunter mused.

He directed her to drive toward the herd, to meet them at their target—the row of black rubber food bowls.

As the herd approached, the horses began to start

vying for the first bowl of feed, pinning their ears back, nipping and kicking.

"Is this safe?" Skyler asked, recalling that the Circle F Dude Ranch hadn't taught her how to handle this scenario.

"Not necessarily." Hunter waved a flag at the herd to back them off from the food bowls. He kept them at bay with the flag as she drove slowly from bowl to bowl, dumping grain. They also dropped bales of hay for the herd before they headed back to her cabin.

"The rest of the hay will go into your barn."

"And then can I eat?" she asked, her stomach hurting from lack of food.

"Then we can eat." As she drove through the gate he had opened for her, Skyler caught a quick smile on the cowboy's face. He was so darn handsome when he smiled.

He directed her while she backed the trailer close to the barn and then she switched off the engine. The bales of hay weighed nearly fifty pounds each and, try as she might, she couldn't lift one bale by herself.

"I've got this." Hunter picked up the bale she had dragged off the back of the trailer. "Do a quick check and make sure they still have water in the pasture."

"Are you sure?" Skyler asked, winded.

"Yeah. Go check on the water and then get yourself some chow." He carried the bale of hay toward the feed room. "We've got a pasture fence to tear down after breakfast."

On her way to check the water, Skyler took her finger and itched beneath the wig. This was an idea she hadn't really thought through; farm work wearing a wig just wasn't practical. It was still early morning—

she wouldn't even be at her desk job at this hour back home—and she was already sweating through her clothes, and her real hair and scalp were soaked beneath the wig. And it itched!

She was half-tempted just to yank off her wig at breakfast and be done with it. The horses thankfully had water, so she wouldn't have to fight the hose to pull it over to the trough. That was a lucky break. She made it to the porch steps and had to sit down.

"Lord, give me strength." Skyler rested her head in her hands. She closed her eyes and let her body enjoy the moment of rest. It was going to take all of her will to keep up with Hunter, but it was also forcing her to build up her stamina more quickly than if she had been at home.

"You okay?" Hunter had finished the chore of stocking the barn with hay; he was brushing the loose pieces of hay off his clothing and arms when he came upon Skyler slumped forward on the front steps of the porch, her head in her hands.

She didn't raise her head. "I'm okay."

He didn't believe her for a second and there was a part of him that knew he had pushed her too hard on her first morning. He knew it because it had been deliberate.

After a second or two of mulling, Hunter extended his hand to her. First and foremost, he had been raised to be a gentleman by his mother, Lilly.

"Let's go rustle up some grub," Hunter said. "I'll show you how to make a real cowboy breakfast."

It took a moment, but Skyler tilted her head up, saw his offered hand and slowly slipped her small hand into his. The bones of her hand were so delicate to the touch that he mentally warned himself not to hold on to her fingers to tightly.

When she stood, she swayed slightly and he caught her under the elbow. He felt terrible.

"Let's get you inside."

Skyler put her hand on her forehead and smiled weakly at him. "I'm just a little dehydrated, I think. I'm not used to sweating so much before it's even noon."

He helped her sit down at the kitchen counter and got her a glass of water. "Just sit there and cool off."

Hunter grabbed some of their ranch-fresh eggs out of the refrigerator, put a skillet on the stove and found a bowl.

"Breakfast hash okay?"

Skyler nodded, taking several big gulps of the water. Her skin had a chalky hue and her eyes looked sunken in her oval face. She didn't look well.

"I'm sorry," Skyler said in a raspy voice.

"No." Hunter frowned, unhappy with his own behavior. He'd been so stuck on the idea of getting rid of her, he'd run her into the ground. "I'm sorry."

Once the skillet was heated, he poured some sunflower oil in the pan, diced some potatoes and onions and threw them in the oil, and then dumped a can of corn-beef hash in the mix.

"That smells good," the tourist said.

"It's gonna be good," he said, frying two eggs sunny-side up. He'd made this meal a hundred times before for his brothers and crew, but never for a lady. But it was the quickest thing he knew how to make in order to get food into her body.

"This will turn you into a cowgirl quicker than anything." Hunter separated the hash onto two plates and then put a fried egg on the top of the hash. He slid the plate her way and then handed her a fork.

"Thank you," Skyler said, loading her fork with eggs and hash.

Hunter sat down next to her at the breakfast bar, hunched over his plate and dug in. He was pretty hungry himself.

"Hmm." He nodded his head when he took his first bite. "One of my better batches."

He looked over at Skyler, who was focused on stuffing as much of the hash into her mouth as she could. Her cheeks were as full as a chipmunk's when she looked up at him, made a happy noise and gave him a thumbs-up.

His companion didn't speak until the majority of her hash was gone. "I've never had this before."

"Do you like it or are you just desperate?" Hunter scooped the last bite of his breakfast onto his fork.

"Both." Skyler followed suit and pushed the last bit of hash onto her fork with her finger. She licked her fingers and then gobbled up the rest of the hash.

Hunter gathered up their plates and put them in the sink while Skyler guzzled down another glass of water. She put down the glass on the counter and he was heartened to see that some of the color had returned to her face.

"Why don't you take the afternoon off?" he suggested.

"Absolutely not." Skyler shook her head. "I feel better now. Tomorrow I need to get up earlier and grab something to eat before you show up at my door, that's all."

"Are you sure?"

"Are you going to rest this afternoon or are you going to work?"

"I'm going to be pulling a fence down."

"Then—" he saw resolve in Skyler's lovely lavender eyes "—I'm going to be pulling a fence down, too."

After breakfast, Skyler excused herself to the bathroom so she could regroup. It really annoyed her to no end that her body, as it had for the last year, had given out on her. Before cancer, she had been tiny but mighty. That's what her father had always said. She hated to feel weak, no matter the cause.

In the bathroom, Skyler pulled off the wig and wet a washcloth, then wiped down her head, scalp, face and neck. She stared at her reflection in the mirror; baby-fine strawberry blond hair had sprouted all over her head. Skyler rubbed her hand over the new growth, grateful to have it at all. But she didn't feel ready to open the topic of her illness with Hunter, so she would just have to find a way to tolerate the heavy, hot wig until she *was* ready.

Skyler put the wig back onto her head, adjusted it and then pushed her cowgirl hat on top of the wig. Honestly, in her mind, she looked one of those L.O.L. Surprise dolls that were so popular with young girls—the wig added extra height to her head, making her face look longer and narrower and her eyes look overly large.

"It's a look." She rolled her eyes at herself before she quit the mirror and left the bathroom.

"Ready?" Hunter was waiting for her outside.

"Ready."

Hunter had her follow him on the tractor while he drove his truck. They headed deeper into Sugar Creek property, heading up a slight incline until they reached a clearing at a plateau. Hunter gestured for her to pull the tractor to the right of where he was parked. He jumped out of his truck and walked over to an old three-railed fence that had been turned a grayish brown by the sun. Many of the rails were broken or split; some of the rails were missing.

"We want to expand this pasture—give the herd some more grazing land to the north."

Skyler rested her arms on the steering wheel of the tractor.

"Where do we begin?" she asked, feeling daunted by the task.

"How do you eat an elephant?" Hunter grabbed some tools out of his truck.

One of her oncologists, Dr. Bryant, always asked her that same question.

"One bite at a time." She swung down off the tractor.

"Exactly."

They worked side by side as the sun beat down on them. Hunter was a quiet worker and so was she. The cowboy would pull off the boards, using a crowbar to wrench them away from the posts, while Skyler did her best to haul the boards to the trailer.

"Do what you can." Hunter was as sweaty as she was. "It's hot and I don't want you to overdo again."

Skyler nodded as she wrapped her arms around the end of a rail and pulled as hard as she could to get it to move a couple of feet. She stopped, dropped it, caught her breath and then picked it up again. Even if she could only haul one board for Hunter, it was better than nothing.

"If you can pull that wire off the boards before I get to the them, that would be a big help." Hunter wiped off his forehead.

Chicken wire had been tacked to the boards to stop the horses from getting their heads stuck in between the planks if they tried to eat greener blades of grass on the other side of the fence. Hunter handed her a hammer.

"Use this to pull the nails out. Keep the nails in your pocket because we don't want them left behind for the horses to step on."

Skyler took the hammer, glad that Hunter had put the earlier episode behind him and was treating her as she wanted to be treated: like an equal.

One by one, Skyler fought with the nails, cursing at times, getting frustrated at times, but also feeling triumphant when she managed to wrench a nail loose and pull a part of the wire away from the post, paving the way for Hunter to do his job.

Skyler locked her fingers into the spaces of the wire, put her boot on the post and then pulled as hard as she could. The wire gave way more quickly than she anticipated and she stumbled backward.

"Careful." Hunter seemed to always be watching her out of the corner of his eye.

She nodded but kept focused on her task. The more she worked, the hotter her scalp became; sweat was rolling down her cheek and the need to itch under the wig only made her feel more frustrated and irritable.

She bent down to take the bottom nail out of the post, and when she did, her hair got tangled up in the wire. When she lifted up her head, it tugged the wig sideways.

"Damn it!" Skyler grabbed the tangled hair and managed to pull it loose, leaving some golden blond strands still wound around the rusty wire.

She stood upright, her fingers balled up into a fist

with her free hand, her other hand gripping the handle of the hammer until it hurt.

"Enough!" she said through gritted teeth. "Enough, enough, *enough*!"

Hunter spun around to face her just in time to see her throw her hat on the ground, yank off her wig, throw it down as hard as she could, stomp on it several times, then pick up her hat and plop it back onto her head.

Her breathing labored from the heat and the hissy fit, Skyler stared at Hunter while he stared back at her. They stood for several seconds, just staring at each other, before he asked, "Feel better?"

It took a moment for his question to register—it hadn't been the question she had prepared herself to answer. She breathed in deeply and then laughed as she exhaled. "Yes. Much."

Skyler knew that this wasn't the end of the discussion between them. But Hunter's willingness to keep focused on the job and ignore the fact that she had just pulled off a wig and stomped it into the ground was exactly what she needed.

"Good." Hunter turned back to his task. "Now let's get back to work."

Chapter Three

Pulling down the fence was more than a one-day job. It was like that on the ranch—some jobs took one shot and other jobs lingered on for months before they were finished.

"Let's knock off for now." Hunter stood upright and then stretched to ease the tension in his back. "It's about time for lunch."

Skyler was wrestling with a plank of wood, dragging it toward the trailer.

"Okay," his helper grunted. "Just let me get this last board on the trailer."

Hunter walked over to where she was struggling and picked up the other end of the plank. Then they carried it together the rest of the way. Together, they lifted it up and dropped it onto the trailer.

"Thank you." Skyler kneeled down in her spot. "That was tough."

"You did real good," Hunter said. "Better than I would've thought."

Skyler didn't move. While she caught her breath, he pulled some cold bottles of water out of a cooler in the bed of his truck. He twisted off the cap of one and offered it to her.

"Drink this."

Skyler stood up, her shoulders slumped forward and her face beet-red, and took the bottle from him. She guzzled the water down almost in one gulp, breathing in deeply after she was finished.

"Thank you," she said again, sitting down on the edge of the trailer.

Hunter was very proud of Montana and the women who were raised here. He had always believed that the women of Montana had certain qualities—strength, gumption and perseverance—that women from other parts of the country didn't have. It was a tough life, and he had seen, time and again, the women in his life step up to the plate and work side by side with the men to keep the ranch running. Skyler had earned his respect today; no matter how tired she was, how out of breath, frustrated or angry, she never stopped moving forward. She never stopped trying.

"My hat is too big now," Skyler complained, pushing her cowgirl hat back on her head. "It fit just fine when I had the wig on."

Hunter hadn't known how to react about the wig, so he hadn't reacted at all. He'd just kept on working like he had been trained to do all his life. "Focus on the job, son," his father always said. But while his hands were busy working, his mind had been working overtime, too. The shorn hair wasn't a fashion statement for Skyler—

she had been sick. And the discovery, even though he hadn't shown any reaction to Skyler, was a kick in the gut. Old memories of a friend long gone and sorely missed felt like someone had ripped out stitches and reopened a wound not yet healed. Now, at least, he understood why Jock was so insistent that Skyler be allowed to have her ranch-life experience.

"I'll see if my sister has an extra hat you can borrow. I bet you're the same size."

Skyler was staring hard at the discarded wig; the wig was covered in dust and dirt, and had been trampled on several times while she hauled wood to the trailer.

Not looking at him, Skyler asked, "Why haven't you asked me about it?"

Hunter finished off his own water, squinted at the sun and said, "Folks in these parts don't go around asking too many questions. We figure if you want us to know something, you'll tell us sooner or later. And if you don't, then it wasn't any of our business to begin with."

She looked up at him, and once again, he was temporarily mesmerized by the goodness he saw in those wide, violet-blue eyes. What he saw in those eyes was a heart of gold, a kind soul and a woman who had seen more than her fair share of hardship. In that instant, he realized that he had been wrong about her from the get-go. She wasn't a spoiled socialite playing dress-up; she was a woman on a mission to save her own life through the hard work and fresh air that could be found on a Montana ranch.

"Let's head back and grab some lunch," Hunter said. "You up for driving the tractor back?"

Skyler stood up slowly, her hat falling forward over her eyes. With a frustrated noise in the back of her throat, she pushed the hat up so she could see.

"I'm up for it," she said and headed toward the tractor, leaving the wig half buried in the dirt.

"I feel human again." Hunter leaned back in the rocking chair, his booted feet up on the porch railing.

"Me, too," Skyler sighed happily.

They had returned to her cabin and made sandwiches for lunch. She hadn't fully regained her appetite before she'd left for Montana, but now it was coming back with a vengeance. She had eaten two whole sandwiches and three glasses of fresh-squeezed lemonade that Hunter's sister-in-law Savannah had made specially ahead of her arrival. It had been the right amounts of tartness and sweetness, and she had greedily guzzled as much as her stomach would allow.

They sat in silence together; it was a comfortable silence, which Skyler didn't often experience. She was typically a nervous talker, always wanting to fill in the silences if her mind wasn't focused on a task. But with Hunter, silence was easy. After a while, Skyler felt ready to talk, ready to fill in some of the silence between them.

Not looking directly at him, she said, "I had cancer."

In her peripheral vision, she saw Hunter look her way. "Had?"

"Yes." A nod. "Had."

"Good news that you can use the past tense."

"Great news, really." Skyler rocked back and forth in the chair. "This trip to Montana was motivation for me."

There was a long pause before Hunter asked, "Is that right?"

"My best friend, Molly, she's the one who arranged the whole thing," Skyler explained. "She knew that I have dreamed of Montana my whole entire life. It started out as a bucket-list trip, but then it became a celebratory trip. My friends and coworkers, family—they started a GoFundMe page so I could fly private out here. I had strangers donate, too," she said with wonder in her voice. "Can you believe that? People who've never met me pitched in so I could get out here safely during the pandemic."

"People can surprise you."

"Absolutely they can," she agreed. "Your father surprised all of us by not canceling."

She saw a muscle work in Hunter's jaw and she almost thought that he had something that he wanted to say on that subject—something he might want to add—but when he kept silent, she thought she must have been mistaken.

"Either way, I'm here now." She rocked back and forth several times, the heat of the day feeling less taxing under the cool auspices of the porch overhang. She breathed in deeply, feeling grateful for the day.

"The wig was not one of my better ideas," she admitted, the thought just popping out of her mouth.

Hunter remained silent on the matter.

"I wanted to feel normal when I arrived," she added.

"You don't owe me any explanation," Hunter said.

"It's not really the best way to meet someone—'Hi, my name is Skyler. I've had a rare form of lung cancer. How you doin'?'"

That made Hunter crack a smile and show those dimples she loved so much.

She turned her body a little toward him. "Now that you know, don't you feel sorry for me!"

"I don't."

"And don't you go easy on me because of it."

This was met with silence.

"Don't you go easy on me because of it," she repeated. "I'm serious. Treat me like you'd never found out."

He looked over at her, squinting a bit. "That's what you want?"

"That's exactly what I want."

"Then that's what you're gonna get."

"Good," she insisted.

"Fine by me."

"Fine by me!" she said more loudly than he did.

That made the dimples come out again. Lord, the man was cute. Sitting on a porch in Montana with Hunter Brand—now this really was her dream coming true. At least the dream she had held dear when she was a teenage girl with braces and a flat chest.

At least the braces were gone.

"So what's next?"

Hunter slipped his hat down over his face and leaned his head back like he was going to take a nap. "After our food digests a bit, I think I want to check out your riding skills. We'll saddle up the horses and go out on the trail."

She hadn't ridden in years, but it had to be like riding a bike, didn't it?

"Sounds like a plan." She titled up her face to catch the rays of sun that weren't blocked by the porch overhang.

After a minute or two, Hunter asked, "I've been wondering...how *did* your friend know about Sugar Creek? It's a bit off the beaten path, isn't it?"

Skyler's stomach clenched a bit and her nose wrinkled as she winced. Somehow she knew this question was going to arise; she had just hoped to have a little more time with Hunter before having to confess.

"*Cowboy Up!*"

Hunter dropped his feet from the porch railing and his boots landed on the wooden planks with a loud thud. He leaned forward, repositioned his hat on his head so he could look at her with a hint of accusation in his bright, ocean-blue eyes.

"I *knew* you recognized me from the show," he said. "I *knew* it."

"Guilty as charged," she admitted. "But what I said at the airport wasn't a lie exactly. I *did* recognize you from the website. I just *also* recognized you from the show."

Hunter didn't sit back in his chair; his shoulders seemed tense as she watched him wipe his hand over his face. He didn't look at her when he asked, "Please tell me you aren't part of one of those fan clubs online."

She laughed. "I promise you. I'm not."

He let out a relieved breath. "Well, that's something, at least."

"Molly and I loved that show," Skyler continued. "We always watched it together. We never missed an episode."

Hunter leaned his elbows on his legs, his head down a bit. "I'm glad you got some pleasure out of it. But agreeing to do that show was the worst mistake of my life. I've wished I could go back a million times and get a do-over. But I can't."

"Really?" Her eyebrows furrowed. "Why? You were great on the show."

Skyler stopped herself from gushing about the countless hours she binge-watched marathon showings of *Cowboy Up!* just to see him ride a horse or sit around a campfire playing guitar with his friends. And she sure as heck wasn't going to confess the many daydreams she had had about marrying him. Judging by his reaction, that secret was best kept in the vault.

Hunter sat back again, seeming to relax. "Being famous isn't what it's cracked up to be, especially if you want to be taken seriously as a rancher in a small town."

Up until that moment, Skyler hadn't realized that she had only been seeing Hunter as a one-dimensional character from a TV show instead of a flesh-and-blood man. It had never occurred to her that *Cowboy Up!* had been anything but amazing for Hunter. After all, being a part of his life, vicariously through the show, had been so amazing for her.

She sought to lighten the mood and set him at ease. "Well, I promise that I'm not a stalker. Just a fan."

"Good to know."

She stared at his profile. "But I do have some posters and T-shirts that I would like for you to sign."

Hunter shot up again, his brow furrowed. "Are you serious?"

"No." She shook her head with a smirk. "I was just teasing you."

"You really spooked my mule, Skyler," he said, the dimples coming out. Then he stood up and raised his arms over his head in a stretch. For the briefest of moments, his button-down shirt raised up, revealing strong, defined abs—the kind that tempted the touch. "All right. Enough resting. You ready to go for a ride?"

She didn't want to let on, but she could do with some more rest. Honestly, she felt as if she had already done weeks' worth of work before lunch and the conversation had tired her out even more.

"Sure," Skyler said with a weak smile. "Lead the way."

At first, when she tried to stand up her legs didn't want to cooperate. She fell back a bit and then tried again. Hunter had his back to her and didn't notice, which suited her just fine. She pushed herself upright, reaching for the railing. In a split second, her world narrowed and the edges of her vision closed in around her. She heard herself say Hunter's name and then everything around her faded to black.

"Why didn't you tell me she was sick?" Hunter whispered harshly into the phone.

"It was her business to tell, not mine," Jock said in his terse manner. "What's going on now?"

"Well, she damn well passed out, Dad." He rested one hand on the porch railing. "I worked her like a man before I even knew anything was wrong."

"You should've eased her in, regardless," his father admonished. "That's just good sense, son."

Yes, it would have been good sense if he hadn't been determined to send her packing back to the city. It would have been good sense if he had a clue that Skyler had health concerns. He didn't have a decent argument so he just moved on.

"Does she need to go to the hospital?"

"I tried to take her and she refused to go. She's resting now," he said. "I think she just got overheated and overly tired."

"Well, that's on you, son. Keep me posted," Jock said. "And let her know we're planning a family get-together—outdoors so everyone can be safe. We all want to make her feel welcome even though we've got this *pan-dammit* going on."

"Yes, sir." Hunter nodded. "I'll do that."

"Take care of her as if she were one of our own, Hunter. I wouldn't expect any less of you."

He ended the call with his father, put his phone in his back pocket and then stared out at the landscape. Jock had pulled the perfect bait and switch on him. He had thought he was getting a bratty city girl who flew around on private jets wasting people's time for kicks. She was in Montana chasing a dream; she was in Montana to regain her life and her health.

The door opened to the cabin while his mind was wandering and he was staring out at the field. He turned to find Skyler standing in the doorway, looking smaller and slighter than before, but the color had returned to her face.

"That was terrible." Skyler had her arms crossed and she sounded, to his ears, embarrassed.

"Do you feel well enough to sit down out here with me?" he asked.

Arms still crossed, she nodded. She sat down in the chair she had occupied earlier. This time she curled her legs up to her chest and wrapped her arms around them.

"I'm sorry I pushed you so hard, Skyler." Hunter was seeking her forgiveness. He had acted like a class-A jerk and he knew it.

"This isn't your fault," she said quickly, emphatically. "I wanted to keep up, show you that I wasn't going to be a burden to you this summer..."

"I didn't want you here, so I made it tougher on you than it needed to be." Hunter decided to just clear the air between them. He felt like he owed her that much.

"I know that." Skyler met his gaze. "And I wanted to prove you wrong. Instead, I made your point for you."

"No. You didn't. Everyone needs time to acclimate

to this kind of work. I ran you ragged and for that I'm sorry. I want you to accept my apology."

"I do."

"Good. Thank you. Now we can start over." Hunter was surprised that she'd forgiven him so easily, so willingly, so completely. He had just told her that he had deliberately run her down and she had nothing but acceptance and friendship in her eyes, which could only be described as lavender with flecks of blue and gray. Lovely eyes. Perhaps the most beautiful he had ever seen. In fact, at times, he found it difficult to break the gaze...to look away from those eyes.

Skyler smiled sweetly at him, yawned and then her eyes drooped down. "I think I'm going to go lie down again. What time should I expect you tomorrow?"

"Let's make is seven." Hunter stood up with her.

"What about the horses, the cows?" she asked, worried.

"I've got them. You just get some rest and we'll go for that trail ride before it gets too hot."

Skyler nodded in agreement as she headed to the front door.

"By the way," Hunter said, "Jock is planning a family cookout. Outside—plenty of social distancing. Everyone wants to meet you."

Skyler smiled that sweet smile at him again. "And I very much want to meet them."

"It's been more than I hoped for." Skyler was propped up in bed video-chatting with Molly. Molly's friendly, pretty face was a comfort to her and she was grateful to Jock for ensuring that she had a solid internet connection in her little private oasis on the ranch. Molly's father was a redheaded Irishman and her mother was a doctor from Haiti; with those genetics, Molly had inherited long, curly sable hair, moss-green eyes and darker skin with the most endearing freckles across the bridge of her nose and cheeks. And her dear friend had the best smile of anyone she had ever known.

"Everyone has loved the pictures you've been posting," her friend said from her micro patio. In the city, Molly's minuscule outdoor space was considered a luxury.

"I've been trying to be kind of low-key about all of the pictures. Hunter doesn't like for his picture to be taken and he definitely doesn't like social media."

"Hunter." Molly put her hand over her heart, fluttered her long, curled eyelashes and pretended to faint.

"Hunter," Skyler repeated in a dreamy voice. "He's so handsome in person, you wouldn't believe it. But, you know…he's better than I had imagined. Nicer."

Molly's eyes widened. "What if you actually marry Hunter Brand? Just think about it. All of those mock weddings we produced between Hunter and you would actually be dress rehearsals!"

That made Skyler laugh. "No. I don't think marriage between Hunter and me is written in the stars. When he first saw me, he looked at me like I was an alien from Mars."

"Well, that wig was odd."

Skyler laughed harder. "I know it was. You tried to tell me."

"Good riddance."

"Agreed," she said. "But now that he knows I've been sick, he treats me like his little sister." She rolled her eyes. "It's *whatever.*"

"Well, I think Hunter Brand would be crazy *not* to fall in love with you."

"Thank you." She smiled; Molly was always there to lift her spirits. "I wish you were here with me. It's like walking on to the set of *Cowboy Up!* The family is going to have an outdoor get-together in a couple of weeks. I'm looking forward to that. By that time, I think all of the quality time with trees and solitude will be getting old."

"I wonder if Chase will be there."

Chase Rockwell was one of Hunter's friends and another dream-worthy cowboy on *Cowboy Up!* Molly had always had a hard time choosing between Chase and Hunter. For Skyler, it had never been a contest: it had always been Hunter. In fact, it still was.

"I don't think so. Hunter says the ranch has been closed up pretty tightly—only essential workers have been coming in."

"And one pretty little redhead." Molly grinned at her.

"I did manage to slip through the cracks, didn't I?"

"It was meant to be," her friend reiterated. "Hey. I've got to run. Make sure you ask Hunter about Chase. Neither one of them are on social media. Find out if he's married!"

Skyler hung up with her friend and slipped out of bed. Alone in the woods, she felt comfortable stepping outside without a bra on. She pulled on a ribbed tank top, a clean pair of jeans and her newly christened dusty boots.

On the front porch, she pulled in a deep breath and then let it out slowly. It was late afternoon and the air was still. Other than some birds chirping and fluttering from one tree limb to another, it was quiet. Slowly, carefully, Skyler made her way down the porch steps, still feeling wobbly from her earlier ordeal.

Across the yard, she made her way to a giant boulder at the edge of the clearing near the gravel drive that led back to the main ranch road. Skyler had been pulled toward this boulder since she had first spotted it. This was the perfect perch for her daily meditation. When she reached the boulder, she ran her hands over the smooth surface; it was covered with swirls of gold and black and white. It had small crevices and places where tiny wildflowers were trying to grow.

Skyler found a foothold and climbed her way to the top of the boulder. There she sat cross-legged, hands resting in her lap, her eyes closed, her chin tilted upward. She wasn't sure how the summer was going to unfold, but she knew that she was in the right place at the right time. She felt it in her gut. As the sun began to set behind her, Skyler began her gratitude ritual, something she had begun during the darkest days of her illness. She sat silently, her body still, and thought of all of her many blessings. Her list of gratitude was a living document; she was always adding to it.

"I am grateful for Jock Brand for allowing me to heal in this most beautiful place. I am grateful for Hunter Brand, who caught me when I was about to fall."

Chapter Four

It wasn't how she would have wanted it, but it took her four days to regain her strength. Hunter refused to let her help with the barn chores, only letting her keep him company while he mucked the stalls and occasionally letting her drive the zero-turn lawn mower. It was something she had learned to use with her father when she was young, and she mowed around the cabin and the other buildings. By the fourth day, she was starting to get restless and she told him as much.

"I feel better." She marched after him as he took a load of manure to the compost pile. "Look at me."

Hunter tipped over the wheelbarrow, dumping the contents onto the pile. "I see you."

"I need to get back to work or I'm going to lose my ever-loving mind," she said, irritated. "I'm not some delicate little baby bird that you have to protect."

"That's not how I see it." The cowboy rolled the wheelbarrow over to the barn and tipped it on its side to rinse it out.

Skyler stomped over to the hose, grabbed it, dragged it over to the dirty wheelbarrow and turned on the water. Hunter made a grab for the hose but she held it away from him with a scowl.

"I'm serious. I didn't come here to convalesce in bed. I've done enough of that. I came here to work, to experience ranch life, and it's your job to give me that experience, isn't that right?"

Hunter's jaw was set and he didn't respond.

"Now, I'm as much to blame for that little episode as you are. More, actually. I knew my body was being pushed beyond its limit and I should have just been straight with you, the consequences be damned."

Skyler finished cleaning the wheelbarrow. Then she shut off the water and threw the hose down on the ground as if to punctuate her words.

"I'm tired of the trees. I want to see some people other than you." Skyler had her hands on her hips. "Take me into town *or* give me the keys to your truck and I'll drive myself."

Hunter stared at her, his arms crossed. She could almost see the wheels turning inside his brain, trying to figure out his next move with her. What he didn't realize was that *she* was going to determine her next move, not him.

Skyler spun on her heel and simultaneously took her phone out of her pocket. "Fine. I'll get an Uber. Does Uber come out this far? Someone has to come out this far, right? We're still in civilization."

"I don't know what you're so worked up about," Hunter called after her.

She stopped and turned back to him. "I'm *bored*. I've seen the trees, I love the trees, but enough with these particular trees!"

"How about that trail ride?" Hunter asked, still planted in his spot.

"Ah, yes. The elusive, promised trail ride," Skyler snorted back at him.

"Let's go get the horses and saddle them up."

A trail ride seemed a much better prospect than town, except for seeing other human beings. When she had imagined Montana for all of those years, she hadn't thought about how lonely it could be. So much land with so few people—it was an adjustment after spending her entire life living in one of the biggest cities in the world.

"Will we see any signs of life other than birds and cows?" she asked, walking toward him.

"I can take you up to the homestead tour," Hunter said. "I can take you up to the main house, ride you by Bruce and Savannah's place, swing by my stake and then finish at Little Sugar Creek."

They brought the horses in from the pasture; Hunter brushed Zodiac, picked out his hooves and sprayed him with fly spray, while she took care of Dream Catcher. She was pleased with how easily her skills came back from her two summers at horse camp. It was like riding a bike; she could only hope that the *riding* part came back as easily.

"You are such a beautiful girl." Skyler combed Dream Catcher's long forelock so it wasn't in the horse's eyes.

Hunter swung a saddle pad and saddle onto Dream

Catcher's back. "She was my sister's rodeo ride for years."

"Your sister doesn't mind me riding her horse for the summer?"

Hunter tightened the girth slowly; Dream Catcher pinned her ears back a bit as the girth tightened around her belly. "She's happy that Dream has a job for the summer. She was over in Australia visiting friends when this whole virus thing happened—she decided to hunker down over there until things calm down."

"I'm sorry I'm not going to get to meet her."

Once the horses had been saddled and bridled, Hunter fit her with a helmet so her head was protected from a potential fall. He gave her a leg up; she swung into the saddle and sat down as gently as she could on Dream Catcher's back. She sat upright and held on to the saddle horn, while Hunter adjusted her stirrups the right length.

"How does that feel?"

"Good." She moved around a little to get the feel of the stirrups and the seat of the saddle. "Comfortable."

The cowboy handed her the reins and then mounted Zodiac. He rode up beside her. "You'll let me know if you need to stop."

"Yes," she promised and she meant it sincerely.

They took a trail that ran behind the cabin; she had walked some of the trail on foot but had never gotten very far. She sat taller in the saddle, feeling more confident in her ability to handle the horse. Along the way, she practiced stopping and backing up and shifting Dream Catcher's direction.

"It *is* like riding a bike!"

"Don't get too cocky," Hunter warned. "An experienced trail horse can spook just as easily as a novice trail horse."

They made their way along the curvy trail, crossing several rock-laden streams and trotting up short hills, which made Skyler laugh with joy. Every now and again, Hunter would hoot and holler, and he told her he was making sure the deer cleared out of their way so their sudden movements wouldn't spook the horses. Skyler joined him in the hooting and hollering, and it felt amazing to yell at the top of her lungs in the middle of Montana.

At the edge of the trail, an expanse of pastureland and fields provided a picturesque foreground for the main house of Sugar Creek Ranch. Of course, she had seen the main house on the show, but to see it in person, to get perspective on the sheer size of the house in relation to the mountains in the background, was another thing entirely.

"Wow." That was all she could say.

"Dad wanted to make a statement." Hunter had stopped Zodiac where the trail met the open field so she could take in the view.

"The statement is 'I have a boatload of money.'" These words just jumped right out of her mouth before she could reel them back in.

Hunter looked over at her and smiled. "You got the message."

Skyler laughed. "Loud and clear."

"You'll meet my parents next week at the cookout." He turned his horse to the northeast.

"I'm looking forward to that." The family had planned the event to be two weeks after her arrival, in order to observe a fourteen-day quarantine. She was totally on board, but had no idea how long fourteen days could feel!

They followed the tree line along the open field. In the distance, a small herd of deer appeared—three mothers with their seven babies dotted the hillside.

"I need to get a picture of this." Skyler shifted in the saddle to pull her phone out of her pocket. "Look how precious those babies are!"

Hunter stopped Zodiac close enough to Dream Catcher that he could take a hold of the mare's reins. His big-city tourist did exactly what he expected her to do: take way too many pictures of every stump, leaf and common deer on the ranch.

But that's where his assumptions of his summer charge ended. She was completely unexpected, from her firecracker personality to her ability to take pleasure in every little thing in life that she did. Everything in the world seemed to hold wonder for Skyler; she didn't just see a leaf—she saw the miracle of nature. And it made him see the world around him—the world he took for granted and often saw as an obstacle or a chore—in a different light.

"Wow." Skyler turned that bright smile of hers on him. And when she did, he felt something odd in his gut, and it was a feeling that he just couldn't explain, other than the fact that he'd never quite felt it before.

"Right?" she said.

"What? The deer?"

"Yes." Skyler looked at him like he just didn't get it. "Of course, the deer! Aren't they amazing? I love their spindly legs and their little white tails."

"Not really. They're all over the place. And they break the fences. I am forever repairing fences that they have broken with their...what did you call them? Spindly legs?"

Skyler ignored his complaints as they rode toward the deer; it was interesting seeing the ranch through her eyes. He had always loved this land, but perhaps he had been taking it for granted lately.

"They are tasty, I will say that," he added.

"Oh!" Skyler winced at the thought. "How could you, Hunter?"

He laughed, something he found himself doing around Skyler. "Easily. Cook 'em right up, add a little barbeque sauce. Finger lickin' good."

"I don't like you anymore." She turned her head away from him.

As they approached the small herd, the adults lifted their heads, alert, their large ears pointed in their direction. They stood stock-still for a couple of seconds before they raced toward the trees.

"Look!" his companion whispered harshly. "Look!"

So he did. He did look. And he watched. The adult females were singularly focused on reaching the trees, while the babies ran in circles, playing with each other, frolicking in the tall grass. One by one, the babies realized that the adults were in the trees and scurried after them as fast as their dainty legs would take them. He had seen that image hundreds of thousands of times since he was a young boy, but he couldn't remember just stopping and really watching them. He couldn't remember just stopping and appreciating the unique beauty of the animal.

Skyler turned her face toward him, her eyes shining with happiness and joy. He found himself thinking a lot about the cuteness of Skyler's oval face. The features of her face were refined and petite; her lips were bow-shaped and her nose was small and straight. He had thought, at first, that her eyes were too large for her face, giving her an odd look. But now he thought they were perfect for her. He didn't care about her shorn hair; in fact, the new growth made her resemble a pixie or a sprite. When he looked at her, he found himself wanting to keep right on looking. He supposed her felt about Skyler the way she felt about those deer: he was fascinated.

Up over a hill and down the other side, the homestead of his eldest brother, Bruce, and his wife, Savannah, was visible in the valley. A pack of misfit dogs, all rescued from one place or another by his brother and sister-in-law, came barreling toward them, tails wagging, barking loudly and persistently.

The pack of dogs followed them as they rode toward the house that Bruce had built with his own hands for the love of his life, Savannah. In the field beyond the house, Bruce was on his tractor mowing and he could see Savannah, with her long, wavy bright red hair, working in the garden behind the house. Hunter's niece, Amanda, just shy of her fifth birthday, spotted him in the distance and started to jump up and down and yell his name.

Savannah stood up, saw them and waved her arms. Following her daughter's lead, his sister-in-law left the garden so she could meet them in front of the house.

"Uncle Hunter!" Amanda had a head full of russet-brown curls, greenish-blue eyes and a face as pretty as her mother's.

As usual, Savannah was in jeans, boots, a loose T-shirt and a big, floppy hat to keep the sun off of her neck.

"Hi!" Savannah greeted them. "We were hoping you'd stop by!"

Hunter made quick introductions, wishing he could get down off the horse and give his niece a proper hug.

"It's so nice to meet you," Skyler said.

"Same here," Savannah said. "We've all been real excited to have you here for the summer. Did you have a chance to try the lemonade I made for you?"

"The lemonade!" his companion exclaimed. "I have never tasted anything that good. Thank you so much for making me a pitcher."

"It was my pleasure," his sister-in-law said. "I'll make more anytime you want and send it along with Hunter."

"Uncle Hunter!" Amanda was swinging from his boot while Zodiac didn't move an inch. "Come and play with me."

Savannah wrangled her daughter. "Come here, wild child. Uncle Hunter can't play right now."

"Why not?" his niece asked with a pout that he found irresistible.

"I'll come and play with you soon," he promised. "I'm going to take her over to meet Bruce and then swing by my place..."

"What place?" Savannah laughed, holding on to her daughter's hands and twirling her in a circle.

"It's rustic," Hunter said.

"Rustic?!" His sister-in-law's voice went way up on the question. "You don't have indoor plumbing! Or a roof! Or walls!"

"Minor details."

She said to Skyler, "It's been a lot of big talk and zero action over there at Hunter's place."

"I've just been waiting for the right woman to come

along and then I'll build her a house just like Bruce built for you."

"Well, it's not from a lack of options. You've got to commit, Hunter. Find the right one and commit." Savannah waved them off.

"'Bye, Uncle Hunter!" Amanda ran beside them, her chubby legs pumping furiously. "I love you."

"I love you, Princess Amanda!"

The truth of the matter was that he came from a family of marrying men. Four of his elder brothers were already married and he always wanted to join the ranks of married Brand men. Lately, he had been casually dating the daughter of a rancher who owned the large cattle spread that shared Sugar Creek's entire southern border. Like him, Brandy McGregor had Montana in her blood. She was a cattleman's daughter and understood what that kind of life entailed. She was as pretty as the day was long, with willowy legs, naturally buxom and thick, light brown hair. She had been on the rodeo circuit with him, and even though she had been four years behind him in school, they shared the same tight-knit group of friends.

Bruce stopped mowing long enough for Hunter to introduce Skyler and then his older brother went right back to work. Hunter understood it—there was only so much daylight a man was afforded each day and always more work to get done than daylight would allow.

"He's got a lot of field left to cut," Hunter explained.

"I see that." Skyler seemed to be sitting straighter in the saddle, her chin up, her shoulders back.

"You feeling okay or do we need to head back?"

"No. I always want to go forward. Never back. Only forward."

* * *

"Wow!" Skyler said. "I really need to come up with a new word to use. But...*wow*."

"Do you like it?"

"Like it? I *love* it! Can we stop and take a look around?"

"We've got the time," Hunter said. "I planned on getting back to the fence tomorrow if the weather holds."

Skyler swung her leg over the saddle, took her foot out of the stirrup and then slid down to the ground. When she landed, her knees ached and she realized that her entire backside was sore. She winced as she straightened up, feeling like she was in her eighties instead of just approaching thirty. Her annoying aches and pains were soon forgotten as her attention was drawn to the stake of Sugar Creek land that Hunter had claimed for his own.

"You can just drop her reins." Hunter walked up beside her. "Dream is trained to ground tie."

Skyler dropped the horse's reins, gave her a pat on her neck and then walked toward the cluster of ancient oak trees at the top of a small hill.

"I call her Oak Tree Hill," Hunter said of his place.

The cluster of hundred-year-old oak trees, with their thick trunks and far-reaching, glorious canopies, beckoned to her. Surrounding the trees was unfenced pastureland lush with grass and indigenous wildflowers. Beneath the trees, the temperature was cooler and the sun was almost entirely blocked.

"Hunter." Skyler stopped beneath one of the oak trees. "This is paradise."

The smile he sent her was different from the others; he appreciated that she loved his spot in the world.

"No one else wanted this spot." Hunter leaned back against one of the trees. "Too far out, too hard to build."

"The harder you have to work, the more you appreciate it." Skyler wandered deeper beneath the tree canopy. "That's what my father always says."

Tucked away in the cluster of giant trees was a small camper with an overhang. Nearby there was a firepit.

"This is where you come when you leave me?" she asked, taking it all in, processing the information.

"Every night," he said. "I've got a vision in my head of what it could be one day."

Skyler opened her arms, titled her head back, spun around and breathed in the scent of the trees. They had a unique, sweet smell that was concentrated in that one area because of the density and age of the trees.

She stopped and opened her eyes; Hunter was watching her. "This is heaven on earth, Hunter."

Hunter ducked his head for a moment before he looked up with a sideways glance. "You think so?"

She leaned down to pick up an acorn, a large seed from the oldest of the group, and put it in her pocket. "I know so. What a gift you will have to give to your wife one day. What an incredible, beautiful gift."

Chapter Five

That night, after he left Skyler at Liam's cabin, Hunter did something that he *never* did: he searched social media for images of Skyler. There was a guilty knot in his stomach; he wasn't exactly tied to Brandy McGregor and there hadn't been any promises made, but before the pandemic had changed everything about their lives, things were moving in a certain kind of direction with her. Their families approved of the match; in fact, both patriarchs thought it would be legacy building to have a marriage join the massive property holdings of the Brands and the McGregors. And if that marriage should produce a grandchild that could one day oversee a conglomeration of the two sets of property? Jock and Beau McGregor, Brandy's father, were salivating at the prospect. Still, Hunter had his doubts. If the pandemic hadn't happened, would he still be with Brandy? She was sweet and beautiful, yet a bit dull.

"There you are." Hunter had to create a new Instagram account, his first, in order to scroll through Skyler's history.

"Now who's the stalker?" he asked himself, enlarging a picture of Skyler before she had cancer. Before she lost her hair, it had been wispy and shoulder-length, a lovely golden, strawberry color that set off her lavender eyes in the most unusual way. With her hair just barely growing in, she reminded him of one of his mother's favorite actresses, Audrey Hepburn. Skyler had that same petite frame and sassy attitude. She was cute in the best sense of the word. Hunter imagined that it would be impossible, in general, to dislike Skyler. He'd certainly tried and failed rather quickly.

He was looking through Skyler's posted cancer journey when his best, and oldest, friend, Chase Rockwell, called.

"What's going on, man?" Chase asked him when he answered the phone.

"Just workin', what about you?"

"Same," his friend answered. Chase had inherited his family's farm and had been doing everything he could to keep it afloat. Chase had grown into one of the hardest-working men he'd ever known. Unfortunately, prior to his death, Chase's father had leveraged every piece of equipment on the farm and had taken out a second mortgage on the property.

"How's it going with the tourist?" Hunter hadn't had time to give his friend an update on Skyler.

"I don't really call her that," he said, feeling bad that he'd ever put that label out there.

"Huh. What *do* you call her?"

"Skyler."

"Give me her last name, man. I'm gonna look her up right now and see why you've done a one-eighty on this woman."

"Sinclair." Hunter didn't bother to play possum with his friend. Chase would just text someone in the family if he didn't give it to him. "I'm just going to send you a link to her Instagram page."

Hunter sent the information to his friend.

"Hold up. Since when are you on Instagram?"

"Since today."

Hunter didn't need to say anything more to Chase; the fact that he had broken his steadfast rule to avoid all things social media following the explosion of press, good and bad, after *Cowboy Up!* told his friend everything he needed to know. Skyler was different. His newfound interest in Skyler was different.

"She's cute. Not like your usual."

"No." He had always gone for tall, lanky, sun-kissed brunettes with rodeo and ranch credentials.

"Her friend Molly is…someone special…" Chase's voice trailed off and then after several seconds of silence, he said, "Ask Skyler to introduce us."

Hunter was floored. Chase hadn't shown much interest in dating since he'd lost Sarah. "You want to have a virtual date with a woman on the other side of the country?"

"Yeah. Why not? I can't do any worse than I'm doing here."

"Why not? I don't know. Maybe the fact that the two of you will most likely never be in the same place at the same time?"

"Maybe that will work in my favor," his friend joked. Then he added more seriously, "I'm tired of being alone.

Everyone here knows my history. Everyone here knows about…" Chase stopped before he said her name. *Everyone knows about Sarah.*

There was some silence on the other end of the line while Chase moved through Skyler's social footprint.

"She had cancer?" His friend's voice had changed.

"Yeah, she did."

Chase let his breath out. "Man."

"I know," Hunter said. "I didn't get why Dad agreed to have a stranger come to the ranch especially during all of this COVID crap going on."

"Makes sense now."

"Yeah, it does."

"Sarah…" Chase said the name that was often spoken silently between them and thought of frequently, but rarely mentioned aloud.

"Sarah," Hunter echoed.

Sarah James had been the daughter of Jock's best friend. The story was that Hunter and Sarah were born a day apart, in the same hospital room, and they shared everything, including a playpen while their fathers played poker. As they grew up, Sarah became a second sister to him. He had never been able to see her as more than a sister, but all of his friends had crushes on her at one time or another. She was beautiful in an approachable, Jennifer Aniston kind of way—an athletic tomboy who felt just as comfortable in a cocktail dress, with a really loud, infectious laugh. But Sarah had only had eyes for Chase and the feeling was mutual.

"It's hard to believe that she's been gone ten years." Chase cleared his throat several times, and Hunter knew him well enough to know that he was fighting back emotion over a loss that was still raw for both of them.

During filming of the last season of *Cowboy Up!*, when Sarah made occasional appearances as Chase's girlfriend, she was diagnosed with a rare form of brain cancer called neuroblastoma. The cancer had been vicious, unrelenting and deadly. Hunter still felt the trauma of watching Sarah deteriorate so quickly and lose her battle with cancer in less than six months. They all did.

Jamie James, Sarah's father, whom everyone called J.J., took his daughter's death the hardest. He drank, he gambled and he got divorced. No one was surprised when J.J. had a catastrophic stroke and followed his daughter into the grave the following year. For Jock, the losses of J.J. and Sarah had been devastating; his father was a man cut from old-fashioned stock and didn't believe that men should ever cry. But Jock would get tears in his eyes at the mention of Sarah and he couldn't even say J.J.'s name without getting choked up.

"Man," Chase said again with a cough and a throat clear. "Heavy stuff."

"Yeah. I know. I'm sorry, Chase." Hunter wanted to redirect the conversation. "How are things going on your end? Did you get that tractor fixed?"

"Aw, I don't know, man." His friend sighed. "I think I'm gonna have to start selling off body parts. Do you know anyone in the market for a kidney?"

Everything hurt. Absolutely everything. Her inner thighs were sore, her butt cheeks were sore, her fingers were stiff from holding a pitchfork and her feet were dotted with blisters from breaking in her new boots. Skyler had taken to walking bow-legged inside of the cabin, hobbling about tenderly, groaning and saying "ouch" as she moved slowly from one room to the next.

"I thought this trip was supposed to make you feel better, not worse," Chester Sinclair said after his daughter ran down the list of ailments from working on the ranch.

"I feel better," she said with a laugh. "And worse."

Hunter had dug several splinters out of her hands before she finally remembered to put on her gloves when they tore down the remaining section of fence. She had also developed a heat rash under her arms that was itchy and burned all the time. At night she tucked washcloths with ice cubes wrapped inside under her arms for some relief. It seemed like she was a walking list of ailments, and yet she felt incredible mentally. She felt more powerful, more in control over her own destiny. She had torn down a fence with her bare hands!

"I'm getting stronger every day." She lifted up her arm and made a muscle for her father to see in the video chat. "Look. A baby muscle! When I got here, I couldn't lift a bale of hay. *Now* I can actually lift and carry it a couple of feet at a time. Just imagine how strong I'm going to be by the end of summer. You'll have to enter me in an iron-woman competition."

Chester smiled in spite of himself; even now, Skyler knew he wasn't convinced that Montana for the entire summer was the right choice.

"You could have done the same thing right here in the home gym with me," he countered, still smiling a bit.

"Anyway, I *am* excited for the family cookout," Skyler said, turning the conversation to a new topic.

"Well," Chester grumbled, "have fun. Be safe."

"I'll be safe. Don't worry."

"I always worry about you."

Skyler smiled. "And I love you for it."

* * *

"Have you ever driven a skid steer before?" Hunter smiled a bit at the way Skyler was walking—like an old, rickety cowboy.

"No."

"Well, hop on up. I'm going to show you right now."

The gravel for the main drive had been delivered, and between the two of them, the job was going to get done today.

"Okay," he said, once Skyler was seated in the skid steer and had the safety bar pulled down. "This is going to move just like the zero-turn lawn mower and the bucket is going to work like the bucket on the tractor. Basically, you know how to drive this thing already."

Skyler nodded; he had taught her how to tie a bandanna around her head so it would catch the sweat and stop if from dripping down into her eyes. Savannah had a spare hat, a dark brown Stetson that turned out to be a perfect fit for Skyler. Today, only two weeks after her arrival in Montana, Skyler looked like a different woman. She had put on some weight—good weight, the kind that came with building muscle. The grayish, pasty hue of her skin had been replaced by a golden, rosy glow. She had taken to wearing tank tops that defined her waist and showed off her slender, petite figure. Her jeans, roughed up and dirty from farm work, hugged her shapely bottom in a way that he found very sexy. In fact, he had to remind himself to focus on the work and not on how kissable he was finding her lips.

"See the green button overhead? Push that," he instructed. He was standing on the bucket of the skid steer, holding on to the safety handles, so close to her really that he could just lean forward and kiss her. It was mighty tempting but he knew it would be a stupid move. Jock would shoot him, stuff him and mount him over the fireplace if he screwed up with Skyler.

"Now turn the key."

Skyler started the skid steer and an elated smile lit up her face. Such a pretty face.

"Cool!" she exclaimed.

While he was standing on the bucket, Hunter had her practice both moving the skid steer forward and backward, and turning it from left to right.

"It's super easy," Skyler told him.

"Now, with your left foot, push your toe down to lift the bucket."

"With you on it?"

He nodded.

"I hope I don't fling you off," she said, biting her lip.

"You'll be fine," he reassured her. She carefully pressed down her left toe and jerked the bucket upward. Hunter held on to the handles tightly while he instructed her to lower the bucket by pressing down her left heel.

"It's counterintuitive," she observed.

"It takes some getting used to, but once you get it, it'll feel natural."

Hunter jumped off the bucket, then taught her how to pick up rock and then relocate it. It didn't take much practice before Skyler was barreling off in the skid steer, picking up gravel and dumping it in the washed-out areas of the long, main drive into Sugar Creek. With the tractor, he took a blade attachment and smoothed out the rock. They repeated this action time and again, working together, until all of the major potholes were filled in.

"My fingertips feel numb." Skyler hopped out of the skid steer after the job was done.

"It's from the vibration. It'll go away." He handed her a bottle of water.

She gulped down the water and then poured some of it on the back of her neck. There was dirt in the crease of her neck and dust covering both of her arms. Her tank top was soaked with sweat, her boots caked with dust and mud. In that moment, Skyler looked like a bona fide ranch woman and Hunter liked what he saw.

"I need one of these." Skyler patted the skid steer with her hand. "I don't know what the heck I would do with it in the city, or where I would park it. But I just really need one."

"You could always park it in the garage."

Skyler laughed. "I *live* in the garage. So *that* is not an option."

They climbed into his truck and he drove them back toward Liam's cabin.

"Look at this!" his companion said to him. "Look what we accomplished. This road isn't making me seasick anymore."

Her enthusiasm over the smallest of accomplishments on the ranch amused him. He'd never taken much pride in filling potholes with gravel—maybe he should start.

"I might've made it a bit worse on you than it needed to be," he admitted.

"I know." Skyler frowned at him playfully. "You wanted me gone in the worst way."

They rode in silence until they reached the turnoff toward the cabin. He slowed down so Skyler could enjoy the ride through the canopy of trees, something she had mentioned to him that she enjoyed.

"I don't feel that way anymore, you know." He didn't want her to think that he wanted her gone. He didn't.

Skyler glanced over at him with a shyness he wasn't used to seeing in her. "You don't?"

"No." He looked straight ahead through the windshield. "You've been a big help to me."

"Really?" She turned her body toward him...as much as the seat belt would allow. "Is that true?"

He nodded. It was true. That fence had been taken down a whole heck of a lot faster with her help, and filling in the potholes had gone quickly. Even when she had to take extended breaks, having her company made the jobs go by faster for him.

She seemed pleased with his confession. "Well, I'm glad. Because I'm having the time of my life."

Hunter dropped her off at the cabin with a promise to pick her up in two hours for the cookout; he watched her walk stiffly away from him. While he was watching, Skyler spotted a rock on the ground, bent down gingerly, picked it up, examined it and then put it in her pocket. She turned her head, caught him watching her, smiled and waved her hand, then continued her short journey to the cabin.

Hunter cranked the engine of the truck and then said to his phone, "Call Brandy."

"Call Brandy? Is that correct?"

"Yes."

"Okay. Calling Brandy."

As he turned the truck back to the main road, the phone rang twice and then Brandy picked up.

"Hey!" She sounded happy to hear from him. "I was just thinking about you."

Hunter drove under the canopy of trees and he looked up at the branches and the leaves. Being with Skyler had just made him more attentive to the beauty unfolding all around him on the ranch. Before her, he never would have bothered paying attention to the branches and leaves in the canopy.

"Then I guess it's a good thing I called," he said to Brandy. "Because I was just thinking about you, too."

"What do you think?" Skyler stepped in front of her phone camera so Molly could see the shift dress she had put on. "Too much?"

"This is just like a romantic-movie montage. You change into a bunch of different outfits and I shake my head and make a horrible face until we land on just the right outfit," her friend said, leaning forward to get a better look at the outfit.

"Except I've just tried on this one dress." Skyler looked down at the gauzy lavender dress with spaghetti straps and a thin belt to highlight her small waist.

"I was with you when you bought that," Molly said.

"I remember." She spun around, letting the skirt twirl around her legs. "What's the verdict?"

"I say yes," Molly responded. Her friend seemed distracted for a moment. Then she said, "You aren't going to believe this."

"What?"

ß´"You said I could give him your number."

"I know, but…" Molly tucked some wayward curls behind her ear. "I guess I didn't really expect him to use it."

"I did. Hunter told me that Chase was really smitten with you."

"Did Chase actually use the word *smitten* or is that your word?"

"My word, I think." Skyler looked at her very short

hair in the camera shot. "I wonder if I should wear my hat."

"He wants to know if he can call me later."

Skyler sat down on the bed and pulled on her socks. She had decided to wear her hat and her cowboy boots with the dress. It was a ranch cookout, after all.

"Say yes," she told Molly.

"I don't know." Her friend looked like she was frozen, but it wasn't a bad connection; she hadn't moved from her spot, seeming to be a bit stunned.

"You don't know?" Skyler frowned. "Why wouldn't you want to talk to him?"

"What if I don't like him? It will ruin countless hours of daydreaming from my youth. Those were wonderful daydreams. Do I really want the real him to ruin my fantasy of him?"

"Hunter says he's a real nice guy. Hardworking. Loyal. A great friend."

Molly fell backward on her bed and said dreamily, "Chase Rockwell."

Then her friend popped upright, a thoughtful expression on her pretty face. "It could be a double wedding, just like we always planned."

Skyler laughed at the thought. Hunter hadn't so much as looked at her with interest since she arrived. If anything, he treated her like an adored little sister. Much of her teenage fantasy of Hunter Brand of *Cowboy Up!* falling madly in love with her had given way to the reality of her relationship with him. Theirs was a budding friendship and she was happy with that. Would it have been nice to come to Montana and find a true romance with a cowboy? Of course. She was a true romance junkie—always had been, always would be. But her illness had taught her how to live in the moment, live for the day and live in reality.

"*Cowboy Up!* cowboys find love in the Big Apple?" Skyler teased her friend. "A sequel to the original series?"

"You never know." Molly refused to let her rain on her parade. "Stranger things have happened. I mean, seriously. A stranger thing just *did* happen!"

"Well, I think you should at least talk to him. It never hurts to have another friend in the world. Let me know what you decide. I love you," Skyler said and then waved goodbye. She went the extra mile and put on some mascara, a light dusting of blush and a clear gloss on her lips. She took some leather cleaner that Hunter had let her borrow and wiped down her boots before pulling them on. The multiple Band-Aids on her feet had made the boots more comfortable and allowed her to walk almost normally. Now if only the rash would go away and the soreness in her thighs and backside would subside.

She shut the front door behind her, still not used to the idea of leaving the door unlocked, and sat down. While she waited for Hunter, she checked her social media, thrilled to see how positive the responses were to all of her Montana posts. Hunter had been a reluctant photographer, but he had managed to capture great pictures of her working on the ranch. The latest picture of her driving the skid steer was her favorite to date. She looked strong. Happy. Capable.

Had she ever really looked that happy before in her life? The end of the summer was far off in the distance, but Skyler was already dreading the day that she had to leave Sugar Creek. How would she be able to go back to her small cubicle at the insurance company, sitting for hours day after day, answering complaints, when she knew that this life existed? How could she, really?

She heard the crunching of the tires of Hunter's truck as it approached. Skyler put away her phone and looked expectantly up the drive, awaiting the first glimpse of handsome Hunter behind the wheel of his truck. Every time she saw Hunter was like the first time—he still gave her the most wonderful butterflies in her stomach.

This wasn't a date. Of course it wasn't. But Skyler hoped that Hunter would like her in her dress. She stood up, put her hands on the porch rail and smiled in anticipation of seeing Hunter appear from beneath the canopy.

Hunter had taken particular care with his appearance for the cookout. He'd shaved his face, put on a clean button-down shirt and belt that displayed one of his most important trophies from his rodeo days—a large, intricately carved belt buckle. He donned a hat that wasn't covered in dirt and stains, and had almost put on cologne but decided against it.

"You look nice," Hunter said, enjoying the pretty sight of Skyler in her sundress as he approached her.

"Thank you." She gave him a twirl when she reached the bottom of the steps. "I didn't know if this was the right thing to wear."

"I think you did just fine," he said as he held out his arm for her. "May I escort you to the truck?"

She didn't hesitate to link her arm with his. "Why thank you, sir. So formal."

"That's how we do it in Montana." Hunter walked her to the passenger side of the truck. "A cookout is a big deal in these parts. I hope you're hungry," he added as he opened the truck door for her.

"Lately, all I can think about is eating."

"Then you're in luck. Because Mom and Aunt Lindsey have been cooking like they're feeding the entire town of Bozeman."

Hunter made sure she was safely in the truck, then shut the door, jogged to the other side and got behind the steering wheel.

"Do you want to take the trail to the main house or our new road?"

"The road that Hunter and Skyler built, of course," Skyler said and then she added seriously, "I really need to figure out how to get my hands on one of those skid steers."

Chapter Six

"I know why you were so insistent about opening the ranch to Skyler," Hunter said to his father.

Jock wasn't a tall man, but he was broad-shouldered and barrel-chested, and held himself with the presence of a man who had scraped and clawed his way to the top of the heap. He had a bright, thick head of white hair brushed straight back from his weathered, deeply lined face. His hawkish nose was a prominent feature of his face, as were his snapping, keenly intelligent ocean-blue eyes.

Hunter hadn't said Sarah's name out loud, but he saw Jock turn his head away and swallow several times, hard, before he said anything else.

"Well, she seems to be a nice young lady," Jock said of Skyler, who was down by the pond with Bruce, Savannah, Amanda and their pack of rescue dogs. Jock completely avoided the subject of Sarah and Hunter decided it was best to move on.

"Yes, she is," Hunter agreed.

Skyler had managed to endear herself to the family without much effort at all. Perhaps it was her pixie-like appearance, or her bright, easy laugh. Perhaps it was how kind and thoughtful she was to everyone around, including, or perhaps especially, the children in the bunch.

"Anything else to report?"

"No." Hunter crossed his arms casually in front of his body. "We've been taking it real slow."

"Good to hear."

"She's a hard worker. A real hard worker."

Jock looked at him sideways with his keen, appraising eyes. "So you've said."

"But she just doesn't have the stamina for this life."

"It takes time," his father noted. "Especially after what she's been through."

"Maybe." Hunter wasn't convinced. Skyler always gave her best effort and never gave up, but he didn't think she was built for Montana life. Not long-term, anyway.

There was a short silence between them before his father asked, "Have you spoken to Brandy McGregor lately?"

"Today," he said, not wanting to go down that road with his father. After speaking with Brandy, Hunter couldn't stop thinking about the fact that he had everything in common with Brandy and very little to say to her. In sharp contrast, at least in his mind, was the fact that he always had something he wanted to share with Skyler. Even after he had spent the day with her, he would go home and think of something he should share with Skyler the next day.

"Your mother and I both hope things are still heading in the right direction in that regard. I know Brandy's father is of a like mind."

"I'm well aware of everyone's feelings."

Hunter could see Jock getting all revved up to harp some more on the subject when his mother, Lilly, thankfully interrupted him.

"Do you think that Skyler would enjoy a pair of moccasins?" His mother held a pair of moccasins in her hands.

His mother was a proud member of the Chippewa Cree tribe and she had learned how to make authentic native clothing when she was a young girl growing up on the Rocky Boy's Indian Reservation.

"I think she would be really honored to receive those, Momo."

A beautiful woman with long, straight silver-laced raven hair, his mother was a gentle spirit who always managed to temper Jock's gruff, demanding ways. Lilly smiled and tucked the moccasins under her arm. "I will wrap them up for later."

Lilly called the family together to take a seat at the picnic tables set away from each other so each family group could safely join the event. Each picnic table had bowls and platters with the evening's fare. It was odd to eat separately from his family; everyone usually sat together in their family group. They were used to gathering every Sunday morning in the dining room in the main house.

"Look at all of this food!" Skyler slipped off her mask and sat down next to him at the table. "This is a feast!"

Hunter enjoyed watching his dinner companion load her plate like she hadn't eaten for months. She piled up mashed potatoes, corn on the cob with a pat of butter, green beans and ribs on her plate, then topped it off with a dinner roll.

"You can have seconds, you know," he said before he took a big bite out of one of his mother's famous homemade butter rolls.

Skyler nodded her response, too busy digging in to the mashed potatoes and gravy. "Mmm. Homemade mashed potatoes."

"Homemade everything," Hunter corrected.

"Lucky." Skyler loaded her fork with green beans. "I was raised almost exclusively on Chinese takeout. My mom, God love her, couldn't boil water."

Hunter noted that Skyler spoke of her mother in the past tense, but didn't want to broach a subject that could ruin the fun she was having devouring his mom's home-cooked food.

"Your family is really great," she said, in between large gulps of Savannah's fresh-squeezed lemonade. "I think I met almost all of your brothers. And their wives. And their kids. And their dogs."

Skyler did have seconds; he didn't know where she managed to put all of that food away.

"I'm stuffed," she said a while later, and put her hands on her belly, which was slightly rounded now from all the food she had eaten. "I can't remember ever eating so much. But everything was just so good."

"It's the ranch work. You're burning calories," Hunter told her. "Mom will pack up some doggy bags for you, if you want."

She wiped her mouth with a napkin. "I absolutely

want. That will be my midnight snack, breakfast, lunch and dinner tomorrow."

"Mom is going to be very pleased that you enjoyed her cooking."

Skyler leaned her elbows on the table now that they were done eating. Her eyes took in the expansive landscape before them. Beyond the pond were cows grazing in the long grass, and beyond that view was the mountain range off in the distance. Skyler sighed beside him.

"What's on your mind?"

"Nothing, really," she said quietly. "Everything."

She breathed in deeply and then let out the breath with another sigh. "I'm here. With you and your family. At Sugar Creek Ranch. It's an incredible privilege. This same time last year, I didn't think I would be alive, much less sitting here in Montana with you and your family. I'll never understand why Jock agreed to this, but I will be forever grateful."

Hunter had thought about telling Skyler about Sarah…and maybe one day he would. But for now, he just couldn't bring himself to talk about his loss with someone who hadn't known her. It was painful enough broaching the subject with Chase.

"I'm sure he had his reasons." That was all Hunter could think to say in response.

As the sun set, the family began to clean up the cookout and return to their homes. Skyler insisted on helping Lilly take all of the bowls and dishes into the kitchen, which was just off the back patio. It was the smaller of two kitchens in the main house and the one that Lilly often used to cook for outdoor family events.

"Thank you so much for inviting me," Skyler said to Jock and Lilly. "Thank you for everything, really."

"We are so happy to have you here with us," Lilly said sincerely. "I think it will be a healing summer for my son and for you."

Skyler glanced over at him curiously. Wanting to move past the moment and not have Skyler ask his mother questions about her statement, Hunter asked, "Don't you have something you wanted to give Skyler, Mom?"

Lilly's eyes lit up. "Oh, yes! Wait right here."

Lilly walked quickly back to the kitchen.

"You've been enjoying yourself?" Jock asked Skyler in his gruff, scratchy voice.

"I have."

"Good. Good." His father nodded.

That was followed by an awkward silence between the three of them until Lilly reappeared with a small box that she had managed to find time to wrap with tissue paper.

"A welcome gift." Lilly held out the box.

"Thank you so much, Mrs. Brand." Skyler accepted the box. "Should I open it now?"

"If you'd like." His mother nodded.

Skyler took the box to a nearby table, and carefully, slowly, unwrapped the paper from the box. It occurred to Hunter that Skyler must take hours to unwrap her presents at Christmastime. After the wrapping paper was carefully removed, and Skyler had folded it neatly next to the box, she lifted the lid and peeked inside.

Joy. That was the expression on Skyler's face when she saw the moccasins. "Oh, Mrs. Brand. They are beautiful."

"She made those," Hunter told Skyler, sure that she didn't realize that they had been designed, constructed and decorated with intricate beadwork by his mother's hands.

Skyler lifted one moccasin out of the box and examined the flower pattern embellishment on the toe.

"You made these?"

"It's a hobby." Lilly had always been humble about her talent, which Hunter always appreciated about her.

"Well... I hate to break up the party, but I'm going to bed," Jock said abruptly. "Young lady—you let me know if Hunter gives you any trouble."

"He's been great to me," Skyler said quickly, and if Hunter was detecting it correctly, a little defensively.

"Good night." His father waved his hand like he was swatting at a fly before he headed back to the house.

"Thank you, again, Mrs. Brand."

"Please, call me Lilly."

Hunter saw how his mother and Skyler were looking at each other—there was a genuine connection there. A mutual affection had grown quickly.

Skyler folded the moccasin carefully into the box and the put the lid back on. She seemed emotional when she said to his mom, "Lilly, I will cherish these for the rest of my life."

A week after the cookout, some of Skyler's aches and pains had subsided and she was regularly getting up in the morning before daybreak without any help from Hunter. In fact, she was usually just finishing up with the barn chores when he pulled in to pick her up for whatever list of jobs he had it in mind to complete that day. There was plenty to love about ranch life and some of it had actually lived up to her teenage fantasies. But the reality of the life was difficult for Skyler to imagine day in, day out for the rest of her life. She missed takeout and Starbucks and Bloomingdale's. She missed her friends and hanging at her father's garage.

Skyler let Zodiac and Dream Catcher out in the paddock after their morning grain and then she quickly mucked the stalls. In the beginning, she couldn't do the barn by herself, and now she could. This was a source of pride for her; she was getting stronger every day. Of course, her dad was right—she could have done the same thing in a gym. She wouldn't have done it, though—that's the truth. She hated lifting weights and riding on a stationary bike. No thank you! But lifting a fifty-pound bale of hay was doing the same thing for her as lifting weights, maybe even more.

Skyler was filling the freshly scrubbed water buckets with water to get ahead of the evening barn chores when she heard the tiniest of meows. She turned off the water and looked around.

"Hey, there." She saw a dainty gray tabby with four white sock feet and a perky, long tail sitting just outside of the barn.

The tabby had pretty green eyes and it made eye contact with her, then meowed again as if to say "hi." Skyler put down the water hose and squatted in the center aisle.

"Come here, sweet thing." She tried to coax the kitty into the barn.

Once the cat realized that she was a friend, it stood up, stretched and walked toward her, its long tail straight up in the air.

"I like to see that you are proud to be you," Skyler

said. "You walk with your tail straight up in the air. Good for you!"

The kitty cat walked right over to where she was squatting, trilled sweetly and then rubbed up against her several times. Skyler reached out her hand to let the feline sniff her fingers.

"Where did you come from?" she asked the loving creature. "You don't have a collar or a tag."

The kitty cat trilled again, threw itself down on the ground, rolled, stretched and began to purr loudly. The cat gazed at Skyler with loving eyes and curled its paws in a show of feline affection.

"You are too sweet, aren't you?" Skyler stood up. "I wonder if you're hungry? You look a little skinny."

She walked outside of the barn toward the cabin, and when she glanced behind her, the cat was following her, hugging the shrubbery and trotting to keep up.

"Okay," Skyler told the kitty. "You stay here and I will get you something to eat."

Inside the cabin, Skyler rummaged in the fridge, grabbing some leftover chicken, a plate and a bowl for water. She finished her chore quickly because she was afraid that the cat would leave if she was gone for too long.

"Oh, good!" Skyler exclaimed when she saw the gray tabby sitting on the porch. "I found something super-delicious for you."

The moment she put the chicken down, the cat began to devour it in a way that let Skyler know that it had missed some meals. Next to the plate, Skyler put down the bowl of water.

The cat seemed to think that Skyler was going to

leave and she moved away from the bowl, anxiously following her and leaving the food.

"I'm just going to sit right here next to you," Skyler explained, sitting down on the top step of the porch stairs. "You eat. I'm not going anywhere."

The kitty ate several bites, then came over to rub up against Skyler for a few moments, then went back to the food. The cat executed this ritual several times until the chicken was gone. After it had cleaned the plate, the cat gratefully climbed into Skyler's lap and began to purr loudly and contentedly, while gazing up at her with love in its eyes.

"You're welcome." Skyler smiled down at the cat. "I love you, too.

Skyler was still holding the cat as it fell asleep in her lap when Hunter pulled up.

"I have a new friend," she said to the cowboy.

"That's one of the rescue cats from the main barn," Hunter said. "She's not the strongest mouser, I can tell you that. I don't think she's caught one since we've had her."

"She was starving, I think."

"May be why she found her way down here," Hunter told her. "I've seen her try to catch all kinds of insects without any success at all."

"Does she have a name?" Skyler rubbed the top of the purring cat's head.

"I think Amanda called her Rosy at one time."

"I don't really like that name."

"Well, she seems to be yours now," Hunter said. "Name her what you want."

Skyler looked down at the slender, small-boned cat

and an image of her mother's favorite flower popped into her head. "Daisy. I think your name is Daisy."

The cat held the eye contact, blinked slowly as a means of communicating love and then meowed.

Skyler laughed and said to Hunter, "She just agreed with the name."

"Okay." The cowboy's eyebrows drew down a bit as he checked his phone. "Are you ready to go?"

"Yep." Skyler gently displaced Daisy. "Now, you stay nearby. I'll be back later."

To Hunter she said, "I need to go into town to get some cat food today."

He nodded. As they walked toward the truck, he asked, "Why Daisy?"

"It was my mom's favorite flower."

"It's just you and your dad now?"

Skyler opened the door to the truck and climbed into what she had begun to think of her spot in the copilot's chair. "My mom passed away when I was nineteen."

"Well, I'm real sorry to hear that," Hunter said.

"Thank you."

As Hunter drove them slowly through her favorite canopy of trees, she asked, "What are we doing today?"

"Worming cattle."

Hunter had been taking it easy on Skyler and he'd put some things on the back burner, but some chores couldn't be delayed and the biannual worming of the cattle was one of those chores. Hunter drove them to a large barn that serviced a smaller herd near the southern property line of the ranch.

"I love the calves with the white faces," Skyler said. "They are too cute."

"I'm not a fan."

"Why not?"

"Those babies belong to the cleanup bull. Which means we wasted a heck of a lot of money and time."

"What's a cleanup bull?"

They met each other in front of the truck. "You see, we bought some top-notch semen—"

"Bought it."

"Yes. We bought semen from what we rated as superior bulls and used that semen to artificially inseminate the females who are in heat."

"How do you do that?"

Hunter squinted at her. "You really want to know that?"

"Sure. Why not?"

"Well, you put them in a chute mainly, put on a plastic protective glove that goes up to your bicep, lift up the cow's tail, stick your hand into the canal... Heck, my arm will go in up past my elbow. Then you slide in this long rod that allows you to inject the semen and then the deed is pretty much done."

"You do that?"

"I have one of the best records in the state for using AI. But just in case the insemination process doesn't work, we use a cleanup bull to come behind us and try to get it done the old-fashioned way," Hunter explained.

"I see."

"I do, too." Hunter nodded toward the babies. "A bunch of offspring of the cleanup bull."

That made Skyler laugh, and her face lit up with humor. "All the white-faced babies belong to the cleanup bull?"

"Every last one of 'em."

"He did such a good job."

Hunter frowned at what he could only see as a giant

waste of money and time. "He brought my batting average way down."

Hunter walked to the back of the truck, pulled some premixed wormer solutions in metal spray bottles out of the bed and headed toward the corral. Skyler tagged along after him.

"Now, you've got to watch yourself in the pen with the cows. Even the babies can accidentally knock you over. They wouldn't mean to do it—they're docile creatures, but they are strong and heavy."

"I'll be careful."

"See that you are," he said sternly. "You could get killed."

Skyler saluted Hunter behind his back and followed him into the holding pen, where a small group of cows and their babies were held. The smell of cow urine and manure was so strong that it made her gag a little bit. When she stepped inside the pen, her boots sank into the mud and manure, squishing as she walked, and made a sucking noise when she lifted her foot, one at a time, out of the muck.

Carefully, she picked her way through the cows, smiling at them and talking gently to them. The babies were often curious, coming up to her and trying to nudge her.

"Hi, sweet baby." Skyler petted one of the cleanup bull's babies. "Aren't you cute?"

"We are going to herd them into this round pen and then, one by one, spray this solution on their backs, along their spines. This will help with worms and lice."

"Lice?" Skyler withdrew her hand quickly from the calf.

Hunter ignored her, focused entirely on moving the

cows into the round pen. He waved his arms and walked slowly toward them, herding them into the adjacent pen. Skyler joined him, waving her arms and herding the cows.

"They all need a bath." Skyler's face was wrinkled up from trying to avoid the smell. "Why are they all so dirty?"

"They're cows. They live outside. They get dirty."

"Ugh." She made an effort to only breathe through her mouth. "I like them very much, but they are stinky."

"It's the cow manure. It's got its own particular aroma."

"Aroma?" she asked. "That's an awfully fancy term for what I'm smelling right now."

Once they got the cows into the round pen, Hunter handed her a heavy metal spray can. "I'll get the first in line and you get the second. We'll get this done double time."

Skyler had her mouth hanging open to avoid the smell and managed to suck a fly into her mouth. She squinted her eyes and spat out the fly, then continued spitting until she was convinced that all of the residual fly germs were out of her mouth. She stood upright, looked over at Hunter, who was waiting for her to get to work, and said, "I'm ready now."

The job went quickly and, although hot and stinky, it wasn't terribly difficult. Her arm did ache from using the same spraying motion again and again and her fingers hurt from holding on to the metal spray canister. But, all in all, she was pleased with her work.

"Now what?" she asked once the last cow was treated.

"We'll let them out in the pasture."

Skyler wove her way through the mooing, slow-moving cows, and encountered a calf, the smallest of the cleanup bull's offspring.

"You know," she said, "you might be a little stinky, but I still love you."

The calf rubbed against her and nuzzled her hand. Skyler bent down to hug the calf. Then something startled the calf, perhaps the sound of Hunter opening the gate, but it bolted to the side and Skyler fell backward with a loud thud and a definitive splat.

Chapter Seven

"Uh!" Her entire backside was covered in the manure-mud mixture. Her arms, her hands, the back of her head, her neck, the back of her pants and shirt—Skyler's whole body was covered with the slimy, stinky concoction. Her hat had fallen off her head and had been pressed into the mud by the calf.

"Oh, no." Skyler pushed herself up to a standing position, her entire hand immersed in the muck. "Oh."

"Are you all right?" Hunter had seen her fall and rushed to her side.

"Am I all right?" she snapped, holding her arms and hands out from her body like she was a scarecrow. "No! I'm not all right. Look at me!"

A family of flies were buzzing around her, trying to land on her clothing and her hair. "Get away from me, flies!"

Skyler swung her arms in the air, trying to dissuade the annoying insects from landing on her. She didn't know what to do; she was a mess. A stinky, terrible mess.

"What am I going to do? How am I going to get home?" She raised her voice, squishing her way to the gate that would take her out of the paddock. "I can't get in your truck like this."

"No," Hunter said with a smirk on his face.

"Quit laughing at me!" she snapped, waving her arms to move the flies away from her.

"I'm not laughing."

"Yes, you are." She complained, "I'm covered in manure and you're laughing at me instead of helping me."

"Okay," the cowboy said, trying to look serious. "We have a couple of choices."

"Which are?" She narrowed her eyes at him impatiently.

"First, you could just ride in the back of the truck and we'll get you home that way."

"Option one, I stay covered in manure and ride in the back of your truck. I can't wait to hear option two."

"We hose you off."

"Hose me off?"

"It's an option."

Skyler couldn't stand the thought of spending one more second in her current condition. "Fine. Where's the hose?"

As they walked together back toward the barn, Hunter, she noticed, kept a safe distance from her.

"I should hug you right now," she said, swerving toward him.

Hunter laughed and tacked to the right, away from her. "I did tell you to be careful. What were you doing?"

"Hugging one of the cleanup bull's calves."

Hunter turned on the hose and let the hot water run out.

"Wash my hands and arms first. Please." Skyler held out her hands, wanting to get them clean ASAP.

The cowboy followed her directive and washed off her hands and arms first before he began the chore of rinsing off her neck and back.

"That's cold," Skyler complained again, jumping around as the frigid water hit her skin and soaked her clothing.

"I don't remember telling you to hug the calves."

"You didn't say *not* to hug them." Skyler scowled at him.

"I kind of thought that might be a given," he said, his voice laced with humor at her expense. "Cover your face with your hands so I can get the back of your head."

When he was done with his chore, her clothes were completely soaked and water dripped from her onto the ground.

"I'm soaking wet!"

"That's the physics of water," he said seriously, but she could see a pleased smirk lingering on his face.

"I can't get into your truck like this." She bemoaned her current state of being. Now she was wet and squishy; the material of her jeans was sticking to her skin, and she felt cold and clammy.

"No."

She stared up at him. "You want me to ride in the back of your truck, don't you?"

He rubbed his chin thoughtfully. "Would you mind? I just had the inside cleaned."

"I'm soaking wet here!" When she waved her arms, droplets of water flew out around her.

"I think I have a towel in the truck," he said, as if he'd just remembered.

She followed behind him, her wet socks slushing inside her boots. He fished a towel out of one of the large toolboxes in the bed of his truck.

She took it gratefully, wiping off her hands, arms and face first. She rubbed the towel over her short hair then she tried to sop up some of the water that was in her tank top and jeans.

"I still reek like cow manure." She sniffed herself.

"Yes, you do," he agreed, too readily for her liking.

"And I'm wet."

"Yes, you are."

After a second or two of thought, she said, "Take off your shirt."

"Excuse me?"

"Don't act scandalized, Hunter. You heard me. Take off your shirt and then turn around. I'm getting out of these clothes."

Hunter's lips quirked up into a half smile and his electric blue eyes sparkled with humor. She could only imagine the things he wanted to say, the sexual innuendos just dying to get out. But, to his credit, he kept them to himself.

Hunter tugged his shirttail loose from his jeans and began to unbutton his shirt. The first couple of buttons exposed the smooth skin of his chest, which was a couple of shades lighter than the skin at his neck, and then the next buttons revealed the top of his six-pack abs. *The man must do sit-ups in his spare time or something,* she thought to herself before she realized, too late, that she was blatantly staring at him while he undressed.

Hunter shrugged out of his plaid button-down shirt, then offered it to her and slowly took his own sweet time turning around.

"Thank you." She took the shirt and then scurried behind the truck.

"Oh, this feels terrible." She pulled off her tank top and bra, watching Hunter to make sure he didn't turn around and catch her in the buff.

She quickly slipped on his shirt, noticing that the shirt held Hunter's woodsy, salty scent. It was a smell that made her senses tingle in the nicest of ways. Next, she pulled off her boots and stood in her socks while she fought to push her wet jeans over her hips and thighs.

"Come on!" she grunted, tugging and pushing and struggling until she was finally able to yank off the jeans.

Her underwear was damp but not completely wet or ruined by the manure. She left them on and tied the towel around her waist like a bathing-suit wrap. Leaving her socks on, she scooped up her dirty clothes and tossed them into the bed of the truck.

"Okay," she said, coming around the side of the truck. "You can turn around now."

Hunter turned around, swept his eyes up and down her body in a way that made her believe that he was looking at her, maybe for the first time, like a woman, and not like his little sister. He smiled at her.

"You look good in my shirt."

She had to be blushing; no doubt about it. "My hat is ruined."

Hunter opened the door to his truck so she could climb in. "Don't worry about it. We'll get you a new one."

"Hunter!" A silky female voice saying his name caught his attention. "I was just talking about you."

Hunter turned around to see Brandy McGregor walking through the doors of the Four Corners Saddlery tack shop.

Brandy, her shiny brunette hair worn long and loose, framing her stunning face, made a beeline for him. She wasn't wearing a mask.

"This is a real treat. All we've had since I've gotten back were phone calls and video dates." His pretty neighbor pouted her full lips, drawing attention to them deliberately, he was sure.

Brandy threw her arms around him affectionately and hugged him tightly. "You know, Dustin has been asking me out but I told him that you had already beat him to the front of the line."

"I've been real busy." Hunter adjusted the bandanna over his mouth. He could see Skyler watching them out of the corner of his eye.

"I know." Brandy made a frustrated noise. "It's not your fault Jock's making you babysit this summer." She reached out and tugged playfully on his sleeve. "Why don't you make an excuse—tell Jock that we need your help over at Boulder Ridge and we can sneak off and have ourselves a little fun."

"What do you think of this one?" Skyler asked, modeling a hat.

Brandy's brow furrowed as her attention turned to where Skyler was standing. "Is that…?"

"That's our guest."

"Oh," his neighbor drawled. "You're calling her a *guest* now. I think I'll go over and introduce myself."

Crap.

Hunter followed Brandy over to where Skyler was trying on hats to replace the one trampled by the cleanup bull's offspring.

"Hiya." Brandy sauntered over to Skyler with her long-legged, stride. "I'm Brandy."

"Skyler."

It was a small space and even though Skyler had her mask on, Hunter was glad that she moved a step or two away from Brandy.

"I like that one," Brandy said of the hat Skyler was trying on.

"Really?" Skyler looked at her own appearance. "I wasn't sure."

"You just have to sit it back on your head a bit." Brandy pointed to her own hat.

Skyler studied her reflection and for the briefest of moments caught his gaze in the mirror. He gave her a thumbs-up.

It was a good color for her; the deep walnut-brown offset her wide lavender eyes.

"You look as adorable as a bug," Brandy gushed. "Doesn't she, Hunter?"

"It looks good on her." He agreed, eager to buy the hat and go.

"Are you enjoying your time at Sugar Creek?" Brandy asked Skyler. "Hunter has just told me oodles and oodles about you. I was hoping I'd get a chance to meet you."

"I'm enjoying it," Skyler said and Hunter noted how

toned-down her response was. Usually, Skyler was over the moon about her time in Montana and she wasn't typically afraid to express it.

"Well, I'm so glad you're enjoying your little summer vacation with us." Brandy rested her arm on his sleeve and Hunter saw Skyler's eyes dart to the hand and then back up to Brandy's face.

"It was very nice to meet you, Brandy," Skyler said after she paid for her hat. "Thank you for the hat advice," she said as she exited.

"Of course. It was my pleasure," Brandy called out as she hooked her arm with Hunter's. "Don't keep me waiting too long," she said, lowering her voice for his ears only. "I'm getting awfully lonesome. Daddy doesn't like to see me lonesome."

Hunter extracted himself from Brandy as diplomatically as he could and then he hurried out of the store, where he found Skyler waiting for him at the truck.

Something subtle in Skyler's body language signaled to him that she felt upset or uncomfortable. How did he know this about her? He just did.

"Don't forget we need to get cat food for Daisy," Skyler said in a subdued tone. She buckled herself into the seat and looked straight ahead, her new hat in her lap.

Hunter drove her to the nearest grocery store and wished that Skyler wouldn't be so quiet. He was used to her chatting his ear off, something he had thought he didn't like. Now that it was gone, he wanted it back. After a quick trip in and out of the grocery store, Hunter asked, "Anywhere else?"

"I want to go home," she said, staring out the passenger window.

"I hope you mean just back to the cabin."

It felt like a sharp, hot poker had stabbed him in the gut when he thought that Skyler might be saying that she wanted to go home to New York. When she didn't clarify her statement, Hunter decided it was best to just leave her to her thoughts. He switched on the radio and turned the music down low.

Every now and again he would look over at Skyler, wishing he knew how to break her out of her current mood. Yes, Brandy had laid it on thick back at the store; no doubt her sugary sweet tone had come off as anything but sweet to Skyler. Brandy had acted like a territorial huntress with Skyler, and he, not knowing *what* to do, like an idiot, had done *nothing*. When they pulled onto the Sugar Creek main drive, his companion still hadn't said a word to him. As he always did, he drove slowly through Skyler's favorite tree canopy, half expecting her to break the silence and point out to him, for the one hundredth time, that the sun filtering through the branches and leaves looked like fireworks in a forest-green sky. But she said nothing.

"We're home," he said, shifting into Park.

Skyler pushed the door open a bit harder than normal and jumped out of the truck. "This isn't my home, Hunter. You know it and I know it."

Skyler slammed the truck door and marched, a little tenderly still, as indignantly as she could toward the cabin.

"Damn it." Hunter held on to the steering wheel until his knuckles turned white.

Instead of doing what he knew he *should* do, he did what he *wanted* to do: he followed Skyler. He hopped out of his truck and jogged after her.

"She's not my girlfriend," he called after her.

"I didn't ask."

"But you care."

Skyler spun around and pointed her finger at him. "Don't tell me how I feel, Hunter. You don't know how I feel."

"Then why don't you tell me?"

"I hate women like that! All of that talking-out-of-both-sides-of-your-mouth, sugary-sweet, mean-girl, butter-won't-melt-in-my-mouth crap! I know that I'm short and skinny and my hair is a weird shade of red. I know I don't have big boobs or any boobs to speak of. I always have to fight against my own negative newsreel! I don't need some random stranger to deliberately try to make me feel bad about myself for no other reason than she's an overly possessive, insecure, jealous wench! If she *is* your girlfriend, you've got real questionable taste!"

"She's not my girlfriend. Not really."

Skyler breathed in deeply and bit her lip hard while she shook her head and looked up at the sky for a moment.

"'Not really' is not a status, Hunter."

"You've never asked me if I have a girlfriend."

"That's right," Skyler snapped. "And you've never asked me if I have a boyfriend."

"Do you have a boyfriend?"

Daisy appeared and trotted up the stairs, where Skyler greeted her gently and kindly. Skyler pulled the cat food out of the grocery bag and tried to rip it open. She tried several times before Hunter walked up the stairs, took the bag from her, opened it and then poured Daisy some food.

"The answer is *no*. I don't have a boyfriend." Skyler crossed her arms in front of her body. "Jeremy couldn't handle my illness so we both thought it was for the best if we broke up. So we did. End of story.

"I have to go take care of the horses now," she said, brushing by him and racing down the steps.

"I'll help you."

"I don't need your help." Skyler picked up the pace.

"Will you just stop, Skyler?" Hunter called after her, frustrated. "You're acting like a teenager."

That got her to stop. She spun around, pointed to her chest and said, "I'm not acting like a teenager. I'm acting *hurt*. I was having a great time with you and then a frickin' Victoria's Secret model, your *girlfriend*, insulted me by calling me a cute bug."

"Adorable," Hunter mumbled.

"What?"

"I think she said adorable."

"Do you want to see adorable?" Skyler asked, holding up her middle finger. "Here's adorable for you."

"Hold up." Hunter picked up his pace; he reached for her hand and caught it, but let it go when she pulled away.

"I don't even know why I feel so mad at you right now." She turned to face him.

"Because you care."

He could see the hurt in her eyes and he was sorry for it. The wires had just gotten crossed between them. They had been developing a friendship—a working relationship—and somewhere along the line, something else had developed between them. He felt it, and now he was certain that she was feeling it, too.

"What if I do?" she asked with a shrug.

He took a step toward her, holding the eye contact. "What if *I* do?"

Disbelief—that was what he read in her large lavender eyes.

"I'm sorry about what happened with Brandy—I didn't know how to react so I did nothing. I was an idiot."

Silence was her response.

"But she isn't my girlfriend. She's home from graduate school because of the pandemic and we've been talking. That's it."

"That's a lot."

"Not to me," Hunter said, exasperated. "I'm much more interested in what's going on right here. Right now. Between us."

"The horses are waiting."

"Let them wait." Hunter had a demanding tone in his voice.

Skyler's arms were crossed in front of her body, but she didn't leave the conversation.

Hunter dipped his head down, lowered and softened his voice.

"I feel a certain way about you, Skyler."

She didn't move; she didn't say a word. She listened, keenly, to what he was saying.

"I don't know exactly what this is, but I want to figure it out." He hooked his fingers with hers; he wanted to test the waters. Would she accept this physical touch from him?

Instead of pulling away, she actively held on to his fingers.

As he held her fingers, he held her gaze.

"I feel connected to you, Skyler." The words were coming out more from his heart than his head. "Connected in a way that doesn't make sense to me, in a way that I've never quite felt before. If you don't feel the same way about me, then tell me now and I'll get one of my brothers to take over for me…"

Skyler's breath caught as she took a sharp intake of oxygen. He didn't need her to say the words; the raw emotion he read in her eyes was enough for him.

Hunter acted on the feeling and kissed her. Still holding on to her hand, he pressed his lips to hers, being gentler and more patient than he had ever been before.

Her lips were soft and the kisses hesitant, but so very sweet.

Hunter took her face in his hands. "You are so beautiful, Skyler."

He read the rejection of that compliment in her eyes.

"You are." He dropped butterfly kisses on her lips. "My lovely, unusual, magical, unexpected angel."

Chapter Eight

Skyler's moral compass was temporarily rendered out of order by the fact that Hunter Brand was kissing her and declaring that he had feelings for her. It was a scene that could be taken out of hundreds of her teenage daydreams. But then reality set it and her moral compass lurched back to center.

"That was a lousy thing to do." She pushed on his chest and took a step back from him. "Brandy is waiting for your call, remember? You're playing both sides against the middle, Hunter. No woman deserves that."

"Is that what this is all about?" Hunter asked, frustrated. "The fact that I've been talking to Brandy?"

Skyler didn't respond; she turned on her heel and headed toward the barn.

"I'll take care of this right now," Hunter said.

She turned around. "What are you doing?"

He held up his hand to stop her from interrupting him while he held the phone up to his ear.

"Hey," he said after the call connected. "Yeah, it's always good to see you, too, Brandy."

Skyler crossed her arms in front of her body; Hunter had actually called Brandy.

"Look," he said, "if you want to go out with Dustin, don't say no on account of me. I think we're better off as friends."

Hunter glanced up at her while he listened to Brandy on the other end of the line. He nodded wordlessly and then he said, "I understand. You take care."

The cowboy put away his phone and walked over to her with long-legged strides. In truth, she didn't know how to react—she didn't know what to do, so she did nothing. She stood her ground and waited.

"That's done," he said dispassionately.

"Just like that." It was both a statement and a question.

"Just like that."

"And how did Brandy feel about—" she snapped her fingers "—'just like that'?"

"She thinks I'm a jackass and she told me not to call her anymore."

"Huh," Skyler said.

Hunter breathed in deeply and let it out with a frustrated noise. "Brandy collects cowboys like a sport. I'm no more important to her than she is to me.

"Now..." he said, dipping his head down, his eyes scanning her face with an appreciation that she couldn't ignore. This man—this cowboy of her dreams—returned her interest, her attraction. "Can we focus on what is going on, right here, right now, between us?"

* * *

It had been completely unexpected, Hunter's declaration of feelings. He had always been polite, solicitous and teasing, but only once, when she had donned his shirt, had she ever sensed that he saw her as an attractive woman.

The kiss. Her mind was always returning to that wonderful, romantic, tender kiss. She had always imagined how his lips would feel if he pressed them against hers. Now she didn't have to wonder. Because it had actually happened. So new was this development between Hunter and her that she hadn't even shared it with Molly. In all the years they had been friends, this was the first time that she had wanted to keep something just for herself. She would, of course, tell Molly—she would tell Molly before she told anyone else. For now, she wanted to savor it, to make it last. She worried, with a tinge of superstition that she had always possessed, that to speak about it aloud would be to risk making it disappear.

"I've got the horses saddled for us." Hunter walked up to where she was sitting on the porch steps with Daisy.

It was nighttime and the moon was full, washing the treetops with a buttery yellow hue. While they spent the day working together, there was no mention of the kiss the day before; there was no mention of the feelings Hunter had confessed he had for her. They kidded and joked and teased, but they kept it light, which suited Skyler just fine. Cancer had focused her mind singularly on the present, but she was very much aware of the future. At best, this would be a summer romance with Hunter. She had a real life back home; it was a smaller, more compact, more mundane life in the city. But it was hers. And there was her dad to think about. Without her, he would be alone. She *was* his family. Unlike Hunter, she didn't have multiple siblings and an extended family in the state. For years, ever since her mother passed away, it had just been the two of them.

"I've never ridden at night before." She picked up Daisy, hugged her, kissed her on the head and then set her down gently on the porch.

Hunter put one boot on the bottom step, leaned forward, held out his hand to her and said, "Our first date should be memorable."

"A moonlight ride." She took his hand. It was the most romantic of first dates. How many women got to say that they rode horses with a dreamy cowboy during a full moon? This would be a moment seared into her heart forever, she was certain of that. Jeremy had actually been a very romantic boyfriend, but not even he could manage a moonlight ride in Montana.

He held on to her hand as they took their time walking to the barn; the air was so clean and crisp that she had to breathe it in deeply several times.

"Are you okay?" Hunter asked.

"I'm perfect." She sighed. "The air smells so good right now."

She saw Hunter take a couple of small sniffs of the air out of her peripheral vision.

"It does?"

She laughed. "Yes. It does. It smells like a Christmas candle. Like pine and wood."

Hunter squeezed her hand in an affectionate gesture. "I don't smell all that, but if you do, and you like it, then I'm glad."

"I do and I do," she said and then breathed in deeply again.

Hunter gave her a leg up on Dream Catcher's back; she had ridden regularly since she had been in Montana, which allowed her to feel more comfortable and confident in the saddle. Recently, her inner thigh muscles had stopped being sore and most of the blisters on her feet had cleared up. Lately, she had been walking like a normal human instead of a rickety robot bolted together by rusty nails.

"Wow," she said, knowing that she still used that word way too much. But how else could she describe the feeling of being on Dream Catcher's back with only the light of the moon to guide her?

"It's a different feeling, isn't it?" Hunter rode up beside her on Zodiac.

"If I could be speechless, I would be speechless right now," she said, her heart beginning to race with excitement and nervousness. "What if there's something out there that spooks the horses?"

"You can handle it," he responded, trying to reassure her. "I wouldn't risk this if I thought you would get injured."

He had been very protective of her ever since she passed out on the first day. If Hunter believed that she could do this, then she had to find a way to believe in her own ability, too.

Hunter pointed Zodiac toward a familiar trail, one that they had ridden together many times. It was so different riding in the dark; her eyes had adjusted and she could make out the basic shape of Hunter's body astride Zodiac up ahead. Through the branches of the trees and the thick summer leaves, flashes of that buttery yellow light from the full moon filtered through, looking like a black-and-gold kaleidoscope that changed and shifted and morphed into something even more beautiful with every step Dream Catcher took. Because of her inability to use her sight, her other senses were heightened. She was keenly aware of the sounds around her—the creaking of the leather, the soft brushing of her jeans against the saddle, the distinctive sound of Dream Catcher's hooves as they hit the ground and the cracking of dried twigs as they snapped beneath the pressure of the horses' hooves.

"You okay back there?" She saw Hunter as a black outline, which changed as he turned his head to look back at her. "You're awfully quiet."

"I feel like I'm in church. Like I need to whisper."

"You do feel a bit closer to God out here, like this," he agreed.

Skyler rested the hand holding the reins on the saddle horn and the other on her thigh. She worked to relax her torso, letting the natural rhythm of the horse's walking gait move her hips back and forward.

"I want to close my eyes," she said quietly.

"Then do it," Hunter said. "Dream knows where to go. Trust her to take care of you."

Skyler followed her instincts and closed her eyes. It felt like she was engaging in one of those trust-building exercises that her company sponsored every year—where she would have to allow herself to fall backward into the awaiting hands of her coworkers, trusting that they wouldn't let her fall.

"Ah." She breathed out the sound of wonder. "I hear so much more—I *feel* so much more."

She mapped the trail in her mind and knew that they

were approaching a corner. After the corner, a small bridge would take them over a stream. Skyler heard the water rushing over the rocks, gurgling and bubbling, and then she heard Zodiac's hooves *clop, clop, clop* on the wood of the bridge. Skyler opened her eyes and blinked several times, trying to hurry up the process of adjusting her eyes. Her eyes adjusted just in time for her to see the edge of the railing for the bridge, and down below the bridge, glimpses of white as the water rushed by. Never in her life had she experienced this feeling of innate freedom, joy, empowerment and bliss. She was smiling broadly and her soul felt like singing. She was happy, content and so grateful to Hunter for always pushing her in the best way.

She wanted to share the feeling with him. "I feel so happy."

She heard Hunter chuckle. "So far I'm not doing too bad for our first date."

That was an understatement—how could any man in her future top this? They would have to rent out the top of the Empire State Building or something outrageous like that. She didn't share this fact with Hunter—no sense laying it on too thick. It was enough that she knew that this was a highlight of her life. Not even in her wildest teenage imaginings of her first date with *the* Hunter Brand from *Cowboy Up!* had she imagined this.

At the edge of the trail, they entered a clearing and the full moon came into view. In the expansive Montana sky, the moon loomed so large and bright that she reached out her hand to touch it.

Hunter stopped Zodiac so she could pull beside him. "This is what I wanted you to see."

Her hand on her heart, she felt tears come to her

eyes at the beauty she was bearing witness to. First her mother had been diagnosed with congestive heart failure, changing the course of her life. She had quit college, taken a job with Molly at a nationwide insurance company and done her best to take care of her mother until her dying day. And just when she thought she had gotten her life stable and her father was sort of back to some semblance of normalcy, they were both thrown back into the fight by her cancer diagnosis. A lung cancer caused by a genetic mutation in young adults, like her, who'd never touched a cigarette.

Tears rolled unchecked down her cheeks and she tried to hide them from Hunter, but a telltale catch in her breathing brought his attention to her.

"Skyler?" He said her name with a concerned undertone. "Are you crying?"

Skyler wiped her tears away with her hand and nodded wordlessly.

"What's wrong? What did I do?"

She shook her head. "You didn't do anything wrong, Hunter. I'm not crying because I'm sad. I'm crying because I'm happy."

"Happy crying?"

The way he asked the question, as if he had asked about something so confusing and foreign to him that he could have been asking her about an alien landing, made her laugh through her tears.

"It happens. To me at least," she explained. "Glorious things make me cry."

Hunter reached for her hand; she put her hand into his, noting the rough patch on his palm where a callus had developed. She had forgotten her gloves and he had given her his; that callus was one of the results of that gesture of care he had shown her. She rubbed her thumb over that callus like she would a worry stone, and they sat together, basking in the light of the moon, while she silently added this special moment to her ever-growing list of blessings.

"Are you ready to move on?" he asked her quietly after many minutes had ticked by. "There's more I want to show you."

Hunter led her to a field of fireflies—acres and acres of tiny green lights blinking like nature's very own holiday decoration.

"Christmas in July," Skyler said in wonder.

"I've never thought of it that way before."

"It reminds me of holiday lights. But there are thousands and thousands of them."

After the field of fireflies, he turned them back into the woods, taking them on the familiar path for her comfort. He always seemed mindful of her experience of his world; he always wanted her to feel safe and secure with him. And she did. She truly did.

"What is that smell?" Skyler closed her eyes for a moment to focus on her nose. "Vanilla! It smells like a sugar cookie. What is that?!"

"Clematis." She could hear the pleasure in his voice. He had surprised her again and he was enjoying his success. "They bloom in late spring and early summer. We have caught them just in time. Soon the scent will be gone."

They ended their moonlight ride at Hunter's stake, Oak Tree Hill. They let the horses graze nearby as they walked, hand and hand, by the light of the moon, to the grand, overarching ancient canopies that were the crowning glory of the property.

"I thought I would start a campfire. Maybe make some s'mores."

"Do you make a mental note of everything I say?" She laughed and leaned into his body. She had mentioned wanting to make s'mores and now it was coming true. It really did seem like to her that Hunter was trying to make all of her Montana dreams come true.

"I try," he said a bit sheepishly.

"You succeed, Hunter," she said, squeezing his hand.

She found a comfortable spot on a bench carved from a log harvested from one of the oak trees that had died. Hunter had cut down that tree with his own hands and then carved a lovely bench for his fire from it.

The bench had a sweet, woody scent and was smooth to the touch as she ran her hands over the surface. Hunter had taken much care with the bench; it was a piece of art, really.

Hunter kneeled down by the firepit, tossed some kindling on the fire and then struck a match and tossed it onto the kindling. He joined her on the two-seater bench; he took her hand and, silently, they watched the fire grow.

"I love this bench," she said to him. "It's actually comfortable."

"You're the first person to sit on it with me."

She looked at him, surprised. "That's not true, is it?"

He nodded, staring into the fire. "I wouldn't lie to you."

"I feel..." She searched her mind for the correct feeling. "Honored."

Then, to break the mood, as she'd always tried to do with her father when her mother was at her sickest, she added, "And hungry. Honored and hungry."

Her attempt at humor had the desired effect—the cowboy laughed. "Let me go grab the fixin's." He stood up. "Don't go anywhere."

She lifted her arms and looked around. "Where am I going to go? I'm a captive audience."

"Exactly." He grinned at her mischievously.

Looking at Hunter never got old; she loved everything that made him *him*—the cleft in his chin, the black-brown hair that he kept cropped short, the strong, straight nose and those sexy, intense, ocean-blue eyes. He had only gotten more handsome with age, and every time—every single time—she looked at him, she felt her heart thump a little bit harder. What she couldn't quite figure is what exactly he wanted with her.

She had always felt puppy love for this man—at least the TV version of him. Now she had a full-blown adult crush on him that was an undeniable fact. But Hunter having feelings for her beyond friendship didn't make logical sense to her. And that wasn't to say that she didn't feel worthy; her illness had given her the gift of self-esteem. She admired her own strength and she was grateful for the vessel she occupied, albeit petite and flat-chested with oddly colored hair that was now sprouting back out of her scalp. She liked herself…she loved herself. She fought the negative demons like anyone else, but she had a keen appreciation for who she was and what she brought to any relationship. And still, Hunter Brand's interest was a bit of a mystery. She realized now that she was a bit more of city mouse than a country mouse; she was like a hothouse flower found in a field of wildflowers—beautiful but oddly placed.

"Graham crackers, chocolate, marshmallows."

"What else could a girl want?" She clasped her hands together in front of her.

"A little company from a cowboy?" He sat down beside her and put the food on the ground in front of them.

"Okay." She smiled and laughed. "That, too."

They had laughed for hours together up on his hill. Hunter couldn't remember laughing with a woman the way he laughed with Skyler. She amused him; she challenged him. She made him think. And she made him see his world through a different lens—a lens that he was beginning to like very much.

"How come I'm always stuffing my face around you?" Skyler put her hands on her stomach with a groan. "I swear I've never acted so much like a swine in front of anyone else."

"You have no idea how much I love that about you," Hunter said. "A ranch woman needs to eat to keep up her strength."

Skyler sat up a little straighter, her chin raised. "A ranch woman. I'm adding that to my résumé."

"You should."

"Cow wormer." She laughed. "Fence tearer-downer."

"You've developed a whole new skill set in a short amount of time." He leaned forward to stoke the fire.

"I really have! I'm not sure how handy this will be in the customer-service arena when my leave of absence is over." She shrugged with a self-effacing smile. "But you never know what life might bring."

Hunter sat back. "Customer service. That doesn't really seem like you."

"I think I'll have just one more," she said when she saw him packing up the food.

He smiled as he skewered two of the giant marshmallows on the stick and held it over the fire to toast. "I'm going to make you the best s'more of the evening."

Skyler rubbed her knees with her hands in anticipation. "I don't mind my job, really. I get to help people resolve their problems. I get yelled at a lot, but those are the ones I feel most proud of when they hang up the phone because I feel like I really cared about finding a solution for them." She addressed his earlier comment about her job. "I took what I could get when I quit college. Mom was sick and Dad needed to keep working full-time at the garage so they wouldn't lose their medical benefits. My income helped make a dent in some of the bills."

Her voice softened a bit at the memory. "I don't regret it—leaving college. I got to be there for the most important woman in my life and I got to be there for my dad, too."

Hunter wanted to ask her about her mother's illness, but she hadn't offered it and he decided not to pry.

"Do you ever think of going back? To college?" he asked instead while he pressed the perfectly toasted marshmallows on top of four squares of milk chocolate and two pieces of graham crackers. He stuck his creation back over the fire to melt the chocolate and then quickly removed it.

"Actually, I had already been accepted to the City College of New York for premedical studies and then—" she shrugged "—my body had other plans for me."

Hunter wished he knew the right words to say when Skyler shared something so personal with him, and yet he didn't. He felt woefully inadequate when it came to feelings and emotions. His special skill set was distraction and deflection. So that's what he did now.

"Madam—" he presented the s'more to Skyler "—your dessert is served."

"My dessert for after my dessert?"

He loved the sound of her laugh, the way her smile always reached her wide, unusual blue-lavender eyes. Perhaps that was her special appeal to him: she did everything to the fullest, even smiling. Even laughing.

"Mmmm." Skyler's eyes got even bigger after the first bite. She had marshmallow and chocolate on the corner of her mouth and it was still there after she popped in the final bite.

"That was the best s'more of my life," she told him.

Acting on impulse, Hunter kissed the corner of her mouth, tasting the sweetness of the marshmallow and chocolate.

Skyler's eyes widened again and she edged away from him for the briefest of moments before she leaned in toward him and kissed him on the lips. He slipped his hand behind her neck and deepened the kiss. He caught her breath in his mouth, tasted the sweetness on her tongue.

"I like the way you taste," he murmured against her lips.

"I like the way you smell." Skyler scooted closer to him, pressing her small, pert breasts against his body. He wanted to touch her; he wanted to feel the silkiness of her skin. She was soft in all of the places he wanted to fill with his hardness.

He easily scooped her up and put her on his lap. He knew, without any doubt, that she could feel his desire for her. Skyler leaned her body into him, took his face in her hands and returned his kisses.

He didn't want to go too far. He *didn't* want to go

too fast. But, God, he didn't want to stop. She was so light and airy in his arms; her kisses were so sweet and sincere. He wanted more of Skyler—he wanted her for always.

Chapter Nine

Always. The last thought that came into his mind—the thought of forever had the same effect as if someone had thrown a bucket of ice water on his head.

Hunter stood up with her in his arms, gently set her down on her feet and took a step back from her. In the process, he almost fell backward over the log bench he had carved for two.

Skyler looked as stunned and confused as he felt.

"I don't want to ruin this by going too fast, Skyler."

She nodded. "I've always been the tortoise, not the hare."

His body was still hard and aching for her, and he willed the bulge in his pants to go down.

"Do you mind if I use your bathroom?" she asked. "My hands are all sticky."

"Be my guest."

He was grateful that she left him in that moment; he

shifted his erection in his pants and felt relieved that it was starting to subside. He had always wanted to be a married man, but he had never found a woman who made him want to commit. In his heart, he had always known it would be a woman born in Montana, raised on a cattle ranch, like he'd been. How could Skyler— a spritelike woman from New York, be making him think of forever for the first time? Could Skyler really fit in with ranch life for the long haul? Would she last decades of harsh Montana winters, with one day running into the next without a break from the work? This life wasn't a vacation and there was rarely an opportunity to have a vacation from the life.

"Thank you." Skyler reappeared with a shy smile on her face, her arms intertwined like a pretzel in front of her body.

While she was in his trailer, he had doused the fire and laid out a blanket for them to admire the moon. He wasn't ready to ride back to the cabin; he wasn't ready for the night to end. He hoped she felt the same way.

"Come join me." He gestured to the blanket. "We'll let our food settle before we ride back."

"I like that plan."

She joined him on the blanket and they lay on their backs, looking up at the full moon above. They held hands, their shoulders and their booted feet touching.

"This was the best first date of my life," she whispered.

"This was the best first date of my life," he replied, echoing the sentiment.

After a while, she curled on her side, rested her head on his shoulder and her hand over his heart. He breathed in the scent of her and hugged her more closely to his body as her breathing changed and he realized she had fallen asleep in his arms. The end of summer would arrive eventually How would he ever be able to let his quirky, enchanting angel go?

Skyler awoke with a crick in her neck and a pain in her back from a jagged rock under the blanket.

"Oh." She winced as she sat upright, blinking her eyes against the daylight. She hadn't slept this late since the first week at the ranch.

"Hunter?" Skyler looked around, wincing every time she turned her neck to the right too far. She stood up stiffly, holding her neck, and continued to look around.

"Hunter?" The fire was going in the pit and there was a pot of coffee cooking, so he couldn't have gone too far.

Just then, the door to the trailer swung open and a refreshed Hunter came through the door balancing a load of eggs, bacon and biscuits.

"Good morning." He shot her that famous, dimpled smile of his. "How'd you sleep?"

"Like a rock." She leaned backward to stretch out the kinks. "And literally *on* a rock."

He laughed and squatted down, setting a well-worn cast-iron skillet on a grate over the fire.

"I didn't have the heart to wake you last night." He poured her a cup of coffee. "Black is the best I can do."

Skyler hunkered down on the bench, wiped the sleep out of her eyes and yawned while holding the tin cup filled with steaming coffee in her free hand. "Wow. That's a first. Sleeping outside under the stars."

In the arms of my dream cowboy.

"Did I snore?" she asked.

"Not really." He cracked the eggs into the skillet. "But you do talk in your sleep."

"I do not."

"Find me a bible." He winked at her with a grin.

"Okay." She slurped the hot coffee, hating the bitter taste but wanting the caffeine to wake her up. "What did I say?"

"Mumble, mumble, mumble... Hunter."

She stopped slurping, her mouth hanging open. "No. I. Did. Not."

"You did." He took a spatula and started to scramble the eggs.

"And, of course, you had to tell me."

"Heck yeah." He laughed, shifting his weight. "Great ego boost for me."

She took another sip of the coffee. "Do you really need an ego boost, Hunter?"

Hunter smiled at her with another wink. "Everyone can use a good ego boost, every now and again. Even washed-up reality TV stars."

Skyler was surprised that he brought up the show; he had always reacted so badly when she mentioned it that she had stopped mentioning *Cowboy Up!* entirely out of respect for his feelings.

"Especially washed-up reality TV stars," he added as an aside.

"Maybe I said, 'hunt.' Maybe I was dreaming about being on a safari." She put her coffee cup on the ground.

"No." He gave a little shake of his head. "It was 'Hunter,' loud and clear."

"Fine, *Hunter*," she said, overemphasizing his name as she stood up. "Mind if I use your bathroom?"

"Mi casa es tu casa." He kept right on cooking the eggs.

By the time she returned, he had cooked up the eggs, the bacon and the biscuits in the same skillet, and she felt more human for having washed her face and rinsed out her mouth with mouthwash.

"Hmm. Smells good." She returned to her spot, her stomach growling in response to the delicious smells emanating from the campfire.

"Gonna taste good, too."

He handed her a plate and fork and she dived right in. Hunter always made her feel good about her appetite—it was something that reminded her of her father.

"What about all of our morning chores?" she asked between bites.

"I put a call in to Bruce—he took care of it."

"It's twenty-four seven here, isn't it?"

Hunter nodded while he chewed. "That's the life."

"A hard life," Skyler noted, putting her empty plate on the bench next to her. "It's not like I imagined."

It seemed that Hunter's body stiffened beside her, but he didn't say anything in response; he just listened to her.

"Where are the horses?" Skyler suddenly sat more upright, looking around. "Did they run away?"

Hunter finished his breakfast, stood up and stacked her plate on top of his. "They're probably on the other side of those trees."

"I think I'll take a walk. See if I can spot them. Okay with you?"

"Do your thing." Hunter headed toward the trailer. "I'll meet you out there after I clean up."

"Would you rather I help you?"

"I've got this."

"Okay." She stood up. "Thank you for breakfast. You are an excellent fireside cook."

"I'll have to teach you."

"That would be a neat trick. My father wouldn't believe it."

While she walked through the field, running her hand over the tips of the tall grass, watching where she was stepping to avoid snakes or other creatures, her father was on her mind. She missed him; when she returned to the cabin, she would call him for a long chat.

She stopped to take pictures of the landscape, always wanting to keep her social media updated with new content for all of the people who were following her on her journey. Many of the people who had donated to make this trip possible were "liking" and commenting on her pictures and videos. It made her feel connected to home; it made her feel connected to all of those people who had sacrificed something—even if it had been a dollar—to make her dream come true.

"There you are!" She stopped and snapped photographs of Zodiac and Dream Catcher nibbling on some leaves from some fallen branches.

After she got the picture she wanted, she walked more quickly toward her equine friends. She had grown to love them both and was happy to see that they'd fared well overnight.

Dream Catcher saw her, nickered and walked toward her, no doubt hoping that Skyler would have a molasses treat in her pocket. Zodiac slowly followed the mare and that's when Skyler noticed something odd about Zodiac's gait. He was walking oddly, swinging his head to the right while his left hind leg was swinging outward.

The only thing that popped into her mind was that he looked drunk.

"Oh, no." Her stomach clenched. She ran up to meet him. "What's wrong, Zodiac? What's wrong with you?"

She checked his legs and didn't see any sign that a snake had bitten him—the skin wasn't broken and there wasn't any swelling. But there was definitely something seriously wrong with him. Shaking with nerves, she fished her phone out of her pocket and tried to call Hunter.

"Pick up! Pick up!" she yelled at the phone. "Damn it, Hunter! Pick up the phone!"

When he didn't answer the phone, she gave up and started to run toward the campsite. Like her US Marine father had taught her, in order to cover long distances without tiring out, she jogged fifty steps and then speed-walked fifty steps, over and over again, until she was in yelling distance of the trailer.

"Hunter!" she gasped, holding her side and out of breath. "Hunter!"

The cowboy came out of the trailer; he must have spotted her.

"What's wrong?" He raced to her side.

"Zodiac! There's something wrong with him. He's walking like he's drunk. Did he have a stroke? Can a horse have a stroke?"

"No. They aren't built that way," Hunter said as he helped her over to the bench and made sure she was settled. Then he grabbed his phone, which he'd left by the campfire, and called his brother Liam, who was a large-animal veternarian.

"I may need you out here ASAP," he said into the phone. "Where are you now?"

Skyler watched Hunter's face carefully while he spoke to his brother. After a moment, Hunter nodded his head.

"Just be on standby for me, brother. I'm going to see if I can lead him back to camp. Could be snakebit."

Hunter ended the call and she watched him grab a lead rope. "Liam is thirty minutes away. I want you to stay right here and wait for me."

Skyler put her head in her hands and prayed for Zodiac. "Please, God. Please. Please let Zodiac be okay. *Please.*"

Hunter made his way to the horses as quickly as he could. The way Skyler had described Zodiac's behavior made him immediately alarmed. She wasn't one for hysterics or exaggeration. There was something seriously wrong with Zodiac, and from past experience Hunter knew there was no guarantee that he would survive.

"Hey, boy." Hunter approached Zodiac cautiously. The horse was still grazing, so that was a plus. If the horse was still eating and defecating, that was a sign that his systems were still functioning somewhat normally.

Hunter hooked the lead rope to the horse's halter and coaxed him forward. When the horse took an awkward, disjointed couple of steps forward, Hunter immediately saw what Skyler had described.

"What the hell?" He searched Zodiac's body, looking for swelling or a sign of snakebite, but he couldn't find anything.

"Come on, bubba." Hunter started the long walk back to the campsite. Dream Catcher kept on grazing, but when they got too far away for her liking the mare snorted and trotted after them.

Skyler met them halfway. "What's wrong?"

"I'm not sure," he confessed, wishing he had a better answer. "Stay back away from him."

She listened to him and backed away from the gelding that was still walking with an odd gait, throwing his head to the right and his left hind leg outward.

"I need to help," Skyler said to him.

"Get Dream Catcher's lead rope and ground-tie her." Hunter understood her need to keep busy. He pulled his phone out of his pocket and called Liam.

"Bring your trailer," Hunter told him. "Get here as soon as you can."

Hunter shot a quick video of Zodiac walking and texted it to Liam.

"He's coming?"

Hunter nodded. "Now all we can do is wait."

"And pray."

He rubbed his hand over his forehead and down his face. She was right about that. All they could do was wait and pray. But Hunter had a bad feeling in his gut. He didn't share his thoughts with Skyler, but there was no way to predict if Zodiac would ever make it back to base camp.

Liam was taller, blonder and had a lighter complexion, but the eyes were the exact same ocean-blue as Hunter's eyes.

"Did you see anything out in the field?" Liam had dropped everything to come to their aid.

"No." Hunter shook his head. "Not that I could see. Not anything that would cause this."

"They were just eating some leaves off of dead branches when I first saw them." Skyler stood away from Zodiac as Hunter had asked her to do.

Both Liam and Hunter snapped their heads up and looked at her. "What branches?" Hunter asked.

"They were over at the edge of the woods," she explained. "They were both eating them."

"Damn." Hunter exchanged a look with his brother.

"Can you show us the branches?" Liam asked her.

Liam rolled the windows down in his truck and they rode together through the field to the edge of the woods.

"Right there." She pointed to the felled branches.

"Is that a cherry tree?" Hunter pointed to a large tree to the left of the branches.

"I think so." Liam shut off the engine and hopped out of the truck.

Skyler followed the men a couple of paces back. Hunter and his brother examined the branches and the leaves.

"The wind must've knocked these branches loose." Liam looked up at the tree. "The leaves are fairly fresh."

"Damn." This was Hunter's response.

"What is it?" she asked impatiently, not understanding what the tree limbs or the leaves had to do with Zodiac's drunken state.

Hunter and Liam headed back to where she was standing.

"Zodiac was eating those leaves?" Liam asked. "You're sure?"

She nodded. "Both of them were."

"But Dream Catcher is fine," Hunter pointed out.

"Maybe she only ate the branches, not the leaves," Liam countered.

"Will you *please* tell me what's going on?" Skyler raised her voice to gain their attention.

"That's a cherry tree," Liam explained. "If the limbs are disturbed..."

"The leaves produce arsenic."

"Cyanide?!" Skyler exclaimed. "Like the poison? *That* cyanide?"

Hunter nodded, his face grim.

Skyler followed them back to the truck, her gut churning with acid and upset. Nothing in Liam's or Hunter's demeanor gave her comfort.

"What does this mean for Zodiac?" she asked.

"I'm not sure," Liam told her with honesty ringing in his tone. "Most of these horses are found dead in the pasture."

Skyler had to swallow back bile that jumped up her throat. She pressed her hands onto her stomach and closed her eyes.

"And the others?" she asked, knowing that she might not like the unvarnished truth she was about to receive from Liam.

"The others are usually put down because they are too dangerous. They can't control their body and could accidentally kill anybody nearby."

"Oh, God." The words tumbled out of her mouth.

Hunter reached back behind the seat, grabbed her hand and squeezed her fingers. "Liam isn't saying that we're there yet."

"Not yet." Liam stopped the truck, shut off the engine and they all jumped out. "We need to see if we can get him in the trailer. If we can, I'll take him to Triple K so I can keep a closer eye on him."

"You're not just taking him away to put him down, are you?" Skyler was shaking with adrenaline and fear.

"No." Liam looked her dead in the eye. "If we have to put him down, we will tell you."

They tried for an hour to get Zodiac in the trailer.

He was normally an "easy loader," according to Hunter, but he wouldn't load.

"His perception is too far off. He doesn't trust his own footing," Liam said. "We can try to lead him back to the cabin or we can treat him here."

"I don't have a shelter in place. No water other than the stream down there by the cherry tree," Hunter countered.

"Then we've got to walk him back," Liam said. "That's the best of the bad choices I'm afraid."

It was an arduous journey back to the cabin. Skyler road Dream Catcher and brought up the rear while Hunter led Zodiac in the lead position. It was painful to watch Zodiac swerving and lurching, uncertain of his footing. They stopped often, grateful that the gelding was still interested in eating and drinking; he had also stopped to relieve himself. Taken together, there was some reason to be hopeful. Skyler had learned that holding on to hope mattered. In fact, it could save a life. It had hers.

It was a relief to see the cabin come into view. They had made it. Zodiac had made it so far. Hunter got the gelding into his stall while Skyler untacked Dream Catcher, rinsed her off with the hose and then put her in her stall. Soon after they arrived, Liam came down from the main house.

"I've made some calls and I've done some research."

Standing next to Hunter, she waited to hear the news.

"No one really knows what to do in this situation. Like I said, most horses don't make it this far."

"Zodiac is a miracle horse," she interjected.

"So far," Liam agreed, but his tone was tempered and cautious. "There is a medicine that has been reported in the literature to work, but I've called around and I can't get my hands on it."

Liam continued. "There have been some studies that report some therapeutic success of vitamin B12 helping if the case of poisoning is mild and caught early."

"That sounds like us." Hunter had his arms crossed, his legs braced apart.

"I can give him B12 and we'll keep him in the stall for now."

"No pasture time?" Hunter asked.

"For now," Liam said. "We are in unchartered territory here. That's all I can say."

Liam treated Zodiac and then left them with a promise to return the next day to check on him and give him another round of B12. Skyler hung over the stall gate, not wanting to leave the handsome gelding alone.

Hunter came up behind her and put his hands on her shoulders. "I'm going to hang around for the next couple of days. There's a cot in Liam's shop."

Skyler turned in his arms, wrapped her arms around his waist and rested her head on his chest, comforted by the strong beat of his heart. Hunter held her tightly in his arms and kissed the top of her head.

"You will stay in the cabin," she told him.

"If that's what you want."

She wrapped her arms more tightly around his body and closed her eyes. "Do you think he will be all right, Hunter?"

"I don't know, Skyler." She could count on Hunter to tell her the truth even if she wanted to hear a lie. "We will just have to wait and see."

Chapter Ten

That night, Hunter had to insist that she leave the barn to get some rest. "Zodiac needs you to be strong for him."

Skyler rubbed the gelding's neck one last time and pressed a kiss on his velvety soft nose. "I will see you in the morning. You will feel better tomorrow. And everyone will know that you are a miracle horse."

"I'm going to let you sleep in tomorrow morning." Hunter had his arm around her waist.

"I do think I need to rest."

"Do not go into Zodiac's stall, Skyler. Promise me. He wouldn't mean to hurt you."

"I won't," she said. "I promise."

They took turns in the single bathroom, each showering off the dirt of the day. They ate a quiet meal, both too tired and too worried to banter. Hunter found some extra pillows and bedding inside an old leather steamer trunk that pulled double duty as a coffee table. While Skyler washed the dishes, Hunter made up the couch.

"I've got to get some sleep." Hunter yawned, his eyes heavy-lidded.

She stepped into his arms and hugged him good-night.

"You won't be mad if I go to bed so early?"

"No." She left his embrace. "You need to get your rest."

Meowing at the door caught Skyler's attention. She hurried to the door and opened it to find Daisy on the other side.

"Where have you been?" Skyler bent down and scooped up the cat. "I have been worried sick about you."

She made sure that Daisy had water and food before she came back inside the house. Hunter had removed his shirt and was lying on the couch, covered by a sheet up to his torso.

"Do you think that Liam would mind if Daisy came inside the cabin? I hate for her to be outside by herself at night."

"You can ask him tomorrow. I'm pretty sure he'll say yes."

Skyler got into bed, turned off the light and stared up at the ceiling. She was exhausted and wide-awake. An hour ticked by and she had tossed and turned until her blanket and sheets were tangled around her legs. Frustrated, she kicked and kicked until she was free. Quietly, she padded out to the kitchen to get a cold glass of water.

"You can't sleep?" Hunter asked the question in the dark and gave her a start.

"You scared me." She filled a glass with water and drank it down. "I thought you were asleep."

"No." He sat up and leaned forward, resting his head in his hands. "This couch is killing my back."

Skyler put the glass on the counter. This was ridiculous. She couldn't sleep; he couldn't sleep. They were both adults. It didn't make sense that they should be apart.

"Come to bed," she said.

Hunter lifted his head and looked over at her. She breathed in, held it and then let out a breath slowly, awaiting his response.

"Skyler, if I come to bed with you, we will end up making love," he said with the honesty she had come to expect from him.

How many seconds slipped by while she absorbed his words. She knew he spoke the truth and her next words would decide the path that their relationship would take. She knew what she wanted—she wanted to be with Hunter, even if they only had the summer.

She put the empty glass in the sink, walked to the couch, held out her hand for him to take and said, "Come to bed with me, cowboy."

Her bravery waned when she found herself alone with Hunter in the cabin bedroom. Out in the living room, she had felt empowered, like a woman in charge of her own sexuality. Once in the bedroom, the lights thankfully off, and *the* cowboy of her dreams outlined by the dim light streaming in through the window by the bed, she faltered.

"Having second thoughts?" he asked her, standing shirtless by the bed.

"No," she whispered. Then, after a moment, she said, "Yes."

Hunter walked over to where she was standing in the doorway, cupped his hand around the back of her neck and kissed the top of her head.

"There're bunk beads in the spare room. I'll sleep there."

"No." She caught his hand. "That room is full of boxes. It's like a storage room. You'd have to move things around just to get to the beds."

"Then I'll go back to the couch," he said. "I don't want you worrying about me. I've slept on the ground working cattle than in a bed."

Skyler grabbed his hand and held on to it.

"I'm serious," he said, trying to reassure her. "This is too fast. You're the tortoise, remember?"

Hunter was doing his level best to make her feel comfortable in an awkward situation. But he was getting it all wrong. She wanted to be the hare; for once in her life, she was determined to be the hare.

"I don't want you to go."

He leaned down and touched his forehead to hers. "I don't think you know what you want right now, Skyler. And that's okay. I don't want you to wake up with regrets. I just know that if I get into the bed with you, I'm going to need to touch you."

Skyler lifted her head so her lips naturally touched his. She lifted up on her tiptoes, put her hands on either side of his face and kissed him. Hunter looped his arm around her back and pulled her tightly into his body. He could lift her and hold her against him with one arm—the strength of the man made her feel womanly. The soapy, clean scent of his warm skin and the feel of this bicep flexing against her back as he held her close to him were heady sensations. The kissed deepened as her breathing became shallow and quick.

"Tell me what to do." Hunter kissed her neck right below her ear.

She shuddered with pleasure, her eyes closed, her fingers in his hair.

"What do you want?" His face was pressed into her neck.

"I want you to stay with me." She raked her fingers through his hair. "I want you to make love to me."

No words from the cowboy, just kisses—on her neck, her chin—and then his strong, firm lips found her softer lips.

"I don't...." She moved her head back an inch or two so she could tell be as honest with him as she thought he was being with her. "I don't feel sexy."

Hunter stopped trying to kiss her and straightened his arms so there was a little distance between them.

"What?" He genuinely sounded surprised. Confused.

"My hair," she said. "My body in general, I suppose. I just don't feel...like *myself* yet."

Hunter stared down at her face, his eyes appearing almost black in the darkened room. "Do I have some say in this?"

When she didn't respond, he asked the question again. "Do I have a say in this?"

"I don't know," she said. "What do you want to say?"

Hunter slipped his hands down, cupped her bottom and pulled her upward into his body. "I think you're sexy, Skyler."

Their groins were pressed tightly together now and she could feel Hunter's rock-hard erection; her body responded with a more intense ache. The moment she felt it, she wanted it. She wanted to touch it, hold it, kiss it. She wanted to get it inside her, sink down on it.

"I think you're *very* sexy, Skyler." Hunter suddenly lifted her up in the air and she naturally wrapped her legs around his waist. He walked them back a couple of feet to the nearby wall and pressed her against it, his hard-on hitting the bull's-eye on her body. He grabbed her arms, lifted them above her head, linked their fingers together and kissed her hard and long.

"Tell me that you believe me." Hunter stopped kissing her and held his lips away from her even as she leaned her head forward, trying to recapture his mouth with hers.

"Tell me." He thrust his hips into hers and she wanted—*needed*—to rip away the layers of material separating their flesh.

"I believe you," she gasped, desiring him like she had never desired another man. She was in pain, a pleasurable, exquisite, throbbing pain she had never known existed before. "I believe you."

With one arm secured around her back, he let her slide down his body until her feet were touching the ground. He kneeled down before her, running his hands down to her backside, then hooked his fingers in the waistband of her simple white cotton panties. She was sure he was going to pull off those panties; she wanted him to rip them off, bite them off, get them off as quickly as he could. But he didn't. He teased her, kissing her mound through the thin material, making her push her body toward his lips, moaning and holding on to his head to keep herself upright on legs that felt like they were made of Jell-O.

Hunter slipped his hands—such large, strong hands—under the short nightie she was wearing, lifting it as he went. He stood up and kept right on lifting the nightie until she had a choice—stop his progression or raise her arms. Slowly, languidly, feeling dazed with so many wondrous sensations bursting all over her body, she raised her arms.

Hunter smiled—she saw the flash of his white teeth—as he freed her from her simple, unremarkable nightgown.

Her chest rising and falling from passion, and with a strip of light illuminating her left breast and the nipple that was tight and hard, Hunter stared at her chest just as she was staring at his.

"You are incredibly beautiful." The cowboy traced the side of her small, pert breast with his finger. "The rarest of flowers."

She caught his hand and pressed it over her breast, closing her eyes at the feeling of his warm palm on her skin.

One hand still on her breast, his thumb gently worrying her nipple, Hunter's free hand cupped the back of her head and he kissed her again. She opened her mouth as she intended to open her body to him. Hunter lifted her with ease and carried her to the bed. She watched as he stripped off his jeans and his underwear. He was unabashed in his nakedness—strong, muscled thighs, corded abs, a beautiful defined chest and a thick, magnificent, hard cock.

Skyler reached for him, heard him gasp with pleasure and surprise. She put him in his mouth, something she knew she would do, and heard him groan at the feeling of her tongue on his skin.

He let her take her time with him, explore him, feel him, dominate him. And then, when she had taken him right to the edge of no return, Hunter stripped off her panties, kneeled down on the ground between her thighs and turned her into a midnight snack.

"Oh, my God." She grabbed the blanket on the best in her fists. "Oh, my God."

"No." The cowboy kissed the inside of her thigh. "Hunter."

"Hunter," she moaned. "Hunter. Hunter."

By the time he was done with her, she was screaming his name, grateful that there were miles of woods between them and another living soul. After he brought her up to the top of the mountain, and she'd shouted his name to the rooftops, Hunter hovered his body above hers.

"I have to go get a condom," he said regretfully.

"The drawer." She flung her hand weakly toward the nightstand. "The top drawer."

Hunter looked at her, surprised, as he reached across her and fished a condom out of the drawer.

The wrapper was soon on the floor, the condom secured, and the cowboy was all the way inside her, making her gasp and arch her back. He knew how to love a woman's body and she just held on for the ride. His movements were long, slow, deep, and he nibbled her ear, sucked on her nipple.

"You're about to come," he whispered in her ear.

How did he know? How could he know?

He pushed deeply into her one more time, his hand beneath her bottom, and then stopped and let her take control of her own destiny. She writhed against him, panting, straining, using him just the way her body needed, until the wave, that glorious wave, crashed over her, again and again, and again.

Hunter had watched her take her pleasure; he was her witness. She opened her eyes, saw him watching her, and to his surprise, she didn't look away. Instead, she watched him. She watched him as he pushed into her body, faster, harder, doing what his body needed... what it craved. He threw back his head and growled loudly as the climax ripped through him. He hadn't felt this before—this intensity, this satisfaction. This love.

They were breathing heavily, their bodies still connected, the air feeling cool against their hot skin.

"Why?" Skyler asked with an emotional catch in her throat.

He understood what she was asking. Why did he do everything in his power to make her happy? Why did he always try to make her every dream, no matter how small, come true? Why had he just made love to her with every fiber of his being? Why he had loved her like he was on a mission to spoil her for every other man who had a thought to touch her?

Hunter lifted his head, closed his eyes and tried to catch his breath. Then, staring deeply into her lovely eyes, he said, "Because I love you, Skyler. I love you."

Skyler was lying on top of her cowboy, who was catching a nap after their second round of lovemaking. Her body couldn't seem to get enough; in fact, instead of her passion waning, it was building. She had a fire in her that Hunter had deliberately lit, and as far as she could figure, it was up to him to put it out.

She kissed his smooth, defined chest, encircling his

nipple with her tongue, and used his hard thigh to ease some of the ache she was feeling.

"Why aren't you sleeping?" He mumbled the question.

"Just one more time." She reached between them and wrapped her fingers around him. He was soft now, but she was well aware of how quickly that could change in her favor.

Hunter smiled, not opening his eyes. "Bad kitty."

She bit his nipple playfully. "One more time."

"If you can get it hard," he said, still refusing to open his eyes, "it's all yours."

It took some effort, but she had always been a goal-oriented woman. Straddling him, she reached for the drawer, pulled out a condom and handed it to him.

Sleepily, he unwrapped it, tossed the wrapper on the floor with the other two, rolled it on and smiled with his eyes closed as she slid down onto his shaft. Her hands planted on his chest, her head down in concentration, she rocked her hips, building speed, moving faster and pushing down harder, until she was panting and climaxing. Somewhere along the way, Hunter had opened his eyes to enjoy the show. The moment she started to climax, Hunter held on to her hips, moving her back and forth on his cock until she felt him stiffen beneath her. With a laugh, she collapsed on top of him, finally feeling satisfied.

He wrapped his arms around her and kissed her on the neck. "For the love of God, Skyler, go to sleep. I need at least a couple of hours of sleep before I get up."

Skyler fit herself into his side, threw her leg over his leg and rested her head on his chest. "Hunter?"

"Hmm?"

"I've always dreamed of you."

"That's nice," he mumbled and she was certain, by his response, that he hadn't been awake enough to register what she had said to him. He rolled his body toward her, tightened his grip on her and added groggily, "Me, too."

"Oh, that's terrible," Molly exclaimed. "I've been so busy with my *stuff* that I haven't called, I haven't texted. I'm so sorry. Is he okay?"

"He is truly a miracle horse." Skyler was sitting on the porch in a rocking chair with Daisy curled up on her lap. "He's been getting better, a little better, day by day."

Molly had her curls gathered up in a single pom-pom on top of her head, so that her pretty, heart-shaped face was highlighted. "I'm so glad, Skyler."

"Me, too."

It had been a week of working and lovemaking and basking in the love she felt for Hunter. It was a love that he seemed to very much return—not just in his words, which were important and lovely, but, more importantly, in his actions. But she still hadn't told Molly and she felt guilty about it.

"I've been kind of radio silence lately," Molly said with a little frown.

"Same," Skyler said, on the verge of talking about her summer romance with Hunter for the first time.

Skyler was about to open her mouth to confess, when Molly said, "I can't believe I've been keeping this from you."

Her eyebrows drew together and her mouth closed. "Keeping what from me?"

Molly gave a little shake of her head. "I'm in love."

"What?!" Skyler sat upright, disturbing Daisy, who complained with a meow before she repositioned herself and closed her eyes.

"I am." Molly smiled softly. "I am in love."

"Don't keep me in suspense a second longer, Molly! Who is he?"

"Chase," her best friend said. "I'm in love with Chase."

"Chase Rockwell?"

Molly nodded, her cheeks flushing prettily.

"When? How?" Skyler exclaimed. "Details! I need details!"

As it turned out, she wasn't the only one having a summer romance. While she was busy finding any excuse to be naked with Hunter, Molly was having a virtual romance of her own.

"We video-chatted one night and that one call lasted for eight hours. I've never in my life had that much to say to anyone other than you.

"We've been texting and video dating, and talking on the phone ever since, and, Skyler—" Molly's amber eyes were sparkling "—he told me that he's in love with me."

"Oh, Molly…"

"He wants to marry me."

Skyler was stunned speechless. She could only stare at her friend, who was beaming with more happiness than Skyler had ever seen before.

"He wants to marry you?" she finally asked.

Molly nodded. "He told me last night."

"How could he possibly know that after such a short time? You haven't ever been in the same state much less the same room."

"He knows." Her friend's body stiffened defensively. She lifted her chin and said, "And so do I."

"Molly." She said the name in a higher-pitched tone. "You don't even know him. How could you even consider marrying him?"

"When you know, you know," Molly said with a frown. "I just know, Skyler. You're the first person I wanted to tell. I wish you were happy for me."

Skyler was taken aback. She wasn't being supportive; she was being judgmental and that's not what Molly need from her right now.

"I'm sorry, Molly," she apologized. "I am just shocked."

"So am I," her friend acknowledged. "But I love him. I do. And I already feel like I'm going to have a fight on my hands with my family. I need at least one person in our corner."

"I'm always in your corner, Molly," she reassured her friend. "Do you guys even know how all of this is going to work? Wait a minute," Skyler exclaimed at a thought that suddenly occurred to her. "Are you moving to Montana?"

"No," Molly said. "Chase knows I just got accepted to law school here. He's going to move here."

Skyler looked past the phone to her small Montana oasis, her mind whirling with thoughts. She wanted to be insanely happy for Molly, but what she really felt was concern.

"Molly," she said after a moment of thought, "I love you and I want the best for you. I just wonder…" Skyler paused, not wanting to offend or upset her dear friend.

"We've never had to hedge our words," Molly reminded her. "Just say what you want to say."

"Could you be confusing how you feel now with how you felt when you were young?"

"Like I only think I love him now because I thought I loved him back then?"

"Yes. I think that's what I was trying to say."

"No." Molly shook her head. "I know my own heart. I know my own mind. I love him."

After a moment, Skyler knew there was only one thing she could say. "If Chase is the one for you, I'm going to be on this journey with you every step of the way. I'm going to give you the most incredible budget bachelorette party New York has ever seen!"

That made Molly laugh and her laugh broke the tension that had been an uncomfortable third wheel during the conversation. "I just want you to be happy, Molly."

"I am happy." Molly smiled brightly at her. "Skyler. I'm going to marry Chase Rockwell from *Cowboy Up!* Do you know what this means?"

Skyler shook her head, deciding to wait and tell Molly about her fling with Hunter another time. This was Molly's moment to shine.

"That psychic I saw on my trip to New Orleans who saw in the tarot cards that we are destined to marry best friends was right. I told you she was right, didn't I? You thought she was crazy and I thought she was a true clairvoyant." Molly was grinning broadly. "Prepare yourself, Skyler. Because *you*. Are. Next."

Chapter Eleven

"How do you know?" Hunter grabbed a bale of hay from the trailer and walked over to the barn at the Rocking R Ranch, Chase's small ranch that bordered Sugar Creek.

Chase followed him with a bale of his own and dropped it in front of the barn. "I just do."

"You're going to marry her?" Hunter adjusted his mask before he grabbed another bale of hay.

Hunter was doing his friend a favor by dropping off some bales of hay they had just harvested at Sugar Creek. Times were tough for Chase and money was tight. Chase would do the same for him—that much he knew.

"I'm going to marry her."

"I don't get it, man," he said. "It doesn't make sense."

"It doesn't have to make sense to anyone else but

me and her," Chase said. "I saw her picture on Skyler's Instagram and I knew I wanted to talk to her. When I talked to her, I knew I wanted to see her on video. When I saw her on video, I knew I wanted to marry her. It's just that simple.

Hunter stacked his bale of hay on the bale Chase had just dropped.

"That doesn't sound simple, Chase. It sounds crazy."

"Crazy is knowing that I have met the woman of my dreams and not doing everything I can to be with her," his friend countered. "I thought I was going to marry Sarah. We had everything all planned out. Right after high school we were going to elope and start a family."

Hunter's gut twisted as memories of Sarah's sharp decline and suffering flooded his brain without his consent. He didn't want his friend to be alone—he wanted him to move on from the pain of losing his first love. But like this? It didn't sit right in Hunter's gut.

Chase took a break from the work and looked him right in the eye. "I'm going to sell the ranch, get what I can out of it. I should be able to get a decent chunk of change. I'll be able to get her a nice ring."

"You're going to sell the ranch?!" The Rockwells had been at the Rocking R for generations.

"That's right."

"Are you thinking about leaving Montana?"

"I'm not thinking about it, I'm doing it."

Hunter looked around the Rockwells' small ranch. Yes, it was showing the signs of neglect—fences were down and weeds were overtaking broken-down equipment that Chase hadn't been able to afford to fix.

"You have a life here," Hunter said with a shake of his head.

"No." His friend jerked the last bale off the trailer. "*You* have a life here. I have an existence. And I'm tired of it, man. I'm over it. My dad destroyed this place—he ran this ranch right into the ground and then had the nerve to up and die and leave me to clean up his mess." Chase had always been a man who knew his own mind, that much Hunter knew. "This place is my past—Molly is my future."

Hunter couldn't think of another thing to say; in fact, her knew that once Chase made up his mind, and spoke it aloud, it was already a done deal. Life as Hunter had always known it, with his best friend living just next door, was going to change. After they finished the job, Hunter knew he had to do right by his lifelong friend.

"If this is really what you want, you know I've got your back. I'll hate seeing this ranch sold, but we've been friends for a long damn time."

"That's true," Chase agreed, wiping the sweat from his brow. "I really appreciate you helping me out with this hay. I'll pay you back as soon as I sell the place."

Hunter brushed aside his offer. He didn't expect to be repaid. This was what friends did for each other. "If you're really serious about selling, I'll talk to Bruce and Dad about buying your herd."

"I'm dead serious about it," Chase said without hesitation. His friend studied the ground for a moment and then said, "I was kind of counting on you to be my best man."

"I'd be honored," Hunter said, pushing aside his own wishes and focusing on his friend's apparent happiness. "You name the date and I'll be there. Heck, I'll even put on a clean pair of jeans since it's a special occasion."

* * *

Liam was working Zodiac in the round pen when Hunter returned from his trip to Chase's ranch. Skyler walked over to meet him, wondering if Chase had said anything to him about Molly.

"How's he looking?" Hunter asked about the gelding.

"Liam says he's still moving in the right direction. We seem to be past the worst of it."

"That's great news."

She nodded, falling in beside him as they headed back to the round pen.

Liam raised his chin in greeting to his brother, but kept his eyes focused on the trotting gelding.

"He's still favoring his left hind at the trot, but I don't think its lameness. I still think its how he's perceiving things," the veterinarian said.

"Will we be able to ride him?" Hunter asked his brother.

"I don't see anything that would indicate that you *couldn't* ride him. But I'd like to see him out in the pasture healing for another couple of weeks."

"I'll bring another horse down from the main barn."

Liam had the gelding slow to a walk, then stop and turn toward him. The veterinarian walked over to the horse, hooked a lead rope to the halter and then patted him on the neck affectionately. "Good for you, pops."

After they put Zodiac out in the pasture with Dream Catcher, Liam took the opportunity to stop by and tinker with the old truck he was restoring.

"How's Kate?" Hunter said, asking after Liam's wife.

Liam rummaged through his tall toolbox and found the wrench he was looking for. "She's hanging in there—her life hasn't really changed. Folks still need their horses trained and they still want to take riding lessons. She's sticking to individual lessons for now. It's Callie I'm worried about."

Callie, Hunter explained to her, was Liam's eldest daughter with Kate. Callie had been born with Down syndrome, but even with an intellectual disability, she was a very accomplished young woman. Callie loved to cook and had a website and blog centered on her passion for creating home-cooked meals. She had lived in a group home in town to gain independence, had been earning her own money working at Strides of Strength equestrian program for differently abled children and was engaged to be married.

"She's upset that the wedding had to be postponed."

"Upset is an understatement." Liam frowned. "She's regressed a bit, having meltdowns and threatening to call of the wedding off entirely. I keep trying to reassure her that the wedding will happen—the country just needs to get past this rough patch."

Skyler was standing a distance away from Liam, watching as he worked on the engine.

"Does she run?" she asked, admiring the 1950s model truck.

Liam threw the wrench back into the toolbox and wiped his hands on a nearby rag. "She did. But she's being moody."

"Typical woman," Hunter joked with a wink in her direction.

"Ha, ha." She rolled her eyes at him. "Very funny."

To Liam she asked, "Do you mind if I take a look?"

Liam appeared confused about the question; he stopped wiping his hand on the rag and glanced between his brother and her.

"You want to take a look?" Liam asked for clarification. "Under the hood?"

She laughed at the question. "Of course, under the hood. Where else?"

Liam stepped back from the truck. "I don't mind."

She saw Liam and Hunter exchange a look, but she ignored it. She was accustomed to the response when she helped in her father's garage. Those who didn't know her always doubted her first.

Skyler pulled a stool over to the front of the truck, stepped up and looked inside the engine. While Hunter and Liam watched, their faces full of misogynistic skepticism, Skyler examined the engine clinically, just as her father had taught her to do. She methodically checked the distributor to see if there was a crack in the distributor cap. She then checked the spark-plug wire to ensure that they weren't cracked or frayed. The wires were secured to the spark plugs, as they should be.

She climbed down off the step stool and asked Liam, "I need to see if you have the right wrench for the job."

She dug through the toolbox, found the tool she was searching for, climbed back up on the stool and reached all the way to the back of the engine. She put her wrench on the bolt that held the distributor in place so she could move the distributor.

"Okay," she called out from beneath the hood. "Get behind the wheel and crank it when I tell you."

With an amused look on his face, Liam climbed behind the wheel.

"Turn it over!" Skyler called out to him.

At first the engine sputtered and clunked while she twisted the distributor, and then the engine started to run smoothly.

"I'll be damned!" Hunter's brother shouted over the loud noise of the engine. He revved the engine several times before he stepped out of the truck to look at the engine. "What did I miss?"

"Yeah," Hunter said. "How *did* you do that?"

"The timing was off." She grinned at them, enjoying their disbelief. "My father set up a crib for me in his office at the garage when I was just a newborn— my first rattle was a ring full of old keys from 1950s-era cars and trucks."

"Thank you." Liam sat back behind the wheel, shut it off and then cranked it again. The engine turned over without any sputtering or knocking.

Skyler leaned her head toward Hunter. "You say cattle is in your blood—well, mechanics is in mine."

"Hey, look!" Skyler and Hunter had just finished the barn chores. Hunter had brought down two geldings from the main barn—one for him to ride and the other, a thirty-year-old retired cow pony, to be a companion for Zodiac when they took the other two horses out to work.

"A four-leaf clover!" She pointed to a clump of cheerful, yellow flowers near the pasture fence. "It's a four-leaf clover! It's been right there in plain sight, this whole time?"

"Just be careful of the tall grass," Hunter said with his typical, slightly bossy tone.

Skyler rolled her eyes and said "yeah, yeah" in her mind. She was born careful.

Sometimes he acted like a parent watching over a precocious child and she didn't like it one bit. She was being judged on that *one* little fainting episode way back on her first day. Now she had the physical strength to match her mental strength. The whole Montana-baby-sitter routine was getting old.

Skyler picked her way through the brush to getter a closer look at the small yellow flowers. She leaned forward and sniffed the flowers. "Hmm. It smells so good."

"Sweet clover. We plant it for the livestock. Savannah makes clover honey every year."

"Oh," Skyler said, disappointed. "It's not a four-leaf clover after all."

"Look…" She held it up for Hunter to see. "Three leaves."

"You superstitious?" He was watching her, as he always did, with a slightly amused expression.

"Only a little." She tucked one of the clover flowers behind her ear.

She was about to embark on a list of reasons why she believed in lucky clovers, but was distracted by a sharp, burning sensation under her pant leg. She glanced down and realized that both of her boots and the bottom of her pant legs were covered in ants.

It took her a second to register in her brain that she was being *attacked* by the miniature insects, but another bite on her skin, which meant that they were also *under* her clothes, made her leap into action. She ran out of the tall grass, and screamed, "Ants! *Ants!*"

She stopped when she was out of the tall grass, then bent over and started to scrape all of the ants off of her boots and pants.

"Get off of me!" she yelled urgently. "Get. Off. Of. Me!"

Hunter was at her side, kneeling down with gloved hands and slapping at her pants to get the clingy, biting creatures off her without them attaching themselves to him.

"Are they off?" she asked urgently. "Are they off?"

"Turn around," he instructed, scanning her boots and her pants. "I think we got 'em all."

The commotion stopped for a moment while Skyler caught her breath. Then she felt a sting on the back of her thigh.

"Oh, crap." She started to hit her thigh with her hand, trying to smash the ant by trapping it between the denim and her skin. The little bugger, perhaps in the last throes of its life, bit her harder.

She dropped to the ground and started to tug on her boot. "I can't get it off. I can't get it off. Get it off!"

She held out her boot for Hunter to pull off. "Get my boot off."

"I'm getting it off," he told her, his voice even.

"Get my boot off!" She felt another ant bite her on her calf. "Ouch, you little bastard!"

"Did I hurt you?" Hunter threw her boot to the side and soon the second boot followed.

"No! The ant!" Skyler jumped up, clawed at the button and zipper of her jeans. Once unhooked and unzipped, she jumped up and down and pushed the jeans, which were sticking to her skin because of the sweat, and finally high-stepped out of the pants.

She turned around in a circle, craning her neck to look at her backside. "Do you see them?!"

Hunter found two more ants on her legs and removed them before they could bite.

"Any more?"

"Hold still."

"Any more?" she asked again, her skin stinging and burning where the fire ants had bitten.

"I'm looking," Hunter said, his tone less even. "Hold. Still."

Skyler stopped moving while Hunter looked her over. "I don't see any more."

"Well, that's a…" she began, just when she felt another bite. "Ow!"

"What?"

Skyler scowled, reached her hand into her panties, scratched her butt cheek several times and then pulled her fingers free of the cotton material to reveal the offending ant smashed between her two fingers.

"I got you." She flicked the insect away from her.

She was standing in her socks, underwear, tank top and cowgirl hat. Hunter looked at her and she looked back at him.

"He bit me right on the butt," she complained.

"You don't say," Hunter said drolly. "Too bad that *wasn't* a four-leaf clover, huh?"

Skyler had been lucky during her ranch experience—most of the days had been sunny with some warm breezes to break the heat. Hunter was forever complaining about the dry days turning all the pastures brown.

"Looks like you got your wish!" Skyler met Hunter at the door a week after the ant attack.

It was still dark and it felt like a monsoon had struck. When she opened the door, the heavy wind was blowing sheets of rain sideways, hard enough that they reached the front door. Hunter's raincoat was soaked with water and he was quickly making a puddle where he stood.

"It's messy out there." He raised his voice loud enough for her to hear over the wind. "Grab your slicker."

"I don't have one."

Hunter stared at her for a second. "You brought five bags."

"Two were pretty small," she muttered quickly. Then she asked, "Do you have one I can borrow."

He shrugged out of the one he was wearing. "Don't argue. Just put it on."

Skyler slipped on his bright yellow slicker made from heavy material. She had to cuff the sleeves so she would be able to use her hands. She felt terrible that he was going to get soaked in a couple of minutes, but when it came to the ranch work, and he told her not to argue, she gave him that respect.

Hunter ran to the truck and together they drove the short distance to the barn. They made quick work of the chores since she was able to match him stall for stall now.

"We'll stop by Bruce's place—he'll have some rain gear I can borrow." Hunter's clothes were damp but not soaking wet when he climbed behind the wheel.

"Maybe Savannah has something in my size?" she suggested.

"That's even better."

Savannah did have a raincoat closer to her own size and she was grateful to have it. The rain was driving down from the sky, pelting them as they tried to get their feeding chores done as quickly as possible. Skyler didn't want to admit it and didn't want to focus on it, but doing ranch chores in the rain was a complete drag. It was muddy, and sloshy; her jeans felt cold and clammy and the damp denim was rubbing across her skin in the most annoying way. It was hard to hear because the rain and wind masked their voices, so they had to yell at each other just to communicate.

Halfway through the first herd of cows, the tractor stopped running.

"What's wrong?" The hood of his rain slicker had fallen back and his black hair was slicked back away from his forehead. He was squinting at her against the rain.

"It just died!"

She tapped several times on the fuel gauge, but it was an old tractor and the fuel gauge was cracked and didn't seem to be operational. With a bad feeling in her gut, she twisted off the fuel cap and looked inside.

"It's dry as a bone in there." She delivered the bad news to Hunter at the same time she was wiping drops of rainwater that were dripping down her nose.

"No." Hunter looked in the tank. "I put diesel in yesterday."

"It's gone now."

"Damn." Hunter kicked at a nearby rock, then stood with his hands on his hips, his head down. He had pulled the hood back up and water was cascading, like a waterfall, over the hood and in front of his face.

"Damn," he said again. "I'm going to have go back and get diesel."

"Can't you call Bruce?" She ducked her head and tried to use the tractor as a shield from the wind.

"By the time he gets here, I could be there and back," he told her. "I'll be fine. I'm worried about you."

"I can make it," she insisted. "I'll just do the marine march my dad taught me and I'll be fine."

* * *

Hunter had to admit that, even in the rain, Skyler had hung in with him. She had insisted on working in the rain and she had insisted on returning back to the tractor to finish the job they had started. He also had to admit that Skyler saved the job; she was able to crack the injectors to prime the air out of the lines to get the diesel back in the cylinders so they could get the tractor to crank. She had been grumbling and low-level complaining about the rain and the mud and the slipperiness of the ground. That grumbling shifted to unvarnished frustration when they made it back to the cabin.

"I'm cold. Wet. Exhausted. Every muscle in my body hurts *still*." Skyler stomped up the porch steps. "I'm stinky and dirty all of the time. I actually found sand in my ear." She held out her hands. "I have this black *gunk* caked under every single one of my nails."

He followed her up the steps not saying a word; he'd been raised up to know better than to interfere with a woman when she was mad as a wet hen.

"I've fallen in manure—that was fun." She pulled at the snaps on the front of her borrowed raincoat. "My blisters have had blisters. I didn't even know that was possible."

She sat down to yank off her muddy, wet boots. "I've been literally attacked by ants. I stink all of the time. Even that clinic strength deodorant I bought the other day has failed. Sometimes I'm so tired when I get home, I'm too tired to take a shower. I peel off my clothing— *peel*, mind you—and fall asleep on top of the covers just stinking to high heaven. What kind of life is this, anyway?"

She looked at him as if to prompt him to participate

in her seemingly one-sided conversation. But he wasn't much in the mood to coddle her; in fact, he was pretty ticked off at how she had managed to spin his world right off its axis.

"Suck it up, cupcake," Hunter said.

Skyler stared at him in disbelief before her eyebrows drew together; her lavender eyes turned a stormy amethyst. She stood up.

"'Suck it up, cupcake'?" she repeated as if she hadn't heard him correctly. "Is that what you said?"

"This is the life." He crossed his arms over his chest. "This is what you wanted."

"Clearly delusional." She walked past him, her soggy socks squishing on the wooden planks.

"This is the life," he repeated.

She stopped, spun around. "I *know*! Don't you think I know that by now? And I hate it! I. Hate. It! *Reality* does *not* live up to the dream—"

"It never does…"

"It's hotter, wetter, muddier, more stinky and more buggy." She pointed her finger at him as if it was his fault that the real Montana didn't perfectly match her fantasy Montana. "*And* there weren't any rabid ants in my dreams!"

Chapter Twelve

They had never quarreled before but Skyler supposed there was a first time for everything. In truth, it was probably a feat that they had managed *not* to fight for as many weeks as they had been thrown together, like two strangers forced to rely on one another on *Survivor* island.

"Ready?" Hunter asked at the bottom of the porch steps. The rain had cleared up, for now, and so had the dark clouds on the cowboy's handsome face.

She could read from his body language that he wasn't sure which version of Skyler he was going to encounter when she walked out the door to greet him.

She had a backpack slung over her shoulder. "Ready."

Daisy was lounging on the top porch step, enjoying the heat of the sun. She trilled when she saw Skyler, turned upside down, curled all four of her paws and gazed at her with love.

"I love you, too." Skyler bent down to pet the cat. "I left you plenty of food and water. And you can always go in the barn."

She stood up to find Hunter watching her as he seemed to like to do, his expression a bit guarded.

"Will she be okay while we're gone?"

"She'll be fine," he reassured her. "I asked Bruce to check on her when he comes to take care of the horses."

Hunter was pulling a horse trailer behind his truck. They were heading to the northernmost part of the ranch to move a herd to a new pasture. The grass was so dry from the lack of rain that the family had decided to rotate pastures early.

"Throw your gear in the back and I'll show you how to load the horses."

Skyler descended the steps quickly, threw her backpack in the bed of the truck and then walked to the barn. Hunter slowly pulled up the barn, parked and asked her to bring Dream Catcher out to the trailer.

"Just walk her straight on in, like there's nothing in the world wrong. If you're tense, she's going to think something's wrong and not want to load."

"Walk straight in?"

"Straight in and then turn around and put the guard bar down."

She looked into the trailer, rehearsed the directions in her head and walked Dream Catcher away from the trailer to get a straight shot in, then walked a line to the trailer. Dream Catcher didn't hesitate or stop; she walked right into the trailer behind her.

"Just like that." Hunter secured the rear guard behind Dream Catcher so she wouldn't back out.

"Did you see that?" Skyler put down the guard and gratefully pet the mare on the forehead. "We did it!"

Hunter walked the gelding named Tricky Dick out of the barn and got him loaded in the trailer. Tricky Dick wasn't as flashy and handsome as Zodiac; he was dark brown with some bleached spots on his coat from the sun and his mane and tail were black and scruffy. Hunter had said, "He's not much to look at, but he's one of the best cow ponies Sugar Creek has ever seen."

"What's in here?" Skyler pointed to the door behind her.

"That's the camper."

She raised her eyebrows with a question.

He opened the door and Skyler was hit with a blast of hot, stale air. Inside, it looked like a mini RV—there was a bed up on a platform, a small kitchenette, a bathroom and a small two-seater dining table.

"I bought this rig from my brother Gabe when he upgraded. Chase and I used to take this on the rodeo circuit."

Hunter shut the door behind them. "This rig's seen some things."

"I bet." She took his offered hand and hopped down to the ground. "Do you guys plan to do any more rodeos together?"

"Naw." Hunter frowned. "I'm pretty sure Chase's rodeo days are over."

Skyler took her spot in the cowboy's truck, certain from his last comment that he was well aware of Chase and Molly's whirlwind courtship. She knew and he knew. And yet neither one of them had wanted to say a word about it.

* * *

The ride to the northern corner of the ranch was a winding, at times bumpy, trek. For Skyler, the trip was an opportunity for them to move past the dustup that had happened between them on the porch. She was a let's-move-forward kind of woman and, luckily, it seemed that Hunter was of a like mind.

"This is a beautiful ride," Skyler sighed, feeling some of the tension of the morning drain out of her body as she breathed the fresh air deeply into her lungs.

A small half smile, one that she had grown to love even more than she had loved it on the reality TV show, appeared on his face, but he kept his eyes on the road. The trailer was heavy with the extra weight of the horses, and Hunter had already let her know that there were several spots on the back ranch road that could be challenging.

She breathed in deeply again and exhaled slowly, leaning her head back and letting the breeze from the open window and the sun filtering through the trees warm her skin. She felt disconnected from the morning when everything seemed so daunting. Now she felt content and relaxed, loving the scenery and peacefulness unfolding all around.

Hunter switched to four-wheel drive, took the rig across a narrow, shallow creek and then around a corner to a clearing. Skyler inhaled again—her breath was taken by the majesty of the mountain. It was closer than she had ever been. Up until now, these glorious peaks had been far off in the distance; now, the mountain was directly before her. She swallowed hard, several times, as she was overwhelmed by the sight before her. *This* was the Montana she had thought about for so many years. This was it. And, to be here, experiencing it with Hunter Brand, was beyond a reward for all of the months she fought so hard to survive.

"This is still Sugar Creek?" she asked, in awe.

"Brand land."

"Incredible." She pushed open the door and stepped out.

Skyler helped Hunter set up the small traveling corral for the horses beneath a shade tree that would give them some shade and shelter. Hunter had loaded the trailer with water for the horses, but they were also close enough to a stream should their stock run out. The camper part of the trailer had been outfitted with solar panels and had a generator to run the appliances, lights, climate control and, most importantly to Skyler, the water heater.

"It's really nice in here." She sat down at one of the bench seats at the dinette. "I've seen apartments in the city about this size."

"I thought you'd prefer this to camping."

She didn't want to say that he was correct, but he was correct. Sleeping on the ground, as she discovered when she had fallen asleep the night of their first date, was not her *thing*.

"You can decide sleeping arrangements," Hunter said, taking off his hat and hanging it on a hook just inside the door.

Skyler stood up; she didn't like the distance her outburst had caused between them. She only had a finite amount of time with her dream cowboy. And even though ranch life had not lived up to the fantasy... Hunter had. He was strong, handsome, sexy and funny. He was a gentleman. A cowboy.

"I would be lonely without you in bed with me." She slipped her arms around his waist and rested her head, as she liked to do, on the part of his chest that housed his heart.

Wordlessly, Hunter wrapped his arms around her shoulders, hugged her and pressed a gentle kiss on the top of her head. He let out his breath and that was when she realized that he had been holding it.

"I'm sorry about...earlier," she said, not lifting her head. This was one of those moments she wanted to savor, burn in the memory bank of her mind and hold on to for the rest of her life.

"I'm sorry." He rested his chin lightly on the crown on her head.

"Our first fight?"

"Bound to happen."

"But we're moving forward."

"That's what I want."

She felt him give a little nod in agreement. After a moment, she lifted her head so she could see his eyes.

"I don't really hate it here."

"I know you don't. You're overwhelmed by reality here."

The fact that Hunter understood her made it easier for her to move past her embarrassment over her mini breakdown. Yes, she was overwhelmed by the daunting reality of ranch life. She was also disappointed. Her Montana experience had been a jumble of incredible highs and muddy, smelly lows. It had been a shock to have her much-loved image of Montana life shredded and patched back together to create a more realistic picture.

Hunter titled up her chin and kissed her gently on the lips. She closed her eyes and melted in his arms, savoring the warm, comfortable, safe feeling of being in the cowboy's arms.

"We'd better finish setting up camp," he murmured into her neck.

It would be too easy for both of them to get lost in each other's arms. It would be too easy to slip out of their clothes and slip into the nearby bed.

"Something to look forward to?" she asked with a small, intimate smile on her well-kissed lips.

Hunter seemed, like her, to need just one more kiss. It was a down payment, a promise, of the lovemaking to come. No one had ever made her feel so desirable, so sexy, so womanly. In the cowboy's arms, she had found a part of herself she hadn't know existed.

Suddenly, Hunter swung her into his arms and walked them both toward the bed.

With a laugh, she hung on to his neck. "We have work to do, remember?"

"It'll wait," Hunter said with that deep growl in his voice that made her feel excited with anticipation of the pleasure to come. "This can't."

The horses, in shadow, were busy eating their hay in the nearby corral. Hunter had given Skyler the choice of cooking in the trailer or building a fire. Skyler chose the fire. She enjoyed watching Hunter in his element—he was manly and capable and that reminded her of her father. Her father was a man's man; Chester wasn't a cowboy and he had never ridden a horse, but he was a United States Marine and a diesel mechanic. He was blue collar and showered after work, not before. Her father had always made her feel safe and cared for—that was the same feeling she had when she was with Hunter.

They were the only people for miles, sitting together at the edge of the fire, with glittering stars, bright and plentiful, strewn across the expansive blue-black sky. The day had ended on a warm note and the warmth lingered in the air, but was slowly being overtaken by a cool breeze coming from the mountains.

"This is what I will miss." Skyler was leaning back against Hunter, her face tilted up to the sky. "You can't see the stars like this back home."

She felt Hunter's arm tense around her. "I'd better check on the horses."

They had just fed them and watered them, and Skyler had the distinct feeling that Hunter needed to put some distance between them.

"Okay," she said quietly.

Their relationship had been like fireworks on the Fourth of July—a sudden burst of sparkling lights in the night sky. But, like fireworks, their relationship was, in her mind and perhaps in Hunter's, destined to be explosive, brilliant and over way too fast.

Hunter returned and stopped next to where she was still sitting by the fire, her knees tucked up to her body, her arms hugging her legs tightly. The cowboy held his hand out to her. "We'd better get some rest. Big day tomorrow."

Skyler put her hand in his—would any other hand ever feel so comfortable to hold? Could she really go home and carry this love in her heart for the rest of her life? Their relationship was still so new, still so fresh, that it didn't seem reasonable to dwell on the end of summer. They had right now and that had to be enough.

And yet there was a voice inside her brain, a voice that couldn't be silenced. She didn't believe, deep down, that she would ever have enough of the cowboy. Could she see herself leaving the city—leaving her friends, her father—and forever exchanging people for trees? She had always believed that she was a ranch girl trapped in a city girl's body. This trip had proven that false. She was a city girl. As much as she loved the endless sky and the fresh air and the babbling, clear streams, it was difficult to appreciate the glory of the landscape when she was wading through cow manure or feeding a herd of horses hours before dawn in a torrential rainstorm.

Hunter had agreed with her let's-take-it-one-day-at-a-time strategy; he hadn't discussed after the summer was over. If he asked her to stay, if he asked her to make Montana a more permanent way of life, what would she say? Was the cowboy worth giving up everything she realized she loved so much about her life in New York?

Yes. The answer was yes. Could she make Montana her home if that home included Hunter?

"Yes," she said aloud even though she meant to only say it in her mind.

"What was that?" Hunter asked, half-asleep next to her.

"Nothing." She curled up on her side and scooted back so she was tucked into the curve of his body. "Good night."

Hunter mumbled something, sneaked his arm around her and pulled her more tightly into his body, like he was holding on to a stuffed animal.

"I love you, Hunter."

"I love you."

The next morning, Hunter let her sleep just past dawn and awakened her with a campfire breakfast.

"How'd you sleep?" He handed her a cup of coffee.

"Actually, not too bad." Once her mind had finally settled down, her body soon followed.

She finished her breakfast quickly; Hunter was already saddling the horses and getting ready for them to ride out to the herd. They had practiced herding cattle several times during her time in Montana, and Skyler was feeling confident in her ability when she mounted Dream Catcher. The most important thing she had learned was when Dream Catcher started to keep a cow from straying, tapping into her natural instinct as a quarter horse, tacking right and then left, Skyler just held on to the saddle horn for dear life and let the horse do her job.

They rode out together as the sun was rising over the mountain peaks. They were lucky—it was slated to be a clear day. They reached the herd positioned near the base of the mountain. Many were lying down while others walked slowly, grazing as they moved, their tails waving back and forth like windshield wipers to shoo away the flies. It was going to be tricky to move the cattle through the lightly wooded area to the pasture that was more plentiful with grass and foliage. There were trees and boulders to avoid and Skyler would have to not let her mind be distracted for thinking of pictures she could capture to show everyone back home this latest leg of her journey out west.

They both took their positions and began to move the cattle to the east. Down a small hill, they followed an overgrown path toward the destination. They carefully crossed the creek, wider here and more rocky, then let the horses and cows break to drink. A horsefly was trailing her, trying to land on Dream Catcher's rump.

Skyler spun around, waved her hand at the large black flying insect, trying to stop it from landing on her horse.

"Let it land." Hunter rode up beside her.

She stopped waving her arms and let the horsefly land. Hunter waited until the horsefly latched on to Dream Catcher's rump and then he slammed his hand down on the bug, killed it and then flicked it with his finger.

"Thank you," she said, taking note of how to kill the nuisance insects. Next time she would take care of it.

Hunter tipped his hat to her, his focus centered on the herd. It was a slow, often monotonous process, moving the herd. But there was also something very poetic and romantic about riding through the woods on horseback, just the two of them, with the sound of intermittent mooing mingled with the chirping of birds in the trees overhead.

"There's a calf breaking from the herd." Hunter pointed to right.

Skyler nodded. She had been trained on this and she was confident that, with Dream Catcher's skill and her ability to hold on, they could get the wayward calf back in line with the herd.

She trotted over to where the calf was curiously sniffing around a nearby tree and then Skyler saw that the calf had found some wild clover to sample. Skyler blocked the calf, whistled and waved her hat so the calf would be persuaded to abandon the clover and head back to the herd.

"Come on, little one," Skyler called out to the calf that was determined to get one more clover before heading back.

The calf suddenly spun around, heading in the wrong

direction away from the herd. Dream Catcher naturally, instinctively, blocked the calf and lowered down, moving to the left. Skyler hung on, remembering to relax her body, not stiffen it against the feeling of just being along for the ride. This was what Dream Catcher had been trained all of her life to do.

The calf turned around and jogged back in the direction of the herd. Skyler patted the mare on the neck. "Good girl."

"Nice work," Hunter said to her when she returned to her position at the back of the herd.

"All the praise has to go to Dream Catcher," she said, but she did feel proud.

Skyler settled into the saddle, letting her hips rock with the motion of the horse, keeping a watchful eye on the herd, focusing on the job, following Hunter's example. They were an hour into the job when Hunter pointed to a small incline.

"It's going to get pretty narrow up ahead."

She nodded.

"How much farther?" Skyler called out to him.

"Just on the other side of that ridge."

Her butt was starting to feel numb and she needed to relieve herself. She had learned early on in her trip that learning how to tinkle in the woods was a necessity and that public restrooms were, in fact, a luxury she had never truly appreciated.

"Just on the other side of the ridge" took another thirty minutes with the slow-moving herd meandering through the trees. As promised, there was an open field past the ridge where the herd stopped to graze.

"This is it?" she asked.

He nodded. "We can head back."

"I'm going to make a pit stop," Skyler said, and after she knew that he heard her, she trotted Dream Catcher back over to the woods.

Like a pro, she got her business done quickly and was back in the saddle in record time. She spotted Hunter up ahead, waiting for her while Tricky Dick nibbled at some leaves on a nearby tree. Skyler closed her legs and asked Dream Catcher to canter; she loved to canter.

Skyler was smiling broadly, sitting in the saddle, directing Dream Catcher, feeling like a real, authentic cowgirl. She had really grown in her time in Montana—in fact, she felt pretty certain that she could ride out her own without Hunter and feel perfectly safe.

Hunter turned Tricky Dick to face them—no doubt he'd heard the sound of hooves approaching. She caught his eye and smiled broadly, imagining how impressed Hunter must be with her riding skills, when she misjudged the height of a tree limb. She had to duck forward, wrap her arms around Dream Catcher's neck, in order to avoid being scraped off the horse's back. Just beyond the tree limb, Skyler sat upright, accidentally pulled back on the reigns, and Dream Catcher did what she was trained to do—she stopped.

Skyler fell forward, once again wrapped her arms around the horse's neck, screamed as she lost her balance, and fell out of the saddle. The horse stood stock while she dangled precariously, her arms wrapped around Dream Catcher's neck. She felt for the ground with her feet, relieved and a little shocked that she hadn't fallen.

"Thank you, Dream," she said, letting go of her grip on the horse's neck.

As she stepped backward, her heel caught on a jagged rock and she fell down.

"Owww!" She winced.

Hunter had galloped to where she was sitting. He dismounted quickly and was at her side.

"Are you okay?" he asked. "What hurts?"

"My butt." She winced, rubbing her backside.

"Anything feel broken?"

"My butt," Skyler said, irritated.

She didn't cry, but she wanted to cry. This moment was a metaphor for her trip to the Big Sky state.

"Do you think you can stand?" he asked, sticking by her side.

She nodded, holding on to his arm. She was going to be stiff, that was for sure, but she could tell that nothing was broken.

"I'm okay." She let go of his arm.

"Will you be able to ride?"

She nodded her head again, biting her lip and hobbling forward.

"You're a real cowgirl now," Hunter said as he adjusted his stride to keep pace next to her.

She winced as she leaned down to pick up Dream Catcher's reins, which had fallen over her neck when she lowered her head to graze and were now lying on the ground.

"How do you figure?"

"Sure you fell off. But you're gonna get right back on. Can't get more cowgirl than that."

Chapter Thirteen

He didn't want to be too obvious or appear to be hovering, because he knew that Skyler didn't like that, but Hunter kept a close watch on her as they headed back to camp. That was a fall that could ruin a person's life. She was lucky—no, *they* were lucky—that she had walked away with a bruised backside and a hurt ego. It could have been a heck of a lot worse.

Hunter knew from experience that the best thing for a fall like that, as long as there weren't any signs of severe trauma, was for Skyler to keep moving—do little jobs to keep herself from stiffening up. She was going to be sore, no doubt about that. But her body would do better if she didn't baby it too much.

After they took care of the horses, Hunter gave her some ibuprofen for the aches and pains to come and then had her jump into a hot shower while he fixed them some lunch. He knew Skyler felt bothered by her fall; he had learned her expressions and her behavior quicker than any other person he'd known in his life. Perhaps he had just paid closer attention to Skyler than he had others.

"How are you feeling now?" he asked when she emerged from the tiny bathroom, her short pixie hair slicked back from her lovely face.

"Better." She sent him a small smile.

She took a seat at the table and waited for him to join her.

"Hope you don't mind grilled cheese," he said, putting a plate down in front of her. "Not much room to bring anything fancy."

"I've never needed fancy," she said, picking up a half of the sandwich he had made for her.

He'd been thinking a lot about what Skyler might need in her life. And if he was honest with himself, he still hadn't figured it out. When he started this romance with her, he hadn't been thinking too far in the future. It was new and exciting and he acted with his heart, not with his head. But, as summer's end approached, he began to realize just how deep in it he was with Skyler.

"You know…" he said after he finished one half of his sandwich. "When I was a kid, I was all dressed up in my new cowboy boots. My new hat. I had on this gun belt with two plastic sharp shooters. I thought I was John Wayne from those old Westerns my father used to watch."

He made her smile with that image of him as a young boy and that let him know that he was on the right track telling her this story.

"My father had gotten me a pony—her name was

Goldie. Now, Goldie lived up to the reputation for ponies—she was mean and ornery and didn't take too kindly to being ridden. Jock did that on purpose, because he wanted me to get a challenge right off the bat. My first ride on Goldie, I got on just fine, I got started just fine, but when I went to canter, she decided that was enough of me. She darted to the side, caught me off guard and I fell off."

"You did?" Skyler said in between bites.

He nodded with a smile at the memory. "But I didn't fall off clean like you did. My new boot got caught in the stirrup and she dragged me through a bunch of buckthorn. Man, did that hurt."

He continued while she listened attentively. Hunter wanted her to feel better and his story seemed to be doing the trick. "Goldie finally—and I would say deliberately—scraped me off on a tree."

Skyler smiled. "That's terrible. I don't know why I feel like laughing about it."

"Because it's frickin' hilarious." He laughed. "But, man, did I hate Goldie for a second or two after that."

"But you became friends?"

Skyler had a tender heart for all living things; it was something that he genuinely appreciated about her.

"Yes. We became friends."

"That's good." Skyler's eyes had a little bit of that sparkle back in them when she looked down at her empty plate. "Is there enough for another?"

After lunch, Hunter helped Skyler stretch her muscles, putting her through the same exercises and stretches he did personally whenever he got bucked off a bull. It wasn't going to fix everything that was heading her way over the next couple of days, but it would go a long way to soften the blow.

"When are we going back?" she asked after they stepped out of the trailer.

"I asked Bruce to take care of our workload until tomorrow."

Skyler squinted against the sun, her eyes turned toward the mountain. "I want to go up to that peak. Do you know a way up there?"

"You want to ride up there now?"

"When am I ever going to get another chance?" she asked.

He picked up a twig from the ground, snapped it between his fingers and tossed it away from him. "It's up to you. Are you sure you're up to it?"

"You said that exercise is good for me and sitting around babying myself will make things worse."

"I did say that."

She turned back to him, her lavender-blue eyes pulling him in and captivating his attention, as they always seemed to do.

"Do you know a way?" she asked.

Hunter always felt compelled to make Skyler's wishes come true. If she wanted to get up to that peak, then he was going to find a way to get there as safely as humanly possible.

He winked at her. "There's always a way."

They packed some supplies and tacked up the horses. This was familiar territory to him and he had ridden to the peak many times. In fact, in his youth, this was one of the spots Chase, Dustin and he would go to drink beer until they were almost too drunk to ride. He didn't miss the hangovers, but he did miss the close friendship he had with Chase and Dustin back when they were all together filming *Cowboy Up!*

Hunter took it nice and slow, picking each path forward carefully with Skyler in mind. It didn't surprise him that she wanted to get back in the saddle and go to the peak. In fact, he had figured out pretty quickly that Skyler was one of the most single-minded, goal-oriented, determined women he'd ever met. He had let her petite, almost fragile appearance fool him in the beginning. He had learned not to underestimate Skyler Sinclair after spending some concentrated time with her.

"We'll tie off the horses here." Hunter found a safer place for them to stop and dismount. "It's too rocky for the horses to go up to the peak."

He was at her side when she dismounted, guiding her down. When she needed help, she was the type of woman who would accept the help, another character trait he found admirable.

"You take the lead," he told her, wanting to stay behind her and catch her if she lost her footing. "Just follow this little path right up past that boulder."

Slowly, and more stiffly than she would have moved before the fall, Skyler hiked the short distance to the peak. He knew the moment when her view became unobstructed because she breathed in and then gasped with pleasure. It was a moment like this—a moment when she was surprised and delighted by her discovery—that he enjoyed the most. It was, he believed, what he would remember most fondly about his time with Skyler.

"Oh, wow." She took out her phone and began to take pictures of the expansive view from the top of the mountain. "Just look at this!"

Hunter stood back and watched her. It pleased him

to see her happy. She turned her head to look back at him, to see what he was doing.

"Come here and look at this view!"

"I'm enjoying the view I have right now." He smiled at her. Whenever he complimented her, she would smile a bit shyly at him, her eyes shining, a pretty blush staining her cheeks.

She finished grabbing the images she wanted to add to her story, put her phone away and then carefully walked over to where he was standing, took his hand and led him back over to where she had been standing.

"I want to share this moment with you," she said honestly.

Hunter found that he just couldn't deny her anything. He stood behind her, wrapped his arms around her and held on to her. She leaned back into his body with a happy sigh and held on to his forearms so they were completely connected.

"I love you," she said simply.

It was so soft, so quiet, the words being swept away from him on a quick gust of wind, that he almost thought he had imagined it.

He turned her gently in his arms; he wanted to look down at her face.

"And I love you." He tilted her chin up and kissed her on that mountain peak. It occurred to him that she was the first woman he had ever kissed here and he was glad for it. He wanted this moment to be special—a moment just for them. He kissed her again, knowing that he would never stop wanting to share kisses with this woman. And yet he couldn't seem to take the leap that Chase had taken. Chase could see himself in the city with Molly; no matter how hard he tried, Hunter couldn't see Skyler living full-time out west. And he knew, without any doubt, that he could not make his life in New York. Sugar Creek was his lifeblood; he was bound to this land and could not leave it.

They had packed a snack so they could sit at the top of the mountain and enjoy the view for a while. Together, they found a flat spot on the mountain face and sat down. Skyler said her tailbone still ached and that she had a feeling that she was going to sport a serious couple of bruises, but she had been in pain before—she had suffered before. The discomfort she was feeling now paled in comparison to the enjoyment she was having and he was glad to hear it.

After she finished her snack, she stood up, allowing him to give her a hand, and then walked over to the edge of the peak.

"Careful." Hunter was right on schedule with his warning.

"I will be," she promised.

Hunter was protective by nature, but Skyler, in particular, he felt the need to protect. Not only because she was an accident-prone neophyte, but also because he loved her so damn much.

She stood with her arms open wide, held back her head and shouted as loudly as she could, "I'm on top of the world!"

She turned around and smiled broadly at him. "Look at me, Hunter! I'm on top of the world!"

"I see you."

This Skyler was entirely different from the woman whom he had met in the airport at the beginning of summer. She had put on weight—she had built muscle naturally from lifting bales of hay, mucking stalls and riding horseback. She was still petite but built more like a gymnast at the height of their training. Her hair had grown back shaggy and messy and she was always pushing at it, but he liked how wild and crazy it was. She reminded him of a wood nymph in a fairy tale, mischievous and full of life. Her skin, once a gray, pasty hue, had turned golden with a rosy undertone. Standing with her hands on her hips, a sweet, shy sparkle in her eye, her feet planted apart with a small smile on her face, Hunter knew that he had never seen a more beautiful woman in his life.

Skyler continued to smile at him, and when he didn't say anything, just kept right on looking at her, she dropped her arms and asked, "What?"

"What?" He was snapped out of his own thinking by her question.

"Why are you looking at me like that?"

"I think you're beautiful. Can't I admire you?"

"If you must," she said with a flirty, sassy tone she was just beginning to use with him. She came over to where he was sitting and made a noise that let him know she had felt some pain when she bent down, which made her laugh at herself before she kissed him playfully. "I hope you don't mind if I admire you, too, cowboy."

That night, Hunter had an odd feeling in his gut. He wanted to savor every moment of their lovemaking, really take his time, memorize the gentle curve of her hip, how soft her skin felt in contrast to the roughness of his own. He loved the firm pertness of her breasts; he loved to suckle those pert nipples until Skyler was panting and digging her fingernails into his arm. He loved the scent of her, the taste of her.

Hunter kissed her between her thighs, lingered there to ready her body to take him in. Then he kissed a trail across her flat stomach and dropped one last kiss on the small, round, puckered scar where the chemo port had brought her life-saving medicine that had saved her and allowed her to come into his life. It had crossed his mind more often than he liked that he could have been robbed of ever having known this incredible woman at all.

"I don't want to hurt you." Hunter was on his side.

"I think it will be better if I'm on top," she agreed.

Hunter rolled onto his back, rolled on a condom and held his arms out for Skyler. Her legs on either side of his body, she sank down on him and they both moaned in unison. He hugged her to him, body-to-body, skin-to-skin, rocking gently together as he covered them with the blanket. He wanted to wrap them up in a cocoon and shut out the world completely. He closed his eyes, focused on the feelings of being enveloped by her warmth, the tightness of her body, how incredible it felt to be inside her, pleasing her as he pleased himself.

It was quiet, her first orgasm. She held on to him, her head tucked into his neck, his hands on her back. He was careful not to run his hands over her backside, as he loved to do. The noises she made as he brought her to climax made him want to join her, but he forced himself to hold off. He didn't want this to end.

"Yes, my love." He held her tightly while she shuddered in his arms.

She was still for a moment, catching her breath. Then she kissed his chest and pushed herself upright. She wanted more of him; she always wanted more. And he knew, more than ever before, that this was the first time in his life that a woman was truly *making love* to him, with him. Skyler was loving him with her body, showing him with every kiss, every moan, every time she caught his gaze and let him see her in her moment of climax, that it was an act of love.

The blanket slipped down her back as she lifted her hands to put them flat on the low roof above the bed. Her breasts white and round, her nipples looking like small rosebuds, she bore down on his shaft, taking him in as deeply as she could and rocking her hips while her strong thighs anchored her to him. He put his hands on her hips and watched his love take her pleasure. Just before she reached another crest, she fell forward into his arms, whispered "I love you" in his ear, and they both rode a glorious wave together. Hunter dropped kiss after loving kiss on her face, on her lips, on her chin, on her cheek.

"You are my first love." Hunter wanted her to know this. He wanted her to carry this knowledge with her always, no matter what happened. "My very first love."

That night, by the campfire, Skyler felt a particular form of contentedness. Yes, her body ached, but her heart was full of love for the cowboy. They loved each other—that was undeniable now. The question remained: What would they ultimately do about it?

"This place seems familiar to me. I can't put my finger on it."

Hunter stoked the fire for a moment before he said, "We filmed *Cowboy Up!* here for several episodes."

Skyler sat up with the realization. "That's it! That's why it seems so familiar."

"We used this same firepit," he added.

She loved the fact that she was sitting at one of the

locations of the show. She didn't express her feelings, sensitive to Hunter's dislike of his history with the show.

Hunter sat back on his haunches, staring into the fire, lost in his own thoughts. After a moment, he chuckled to himself and then sat back on the ground.

"What?"

"I was just thinking back to something that happened during filming one season," Hunter said with another laugh. "I went off into the woods to relieve myself— I went pretty far out in the woods because we had the film crew with us and I don't know..." He shrugged. "I didn't really trust them—they were from LA."

"City folk can be suspicious," she interjected teasingly.

He smiled as he continued. "I was just about done and I look down and realize that I had been relieving myself on a snake."

Skyler wasn't expecting him to say that. "Oh, no!" She laughed, surprised.

"I jumped back like I had been bitten for real," he said. "I didn't have to pee anymore, I can tell you that. The snake was about four feet long, impressively thick..."

"Venomous?"

He nodded. "I had taken a whiz on a prairie rattlesnake."

"Was it asleep? Why didn't it move?"

"I was wondering the same thing," he said. "So I found a sharp stick and poked it. Probably not the smartest idea, but that's what I did. It was dead, so I stabbed it with the stick and carried it back to camp. Told everyone that I killed it."

Skyler laughed along with him, enjoying this storytelling side of Hunter.

"Hey…wait. I remember that episode. They filmed you with that snake."

He nodded, his smile dropping just a bit. Then he flashed her a self-effacing half smile. "I never did tell them that I found it dead. You're the only one who knows that secret."

She crossed her heart with her finger. "I'll never tell."

After a minute, Hunter added, "You know, the first thing that I thought when I saw that I was peeing on a snake?"

"What?"

"That if I got bit by a venomous snake on the head of my *snake,* as it were—" he grinned at her with good humor "—there wouldn't be anyone back at camp who would be willing to suck the venom out."

Skyler laughed so hard that her stomach hurt a bit.

"Not one of them would have taken pity on me," he told her.

"Not even Chase?" she asked, still laughing.

"Heck no," Hunter said. "He'd say 'Sorry, bro— you're dead.'"

They continued to laugh together and then Skyler asked, "Wait. Wasn't there a girl on the show? What was her name?"

Hunter stopped laughing and she regretted even bringing it up. Up until then, they had been having a great time. "Sarah."

"That's right," she said. "Sarah."

The cowboy breathed in deeply and then let it out. He stared into the fire for a good long while before he seemed ready to talk again. She could read Hunter well—as well as she could read Molly or her dad, but it had happened in a much shorter amount of time.

"You asked me once why Jock let you come here."

She nodded. She had always wondered that. It would have been so easy to cancel on her.

Hunter looked at her over the fire, his brilliant blue eyes catching the yellow and orange light from the fire. "He let you come because of Sarah."

She didn't understand and she told him as much.

"Sarah was one of my best friends—we grew up together. She was the daughter of Jock's best friend." He was staring at the fire now. "She was also Chase's girlfriend."

Skyler's stomach tensed as she anticipated something she didn't necessarily want to hear. Why would Jock let her come to Sugar Creek because of someone named Sarah?

"Sarah wasn't there to film that show—the one with the snake—because she had just been diagnosed with cancer."

"Oh," Skyler said softly. "I see."

"Brain cancer."

"I'm so sorry, Hunter." She said it and she meant it. "I am so sorry."

He swallowed hard, lowered his head and gave her a quick nod.

"It wasn't six months later and we lost her," Hunter continued, his head still down. "We all lost Sarah. Sarah's father took it the hardest and it wasn't too long before he joined her in the grave."

Skyler put her hand over her mouth, saddened for Hunter and his family. His friends.

Hunter looked up at her then. "I believe Jock invited you here to help me."

"To help you?"

"I've never quite gotten over Sarah's death. She was my sister..." His voice had a catch in it. "Not by blood but choice."

The picture came into focus for Skyler—Hunter hadn't been able to save Sarah, but Jock believed that he could find some closure by helping her heal.

"Did it work?" she asked.

He looked up again this time with a question in his eyes.

"Did I help you?" she persisted.

Hunter stared across the fire, his eyes so intent on her face. "You've helped me more than anyone in my life, Skyler. For the first time, I feel like I can finally let Sarah rest in peace."

Chapter Fourteen

Skyler had difficulty sleeping that last night they were away from home base. Hunter slept beside her—he seemed to fall asleep so easily—while she stared up at the low ceiling, thinking. The subject of Molly and Chase's relationship had still not been broached. After the discussion about Sarah, something that seemed to be a gut-wrenching subject for Hunter, Skyler had decided to not raise the question she had regarding Chase's sudden attachment to Molly. But there were many questions on her mind.

The next morning, they had packed up the campsite and loaded the horses. Their work was done and so was their minibreak from the routine of their ranch chores.

"Time to go." Hunter got behind the wheel. He glanced over at her. "Ready?"

She had her elbow resting on the open window, taking one last look around, wanting to commit it to memory. "Ready."

Once they had crossed the stream and Skyler knew the toughest terrain was behind them, she turned her body slightly toward Hunter.

"Can I ask you something?"

"You can ask me anything you want."

"Do you know about Chase and Molly?"

He hesitated, and in that hesitation, she knew that the answer was yes. He did know.

"Yes. Chase told me."

She waited a moment to see if he would say anything else. When he didn't, she prompted, "And…?"

Hunter shook his head as if he was having his own conversation with himself. Then he said, "I don't know what to think about it, to be honest."

He glanced over at her. "What about you?"

"I think it's too fast."

"I think so, too."

"I think that they've never been in the same place at the same time."

"I said that to him."

"I said it to her." She braced her hand on the dashboard when they hit a deep bump in the rustic road.

"And?"

"She says she loves him."

"He said the same."

They were both quiet for a moment before Skyler asked, "Last night you told me about Sarah."

He nodded.

"Do you think Chase has told Molly about her?"

"I don't know."

"I don't want to offend you, Hunter, I just want to protect my friend…"

"You won't offend me."

"Do you think that Molly is some sort of rebound for him? I know it's been years, but time doesn't always heal."

"I don't think it's a rebound," Hunter insisted, but she still didn't feel reassured.

"Do you think he really loves her?"

"He sounded like it." He glanced over at her curiously. "Do you think she loves him?"

She breathed in on the thought, then exhaled and said, "Yeah. I think she does. Or at least she thinks that she does."

The conversation waned and neither of them seemed too eager to pick it back up. As they approached the settled part of the ranch, with Bruce and Savannah's small stake appearing in the far-off distance, Hunter said, perhaps as a way to button up the subject, "I hope it works out for them."

"So do I," she agreed and she meant it sincerely. Molly deserved to have a lifetime of love and she hoped that Chase turned out to be the man who could give that to her.

"We are sitting in a glass house," she openly mused.

"Meaning?"

"Maybe we don't have much of a leg to stand on, really. We jumped in pretty quick without much of an exit plan."

That brought his eyes, a bit narrowed, to her face. "Yes, we did."

There was an odd silence between them, but it wasn't

comfortable, like most of their lulls in conversation were. This felt different.

"Maybe we need to fix that." Hunter's hands had tightened on the wheel, the knuckles on his hands turning white. Then he loosened his grip.

She waited, holding her breath for a second before letting it out. Did he mean "fix it" as in figure out their exit plan? Or was this the beginning of some sort of proposal?

He turned them toward Liam's cabin, his eyes steady on the ranch road. "Do you think that you could ever see yourself here...full-time?"

It was a question she had asked herself so many times and recently she had gotten to *yes*. Geography couldn't be the reason for the love she felt for Hunter to be lost— the only thing that really gave her pause was the idea of leaving her father entirely without family. He was a widower and she was his only child—the thought of leaving him alone hurt her heart.

She was formulating her response when her phone started to go crazy. She fought to fish it out of her back pocket and then looked at the screen. A slew of text messages and emails from several days ago were loading into her phone now. And there were missed calls.

"Oh, no!" Skyler read the first text message and then the next.

"What's wrong?" Hunter's phone was chiming, as well.

"My father." She was already dialing Molly. "They think he had a stroke."

Hunter felt unmoored and odd as he pulled up to Liam's cabin for what would be the last time he would come to pick up Skyler. He reflected back on the first time he had brought her to what she called her oasis in the world. He had resented her; he had wanted to be rid of her. And now all he wanted to do was hold on to her, to keep her close.

He shut off the engine and studied Skyler sitting on the front porch, her antique-wallpaper luggage stacked near the steps. Daisy was curled up in her lap. Skyler looked over at him, caught his eye, but her usual smile was not present.

"Everything set for today?" he asked when he reached the porch.

She nodded. "They couldn't get a charter on such short notice but I got a seat on a commercial flight."

The doctors had confirmed that Chester Sinclair had experienced a stroke and Skyler didn't hesitate to cut her time in Montana short.

"You'll be okay?" he asked, picking up two of her bags to load in the truck.

"I'm stronger now," she said. "I'll be okay. I have to get home to my father."

He packed up her luggage and she was still on the porch with Daisy curled up on her lap. There were tears in her eyes when she looked up from the cat. "I shouldn't have started a relationship that I couldn't finish."

It struck him that the same could be said for their relationship, and perhaps, she was saying that, too.

"How will she be okay without me?"

"I will take her to Oak Tree Hill with me," he promised. Daisy had become a part of Skyler, so naturally, she was a part of him.

"Okay," she said, hugging the cat to her chest. She kissed her on the head, then put her down next to the rocking chair. Daisy meowed loudly and gazed up at Skyler.

"She knows something's wrong," she told Hunter.

There wasn't anything he could say to make it better, so he remained silent. Skyler stood up and looked around.

"What about the horses?"

"I'll take them back up to the main barn."

"Even Zodiac?" she asked. Liam was still monitoring him and hadn't cleared him for work.

Hunter wrapped his arms around her, rested his chin on the top of her head, as he liked to do, and gave her a shoulder to lean on.

"Don't worry about the animals right now. I've got them covered. Let's just get you home to your dad."

Holding hands, Hunter escorted Skyler down the stairs to the truck.

She paused and looked back at the barn. "I wonder if I should just say one more goodbye to the horses."

"No." He coaxed her forward. "It will never be enough."

"No," she echoed, looking around, seemingly to make a mental recording of her ranch oasis. "It will never be enough."

He opened the door for her and waited for her to get in and buckle up. Then he shut the door firmly behind her. He didn't feel as strong or confident as he was showing to Skyler; she needed him to be the backbone for them both right now. Inside, he was torn in two. He hadn't expected to say goodbye so soon. Hunter hadn't had time to prepare himself; he hadn't had to time to work through their geography problem. And now she was returning home and he had no idea if their romance, so new and unexpected for both of them, would be able to survive the distance.

"Do you know, we don't have a picture of us together," she said as they pulled onto the highway, leaving Sugar Creek land.

Skyler had been very considerate about his aversion to social media. He still got a knot in his gut when he remembered what it felt like to be a teenage kid on the receiving end of so much simultaneous obsession and venom. He had been very careful about his image once the show was canceled. And Skyler, to her credit, hadn't taken pictures of him while she was photo-journaling her trip for her supports, coworkers and friends back home.

"That's my fault," he admitted.

"It's like we didn't exist at all."

"You don't really believe that," Hunter said more sharply than he had intended.

"I don't know what I believe." Skyler rubbed her hands over her face, dark circles from stress and lack of sleep noticeable beneath her eyes. "This isn't how I expected things to end between us."

He glanced over at her; he wished that he wasn't driving while they were having this conversation. He wished that it didn't feel inappropriate to discuss a heavy subject like their geographically challenged relationship when she was so worried about her father.

"This isn't goodbye," he said, and he heard the certainty resonated in his own voice.

"It isn't?" she asked doubtfully.

"Not for me." He took his hand off the wheel for a second to squeeze her hand reassuringly. "It's not goodbye—it's 'see you later.'"

That got a small smile out of her. "Okay."

At the airport, Hunter pulled in front of the terminal to unload the baggage. Before he took the truck to the parking lot, he asked the baggage handler to take a picture of them. They took off their masks and posed for the picture.

Skyler put her mask back on and took her phone from the gentleman. "Thank you."

Skyler looked at the picture and then showed it to him. "We look good together I think."

"I think so."

After she was checked in, Skyler wandered over to the carousel where he had seen her for the first time.

"I never did get a chance to go to the museum."

He turned her around and wrapped her up in his arms. "Hey. Montana will still be here. The museum will still be here. I will still be here."

They stood together for many minutes, the world going about its business while they were stuck in that one moment together. When boarding for her flight was called, Hunter tightened his hold on her.

"I love you, Skyler." He looked into her eyes so she would see that he meant it.

"I love you."

For the briefest of moments, they slipped down their masks and kissed.

"Remember," he said after he pulled his mask back up. "It's not goodbye. It's 'see you later.'"

She nodded and began to walk away from him.

"Don't forget me, Skyler," he called after her.

She turned around. "I've loved you almost all of my life, Hunter. How could I ever forget you?"

* * *

"Molly!" Skyler was relieved and grateful to see her friend awaiting her arrival. "I'm going to hug you," she said to her friend.

"I get tested every day at my new job," Molly told her. "Hug away."

They hugged each other tightly. Skyler was grateful to have Molly, the closest thing to a sibling she had in her life, to help her navigate the next several days. They managed to MacGyver her luggage into the early model Toyota Molly had borrowed from her aunt.

"I'm so sorry about your dad," Molly said as she navigated out of the parking garage and pointed them toward home.

"I still feel like I'm in shock," Skyler said while sending Hunter a text that she had landed safely.

"Of course."

"First Mom dies from complications related to COPD, and then Dad has to handle my diagnosis without her, and now he's in the hospital with a stroke? He doesn't deserve it."

"Neither do you," her friend said.

Skyler couldn't deny that it felt like the worst kind of luck, but she couldn't dwell on it. She needed to dwell on how to make her father whole.

"How does it feel to be back?" Molly asked.

"Weird," Skyler admitted. "Different worlds."

"I bet," her friend said. "You look amazing."

Skyler touched her hair. "I need a haircut. It feels really good to be able to say that again."

"Mom will do it for you. She's been cutting the neighbor's hair on the balcony. Strange times."

"If she'd be willing, I would really appreciate it. I'm starting to feel like a Muppet."

They arrived at Skyler's 1930s single-family two-story house in Queens—it had seen better days. The whitewash paint was more gray than white and the roof had needed replacing for years. Her mother had always been the iron fist when it came to maintaining curb appeal. Molly helped her drag her heavy bags up the steps to the house.

"You packed a ton." Molly lugged the last bag up to the top step.

"I didn't wear half of the stuff." She put the key in the door. "I could've taken one suitcase and a carry-on."

Once inside the front door, which opened directly into the living room, Skyler turned on the lamp just inside of the door and looked around. There were papers strewn on the floor near her father's favorite recliner chair and a bowl of half-eaten popcorn on the scratched, 1970s coffee table that her father had refused to let go.

"I wish I could stay." Molly sent her a regretful look. "I tried to get out of my shift."

Skyler hugged her friend tightly. "Thank you, Moll. I'm so lucky to have you in my life."

"Same." Molly squeezed her tight. "Keep me in the loop. I check my phone on breaks."

"I will."

"And I'll be back tomorrow."

Skyler shut the door behind her friend, locked it and then looked around with a heavy sigh. She had called her father on the way home from the airport and he sounded in good spirits, except for the fact that he was upset that she had cut her trip short. Over the course of the summer, her father had come to believe that her trip out west was exactly what she had needed to reboot her life.

"Don't come home," he had told her in a complete 180-degree reversal of his initial response to her trip.

"I'm coming home," she had said in a tone that brooked no argument. He hadn't convinced her *not* to go and now he wasn't going to convince her to stay while he was in the hospital.

Skyler moved around the two-story house in a bit of a daze, picking up papers and putting them in the recycling, gathering up random dishes and stacking them in the sink. Her father had returned to bachelor life in her absence—not completely messy, but not overly concerned about keeping a tidy house. Room by room she made her way through her childhood home, finding a shirt or a pile of grease-covered uniforms from the garage along the way. The house felt empty and sad, and she knew that she would need to keep herself busy straightening the house and unpacking her bags while she awaited her father's release.

The dishes had been washed and were drying in the dish drain; the uniforms were in the washing machine. Skyler rolled her largest piece of luggage through the house to the back door. She opened the door and was greeted with the concrete slab between the house and her garage apartment. Weeds pushed up through cracks in the slab and it was odd that this was one of the only splashes of greenery she could see.

In that moment, she missed the trees of Montana, so plentiful and fragrant, desperately. Or perhaps she just missed Hunter desperately. As if he had picked up her thoughts on some mutual wavelength that connected them, no matter how many miles separated them, Hunter called.

She quickly picked up the phone on the first ring. "Hi."

"Hi," he said back. "I miss you."

"I miss you so much," she said, juggling the phone and the suitcase as she continued on her path toward her apartment.

"I have Daisy with me," he told her.

"Thank you, Hunter. I need her to be okay."

"She is," he reassured her. "The question is, how are you? How is your father?"

She wrestled her suitcase through the door to her apartment and then collapsed on the couch. She had, in fact, missed her couch. It was the perfect fabric and so comfy. She sat up long enough to kick off her shoes before sinking back, with a happy sigh, into her couch. They spoke for an hour with a promise to speak the next day. One by one, she got her bags into the apartment. Before Sugar Creek Ranch, she would not have had the strength to travel across country, begin to clean her father's house and still get her bags to the apartment.

But now she was tired, and all she could think about was crawling into her own bed, getting some sleep and then going to visit her father as soon as visiting hours started the next day. Thank goodness the hospitals were now allowing visitors.

A quick shower later, Skyler set the alarm on her phone, then ran her fingers over the only picture of her and Hunter together that she had set as her home screen wallpaper.

A text came through from Hunter in response to

her text letting him know that she was going to sleep. Sleep well, my love.

The bed, her wonderful mattress, felt like home to her. Her pillows, her blanket, her sheets. But the bed was lonely without Hunter. She missed his body making everything too hot; she missed fighting over the blanket, each accusing the other of being a blanket hog. She missed being able to curl up next to him, put her hand over his heart and smell the wonderful scent of his skin. That night, as the sounds of her neighborhood kept her up instead of lulling her to sleep, Skyler wished she could get Scotty to beam Hunter right into her bed. No, that wasn't true. She wished that Scotty would beam her, and her bed, back to Montana. Somewhere along the way, the real Montana—the one with the rabid ants, giant horseflies, mud and manure, had begun to feel more like home than New York. She didn't know it before she left Sugar Creek…but she knew it now. Montana was Hunter's home; and for her, wherever Hunter was, that was home for her, too.

Chapter Fifteen

"I'm okay, Sky." Chester Sinclair slumped into his recliner.

Skyler watched as her father tried to use the lever to recline the chair; her father had had a stroke on the right side of his brain, which had caused some weakness on the left side of his body.

She rushed over to his chair, helped him recline and then didn't take offense when he growled at her for helping him when he didn't need it. Her father was a lefty, which made this stroke a serious blow. Yes, he had other mechanics that worked in his shop, but with the pandemic and people driving less, business had slowed and he was already struggling to make ends meet. In order to not lay off any workers, Chester had been taking in some overflow clients from a company that had some older model diesel trucks. Now he was going to have to give up that revenue stream, and if he couldn't come up with another solution, he would have to start furloughing workers.

"Dad." Skyler kneeled by his recliner, acutely aware of the fact that at the beginning of summer, and not all that long ago, he had been the one kneeling beside her chair. "It's going to be okay."

Chester put his hand on her face, looked her over real good. "You're better. That makes everything okay for me."

Skyler had a ton of ideas about how to keep them afloat while Chester was recovering, none of them her father was going to like. So she decided it would be best for her to let him settle in to the routine of physical and occupational therapy for his left-side weakness and then she would broach some touchy subjects with him.

"Here's the remote." She brought him the control for the TV. "Molly and I will be in the apartment if you need us."

"I'm glad you're home, Mr. Sinclair." Molly had her hip leaning against the kitchen counter. When she had first come to this house for a sleepover, Molly had to stand on her tiptoes to reach a plate of cookies Skyler's mom had made for them.

"Thank you, Molly." Her father always had a smile for Molly.

Skyler leaned down, gave her father a kiss on the cheek and then she and her friend walked to the back of the house toward the apartment.

"He's going to get better," Molly said, her hazel eyes concerned. "He'll get some therapy and he'll get better."

Skyler sent her friend a brief smile while she unlocked the door to her apartment. She did believe that her father was going to get better. He was strong and determined, and she had seen life knock him down plenty of times before. Chester Sinclair had always gotten back up and worked so hard that he was even better off than before.

"I have to learn how to cook," Skyler mused, looking at the pile of luggage still yet to be unpacked. "No more takeout for him. He has to be on a healthy diet."

She exchanged a look with her friend and said, "He's going to hate that."

They both laughed. Chester was a steak-and-potatoes kind of guy—getting him to change his diet and start to exercise was going to be a challenge. But if she could worm and herd cattle, she believed she was more than up for the task.

"Do you want me to help you get this done?" Molly nodded toward the luggage.

Skyler lifted her shoulders with a sigh. "No. I'm not ready to tackle this. I actually wanted to talk to you about something."

Molly knew her well enough to know that they weren't about to discuss something frivolous. Her friend took her typical seat on the sofa and curled her legs beneath her.

"What's going on?"

Skyler joined her on the couch, sitting cross-legged and facing Molly. "I don't know why I've waited to tell you this."

Molly waited for her to finish.

"But Hunter and I…" She stopped for a moment to find the exact right words. "Fell in love."

Molly's heart-shaped face went from surprised to

joyous quickly. She stood up, sat down next to Skyler and hugged her tightly.

"I'm so glad," her friend said. "I was so worried that I would have Chase and you wouldn't have your own cowboy."

Now she was glad that she waited to tell Molly. This was the kind of moment she could look back on with a smile for the rest of her life—the day she told Molly that she was in love with Hunter Brand, and now Hunter Brand was in love with her!

Molly, of course, asked the obvious question. "But why didn't you tell me sooner?"

"I don't know," she said honestly. "I think it was so new and so unreal that I couldn't bring myself to talk about it. Not even with you."

She reached out and squeezed Molly's hand. "I'm sorry."

Molly shook her head quickly, her wild curls dancing about her shoulders. "Don't you worry about it for one more second, Sky. I'm just happy. For both of us."

Her friend sat back, her face beaming. "We both got our cowboys. It really happened for us."

"Well..." Skyler wanted to temper Molly's enthusiasm. There hadn't been any promises or proposals and even plans between them. "I'm not sure there's a cut-and-dried status category for us. He has his life at Sugar Creek and I have to make sure that the bills get paid around here."

"It's going to work out for you." Her friend had always been an optimist. In fact, Molly had never faltered in her belief that she was going to survive cancer.

"You know what makes me feel happy right now, Moll?" Skyler said. "To see you so happy with Chase."

She meant it sincerely. She didn't know where her relationship with Hunter was going to go, and that was just the reality of the current moment. But to see Molly glowing from being in love with Chase was just as rewarding as if it was happening to her.

"Your cowboy is coming," Skyler said with a smile.

"Your cowboy is coming, too," her friend said emphatically. "Just you wait and see."

They talked for nearly two more hours, bouncing from one subject to another, and then Molly had to go home and get ready for work. Skyler was still on leave from the insurance agency; she had some serious thinking to do about her next steps. Unfortunately, none of those next steps would lead her back to Hunter anytime soon.

"We've been missing you at the family events." Hunter's eldest brother, Bruce, had come up to his place among the ancient oak trees. It was a rare visit to his remote and private stake on Sugar Creek.

"Is that right?" Hunter was sitting on the two-seater bench that he had carved with Daisy curled up next to him.

Bruce had grown a beard and he needed a haircut, but his ocean-blue eyes, the same as his own, were both curious and concerned. As the eldest of the siblings, Bruce was expected—by Jock—to wrangle his brothers and sister if they looked like they were straying from the herd.

"Mom is worried about you."

That was a punch to the gut; he never wanted to upset his mother. And yet that knowledge wasn't enough to make him want to break out of his self-imposed isolation. After Skyler's trip was abruptly cut short, and his life returned to the way it was before she had arrived, Hunter found that his preference to be alone now extended to his family, too.

"And Dad?" Hunter asked, knowing that news of Brandy and Dustin's relationship had burned through the gossip wires in Bozeman like a wildfire.

"Pissed off."

"That's about right." He looked down at Daisy and the cat lifted her head, gazed up at him lovingly and then meowed.

Bruce lowered himself to the ground, grunting a bit. "You need something to sit on around here."

"I don't get many visitors," Hunter countered.

"Nothing to visit, really." His brother looked around.

They didn't speak for a while; Hunter waited for Bruce to say what he was really there to say.

"You look like hell, bro," Bruce noted.

Hunter reached up and scratched his scruffy facial hair. He could use a shave. And he could put on some clean clothes.

When he didn't add to the conversation as he knew Bruce expected him to, his brother said, "Everybody— Mom, Dad, me—thinks you got involved with the woman from New York."

"Her name is Skyler."

Bruce knew right then—Hunter could read it in his face—that the family's suspicion about the nature of his relationship with Skyler was true.

"So it's true." His brother had a grim expression on his face. "What about Brandy?"

Hunter stood up, frustrated, disturbing Daisy. The cat got up, executed a Halloween-cat stretch and then turned around in a circle several times before she curled back up on the bench.

"Brandy doesn't want anything to do with me and the feeling is mutual. She was a pain in the butt when we were kids and the only thing that's changed now that's she's older is that she's a heck of a lot prettier than she used to be. But still a royal pain in the ass."

Hunter paced a little beside the firepit. "And the fact that Jock got his hopes up that I was going to marry Brandy and then have a grandchild that would tie the two ranches together was nuts!"

He stopped pacing. "You see that that was nuts, right?"

"You and Brandy could've hit it off," his brother said.

"Well, we *didn't*."

Bruce held up his hands. "Okay. So you didn't. That still doesn't explain why you've been living like a hermit out here with that cat."

"I'm figuring things out."

"Like what?"

"Like," Hunter said pointedly, "how I'm going to get Skyler back home where she belongs."

The visit from his brother did have the benefit of "snapping him out of it." After Bruce left, Hunter got himself cleaned up. He shaved, put on clean clothes and headed over to Chase's ranch. Chase was the person in his life, a brother from another mother, who would understand his dilemma with Skyler.

When he pulled onto the neglected driveway to the Rocking R Ranch, Chase was near the fence putting up a For Sale by Owner sign. Hunter got out of his truck and walked over to his friend.

"This makes it real," he said.

"Yeah." Chase had been hand-digging a hole for the wooden signpost. "It's real. Molly told her folks about us last night."

Hunter helped Chase lift up the heavy signpost and together they put it into the hole.

"Oh, yeah? How'd that go?"

They both pushed dirt into the hole, helping the signpost to be more secure. Then Chase used the shovel to tamp down the loose dirt.

"Not too bad, considering." Chase leaned on the shovel for a moment. "I think they were hoping for a more of a white-collar kind of guy for Molly."

Hunter nodded his understanding. A lot of parents had a certain idea of who they wanted their adult children to marry—he was living proof of that.

"Six years in the army did help soften the blow for them." Chase threw the shovel in the back of Hunter's truck.

After the show got canceled, Chase had joined the army. He might have gone far in the armed forces if his parents hadn't desperately needed his help on the ranch. Chase's father had been a great guy, but he was lousy with money. When they were growing up, everyone knew that the Rockwells were always on the brink of financial disaster. All of Chase's money from the show had gone to his family and even that hadn't been enough to save them.

Hunter drove them to the house. The Rockwell house had been built in the 1920s—it was a small two-story house with whitewashed boards and a rusty tin roof. There was a front porch with an old swing where Linda

Rockwell, Chase's mother, had treated Hunter with homemade root beer.

As he parked, he stared at the house, memories of his childhood—great memories—rushing over him.

"We had some good times here, didn't we?"

"We did," Chase agreed. His friend didn't say it, but Chase had also had plenty of bad times in that house, too. When he drank, his father could get mean. When he drank, his father had a temper.

When he got out of the truck and looked around, something hit Hunter's gut. There were crossroad moments in a person's life—this felt like one for him.

Inside the farmhouse, they sat at Linda's kitchen table, a bit wobbly now as it was sitting on floorboards that had sagged over time.

"What's the news?" Hunter asked his friend.

Chase popped the top off a bottle of beer and handed it to him. After he grabbed a beer for himself, his friend joined him at his mother's wobbly table. The table, like the kitchen, seemed so much smaller than he remembered. But then again, most of the time he had spent at this table, he had been a kid.

Chase held up his bottle of beer. "To Molly and Skyler."

Hunter touched his bottle to Chase's. "To Molly and Skyler."

Chase was the first person he had told about his relationship with Skyler. To his mind, Chase was the only one who wouldn't judge his feelings for her. After all, he had fallen for Molly in record time.

"Molly sent me some ideas for a ring," Chase said. "As soon as I sell this place, the first thing I'm doing is buying her the best damn ring I can afford."

Hunter took a swig of his beer then put the bottle down on the table. The table wobbled again.

"How can you stand not to fix this?" He stood up, grabbed one of the bottle caps on the counter, kneeled down and put the cap under one of the table's legs.

"This table is the least of my problems," Chase said.

Hunter jiggled the table to see how well the bottle cap had worked. Satisfied, he sat back down.

"What's the news on your end?" Chase asked him, milking his beer, as he had done for years now.

Hunter breathed in and let it on a frustrated sigh. "We're stuck, bro. That's the news. As long as her dad is laid up, she's not willing to even consider coming back here."

"Is she worth the wait to you?"

Hunter finished his beer. "Yeah, she's worth the wait. Problem is, I miss her."

They sat together in silence, each occupied with their own thoughts. Sometimes a person just needed a chance to see a problem from a different angle—that's what coming to the Rocking R had done for Hunter.

"I'm going to help you get the money for that ring right now," he told his friend.

Chase raised an eyebrow at him, his fingers busy peeling the wrapper off the bottle.

"I haven't spent a dime of my *Cowboy Up!* money."

His friend shook his head. "I'm not taking another dime from anybody. Not even you."

"I'm not talking about borrowing."

"Charity."

"Not charity. A business transaction."

"Come again?" Chase said, but Hunter knew he had his friend's full attention now.

"I'm going to buy the Rocking R."

Just now, sitting in the Rockwell kitchen, Hunter finally knew what he wanted to do with all that money he had made from a show he had learned to regret. If he could buy the Rocking R Ranch, which would allow Chase to get that ring for Molly and help him establish his life in New York, then being on that damn show would actually have been worth it.

Chase stopped peeling the label and sat back in his chair. "You want to buy this place?"

"I do," he said. "I'll take the whole damn lot. What's your price?"

His friend did not respond the way Hunter had expected. He had expected Chase to be excited, relieved and, of course, to think that he had actually saved the day. Instead, Chase frowned and shook his head.

"Nope," he said.

"What do you mean *nope*?"

"Nope," Chase repeated. "I'm not going to let you buy this place just to bail me out. Forget it."

"I'm not buying it to bail you out."

Chase shot him a skeptical look.

"Okay, I admit that one of the results of buying this place would be to bail you out. But that's not the only reason."

His friend finished his beer and stood up. "Give me another reason."

"I'm years away from building on my stake at Sugar Creek. I could move right into this place. I could move Skyler right into this place."

Chase put another beer down in front of him, grabbed his empty bottle and put it in the sink. His friend didn't get a second beer for himself.

"You want to live with Skyler here?"

"Yeah. Why not? I'll look a heck of a lot more tempting with an actual house instead of a trailer. Right?"

"I can't deny that." Chase laughed. "That trailer is not exactly a benefit to marrying you."

Hunter wasn't offended by his friend's friendly ribbing about his trailer; after all, it was true. He wanted to have a place for Skyler, a place where they could start their lives. They could save and design their perfect miniranch among the ancient oak trees while they occupied their time refurbishing the Rocking R.

"You really want to buy this place?" He could tell that his friend was starting to warm to the idea.

"Yeah," he said after he swallowed a swig of beer. "I can't let this place be sold to strangers. That way, it will stay in the family. And you'll always have a place to come home to when you bring Molly out to Montana for a visit."

"We can settle on a price that's fair," Chase said and that was when Hunter knew that his friend was on board with the idea.

Hunter held his hand out over the tabletop. "Do we have a deal?"

Chase shook his hand with the grip of a man who had done hard work all of his life. "We have a deal."

Hunter finished his second beer, stood up, tossed the bottle into the sink and then said, "Let's go take that damn sign out of the ground."

Chase stood up with a sigh, "Bro, I wish you had figured all of this out *before* I dug that hole."

"I like your hair," Hunter said to Skyler.

She reached up and touched her newly cut hair. "Do you? Molly's mom cut it for me."

"I like it short," he told her, wishing that he could reach through the screen and touch her.

"I kind of do, too," she agreed. "I always wore it long but now I think it suits me."

Once Hunter came up with a plan, he didn't want to wait to put it in action. While Skyler was busy getting her father set up with therapists, he had been busy buying the Rocking R Ranch. It had been a simple transaction—he was a cash buyer, not negotiating on the terms and he didn't give a damn about an inspection report. He knew the Rockwell home inside and out; he knew where all the bodies were buried in the plumbing, in the foundation and the roof.

"I have some news," he told her.

"Oh, yeah?" She settled back on her couch, which was her usual position when they talked.

"I bought the Rocking R Ranch."

Skyler's lavender-blue eyes widened. "You did?"

He nodded. "It's ours."

"Ours?" She repeated the word.

"It's a place to start."

Skyler had a confused look on her face. "Hunter—a place to start what?"

"Our lives together," he said directly.

"But we've talked about this," she said with a frown. "You know I can't even consider coming back to Montana until things are more stable around here. And even then…"

"Even then what?" Hunter asked, wondering why neither Chase nor Skyler had been as enthusiastic about his grand plan as he was.

She bit her lip, something she did when she was hesitating to say something to him.

"Even then what?" he repeated, prodding her to open up to him.

"I'm not going to move my whole entire life to Montana unless we were going to get married, Hunter." She held up her hand quickly. "And I'm not saying that to prompt some proposal out of you…"

"Is that all?" he asked, a light bulb coming on his brain. In his excitement, he had missed a vital step with Skyler.

"Is that all?" Now she was repeating the question. "It's kind of a big thing."

He leaned forward so she could see him more clearly in the video. "You want to marry me, don't you?"

When she didn't answer him right away, he came at it from a different angle. "I want to marry you."

"You do?"

"Of course I do. I thought you would have picked up on that by now."

"You have never mentioned marriage to me. Not once," Skyler told him.

"Well, let's fix that right now," Hunter said, and at that moment, Daisy jumped up on the small table in his trailer, walked in front of the camera and hit him in the face with her tail.

"Daisy!" Skyler exclaimed. "Hi, baby girl!"

Hunter gently moved the cat out of the way. "Will you marry me, Skyler?"

He couldn't read Skyler's expression—was she happy or mad?

Daisy had turned around and was rubbing up against his chin, purring and blocking the camera shot with her body.

"Damn it, Daisy. I'm trying to get something done here."

Hunter scooped up the cat and put her down on the floor with a quick pat he hoped would satisfy the feline for a moment or two.

"What do you think?" he asked, wondering why Skyler hadn't yet responded to his proposal.

"Well…" Skyler said slowly, thoughtfully. "I think this isn't the most romantic proposal on record. But yes, Hunter. I want to marry you."

A huge smile came to his face.

"But—"

"No buts."

"*But* we have to talk about my health, Hunter. Whenever I've tried to bring it up, you change the subject."

"You're in remission. Subject closed."

"Hunter—it's not that simple. I need to have regular checkups. I'm in remission, but there aren't any guarantees. If it…" She paused, swallowed her own worries back and then restarted. "If it comes back, can you handle it?"

"I can handle it, Skyler," Hunter said seriously. "In sickness and health. Remember?"

She smiled at him then. "Yes. In sickness and in health."

"So, is that a 'yes, I will marry you' smile?"

"Yes." Her smile widened. "I will marry you, Hunter."

"Hot damn." The cowboy grinned at her. "We're gonna get married, you and me."

"But we have to wait until after I get things settled with my dad, Hunter. You understand that I have no idea how long that will take."

"That's okay," he said. "You're worth the wait."

That brought a lovely smile to Skyler's lovely face. "Thank you, Hunter. You've always been worth the wait for me."

Chapter Sixteen

"Hey, Dad," Skyler said as she picked up the phone. "Everything okay?"

"Everything's fine," her father said with an annoyed sigh. Her hovering had increasingly annoyed Chester and she had really been working hard to hide her worry from him. "Come to the house when you have a moment."

"I'll be right there." Skyler had been taking care of the garage's bookkeeping from home and she was just at the point where she could take a break. Her father hadn't objected to her taking care of the books for now, but he had been diametrically opposed to her going back to work in the garage.

Skyler crossed quickly to the house, hurriedly opened the back door and headed toward the living room, where her father spent most of his time. She rounded the corner and then stopped in her tracks.

"Hi, Skyler."

There he was—the cowboy of her dreams, standing in her living room. Wearing, as he always did, his boots, jeans and button-down shirt, tucked in. And his hat was on the couch next to where he had been sitting.

"We have a visitor," Chester said casually from his recliner.

Skyler put her hand over her mouth and swallowed back happy tears.

"Do you know how easy it is to get a COVID test around here?" he asked, walking toward her.

She nodded and met him halfway. They embraced, but he didn't kiss her, which was how she wanted it. They would kiss later, when they were alone.

After they hugged, he looked down into her face. "Surprised?"

"Floored," she admitted. "What are you doing here? How did you pull this off without me knowing?"

"He got in touch with me," Chester said, turning the TV on mute.

Together, Skyler sat down on the couch with Hunter, their hands intertwined, their shoulders and thighs touching. She couldn't stop looking at him; he was real.

"Your dad helped me keep it a secret," Hunter said. "Chase has come to propose to Molly."

"Oh." She welled up again. "I'm so happy for her."

Chester didn't seem surprised when Skyler suggested that she give Hunter a tour of her childhood home.

"Where are you staying?" she asked him.

"I have a hotel room with Chase. But I have a feeling he's going to be wanting some privacy."

"Yes." Skyler nodded.

"So your dad said I could stay in your old bedroom upstairs."

That made Skyler laugh. Of course, her old-fashioned father would agree to Hunter staying with them, as long as he wasn't staying with *her* in the apartment. No doubt Chester knew that they had been intimate, but he wasn't modern enough to condone it under his own roof.

She showed him the upstairs, including her very girly room, still decorated from high school, with small pink-rosebud wallpaper, antique lace curtains and a twin-size bed. Hunter sat down on her bed and looked around curiously at her room.

"I've never had a boy in this room before," she noted.

Hunter brought his eyes back to her with a possessive glint in his eye; she could tell he liked the fact that he was the first.

"I have to show you something," she said, "but you have to promise that you won't judge me and you won't let it influence, in any way, your decision to marry me."

The way he grinned at her let her know that his interest had been peaked. "What is it?"

Skyler opened her closet door, raised up on her tiptoes and pulled out a large photo album at the bottom of a stack of books on the shelf. She held the photo album tightly to her body, protectively, as she turned toward him.

"This might be a huge mistake."

"Well," he said. "Now you *have* to show me."

She walked over to him slowly and then held out the heavy album to him. She sat down next to him and leaned into his body as he opened up to the first page of the album. The only thing on the first page was a large signed promotional picture of him on the show *Cowboy*

Up! with a large heart drawn around it in sparkling red ink. Hunter stared at that picture, a picture that he had signed so many years ago.

"I wrote to you for an autographed picture and you actually sent one to me," she told him, feeling a mixture of embarrassment and wonder that she was able to show him the picture now.

Still silent, Hunter turned the page and found the letter that he had sent along with the picture.

"I wrote this," he said, examining the letter more closely.

"You did?" she asked, unbelievingly. "I always figured your manager wrote it and you signed it."

"No." He shook his head. "This is my handwriting."

Hunter continued through the album that she had dedicated to the object of her affection: Hunter Brand from *Cowboy Up!* After they looked through all of the pictures and articles printed from the internet, Hunter closed the book, left it sitting on his lap and looked over at her with a strange expression on his face.

"I had a big crush on you," she said by way of explanation to fill in the awkward silence. "Well, not *you* really. The TV-show version of you."

Hunter appeared to be rendered speechless.

"Did I scare you?" She tugged her book out of his hands and carried it back to the closet. When she turned back around, he was standing up. In the small room, it was easy for him to reach for her and pull her into his arms. With a smirk on his face, he kissed her, long and deep.

"You don't scare me," he said, looking into her eyes. "Being without you scares me."

She wrapped her arms around him, so happy to be

back in them. He took her face in his hands, wanting more of her kisses.

"Where is this apartment of yours?" he asked against her lips.

"Out back."

"We have to go there now." He buried his face in her neck. "Unless you want to finally christen this sweet little bed of yours."

The next night, Chester ordered takeout and invited Chase and Molly to join the three of them for dinner. Molly had a postengagement glow; Chase had given her the exact proposal she had always wanted—he got down on bended knee in Central Park. The conversation flowed easily and for the first time in a long time, the house was filled with laughter. Skyler could tell that Chester liked both of the men sitting at his table. Her father's approval of her future husband wasn't essential, but it was important.

"Pass me some of those potatoes," Chester said boisterously, noticeably uplifted by the company in his house.

Skyler didn't say a word. This night wasn't about trying to regulate her father's diet, a bone of contention between them—it was about celebrating Chase and Molly's engagement.

"So when are you two going to tie the knot?" her father asked Molly and Chase, using his right hand to scoop up potatoes instead of his left.

"Not for a while," Molly said as she and Chase exchanged a smile. "I want a big wedding. Lots of planning."

"And I have to move out here and find a job," Chase added.

"What kind of work will you be looking for, son?" Chester asked before he took a big bite of potatoes loaded with gravy.

"I'm not sure. Whatever I can get to get myself established."

Hunter said, "Chase was a mechanic in the army."

Chester and Skyler turned their keen attention to Chase.

"What kind of training do you have?" her father asked.

Chase wiped his mouth off with a napkin before he answered. "Diesel mechanic. I worked on M1 Abrams tanks and every truck that the army owns. If it's a diesel I can fix it."

"Well…" Chester sat back in his chair and Skyler could tell that his wheels, like hers, were turning. "You didn't get marine training."

"No, sir." Chase smiled.

"But I imagine the army taught you how to at least hold a wrench right."

"Yes, sir. They did."

"I've got a job waiting for you if you want it." Her father rested his forearms on the table and looked Chase directly in the eye. "But I'll need you ASAP. I'm laid up for a while and I need a solid diesel mechanic to pick up my slack."

Molly reached for Chase's hand. "I'd be honored to work for you, sir."

"Call me Sarge," Chester said.

After dinner, Skyler had shooed him out of the kitchen while she cleaned up, and Hunter took the opportunity to speak with Chester alone.

"I appreciate the hospitality," he told Skyler's father.

Chester was a good man—stern but fair. And it was obvious that Skyler was the apple of Chester's eye.

"Well—" Chester turned the TV on mute "—I appreciate you taking such good care of Skyler while she was in Montana."

Hunter nodded, finding now that he was alone with Chester again that it was difficult to formulate the words he needed to say.

"I'd like to be able to take care of Skyler…" Hunter said quietly. "For the rest of her life."

Chester looked over at him, his eyes narrowed a bit, before he turned off the TV. "Speak your piece, son."

"I'd like your permission to marry Skyler."

Chester thought for a minute or two, time that seemed to stretch out much too long for Hunter's comfort.

"I'd like for Skyler to go to college. She left to help me take care of her mother. I've always regretted that for her," Chester said. "You got a problem with that?"

"No, sir."

"Are you planning on setting up house in Montana?"

"Yes, sir," Hunter said, not sure if Chester would be happy to hear this news or not. "I just bought a little place outside of Bozeman. A place that we can make our own."

"Good. Good." Chester nodded. "She was better in Montana. Happier. And, she couldn't—" Skyler's father waved his hand "—hover over me like she is now. I don't want her to waste her time trying to manage my life when she should be out living her own."

Chester pushed forward so the recliner was upright; he looked over at him. "I'm too damn old to have my daughter telling me to eat my vegetables."

Hunter laughed. "Yes, sir."

"Come with me." Chester stood up, a bit unsteady at first, but he found his balance quickly. Hunter followed the man to a bedroom down a hallway. Chester opened the top nightstand drawer, grabbed a box and then handed it to him.

"Give this to Skyler when the time is right."

Hunter opened the box and inside was a diamond ring. A round cut stone set in antique platinum.

"It was her mother's ring."

Hunter closed the box and tucked it into his pocket.

"Thank you, sir," Hunter said. "I love your daughter very much."

"Good." Chester nodded, turning his head but not soon enough. Hunter saw tears in the man's eyes. "Very good."

Chester cleared his throat several times before he brought his eyes back to his, "You understand that she's going to need doctors, specialists—we aren't completely out of the woods with this damn cancer business."

"I've already got doctors lined up for Skyler, sir. We can set up appointments for right after she arrives. Get her established."

Chester put his hand on his shoulder for a moment. "You'll take care of her."

"Yes, sir. I will."

"I'm counting on you," Skyler's father said. "Make her happy, keep her healthy."

They walked out to the living room and Chester stopped by the kitchen. "Come join us."

Skyler looked at Hunter curiously and wiped her hands on a nearby dishtowel. "Okay."

She sat next to Hunter on the couch while Chester eased back into his chair.

"I want you to go back to Montana with Hunter."

Skyler's eyes darted between her father and Hunter. Hunter looked legitimately shocked because he hadn't discussed a timeline with Chester.

"Dad—" Skyler began to protest.

"No." Chester cut her off. "You get your way with me all the time, Sky. This time it's my turn. I can't have you wringing your hands and micromanaging my appointments or counting my calories. You've always been so busy telling me how grown you are—well, in case you haven't noticed, I'm pretty damn well grown, too."

Skyler opened her mouth to say something, but Chester was determined to stay on center stage.

"Now, Hunter here is a nice young man. I like him. And even though he didn't have to, he's asked me for your hand in marriage and I've said yes."

The longer Chester talked, the younger Hunter felt. It was like the two of them were sitting in the principal's office after they'd got caught making out in the bleachers.

"Hunter tells me he bought a nice little place for the two of you. So go on and get on with it."

"Dad…" Skyler began again.

Chester looked lovingly at his daughter; this look tempered the gruffness of his words. "I love you, Sky. You were happy in Montana—when you're happy, I'm happy. If you want to do something to help me get better, go back to Montana. Go be happy."

Wordlessly, Skyler stood up and hugged her father. "I love you, Dad."

It was a long, poignant hug, a hug between two people who had leaned on each other to navigate some of their darkest days.

"Okay." Chester patted her on the back. "Now you two go on and try to stay out of trouble. My show is on."

"Molly, you aren't going to believe how perfect this house is for me." Skyler was video-chatting with her friend from the Rocking R Ranch.

"We can't believe that we got to move into your apartment!" Molly laughed joyfully. "We swapped."

"We did swap!" Skyler laughed, happy to be back in Montana with Hunter. "You've requested time off for the wedding, right? You have the dates?"

"Already taken care of. We will be there," her friend said. "I love you, Sky. I'll see you in a couple of months."

Skyler hung up the phone and looked around her new—*old*—farmhouse. This was to be her first home as a married woman and she couldn't feel luckier. With a lot of love, time and sweat equity, Hunter and she intended to restore the farmhouse to its original glory. Skyler finished washing the breakfast dishes and looked out the kitchen window to see Zodiac and Dream Catcher grazing in the pasture. Hunter had moved the horses to the property soon after they landed in Bozeman.

In the distance, she saw her husband-to-be walking toward the house carrying some tools he had used to repair one of the pasture fences. Eager to share the news from back home with Hunter, she grabbed her hat and raced out the front door. On the front porch, Daisy was sunning herself happily. The cat executed a barrel roll and then stretched out her legs and her toes. With a laugh, Skyler rubbed the cat's belly, so happy to have her feline friend living with them at the Rocking R. She skipped down the steps and met Hunter in the yard.

They greeted with a kiss and a hug, which was their way.

"I just heard from Molly." She fell in beside him as he walked toward a nearby barn that he had turned into his work shed.

"How's everything on their end?"

"They love the apartment. How awesome is it that we actually got to just swap houses?"

"Pretty awesome." He smiled at her.

"Chase is doing an incredible job for Dad, so he doesn't have to furlough any workers. And Dad is getting rent from Molly and Chase so…"

Hunter put his tools in his toolbox. "All is well that ends well?"

She wrapped her arms around him, not caring that he was dirty and sweaty. "Exactly."

Arm and arm, they walked together across the yard. She asked him, "What's on your agenda for today?"

"I actually want to head over to Sugar Creek. Go pick some stuff up from the trailer. Did you get your application for Montana State done?" He held open the front door for her, the screen door creaking loudly. "I need to fix this," he said, fiddling with the latch.

"You've got to fix a ton of stuff," she agreed.

"So," he said, taking his hat off and hanging it on the hat rack. "Are you done with your application?"

"I was just about to hit Send when Molly called."

"Why don't you finish it while I take a shower? Then we'll head to Sugar Creek."

Her application to college completed, Skyler walked out to the pasture to visit with Zodiac and Dream

Catcher. Jessie, Hunter's sister, had given Dream Catcher to her as a prewedding gift.

"Hi, sweet girl." The mare walked over to the fence where she was standing. She rubbed the horse between the eyes and then fed her a molasses treat out of her pocket.

"We are going to be together for the rest of your life," Skyler said to the mare, still in awe of the way her life had unfolded.

Soon Zodiac meandered up to the fence, poking his soft nose into her hand looking for a treat. She laughed, happy that Zodiac was still her miracle horse. According to Liam, he had made a miraculous full recovery and was cleared for easy trail rides. Hunter promised that they would go on their first trail ride as soon as he finished fixing the fence.

"There you are." Hunter found her watching the horses as they walked out to the middle of the pasture.

He put his arm around her and they stood together, in silence, gazing out at their new home. Skyler leaned her head over and rested it on his shoulder. "I feel happy here."

"I'm glad," he said, tightening his hold on her. "You ready to take a ride over to Sugar Creek with me?"

She nodded with a smile, knowing that this beautiful view was hers to enjoy for the rest of her days. They walked together to his truck, arm in arm, discussing, as they liked to do, their plans for the Rocking R. Inside the truck now, in her spot, Skyler buckled her seat belt.

"I think we need to start painting the inside of the house next week," she said when he joined her in the truck.

"We'll see." He cranked the engine. "Let me get things straightened around outside first."

"I'll help you straighten things around outside and then we can paint together next week."

He smiled at her as they left Rocking R land and pulled onto the highway that would lead them a short distance to Sugar Creek. "Sounds like a plan."

"Our gravel is holding," she said excitedly when they reached the main Sugar Creek Ranch road.

"You did a good job."

"Yes, I did!"

Hunter took the roughly hewn road that would lead them to his trailer. Skyler hadn't yet been back to the ancient Oak Tree Hill, where they had had their first amazing date. This was the place, she believed, that she truly fell in love with the real Hunter Brand.

Hand in hand, they walked beneath the canopy of the oak trees, and Skyler reveled in the cool breeze and sweet-smelling air that met them as they walked deeper into the embrace of the old trees.

"I love it here," she whispered, always feeling a reverence for this unique spot in the world.

"I love you." Hunter let her hand drop and he stopped walking. "And I really wish I could have given you a more romantic proposal."

"That's okay." Skyler turned around and discovered her cowboy kneeling before her.

"Skyler." Hunter held up a closed box. "Will you marry me?"

Her eyes immediately filled with tears as she nodded her head, too emotional to even get the word *yes* out of her mouth. Hunter flipped open the box and that was when she saw her mother's engagement ring inside.

Tears of joy and sorrow for her lost mother flowed freely down her cheeks as Hunter stood and slid the ring onto her finger.

"Your father told me to give this to you when the time was right."

Still crying, Skyler gazed at the ring on her finger—a ring that symbolized a happy marriage between her mother and father. The ring also symbolized her father's approval of the man with whom she intended to spend the rest of her life.

Hunter wrapped his arms around her, hugged her tightly and then kissed her gently on the lips.

"Thank you for my proposal do-over, Hunter," she said between kisses.

"Anything for you, my love." Her dream cowboy said, "Anything for you."

Epilogue

Theirs was a simple ceremony beneath the canopy of the ancient oak trees where they had first fallen in love. Dr. Bonita DeLaFuente-Brand, Gabe's wife, arranged for her father's private jet to bring Molly, Chase and Chester to Bozeman, Montana, for an early fall wedding. The air was crisp and Skyler, to Hunter's mind, was the most beautiful bride Montana had ever seen. Her simple, unembellished white satin gown, complete with pockets, emphasized her narrow waist and complemented her short reddish-gold locks. His mother had handcrafted a pair of white leather moccasins, at Skyler's request, for the wedding. It was a gesture that had touched Lilly's heart, as it had touched his own.

Together, they stood hand in hand beneath the oldest of the ancient trees on his hill, with his family standing in a circle around them while the pastor had them read their vows. While Skyler was reading her vows to him, all Hunter could do was focus in on the softness of her lips, the pertness of her small nose, the little freckle on her left cheek and the darkness of her long lashes surrounding her unusual lavender-blue-gray eyes. She was the true love of his life—his first, only and forever.

"I now pronounce you husband and wife," the pastor said. "Hunter. You may now kiss your bride."

She smiled at him, her smile so warm and full of promise of the good years to come. He leaned down and pressed his lips to hers. It was a sweet kiss, tender and kind.

"I love you," Skyler said, holding his gaze.

"I love you," he said, stealing one more kiss before they faced, for the first time, their friends and family as husband and wife.

The Rocking R Ranch was right now, but one day, they would build their dream home right here on this hill. One day, their children would race across those fields, carefree and completely loved. One day, Hunter would meet his grandchildren—a new generation of Brands with his determination and Skyler's kindness.

They had decided on a picnic-style reception at the main house. Next to Skyler, Hunter sat at a table for two at the top of a horseshoe shape of tables.

"What did you get Skyler for a wedding present?" Savannah called out to him.

"I got her what she asked for," he said, and Skyler was beaming as she thought of her wedding present. "I got her a skid steer."

"It was the best present of my life!" she called out to her friends and family. As their wedding party laughed, Skyler turned her pretty violet eyes to him.

"This feels like a dream," his bride said with a happy sigh.

He took her lovely face in his hands, her eyes so full of love for him. Hunter said, "My beloved Skyler. You are my every dream come true."

* * * * *

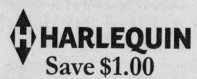

HARLEQUIN

Save $1.00

on the purchase of ANY Harlequin book
from the imprints below.

*Heartfelt or thrilling, passionate or
uplifting—our romances have it all.*

PRESENTS INTRIGUE

DESIRE ROMANTIC SUSPENSE SPECIAL EDITION

LOVE INSPIRED

Save $1.00

on the purchase of ANY Harlequin Presents, Intrigue, Desire,
Romantic Suspense, Special Edition or Love Inspired book.
Valid from June 1, 2023 to May 31, 2024.

52617414

Canadian Retailers: Harlequin Enterprises ULC will pay the face value of this coupon plus 10.25¢ if submitted by customer for this product only. Any other use constitutes fraud. Coupon is nonassignable. Void if taxed, prohibited or restricted by law. Consumer must pay any government taxes. Void if copied. Inmar Promotional Services ("IPS") customers submit coupons and proof of sales to Harlequin Enterprises ULC, P.O. Box 31000, Scarborough, ON M1R 0E7, Canada. Non-IPS retailer—for reimbursement submit coupons and proof of sales directly to Harlequin Enterprises ULC, Retail Marketing Department, Bay Adelaide Centre, East Tower, 22 Adelaide Street West, 41st Floor, Toronto, Ontario M5H 4E3, Canada.

U.S. Retailers: Harlequin Enterprises ULC will pay the face value of this coupon plus 8¢ if submitted by customer for this product only. Any other use constitutes fraud. Coupon is nonassignable. Void if taxed, prohibited or restricted by law. Consumer must pay any government taxes. Void if copied. For reimbursement submit coupons and proof of sales directly to Harlequin Enterprises ULC 482, NCH Marketing Services, P.O. Box 880001, El Paso, TX 88588-0001, U.S.A. Cash value 1/100 cents.

5 65373 00076 2 (8100)0 12532

© 2023 Harlequin Enterprises ULC

HSERIESCOUP0623